Dan Hanks

SWASHBUCKLERS

ANGRY ROBOT

ANGRY ROBOT
An imprint of Watkins Media Ltd

Unit 11, Shepperton House
89 Shepperton Road
London N1 3DF
UK

angryrobotbooks.com
twitter.com/angryrobotbooks
Don't Cross the Streams

An Angry Robot paperback original 2021

Cover by Karen Smith
Edited by Eleanor Teasdale & Paul Simpson
Set in Meridien

ISBN 978 0 85766 938 4
Ebook ISBN 978 0 85766 939 1

Printed and bound in the United Kingdom by TJ Books Ltd.

9 8 7 6 5 4 3 2 1

PRAISE FOR DAN HANKS

"Combines sci-fi and fantasy elements into an energetic cross-genre romp."
Publishers Weekly

*"Packed with heart, wit, and plenty of action, Swashbucklers is the sequel
to all your favourite childhood adventures. Hanks at the top of his game!"*
Reese Hogan, author of *Shrouded Loyalties*

"It reads like Stephen King on steroids. Stranger Things *meets* It *meets*
The Goonies. *I want to hear this story told late at night over a campfire,
while the marshmallows go all gooey."*
Caroline Hardaker, author of *Composite Creatures*

*"Brings all the magic of the 80s back to life, and delivers a fun, action-
packed tale with heart."*
Fantasy Hive

*"Proves it's not always possible – or wise – to put aside childish things.
A great read!"*
RWW Greene, author of *The Light Years*

*"A nostalgia-inducing, pop culture acid-trip where the hometown kids
reunite as middle-aged Goonies."*
Patricia A. Jackson, author of *Forging a Nightmare*

*"Hanks puts forty year-old characters in an action-packed fantastical
story designed for the fitness level of teenagers and sees if they can keep
up. They can't. And it's an awesome formula for fun."*
Chris Panatier, author of *The Phlebotomist*

*"A team of world-saving teenage misfits is again called upon in their middle
age to once more face the nightmare-inducing villain, while juggling school
runs, work and housework. Hilarious and poignant, loved it!"*
Gabriela Houston, author of *The Second Bell*

BY THE SAME AUTHOR

Captain Moxley and the Embers of the Empire

To Elliott and Noah, and all the adventures that lie ahead

PROLOGUE

Gerald heard the whispering on the baby monitor five minutes before he died.

He dismissed it instantly, of course, and kept drinking as he watched the evening match. The little flash of red, blinking from the box on the shelf, was just another twinkling light in their very festive living room. Barely even noticeable against the glowing Christmas tree and all the flickering fake candles. It was probably picking up interference from another wireless contraption on their street, the signals cutting into the sweet sound of his daughter gurgling happily to herself as she fought sleep.

Certainly nothing to get him off the couch to check on her. Even if the sound had made his heart race that little bit faster and his hands grow clammy.

Then it happened again.

"Shhhhhhh."

The light seemed to flash more urgently, as if in warning.

He frowned and hit mute on the remote. The football continued silently, as he fixed his gaze at the bookshelf where the monitor sat, waiting for confirmation he'd heard what he'd heard. For a second, nothing happened.

Then the red light flashed permanently.

"...tubby little..."

Not only had something just shushed in his daughter's

room, but the musical mobile over her cot had started playing.

The mobile his daughter definitely couldn't reach to turn on.

"...stuffed with fluff..."

The cushions fell aside as he leapt up and scrambled up the stairs, beer spilling all over the carpet, leaving a trail his wife would later find when she returned from Pilates to discover his eviscerated corpse.

"Sarah!" he cried out, despite knowing full well his four-month old wasn't going to respond to him. "Sarah, don't worry, I'm–"

He never got to finish his sentence.

Sliding into the nursery, he ran face first into a wall of fur. Half-cursing, half-spitting it out, he collapsed backwards and landed on his bum, as the life-sized toy he had bought only last week loomed over him. The soft toy of Sarah's favourite children's TV show.

"Let's see what they stuffed *you* with," Daphne the Disco Duck squawked.

He screamed as the thing fell on him and ate.

In the cot on the other side of the room, his daughter gurgled like her daddy was now doing, before she finally drifted off to sleep as the blood rained down around her and the mobile continued to spin and play.

CHAPTER ONE

Sequels

Dark Peak hadn't changed in thirty-two years.

Cisco wasn't sure if he had expected that. Ever since deciding to come back, he'd been playing the scene over and over in his mind, like repeats of his favourite show.

Most of the time the fantasy consisted of a slow summer drive through the high street. He'd stare with distaste at the new buildings where old stone terraces had once stood. He'd shake his head at the high rises going up in what used to be little parks or fields around the town. He'd probably frown as he saw the bustling new bars vomiting up tables and chairs into what had once been quiet countryside streets.

Of course, like a goddamn pro he would take all this newness in and say nothing. He'd channel his unflappable weird-kid-returns-home-as-awesome-adult *Grosse Point Blank* composure, pull up to the pavement and get out. Heads would turn his way as he slammed the door. Childhood friends who'd never left the town would recognise him and run over and slap his shoulder as though he was some kind of soothing ointment to their tired lives. Old jokes about what had once happened... well, they'd be long forgotten, surely? There would be nothing but respect.

"Cisco Collins!" they'd say. "Great to see you again, mate. Welcome home!"

Maybe they'd go for a beer and catch up. Or he'd just give them a cursory nod and slip on past as enigmatically as possible.

Of course, that wasn't how things ever went in reality. And in this reality especially, it was clear the timeline's dial had been knocked from "pretty normal" to "perpetually ridiculous". Which meant he should actually have been relieved his wintry return to Dark Peak was initially met with no more fanfare than the harsh December squall whipping around the town square and a swaying Christmas tree that was spooking the pigeons.

In fact, as he stood there, back in the location where everything had changed – the site of the infamous 1989 Halloween gas leak that had left most Dark Peak residents seeing monsters and several people dead – he felt a strange sense of happy nostalgia warm his insides.

Because after all this time, nothing had changed.

Same old buildings.

Same old people.

It was almost like stepping back into a cosy memory or returning to a treasured world in a sequel.

Except that sequels were never quite as good, were they?

"Oi, Gasbuster!" a balding man in a bright yellow puffer jacket yelled across the gardens, as his three screaming kids chased each other around the grass and muddy flowerbeds. Cisco shouldn't have turned at the name. But there's a sadistic instinct in humans that makes you do things when you know you really shouldn't, and he had already locked eyes with the man before he realised his mistake. The man grinned like a fisherman who'd just hooked his first idiot of the day. "Yeahhhhh, I knew it was you! The kid from the gas leak!"

Cisco swore under his breath and let the wind carry it away, as the man grabbed his eldest daughter and pointed as if Cisco was some kind of festive attraction.

"Look, honey, that's the bloke from the bedtime stories your mum tells you. The gas leak boy. I told you he was real!"

The girl laughed joyously and waved to him. Grim-faced, Cisco waved back.

A hand tugged at his jeans.

"Who's that?"

Cisco reached down and gently squeezed the mittened hand of his eight year-old son. "I've no idea, George."

The boy's flushed face, squashed in between his knitted beanie and the scarf around his neck, tilted up at him with a puzzled expression. "Then why are you waving to her?"

"That's what you do when kids wave to you. It's the law."

"There's a law about waving?"

"Uh-huh, a parent's law." Why did he often find himself lying to his son to get out of answering a perfectly reasonable question. *I don't have the energy for the technicalities of a discussion that could spawn a thousand more questions and last forever,* came the well-worn reply from his brain. "When you become a parent, George, you absolutely have to wave when kids wave at you. I would expect the same if you did it to someone else."

Of course, George instantly began waving to the man. Cisco thought he recognised him now. He fumbled in the closet of his mind where he'd shoved a lot of past trauma. Dean someone?

Most-likely-Dean laughed again nastily and didn't bother waving back to George.

"OK, not everyone knows the law, I guess," Cisco said, gently putting the boy's hand down.

George seemed to mull that over for a moment. "What did he mean by Gasbuster? Shouldn't it be Ghostbuster?"

"It should have been," Cisco admitted, unable to help the regret seep into his voice. "But that's not what everyone ended up remembering."

"Why?"

"Oh, it's a long story."

"But why?"

Cisco sighed, not fancying that conversation right now. He looked around for a distraction. Distraction and lying, that was his parenting style.

There was a little café on the north side of the square, its windows finely decorated with colourful festive scenes and golden angels and falling snow. A cosy, beckoning light shone through the steamy glass. The Pepino Deli sign above the door had been draped with colourful lights that were blinking on and off.

"Need a wee?" Cisco asked, pulling George in that direction.

His son resisted. "No, I'm OK."

"How about a cake?"

"Let's go faster!" George said, leading the way.

They headed up the uneven flagstones, trying not to slip on the wet brown leaves and fighting the sleet that was now beginning. Cisco could hear the name again, "Gasbuster!", carried through the squall, but couldn't tell if it was the man or his own brain gleefully playing tricks on him.

The trouble wasn't so much the name, he reminded himself, following quickly after George who was now suggesting that maybe he'd like a hot chocolate with his cake. Yes, living with the humiliating moniker had been annoying in the aftermath of that particular Halloween night. Having it haunt him like a particularly irritating poltergeist. Hearing it in whispers behind him in class or in assembly or in the dinner line. At least until he'd been able to convince both his mothers that maybe, *maybe,* they might want a change of scenery for his final year at school? A change that was as far away from his childhood home as possible.

But, really, the name was just that. A name. He'd been called far worse.

What really bugged him about the whole thing was that the name implied his heroic efforts had been for nothing. It suggested something very mundane had actually happened back then. That the monsters everyone remembered for weeks and years afterwards were some kind of mass hallucination brought on by some ridiculously implausible gas leak – when they had been very real indeed.

Real enough he could still feel the manifestations pouring through him, after his body had been turned into a gateway to hell. Real enough to have driven him out of his beloved hometown so he could attempt to live a half-decent life away from the whispers and stares and rumours. Real enough to have given him scars on multiple levels.

All those classic 80s movies had led him wrong for so long. Saving the day wasn't always met with a happy, heroic ending for the teenagers, before the credits played out to some great power ballad. Sometimes the grown-ups just didn't understand what sacrifices you'd made to protect everyone from the supernatural. Sometimes it was easier for them to make up some more plausible explanation for what had happened, blame *you* for the chaos, and then leave you to deal with the fallout. And even though you waited for those damn credits to roll, just to end your suffering, you were left with the horrible realisation that they never roll in real life. The treadmill just keeps going. And if it's smeared with crap you don't get a chance to step off for a moment and clean everything up… you just have to keep running, getting messier and messier, until you are only age and shit, and there is nothing else left of the person you used to be.

"Happy Christmas!" the hand-painted sign on the café door read, not picking up on his mood at all.

Cisco let his son lead him in. The boy saw the cakes on the counter and slipped out of his grasp, leaving him alone to search for a table.

At which point he saw her.

A blast from the past. His very best friend in forever. Until he'd left her behind like he'd left everyone else.

Doc saw him. Her eyes widened. And not for the first time in his life, Cisco wondered if adulthood would be easier all round if the hell portal he had once helped close would open up again and swallow him whole.

I should have told her I was coming back, he thought, far too late.

"Cisco?" Doc said, removing her headphones and sitting back from her table as if needing more room to take in the unkempt mess he knew he'd become. "Now there's a sight I didn't expect to see blowing in on the winter winds like some scruffy, middle-aged Mary Poppins."

Maybe it was the instant warmth of the café after being outside in the winter chill, but Cisco's cheeks were burning.

"Hey, Doc," he mumbled.

Dorothy Constance Forbes, Doc to her friends, stood up and walked between the tables, continuing to look him up and down, still wearing that enigmatic smile of hers.

"I know in these situations it's usually polite to lie and say you haven't aged a bit, but man, you *got old*!" She touched his hair. "Look at those streaks of grey. And some kind of beard, too. I have to say it suits you. The age *and* the beard."

Standing face to face for the first time in a long time, he realised with secret joy that just like the town Doc had held onto all these years, she hadn't changed much at all either. Still an inch taller than him, vibrant dark curls framing her glowing black skin and mischievous eyes. And there was still a presence to her, an energy that only a few people you ever meet in life have.

They leaned in awkwardly for a hug, before he was immediately pushed back by the point of her finger as she jabbed it in his chest.

"Now, what the hell are you doing here?"

"Huh?"

"We haven't talked in forever, haven't seen each other in longer, and now you just show up? Waltzing into my favourite café without a bloody word of advance notice, even after all the invitations I sent your way to come and see us. Why?"

He glanced around to make sure George wasn't in earshot. The boy knew a little about what was going on with his mum, but again the warning *no energy for questions* flashed repeatedly in his head. "It's complicated," he said, dropping his voice. "This seemed as good a place as any for George and I to squirrel ourselves away for the winter to survive the transition back home."

"Like the nuts that you are," Doc replied good-naturedly. She took the hint though, as he knew she would. Any time *it's complicated* reared its ugly head, it was a good bet to nod sympathetically and

back the hell away from whatever the real details were – which
in this case was Cisco's soon-to-be-ex absconding with her gym
instructor. A cliché, sure, but there was a reason clichés were
clichés. They were prone to happening. Especially in gyms with so
much spandex and adrenaline.

Thankfully he hadn't really been all that bothered by what
she'd done. There was a part of him that had always known it
wasn't right. They wanted different things, saw the world in
different ways. She liked being fit and active, he really didn't. She
liked going out with her friends all the time, he preferred binge-
watching TV shows on Netflix. All the usual stuff you discover far
too late, before realising you should have been listening to that
gut feeling that kept nagging you all that time – even if that gut
feeling had always been searching for someone it wasn't even sure
existed. A love just beyond touching distance, as though maybe it
might just have been from a dream or some movie he saw once or
a forgotten friendship from childhood.

He wondered suddenly if maybe he could open up, now he
was safely back home. To spill everything out to his best friend as
he'd done as a kid. Doc was always the first person he told when
anything remotely interesting happened: getting his first games
console, that time he was shoved into the boiler room at school as
a prank, the night Rebecca Miller finally accosted him and shoved
her tongue into his mouth, whirling it like a washing machine and
causing him to gag.

And now he'd returned home because interesting things
were happening again, weren't they? Not the divorce, that was
almost mundane in comparison. No, it was more the recurring
dreams of a familiar woman trying to give him a message. The
unshakeable anxiety of a threat on the horizon, like dangerous
clouds threatening an unrelenting snow.

The murder.

Yet as quickly as the urge came over him to spill his thoughts
and feelings out to her, the responsible adult part of him pushed
it back. Now wasn't the time and this definitely wasn't the

place. So he didn't offer any more details, only a tired smile.

"Where are you staying?" she asked, never one to press for more information than she needed. He loved her for that. "We have room with us if you need a place to crash for a while? You know Michelle would love to see you. Cecilia, too."

"Oh, thanks, but Jake offered–"

"That little shit knew you were back before me!?"

Cisco couldn't help his smile growing wider at the stirrings of that old animosity. He'd missed that. "I might have grown old in all the worst ways, Doc," he said, "but it's nice to see *you* haven't changed a bit. Yes, I told Jake I was coming back. We're going to be staying at his place with his family. But it was a last-minute thing and… well, I asked him not to tell you or Michelle."

Doc glowered and turned on her heels to return to her table. She hadn't punched him out though and he took that as an invitation to join her. He whistled to George, gesturing for him to stop prodding the cakes, and pulled the seat out opposite her.

"Look, I'm sorry. I should have told you, but I just figured you were busy with work and everything."

She frowned. "Did you just whistle at your son like a dog?"

As George came running over, Cisco kicked aside the chair next to his and gestured for him to sit.

"It's the only thing that cuts through the excitement in the circus of his mind and I'm at the stage of being a dad where I do whatever gets the job done. Judge all you want."

She picked up her drink and eyed him over the rim. "Oh, I am." Then she took a sip, put it down again and turned to George. It was like switching on a light. Suddenly she was all warmth and a beaming smile and those twinkling eyes again. She reached out a hand and they shook.

"You must be George, nice to finally meet you. I'm betting you're here to learn all about the place where your Daddy grew up, huh?"

"I guess."

"Find out anything fun so far?"

The boy shrugged. "He used to have a lot of gas."

As Doc began laughing, Cisco joined in. A long, loud laugh of letting everything go that turned everybody's heads and had his son shrinking into his coat with embarrassment beside him. Yet it felt good. As though he hadn't laughed in years. Which come to think of it he probably hadn't. He hadn't found anything this funny in a good long time.

"Ah, that's fantastic," Doc groaned, wiping her eyes. She put her hand on George's arm and leaned in. "Yes, your dad had a lot of gas. You heard the name then? Gasbuster. Like a Ghostbuster, but with more farts."

George giggled.

"Doc, you're not helping."

She grinned over the small table. "Then tell me the truth, Cisco. Why didn't you want me and Michelle to know you were coming back? We love you, you silly oaf. And you would have given us something to get excited about! Not that married life isn't exciting, of course. That girl still gives me chills in all the right places, if you know what I mean."

George frowned. "What are chills?"

"Why don't you go and have a look at the cakes again and pick all three of us something nice?" Cisco replied, giving his son some money as he scowled at his friend.

Doc just laughed again as the boy ran off.

"Sorry, I'm usually a little more subtle but yeah. It's just that, you know, it's *you*, Cisco. You're back in Dark Peak! We honestly never thought we'd see you here again after everything that happened. With the…"

Her voice trailed off.

"Gas leakage incident?" he offered.

She held up her hands in immediate surrender.

"Let's not get into that again. Whatever it was we went through back then – and thankfully I've been able to forget the entire charade for the most part – it's just good to see you back here where you belong. You fancy joining us for dinner one night, to regale us with tales of your lives and the real reason you've returned?"

Cisco dropped his eyes away, a little taken aback she'd seen through him that clearly. But before he could reply, the person at the next table got up, folded their copy of the *Manchester Evening News*, and left it on the table as they made their way out of the coffee shop. And there, on the front page, was the real reason he had come back to Dark Peak. The beacon of darkness that had lured him here, instead of going to literally any other place on Earth where he might have been safer for a while longer.

Baby monitor murder, the headline screamed. *Costumed attacker at large.*

Steeling his jaw, Cisco's gaze dropped to the artist's reconstruction attached to the story. A terrifying drawing of a giant fluffy duck with glowing red eyes that witnesses described fleeing the scene after murdering some poor father in the village just down the road.

Dressed as a popular children's television character, they'd said.

Cisco didn't think it was a costume at all.

Looking away from the story, he regarded the woman opposite. The woman who had once saved him from a similar fate at the hands of a two hundred year-old pirate and all manner of wretched fictional monsters only he seemed to remember.

"Sure," he replied, wondering how Doc, Jake and Michelle were going to take being told they were all in mortal danger once again. "Dinner sounds good."

CHAPTER TWO

Memories

Jake's four-bedroom, detached, countryside home was, unsurprisingly, everything Cisco had thought it might be – a huge sandstone beast of a property at the bottom of Dunmow Hill, the gloriously overgrown rise marking the edge of town and the beginning of the Peak District. Capped by a thatch of fir trees, resplendent with huge oaks, a field of wild grass and trampled footpaths and blackberry bush borders, the Hill still bore the hallmarks of the painful cross-country runs Cisco remembered doing here as a teenager. Except now at the foot of its wet, wintry slopes was a perfectly designed estate full of family homes, pristine pavements and gardens currently full of light-up reindeers and jolly snowmen and signs saying "Santa, stop here!".

It was a home that encapsulated everything Jake had grown into. Perfection.

Cisco fondly remembered his quiet friend with the incessant scientific curiosity and the social confidence of a hedgehog. Always pushing his glasses up his nose, curling up into a ball in the presence of girls, and generally making Cisco feel a thousand times more confident than he ever had any right to feel.

Now? Jake was at least half a foot taller than Cisco, wore contacts, and had a glow that spoke both of his acquaintance with the local gym and a generally optimistic attitude to life. He was currently swinging George around their gigantic living room, while his wife Natalie and their three teenage girls laughed along and Einstein the dog – in true Jake fashion, named after the actual scientist, not after the famous movie canine – barked and rolled over for a tickle.

"Who's glad to see me then, eh?" Jake cooed to Cisco's son, as George giggled himself silly. "Who's glad to see Uncle Jake?"

"Let me down!" George screamed happily, not wanting to be put down at all. As soon as Jake dropped him gently to his feet, he held up his arms as Cisco knew he would. "Again, again, pleeeeease!"

Cisco fidgeted on the couch, nursing his beer and scratching Einstein's belly with his foot. It didn't hurt to let his son have a bit of fun with someone else. It would do him good. Much better than for them to return to their plot arc of constant arguing that had been the essence of their father-son relationship recently.

Just put on your coat, eat your dinner, yes you did ask for jacket potato not mash, no you can't play the PlayStation for just another ten minutes, I've just made you chocolate pancakes so is this really the worst day of your life?

As if to drive the point home, George ran over and jumped straight into his crotch, causing him to spill his beer.

"F...or goodness' sake, George!"

Cisco pushed him off, feeling the alcohol seep onto his jeans and pool on the sofa, which Einstein immediately jumped up to drink. Thankfully, Emily, Jake's youngest at thirteen, was already running into the kitchen to grab some paper towels, before shooing Cisco, George and the dog away, and cleaning up.

Cisco blew out his cheeks as her parents beamed with pride. "Seriously, how did you two raise such brilliant children? What's your secret?"

"It's all Nat's doing," Jake said, slipping his arm around his wife's waist.

Looking down to his son, Cisco saw George was pale faced and mortified at what he'd done, his little brown almond eyes adorably heartbroken beneath his sweep of black hair. "Up you come," Cisco said, swinging him up onto his hip and beginning to sway him back and forth as they hugged. "It's fine, don't worry about it."

Natalie grinned.

"What?"

"Oh, it's just nice to see the baby sway again. Jake used to do that with the girls." She squeezed her husband back. "Although to be fair, he still does it with the dog sometimes."

Cisco laughed. However, as he kept rocking his son – as he'd done ever since George had been a baby – a niggle in the back of his mind told him the boy was feeling heavier than ever. The day was coming when he'd put his son down and never pick him up to do this again. He needed to make the most of this parenting thing, before these moments were gone forever.

"Right," Jake said brightly. "Dinner's going to be ready in a minute. George, why don't you go with Aunty Nat and see your room? She and the girls have set it up all nicely for you. They've even loaned you some of their old toys."

"Thanks so much, Natalie," Cisco said again. "We really appreciate you letting us stay and going to so much trouble to make us feel at home."

Natalie smiled as she walked over to take George's hand.

"What toys do you have for me?" he asked. "Dolls?"

"Erm, maybe?"

The boy considered it for a moment, then nodded. "OK. Cool."

Hand in hand, she led George and her daughters upstairs, while Jake picked up his beer from the mantlepiece, looked over to his friend and raised it in salute.

"To the simplicity of childhood."

"Amen to that."

They both downed their drinks. Then Jake went to the fridge and opened two new beers. There was a sudden un-Jake-like twinkle in his bright blue eyes.

"Speaking of which, want to see something rad that'll take you back the thirty years or so since you were last in town? Or since anyone last used the word 'rad'?"

Cisco felt the alcohol take the edge off his dour mood ever so slightly. He took a swig of the new beer, hoping it would help some more.

"Can't hurt?" he replied, wondering just how true that was.

Jake swung back the fake bookcase in their converted third-floor loft to reveal a secret room behind, full of Cisco's childhood.

A doorway back to the 1980s.

Holy shit, was Cisco's only thought, his mouth gaping at the sight that lay beyond.

Hung on the far back wall were four battered machines – each a mishmash of separate video games consoles, the best and the worst of the 8-bit era, and all full of scuffs and scorch marks. Three of them had black cords spiralling out of them, to which arcade light blasters were attached. The fourth had a giant plastic glove resplendent with crude buttons on the wrist, a relic that was somehow still intact despite looking like it had been rather too close to a fire and was covered in supernaturally blue stains.

"All this time?" he gushed, as Jake gestured for him to step into his past, only to be confronted by a wall of familiar game cartridges stacked up to the side of weapons. A sight that sent a cascade of feelings through him he couldn't keep up with. He ran his eyes over them, then back to the blasters, reaching over to caress the cheap, cold plastic that had often saved his life. He knew instantly the one underneath his fingers – the one connected to a console with a sword cut in the side – had been his. Worn from battle to battle across Dark Peak all those years ago. "You kept the War Wizards all this time?"

Jake shrugged sheepishly, as though both delighted and embarrassed by Cisco's reaction. "It felt like the right thing to do, you know? Sure, none of what we went through ended well from the little I remember of the whole gas leak, but it seemed important to keep them for some reason." He idly scratched his cheek, his gaze lost in the distance, as though trying to visualise something that kept slipping away. "Besides, I seem to remember it took me bloody ages to cobble these things together for our Halloween costumes."

They weren't costumes, Cisco almost replied. But he let it slide as his gaze left the consoles and drifted across the rest of the room – which consisted entirely of bookshelves lining the walls, leaving only a gap for the window that gazed out over Dunmow Hill behind the house. The crescent moon was shimmering low in the sky, splitting the clouds and spilling silver over the trees and fields. There was a blur in the night as something dashed across the garden, but Cisco paid it no mind. Probably just a cat. He was too lost in the unfolding realisation at what else Jake had preserved in this tomb to all their childhoods.

The bookshelves were full. Stacked with an 80s child's dream of books, comics, toys, models, shows, and games. What looked like an entire *Power Pack* collection. Models of the Thunderfighter from *Buck Rogers,* next to his robot companion Twiki. A *Battlestar Galactica* Viper. X-Wings. Big Trak. A poseable Gizmo. Zoids. Cabbage Patch Dolls. A Viewmaster. The *Ghost Castle* board game. A mini-CD of Prince's *Batman* soundtrack. A bunch of *Choose Your Own Adventure* novels. The entire set of Nancy Drew mysteries. VHS cassette recordings of everything from *Xanadu* and *Aliens* to *Red Dwarf* and the *Dungeons & Dragons* cartoon. And so much more.

Everything Cisco remembered from their hangout in Doc's father's basement was here. Mr Forbes' entire, original collection of geeky treasures.

"You kept it *all*?" he whispered.

Jake shrugged, as though he didn't understand it either.

"When Mr Forbes moved to the care home a couple of years ago, Doc had a big sale. Said she wanted to be rid of it. But I saw everything boxed up in her garage and couldn't help myself. Something made me take the lot. Although, between you and me, Doc still doesn't know, so can we keep it quiet? I had to send a friend to pay and pick it all up. No way would she have let me take it had she realised."

Cisco could feel his face pulling between the joy of a rediscovered feeling and utter confusion.

"But you were never that into any of this! I know full well we used to bore you senseless making you spend time with us when we were hanging out reading comics and playing games and constructing models. Why would you save it?"

It was a question that seemed completely inadequate for what he was seeing. Doc's basement had been a cornerstone of Cisco's childhood. Most of his happy memories in life were still derived from his time spent in that basement and so many of his teenage emotions were imprinted forever on the artefacts now lining the walls of this secret loft room. He felt a lump in his throat. Suddenly all the feelings he'd been suppressing lately rose to the fore and he struggled for control of the moment.

"I honestly couldn't tell you," Jake replied. "It's not like I remember much from those days and I'm definitely not the Nostalgia King like you are." He grinned. "Maybe it was your voice in my head, telling me to do it? I don't know. But I'm glad I did. It might not have been my own personal treasure trove, but it was a part of who we were. I guess I just didn't want to let go of that part of our childhood yet."

Cisco understood that all too well. "There's a lot of that about at the moment."

"Right!? Nat said as much the other day – how everyone is rehashing stories they remembered growing up. It's all reboots and remakes and re-whatevers. Some of it is amazing, obviously. Have you seen *Cobra Kai*?" He waved an apologetic hand as Cisco pulled a face. "Sorry, of course you have. It's great, isn't it? But still, everyone's out there trying to capture the feeling of being a kid again. Which is ridiculous, because the science of life is you can't ever go back. Only forwards. I don't know why we're so obsessed with it, to be honest."

Cisco nodded politely, unwilling to openly disagree. In truth, the illusion the 80s had returned were one of the few things that had kept him going in recent years. The nostalgia might have held him back, but it had also kept him alive.

"Anyway," Jake continued, looking around with the casual eye of someone who didn't really understand the beauty before him. "Nat agreed to let me store everything here and we obviously had to hide it to keep it secret from Doc, but also to have it available in case any of the girls wanted to enjoy it one day. Hence the secret bookcase." His shoulders hunched a little nervously, an old mannerism which was out of place on his strapping, tall frame. "Do you like it then?"

Cisco walked over to one of the shelves and picked up a small, thin and well-loved book. One he'd read hundreds of times as a kid. He touched a finger to the faded cover, tracing the image of a boy and a cat, flying high above the world on a broomstick.

"Like it? I'm in *love*, Jake." He stared at the picture, feeling the same rush of excitement he'd had the first time he'd ever seen it. "I can't believe you've done this. Yet I'm so grateful you were here to save it all. Thank you, mate. Truly. Thank you."

Jake's cheeks grew a touch red. "Oh, good. That's a relief. I hoped you'd appreciate it. And, hey, I know it's been tough for you lately, but it's really good to have you and George back in town. I know Michelle and Doc will think so too, although I still think you should have let me tell them sooner, rather than risk you bumping into them by accident. How did Doc react anyway?"

"Gave me some shit. The usual."

Jake smiled, then, hearing someone call his name from somewhere else in the house, he took a step back towards the doorway. "Right, I think dinner is a go. Let me go take care of things downstairs to set up. Will you be OK up here by yourself for a bit?"

Cisco kept staring at the book in his hands. It felt warm and worn, like family.

"I know you can't really hang onto your childhood," he said quietly, "but there's a longing I keep having. For that feeling you just talked about. Not just about being a kid, but a specific, undefinable moment from back then."

"What'd you mean?"

"I'm… not sure? I wish I knew. Maybe it's a kind of magic. The excitement of the unknown future. Or that first realisation when you understand just how many possible adventures lie ahead. And always, *always*, you'll choose the right path and you'll get to save the day, defeat the bad guy, get the glory, kiss the person of your dreams, and everything will be OK in the end." He took a swig of beer and stared out of the window at the treetops scattered up the hill, still bathed in moonlight. "Then you grow up. You discover life doesn't work out for most people, you'll fuck up, you'll have regrets, the nightmares you had will never truly leave you, but those friendships you treasured will. And that magic you remembered so well? It's just a memory now. A feeling you can't really explain and can't ever get back."

There was a moment of silence. For a second he wondered if Jake had already gone, bored by his rambling, but there was an uncomfortable shuffle of feet in the doorway.

"I'm still here, mate. And so are Doc and Michelle. We always were here, whenever you needed. Don't forget, we're not the ones who left."

Cisco kept staring out of the window, picturing shadows in the darkness.

"I had to go, Jake. I forced my mums to move because I was the only one who remembered what happened. Everyone else bought the bullshit gas leak because it was easier to swallow than the truth and that's what allowed you to stay and grow up and be happy. I'm the one who believed it was real, so I had to go. Although…" he laughed, "…obviously it didn't help! I well and truly anchored myself to the past, forgot the present, and ended up in between. I absolutely limboed myself."

Jake wrapped his fingers around the door handle as he backed out.

"Tell you what, we'll look after George and get him started on his dinner, then after that we'll let him put the rest of the Christmas decorations up. Why don't you hang out up here for a bit? Finish your beer and get reacquainted with these old friends of yours?"

Cisco smiled gratefully as Jake left. Yet, for the first time in ages, he didn't feel alone. He was nestled in the heart of his childhood again, in the place he'd been struggling to reach for most of his life. Everywhere he looked were long-lost emotions. Breadcrumbs back in time, to those elusive moments in the past. Memories even he couldn't really remember properly, but felt in his very core. This stuff was the DNA of everything he had been as a child and everything he had wanted to be as a grown up.

The old copy of his favourite story in his hand, he wandered the bookshelves. His fingers ran lovingly across broken spines of books he had once read and over the plastic models he used to play with, trying to reestablish the link to the boy who had loved life. The boy who had then grown up, never achieving what he thought he might, and being far from the kind of father he'd always wanted to be. Unable to give his beautiful son the best of himself, because he didn't know where it was. Only that he had lost it somewhere along the way.

He slumped in the velvet green reading chair in the centre of the room and was about to tip the rest of the beer down his throat when there was a noise.

A scratching.

It came from the direction of the window.

A cold fear gripped his insides as he swung his gaze slowly towards the darkness outside. Tears began to sting his eyes and he had to blink them away to focus, only for the hairs on the back of his neck to stand on end as he saw the night shift and ripple through the glass.

The noise came again.

A scratching, like claws.

He lowered his beer, but tightened his fingers around the bottle. He had visions of a face emerging in the window. A pirate's gaunt and grimy face. Just as it had once upon a time. Just as it had many times since, in his nightmares, waking him up in twists of bedsheets and sweat.

Sitting up in his chair, feeling the cold sweat return, he prepared to fight or run.

Yet, in the end, all he could do was freeze, when to his utter horror a pair of non-human yellow eyes appeared and stared unblinking at him, above a slowly widening mouth full of razor-sharp teeth.

CHAPTER THREE

Tabitha

Cisco could remember enough of his past to know that anything appearing at the third-floor window of a house at night in the middle of winter wasn't something you wanted to engage with. Especially something that looked like it could tear your fingers from your hand.

But though he was with a cold, seeping fear through his entire being, a small part of his brain decided this was a good thing.

If he survived it, a monster attack would prove to the others it hadn't been a gas leak in 1989. That he was right to worry things were happening again, just as they had back then. That they *had* saved the town – possibly the world – and he had been right to keep that memory close, even when everyone else had let it go.

If he survived it.

Yet as the face pressed closer against the window, Cisco saw that it wasn't a monster at all. Sharp teeth, yes. But the lips curling above them didn't seem to be growling in hunger.

They were smiling.

At him.

"Are you ever going to open the window?" the beautiful black fox called to him, pressing her pointed snout further against the glass and scratching with her paw again.

Cisco stared, his mouth gaping open like a dope. His eyes flicked down to his bottle of beer to check the percentage of alcohol, making sure Jake hadn't given him a super-strong European ale by accident. Then he looked back to the window and tried unsuccessfully to make his mouth work.

It didn't.

The fox twitched her ears, looking increasingly impatient and cold. "It's truly good to see you again, my friend. But if you would be so kind as to let me in, I would appreciate it. The wind is strong at this height and I do not wish to ruin myself with a needless fall. I am not a cat and I do not have any spare lives to give."

A talking fox, Cisco thought on repeat in his head. *There is a talking fox outside the window.*

Shaking himself to move, he stood, kept his beer bottle handy – just in case – and leaned over to open the window, before snatching his hand back and stepping away again.

The fox purred with relief as she slunk inside, curled up her thick, bushy tail and sat on it on the windowsill. "Ah, that's better. Thank you, Cisco. Honestly, it was quite a climb to get up here, I'm glad it wasn't for nothing." Those teeth reappeared as she grinned again. "Do you remember the first time we did this? You hid under your covers for ten minutes! Took me three nights balanced precariously on your window ledge to get you to talk to me."

Cisco smiled awkwardly, wondering if he was possibly having a breakdown of some sort.

"I don't understand," he said.

Understatement of the year right there, his brain added.

"I see," the fox said.

"Are you really here right now?"

She looked around and seemed to shrug. "I think so."

"And you know my name?"

"Why wouldn't I? We are old friends, you and I. Comrades in arms, you could say."

Cisco felt his left eye twitch. He looked again at the beer bottle and decided to put it down, placing it carefully on a shelf next to a miniature Batmobile toy from the old TV series.

"Listen, you seem lovely. And I've seen a lot of strange things in my life. But I'm sure I would have remembered a talking fox?"

She inclined her head slightly, perhaps stifling a laugh. "Admittedly, you always told me you were a dog person. But we were definitely friends. Tabitha. My name is Tabitha."

The name struck a chord of sorts in the back of his mind, bringing with it a whole host of feelings he couldn't quite pin down long enough to grasp. Until he saw he was still holding the book he loved. The one with the boy and the sleek black cat on the front.

He looked up in shock.

Tabitha smiled again. "Yes, a bit like in that book. You'd be surprised by how many stories you humans read that contain little trails leading back to the truth of the world you live in. As it happens, that author and I were friends once too." Her little whiskers blew out in a sigh and she rearranged her tail to sit back and think. "You really don't remember me, do you? Or the adventures we had together? Hmm, well, that is not unexpected considering. Sometimes memories do not travel across the divide so well. But that does make what lies ahead a little more difficult."

"I remember that Halloween," Cisco replied quickly, not wanting to upset the fox. He'd been holding onto those memories of the ridiculous and magical all his life and here, finally, was someone – or something – he could converse with about it. "The monsters we fought. The battle against the pirates. Sealing the portal in the school gym. All of it. Nobody else remembers properly, but I do. They all believed it was a gas leak, just like the papers told them to believe. But I knew. I *knew* it was real."

"Then that is a start," Tabitha said kindly. "Do not fear, Cisco. We all have adventures we forget. Our lives are full of them. Not always fun, some darker than others, and we often remember so very little of them, or we put up walls to shut them out if we need to, yet they are still there somewhere. Locked away until the time is right to reveal them again."

Was now that time? Cisco wondered, glancing up to the window to check the fox's reflection was there and that he wasn't talking to himself. Because of all the questions he had ever asked in his life, he suddenly knew this was the most important. As if someone, somewhere, had rolled some dice and they were about to land.

The creature sat up straighter.

"We have been keeping an eye on you all these years, hoping you could see out the rest of your lives in peace. But, alas. The time has come to fight again."

"Fight what?" Cisco asked, panicked. Then he frowned. "Wait, you've been *watching* us?"

"For your own safety, you understand. Most of the time you won't have known it, but perhaps there will have been moments you felt the hairs on the back of your neck stand on end, as if you weren't alone. You might have turned to find a bird perched nearby, head tilted your way for a moment longer than necessary, before flying off. Or perhaps you would see nothing but the rustle of undergrowth or a glimpse of a shadow within the leaves of a tree."

"Creepy."

Tabitha laughed. It was a perfect little croaky growl. "It was for your own benefit. Most of the time, anyway. Admittedly, your old friends would occasionally come and check in because they missed you."

Cisco wasn't sure what to say to any of that. *Old friends? What old friends?*

"And what exactly did we need to be kept safe from?"

The fox's good mood soured. "What do you recall of Deadman's Grin?"

Cisco's entire body convulsed in a shiver.

Deadman's Grin. It was the first time he had heard the name spoken aloud in over three decades, and suddenly the two words rattled around his insides, pulling him this way and that, scratching at him like they were cold, decomposing fingers trying to claw their way out of the underworld through his skin.

Given what had been done to him in the past, he couldn't be sure they weren't.

"I remember enough," he said shakily, feeling clammy and nauseous, thinking back to the distinct tricorne hat that had accompanied the ghostly silhouette in every nightmare he'd had over the years. "I remember we fought him and killed him. I remember he tortured me." He touched a finger to his chest. "I remember all that very well."

Tabitha bowed her little head in a silent acknowledgement, then got up and circled back through the window onto the ledge. There she perched against the night, her black fur gleaming beneath the silvery moon. She glanced once over her shoulder. Watching for something? Or considering her next words?

"I'm afraid that the battle is not over yet. The evil you once faced is stirring again and the attack the other day, in the town not too far from here, is only the beginning. I know that is why you were drawn back to Dark Peak, Cisco. I know that you have been watching and waiting for this moment again and I also know you must be scared of what lies ahead. Yet I am glad for all our sakes that at least some part of you remembered enough to return you to us. For we have need of you and your friends again."

"My friends don't remember like I do, though. I've tried to convince them, but they refuse to believe anything beyond the excuses we were all given as kids. The lies the adults told us."

Tabitha seemed to start coughing up a fur ball, until Cisco realised the fox was laughing again, louder this time.

"Look around you, Cisco! Look at the room you're in. Jake has pieced together the past you shared, despite not understanding exactly what he was doing. The memories are right here. He collected them all. You just have to help your friends unlock them." She raised her nose into the night and sniffed. Her little paws shuffled, seemingly eager to be off. "But, first, you must help yourself. Come with me now. I will show you the worlds we once journeyed together and maybe it will help you remember the part of your past that you yourself have forgotten."

He felt a rising panic mixed with excitement.

"Come with you? Out there?"

He looked from Tabitha to the shadowy hill behind, then to the significant drop from the loft window. After everything he had been through, the breakdown of his marriage, realising he wasn't the father he wanted to be, the daily struggle of just surviving in the chaos of recent years... well, Cisco wasn't surprised to find himself taking a step towards an escape.

A talking fox? Other magical worlds he used to visit as a kid? It was a direct route back to everything he missed. He had done his best to hold onto the person he had once been and royally screwed that up. The responsibilities of being an adult had made it all so much harder to stay on the safe road through the woods, away from losing himself in the magic on either side. Now was his chance to be led back. To be shown the way home.

And he so badly wanted to go. To fully embrace that feeling of excitement building in his chest, the anticipation of rediscovering himself. While also fulfilling the vow he'd made to himself when deciding to return – to learn more about the evil he had once defeated and put it down for good this time.

To discover he hadn't been alone back then after all and would not be this time either? Well, the relief almost convinced him to go. To slip out of the window like he was a child again, following the magic and remembering what he had forgotten.

Except.

He was already at the window when he knew he couldn't leave. Not now. His hand rested against the frame, holding on tightly to prevent him following the fox back into his childhood – every instinct inside him suggesting there was a chance he might never want to return.

"My son," he said, frowning and feeling a little sick at the resentment that briefly flickered into being inside him. "George.

We're about to have dinner and I can't just up and disappear. Not like I used to. He needs me."

It explained nothing and everything.

Outside, an owl hooted from a distant tree. Something slunk in the bushes at the bottom of the garden, rustling through the leaves. And up on the roof, in the light of an attic window, Tabitha sighed.

"You are a father now, Cisco, with responsibilities you didn't have before. I understand that... and yet time continues to run out. Deadman's Grin is growing stronger. He is trying to come back."

"But we killed him?"

"Death is a human construct. In truth, what dies isn't always dead. The attack the other day is a sign the pirate is beginning to rouse from his otherworldly slumber. It was a random, uncoordinated lashing out of his powers, yes. Yet also a sign of worse to come. Please, as you once did before, trust me, Cisco. Climb out of the window and let us travel and prepare you. I will have you back before morning, as we used to, I promise."

There was a shout up the stairs. Then the thumping of someone coming up.

Cisco looked to the window, out to the darkness, where the promise of adventure and answers lay once more.

He stepped back.

"I can't," he said, his stomach sinking. "I'm sorry, Tabitha. Whatever I was able to do back then, whatever we did when we were kids, that's changed. I can't just do a runner from my friend's loft window. I can't just vanish and leave George behind right now. Not even to run off with a talking fox to an enchanted forest or wherever the hell you want to take me."

"Technically all forests are enchanted–" she began, her tail swishing back and forth.

"Please," he urged. "Go now before someone sees you. I'll come another night, I promise. Just let me know ahead of time so I can arrange a babysitter?"

Tabitha tilted her head, relenting. "Another night, then.

Although I will have to see if I can convince you another way in the meantime." She slipped back through the window and onto the roof tiles, muttering to herself, "I wonder if she'll have more luck..."

For some reason, Cisco immediately pictured a blonde woman. The same person who had haunted his dreams for years now, first as a girl, then older, always about the same age as him. Her anxious face reappearing every now and then. The way she shook him as though frustrated that he was never able to stay asleep long enough to learn what it was she wanted. Calling him without any sound ever reaching his ears.

"Wait, what'd you mean by that?" he called to the fox.

Tabitha, though, was already gone. His words drifted out into the night unanswered.

Jake poked his head into the room. "Kids are eating and our dinner's ready now too," he said, glancing around not so subtly for whoever Cisco had been talking to. Seeing nobody, he managed to bury his concern beneath a well-practiced smile. "Fancy another beer with it?"

Cisco glanced one more time into the cold, dark night, and shivered.

"Good idea," he said, shutting the window and locking it tight.

CHAPTER FOUR

The Pirate

The next day Cisco woke in a strange, yet comfortable bed, feeling weird and not entirely at ease.

He hadn't had a great sleep. The woman in the dream had returned, as he thought she might, confronting him in the middle of an otherworldly jungle, shaking him as though trying to wake him up.

Except now he'd heard her.

It's almost time, she'd said. *He's almost back.*

The dream had been stronger, if that was a thing. More realistic than before.

Whether or not the extra beer he'd had with dinner had anything to do with it, he wasn't sure. But he'd needed it and to be honest where was the harm, really? Being confronted with his past in the form of Mr Forbes' old collection had shaken him enough. But everything that had come after that, well, he didn't know where to start.

Had a talking fox really encouraged him to run away into the night and relearn what he was up against? What did it mean if it had actually happened?

There was always the chance he'd got drunker than he'd realised and conjured up an imaginary character like the one from a beloved childhood book, in order to deal with the nostalgic trip of finally coming home. Jake would appreciate that explanation. It felt scientific.

Yet all Cisco could think was that he and his friends had indeed played a part in a much bigger adventure than he'd considered when they were kids. And even though he'd remembered some of it – the run up to that Halloween in 1989, the battles with ridiculous monsters, the duel with Deadman's Grin himself – there had apparently been a whole magical part of that story that had fallen out of his brain.

He lay in bed pondering all this as the low, mid-morning December light peeked through the curtains, while listening to George bounce about on his bed in the room next door. His son was playing with Emily again, who had clearly taken a shine to him. They were discussing what they were going to cook for breakfast on the toy kitchen in his room.

"A veggie breakfast, just like your dad makes?" Emily suggested, her voice muffled through the wall and in between the excited gasps of George as he kept bouncing.

"No," George said, getting more and more out of breath. "Pancakes!"

Emily laughed and then so did George.

"Pancakes it is then!"

The laughter continued as they began to collect all their pretend ingredients and Cisco lay there smiling to himself for the briefest of happy moments, clinging desperately to this thread of reality, even as his mind ran itself in circles trying to understand the other realities he'd been presented with.

Then his phone momentarily brightened up the gloom with a Twitter notification.

Rolling over, he tilted the screen towards him and gazed blearily at the little blue box, hoping it was one of his friends saying hi or just a funny video or something positive and light.

Nope.

Bizarre attack in Manchester as costumed cannibal snowman partially EATS homeowner.

Cisco let the phone drop and rubbed his palms over his eyes.

"Fuck," he groaned, before getting up and beginning to formulate a plan.

The others in the house were all gathered in the kitchen when Cisco eventually made it downstairs. Jake was at the stove in a Father's Day apron, doing his best to flip pancakes. Natalie was teaching George how to smother them with margarine and maple syrup and sliced bananas. And the three teenagers were all reading books.

There wasn't a phone or tablet in sight. Just like it used to be, back in the day.

Of course, after he kissed his son on the top of his head to say good morning, Cisco immediately sat down at the table and doomscrolled through his own social media feeds.

"Good sleep?" Natalie asked.

"Uh-huh," he replied, as George slid across to his lap and started bouncing on his knee. He gave the boy a squeeze, then moved him straight into his own chair. "I don't know whether it was the beer or the amazing mattress, but it worked a treat, thank you, Natalie." He put his phone down and nodded to Jake, who slid a couple of fresh pancakes in front of him. "You know, I could get used to this, buddy."

His friend grinned. "You're both more than welcome to stay as long as you need."

"Can we *live* here?" George asked hopefully.

"Oh, well, we're only visiting for the moment, Georgie-pops. Just until I figure out what's going on with... well... everything."

Jake grabbed his own breakfast plate, which was more fruit than pancake, and sat down opposite. "And did you get anything figured out last night? You were up in that room for a while and I could have sworn I heard you talking to yourself."

Cisco opened his mouth, wondering if he should just be honest. But George was looking up at him curiously, so he simply shook his head. "I was just a bit gobsmacked by the collection. You really went and saved it all, didn't you? Mr Forbes would be pleased."

"We both know he would have preferred that you have it. Out of the four of us, you were always the one who appreciated his geeky tastes for entertainment. Kindred spirits and all that."

"Oh, he didn't like me at all," Cisco said through a mouthful of pancakes. "He was terrifying."

"He just thought you were mucking about with his daughter, that's all," Jake teased. "Anyway, I'm glad I could keep it in the family. Did you see anything up there that caught your eye? I'm more than happy to let some of it go to a better home with you and George here, when you get settled."

"Me too," Natalie added quickly, putting on an air of fake exasperation that Cisco knew wasn't entirely made up. "Whatever you want, take it. I'd like my loft back one day."

Cisco wiped away a dribble of maple syrup from the corner of his lips. He had been hoping they'd say something like that. It would give him the cover he needed for his plan. Not that it was really a plan with any kind of sense behind it, but it would make him feel like he was actually doing something – at least until his brain conjured up another talking animal.

"That's very kind of you both. Maybe I'll go and have another look this morning? It'll give me something to do."

"OK, but don't be long," Jake said, polishing off the rest of his fruit, then gesturing to his kids. "I've promised Emily and Nat a trip into Manchester to see the Christmas markets this afternoon and we're dropping off Lea and Anne at their friends on the way. You and George are coming too. We'll make an evening of it?"

"Sounds good," Cisco replied, his heart skipping a beat. This was almost too perfect. A drive into Manchester would take them near the scene of last night's attack. He could come up with an excuse to ask Jake to make a detour on the way back, maybe look for other signs of the supernatural, and judge for himself if there was any connection between these events and what he'd once experienced.

As Jake's girls all went off to get ready with barely a word of prodding from their parents, Cisco gave George a big warm smile.

"Shall we go and get ready too?"

"Nah."

George poked Cisco's remaining pancake with his finger and pulled it away, dripping maple syrup across the table.

"Did you not hear, we're going out to see–"

"I don't want to go out."

Cisco sighed. "But it's the Christmas markets. You'll love it."

"I don't want to go out!"

Jake leaned across the table and whispered conspiratorially, "Come on, George. It'll be fun."

"OK!" George said brightly, got down from the table, and ran off to the bathroom from where the gentle brushing of teeth could soon be heard.

Cisco narrowed his eyes at his friend.

"Seriously, how the *fuck* do you do it?"

Jake gave a humble shrug. Still shaking his head, Cisco excused himself and skulked straight to the loft to grab what he needed, hoping Tabitha was wrong about what was happening, while also hoping the War Wizards were still working in case she was right.

Manchester city centre was abuzz with festive cheer.

The crowds ebbed and flowed through the slick, neon-lit streets, pulsing with laughter and excitement that felt even more joyfully intense since the pandemic conditions had been lifted. People gathered with rosy cheeks above thick, colourful scarves, milling around the Alpine stalls, clinking mugs of mulled wine. And the air was thick with noise and the salty waft of fried onions and gravy, sweet-smelling cakes, and spices to make your eyes water.

Even Cisco had to admit he was enjoying himself.

Watching George embrace the chaos was a treat in itself. Where they had previously lived wasn't anywhere close to a city. Especially not a vibrant, beautiful city like Manchester. And even though he'd taken George down to the bustling chaos of London before, mainly to go visit the *Diplodocus* in the Natural History Museum, nothing beat the chaos of this fine northern town at the beginning of December, when the markets arrived, the nights were cold and dark, and the city centre became a glowing Christmas metropolis.

Jake had driven them in, which had given Cisco the chance to stow the old War Wizards in the boot of the car, under a pile of coats. He almost felt silly doing so, but the notification from earlier kept running through his mind. If he was going to try to find out what was going on, while bringing everyone along for the ride, it seemed like the responsible thing to do to be prepared to protect them. Even if that meant taking a gamble on the battered console weapons that hadn't been used in all the time that most people in the crowd had been alive.

What Cisco discovered he *wasn't* prepared for, was the addition to their party. When two familiar faces materialised from the crowd and waved to their little group, he stuttered and stumbled to a halt.

"Surprise!" Jake's tall, beautiful sister Michelle enveloped him in a hug, smothering his face with her deliciously perfumed scarf in a way that felt like being accosted by a cinnamon bun. "It's been *way* too long, Cisco. I still can't believe you're back. Or that you told Butthead here not to tell us."

He tried to say something in Jake's defence, but Michelle had already moved onto George, crouching in front of him and booping his nose.

"And you must be the George I keep hearing so much about! Well, aren't you just as cute as your father?"

George blushed and snuggled closer to Cisco's leg. Cisco ruffled his hair, also blushing.

"Yeah, I'm the worst," he said. "I'm sorry I didn't say anything, Michelle. It's a bit complicated. But lovely to see you, as always. You haven't changed a bit. None of you have, in fact."

His gaze drifted to Doc, who gave him a good-natured tongue poke, before she, too, made a fuss over George and introduced her to the curly-haired girl of a similar age hanging onto her leg: their daughter, Cecilia.

Jake theatrically ran a hand through his perfect hair while pretending to flex his bicep. "I like to think I grew up a bit since we were all last together, thank you very much."

"You'll always be the nerdy little dipshit to me, no matter how much time you spend in the gym," Michelle said, punching him hard in the shoulder.

"Come on, there's no harm in looking after yourself, right, Cisco?"

Cisco offered a smile of solidarity, trying to ignore how well the other three had aged, while he felt a bit like a schlub, who couldn't remember even seeing a gym, let alone being in one.

"I'm famished, let's eat," he said, deciding to play to his strengths.

An hour later the group lounged around the booth table in the busy pizzeria, amid scatters of crusts, doughballs and with a comforting cloud of garlic hanging over them. Outside the window, the city continued heaving like an ocean of excitement, while the good cheer had spilled inside, too. Doc and Michelle were teasing Jake for his piss-poor Italian pronunciation of Giardiniera. Natalie was still laughing at all the stories they'd been telling about each other from when they were kids. And, to one side, sitting silently opposite one another, George, Emily and Cecilia were quietly getting on with being hypnotised by the glowing screens of their tablets as they played online via the poor pizzeria Wi-Fi.

"Not too much longer on that thing," Cisco said quietly to George.

The boy grunted a brief, "OK, Dad," which was what he'd done the three times in the last ten minutes Cisco had said exactly the same thing. They both knew it was just something to say for Cisco to make himself feel like he was a caring parent, while being too much of a coward to actually stop the gaming and deal with the fallout. It would come soon enough, when they made the move to leave.

In the meantime, the adults were finishing up their drinks and telling tales of teenagers doing teenagery things.

"You actually got kicked out of the cinema?" Natalie asked Doc, wide-eyed as she swung her glass of wine between Doc and Michelle. "What did you two do? Were you making out? Oh, please tell me you were making out! I remember the woman who used to run the Broadway and she was such an old curmudgeon. I bet you gave her a shock."

Michelle flashed her perfect smile and put her arm around her wife. "Oh, we gave her a shock all right."

Cisco was surprised to see Doc's gaze drop to the table, her cheeks flushing fiercely. It was exactly the same smitten and nervous look she always had around Jake's sister as teenagers. He loved knowing that hadn't changed in all these years, even after they'd got married and had a child. They'd somehow kept the magic.

It was nice to know it was still possible.

"We weren't making out though," Doc said, managing to find her voice, even as she nuzzled into Michelle's embrace. "At least, not on that occasion." She blushed some more. "I think we were watching *Arachnophobia* and what happened was I'd dropped my Milky Bar behind the seat when that spider jumps at that dude, and I then had to use my lighter to try and find it. The attendant thought I was trying to set the seats on fire."

Natalie pulled a face. "You used to smoke?"

"Hell no, I just liked having a lighter on me! I guess I always thought it could be useful if we ever got stuck anywhere dark."

Doc's lips lingered on that last word, savouring it as though tasting something familiar. She frowned and her gaze drifted to Cisco, before immediately flickering away again, almost guiltily. For a moment, he could have sworn he saw something in her eyes. A flash of recognition. A half-remembered memory. But in an instant she was back to reminiscing about far less concerning parts of their childhood.

"Anyway, that was the story of how I ended up being turfed out of the Broadway."

Jake smiled. "I bet you were gutted to have to leave. I mean, it *was* fifty pence of pocket money you'd never get back."

"Oh god, that's right!" Michelle said, grabbing the last piece of garlic bread and snapping it in half. "Only 50 pence a ticket. You could slide a pound under that ticket window and get half back and then blow it on sweets. A whole night out for a quid." She gestured with half the bread to Natalie, as she spoke while chewing the other half. "How much… was it… the last time we all went out to the cinema together?"

"Enough to make Jake turn whiter than he normally is when he had to hand over his credit card," Natalie said dryly, giving her husband a loving nudge in the ribs. "We had to remortgage the house to cover it."

They all laughed.

"Seriously though, those were the days, eh?" Doc said wistfully, her gaze sweeping across them all before losing itself in the bottom of her bottle of Peroni. "That cinema was magic. Totally old school. Balcony up top. Shitty seats. And all the best movies came out in the 80s too. Do you guys remember seeing *Big* there? *The Last Crusade? Batman?*"

Cisco swirled the last of his beer around happily at all those scenes playing out in his head. "I'm pretty sure we saw everything there, Doc. It was our go-to place after the bowling alley and the ice rink, after all. We basically never left. I'm sure our bum imprints are still in those seats in the back row."

"Ah, you don't know," she said sadly. "Yeah, they probably would be if the place was still there, but the Broadway became a pub ten years ago."

"Another pub? Aren't there, like, fifteen of those in Dark Peak already?"

"Twenty-six," Jake confirmed. "Worse still, the bowling alley is now a swanky bar and the ice rink got bulldozed for an apartment block. Although I suppose that's more our style, now we're all old and property conscious?"

"None of us could last a minute on that ice now, anyway," Michelle added. "Not without breaking something."

Cisco lifted his nearly finished drink in the air over the table. "To the good old days."

They clinked glasses. A sparkling sound, almost magical in its melody. A musical chime that, to Cisco, in that moment, spoke of finally coming home. Because, he suddenly understood, as he took in all their faces, sometimes it wasn't just about the place you returned to. Sometimes home was also the people who were there to greet you.

He put the glass down and signalled for the bill. It was time. He took a breath, grabbed George's tablet and flipped the cover over to shut it down.

"Come on, everyone," he said, over the loud whine his son suddenly began to emit, like an angry car alarm. "Let's go get Christmassy."

Outside in the cold, their breaths fogged the air but did little to mute the bright lights and decorations swallowing up the city around them. Doc held out her gloved hand to George – who was still complaining about losing access to his game – and wiggled her fingers at him. "Come on, kiddo, you don't need a tablet where we're going. You can walk with me and we'll keep an eye out for Father Christmas and his elves. They're bound to be around here somewhere."

"Cool!" George said, instantly distracted as Doc led him away talking about all the decorations they could see. Michelle wandered after them with Cecilia and took his other hand and within seconds he was already making them swing him in the air – much to little Cecilia's disgust.

"That went well," Jake said, clapping Cisco on the shoulder. He gave Natalie and Emily a nod as they wandered after the others, while he and Cisco held back. "Sorry I didn't tell you we were meeting them, but I wasn't sure how you'd react."

Cisco shrugged as he shrank into his jacket, trying to seem put out but failing miserably. It had been the best night he'd had in ages. A throwback moment he wouldn't forget in a hurry.

He still didn't know why he'd asked Jake to lie about his return to Doc and Michelle. It made even less sense now they'd all clicked back into place as if they'd never been apart. Sure, maybe he'd been worried about telling them the real reason why he was here. But, more likely, he wondered if he'd just been too scared to discover they didn't actually care? Either way, they were together again now and it felt good. *So* good. The weight was lifting from his shoulders and he felt an injection of pure joy into his aging heart as he and Jake began to trail after the others into the maelstrom of festive colours, delicious smells and cheerful noise.

"You know," he mused, "this was always my favourite time of year. Behind Halloween, of course."

"Christ. Even after *that* Halloween?"

Cisco laughed. "Yeah, I know. It doesn't make sense given what you thought happened and what I thought happened… and the fallout afterwards. But there's just something about that time of year, I guess."

There was no guessing about it. He knew why. Despite the battles with evil, despite the near-death experiences, and even despite the hell mouth he'd been turned into, none of it dulled the joy of being with his friends through it all. That kind of experience left a mark on a person. He would forever associate pumpkins and scatters of autumn leaves – and ghosts and haunted mansions and underground lairs, of course – with these people who made up the best days of his life.

Jake tried to sound understanding, while remaining completely unconvinced. "I'll let you have that, but it's Christmas for me, thanks. Always and forever. The cheer, the bright colours, the lack of everything being associated with dying. Halloween can suck it."

Cisco nodded solemnly. "Oh yeah. For you, Christmas makes sense. You're definitely more of a jolly sort, I'll give you tha–"

He stopped talking as his body was seized with a bone-chilling cold. He dropped to one knee in a puddle of decomposing mulch and soggy chips. His palm smacked against the paving slab as a wave of nausea hit him, sending his stomach into spasms and forcing him to squeeze his eyes shut through the agony.

It was like dying, only without the dying part.

Then, as quickly as it had started, it stopped again. Everything went suddenly numb. And he opened his eyes to see a reflection in the ripples of the puddle he was slung over.

A shadowy figure in a long black coat, his pale, grim face hidden by a tricorne hat.

I'm coming for you, he rasped.

Then he vanished.

"Cisco?" Jake urged in a panic, crouching beside him as people around began to notice and back away quickly. "You OK? You look like you're going to spew!"

"F- fine."

Cisco waved him away. It had certainly felt like he was about to upchuck, and perhaps burst into flames, but the feeling was already gone again. As though it hadn't really happened in the first place.

The fear though. That was still real.

"Jake, what do you remember from 1989?"

"Jesus, what?" Jake yanked Cisco to his feet and then looked him up and down carefully. "Why? You don't want to go over that again now, do you?"

"I'm not sure I have much choice." The Christmas colours of the market swam in Cisco's vision as he leaned into his friend and grabbed his jacket, as much to steady himself as get him to listen. "That Halloween was when Dark Peak lost its shit and never got it together again, right? Just tell me what you remember. Because you always maintained that it must have been the gas leak as we were told, but while the others believed it, I know you. You're too scientific to trust that kind of bullshit excuse. Mass hallucinations across an entire town over a couple of weeks? Come on, that's not possible. We all would have died."

Jake glanced between his clearly disturbed friend and where the others had congregated around a stall selling handmade baubles. He sighed as if finally giving in.

"I don't remember much. But, yeah, there was always something niggling in my head about it. Felt like a jigsaw puzzle where the pieces have been hammered together to fit into a neat shape, and the picture they show is..."

"Wrong?"

"Yep."

Cisco managed to find his balance again and let his friend go. "And?"

"Dad was the one who came up with the gas leak theory. He said the town needed answers and this was the only one he had. The police needed him to solve it. So he solved it."

"Yet you knew he was wrong, didn't you?"

Jake looked uncomfortable with that accusation. Cisco wished he had the time and energy to tackle this conversation properly, putting the words in a better and less blunt order, but he was worried now. Something was about to happen and he needed his friend on side.

"I don't think he was wrong," Jake said firmly. "I think he did what the town needed to be done. That was the narrative that made the most sense and the longer we went on saying it, the easier it became to believe. Whatever I thought didn't really matter. It was all a bit fuzzy anyway."

Cisco tensed, standing absolutely still in the midst of the crowds.

There had been a tremble in the pavement.

"Jake, I need you to remember something specific now. When your father got to the school, he found someone else with us. A tall man in old fashioned clothes and a pirate hat." Jake nodded slowly and Cisco felt his pulse race as he finally closed in on the truth. "What happened to him, mate? They say he died, but I don't know if that's true anymore."

Jake's brow knotted in that way it did when he had been a child trying to figure out a particularly complex scientific conundrum. He even raised a finger to the bridge of his nose, before remembering he no longer had any glasses to push back up.

"Deadman's Grin?" he whispered.

There. He remembers too.

Cisco felt the relief sag his shoulders, despite the simultaneous cold shiver that ran up his spine as the words were uttered aloud for the second time in the past twenty-four hours.

Jake had finally given the name life again on his own lips, without any prompting. What was it that Tabitha had said: that his friends' memories were still there, they just needed to be unlocked? Was that what was happening now? Cisco could have cried with happiness.

"Yes, that was his name, Jake! The pirate responsible for everything that Halloween. You're remembering!"

Jake opened his mouth, looking for all the world like he was about to confirm it.

But nothing came out.

Another thud shook the ground. The hand-carved wooden decorations on the stall next to them jingled and shook. A little girl beside it dropped her roasted marshmallow in surprise and began to cry.

Then the screaming started and they both turned to see something moving across the rooftops of Manchester.

A giant, illuminated figure with a beard and a floppy red hat.

"What the hell is *that*?" Jake asked weakly.

They watched as it beat its chest, then jumped from the Town Hall to crush a couple of stalls beneath its oversized black boots.

"Holy god," Cisco breathed, as the city's beloved inflatable decoration lifted its head and roared into the night. He turned to Jake, aghast. "It's Father Christmas!?"

CHAPTER FIVE

The Battle of Christmas

"He's real, he's real!" George shouted excitedly as they ran for their lives.

There had been no time to explain the situation properly. Cisco and Jake had simply grabbed the others and made them leg it. George was still under the impression this was part of the festivities, even as people around them were crying out and tripping over each other in an effort to get away, diving into shops and pressing their terrified faces to the windows as the giant Father Christmas stomped down Cross Street towards the Arndale Shopping Centre. The boy kept pulling at Cisco's arm, wanting to stop and tell the big man what toys he wanted, until Cisco finally scooped him up into his arms and carried him along faster.

Doc wasn't as easily placated. Carrying Cecilia, she kept looking back over her shoulder and then to Cisco.

"Don't even say it," she insisted, running alongside him now. "Don't you dare. There has to be some normal explanation for this. A malfunction or... something? I don't know. But don't even think of saying you told us so. This has nothing to do with what happened when we were kids. *Nothing.*"

Cisco gestured to the giant Santa ripping out a lamppost and swinging it like a hockey stick. A policeman who'd gone to help went flying across the square. Two men trying to get selfies with the monster were then splattered across the street.

"Explain *that*," he shot back.

She glowered but couldn't reply. Because of course she couldn't. There was no normal explanation for any of this, only the nonsensical, supernatural explanation that had once driven him out of town and had now driven him back.

Thankfully he had prepared for such an occasion. Perhaps not expecting as big an occasion as the one currently chasing them through the streets of Manchester, but they were going to have a better chance of defending themselves than anyone else here.

"We should take cover!" Michelle shouted, as a police van rushing towards the giant was speared to the tarmac by the lamppost being slammed through their vehicle.

Natalie nodded in agreement. "Yes, cover."

"Where?" Jake asked, carrying a sobbing Emily in his arms.

Cisco grabbed Doc's arm and leaned in.

"Back to the car," he gasped, feeling his lungs burning and the weight of his son growing heavier by the second. "Jake's car. Arndale."

"I don't think we'll make it. We should hide while we can."

"No time to explain. Please?"

There must have been something in the desperate look he gave her that got his message across.

"Right, keep going," she said, still cradling her daughter, while pulling along Michelle and giving Jake a look that said he better not argue. "But off Cross Street. Quickly, down here."

They pulled off the main street into an alley. It cut around the back of the chemists and was more of a rat run to get back to the car park, but Cisco figured it for a smart move. The towering inflatable wouldn't bother coming down here.

An unearthly, blood-curdling roar shook the windows around them and sent flocks of pigeons flying for their lives. Cisco looked back to see Santa's glowing red eyes fix on their little group of escapees, ignoring the other people scattering around his boots.

It's us he's after.

Shit.

"Go, *go!*" he yelled, as Father Christmas jabbed a car-sized mitten between the brick buildings, only just missing them. As they hurried further into the maze of alleyways, past overflowing dumpsters and bin bags, there was another furious shaking. Suddenly a shadow loomed overhead and a telegraph pole slammed down just behind Cisco's feet. He stumbled a few yards and only just caught himself before he and George fell into the rubbish.

"Cisco!" Doc cried, but he waved her on.

"Keep moving, I'm still here."

Emily was full on wailing now, her head buried into Jake's neck. Cisco risked a quick look at his son to find George sleepily grinning from ear to ear as his head bobbed against his dad's shoulder, still thinking it was some kind of Christmas game. It was quite something to behold. All that energy Cisco often wasted trying to get George to be engaged with the real world outside of computer games and *this* is what he ended up enjoying? Kids made no sense sometimes.

"Market Street!" Michelle announced.

She led the group out of the alley into the pedestrianised section of the city famous for its chaos. They ran up the cobbles, towards the entrance into the Arndale. Two buskers gaped in horror as they saw what rose on the skyline behind, then dove out of the way as Father Christmas dropped from the air and cracked the street beneath them, crushing a man with his clipboard and questionnaire who had been pestering shoppers.

Blood spilled out from beneath the monster's jolly black boots as Cisco and the others darted around them and through the double doors into the bright interior of the shopping centre.

"Up... escalator," he said, his voice barely a whisper now.

Behind them the giant beat his fists against the walls and howled his rage. Decorations began to fall around them. Glass windows shattered as they passed.

Yet, for the moment, he couldn't get in.

Up past the shops and through the food court they ran. Slower now. Much slower than they had been. Had this been easier when they'd been kids, running through the tunnels under William House, or through the streets of Dark Peak? Cisco knew it must have been. He certainly didn't remember his lungs hurting this much or his muscles threatening to explode. Age and laziness had taken their toll. Every part of him ached. He badly wanted to sit down. Or sleep. Or just die quietly in a corner somewhere.

Yet still he pressed forward, into the car park.

A glance to his shoulder revealed George was now drifting off to sleep.

He almost laughed. Couldn't get the boy to sleep normally, but, sure, pitch him into a chase across the city with a maniacal Father Christmas trying to kill them and he was out like a light.

"Three C," Jake called out, pointing to a sign on the wall. "The car should be around here."

"There!" Natalie answered, spotting the silver SUV and heading towards it.

As they drew up, his friends instinctively looked to Cisco. It was a moment he remembered all too well from their Halloween experience. He had been the unofficial leader, after all. Definitely not the bravest among them or the cleverest or even the coolest. Just the one who believed enough.

He tried to open his mouth to offer some stirring words of wisdom, only to gasp and dry heave.

Handing George to Michelle, he bent double, feeling his head go light. "I'm OK," he insisted. "Just get the kids in the car. Natalie, can you stay with them?"

Natalie seemed to have no problem with that. She helped Emily into the front seat, while Doc strapped Cecilia in the back and the now softly snoring George next to her.

Cisco then beckoned his old friends to the back of the vehicle.

"We can't just drive away," Doc said firmly. It took him a little by surprise, though it was a welcome one. The old Doc wouldn't have left a fight like this either. And even though she still clearly didn't have a clue what was going on, there was enough of that spirit guiding her, even now. "People are dying out there. We have to help somehow. We can't run."

"We're not going to run."

"Then what?"

Cisco answered her by opening the boot and taking great delight in the shocked expressions on all their faces as they saw the four battered and battle-scarred 8-bit games consoles he had tucked away beneath some spare coats.

He picked up his War Wizard and with only a modicum of embarrassment undid the straps to their maximum length and squeezed it onto his back.

It was tight and only just fit.

But it *did* fit.

"We're not going to run away from this," he said. He felt an inane grin spreading across his face, much like the one George had been wearing for the duration of the chase. He gestured with his blaster for the others to suit up. "We stand and fight. Because we're–"

He was interrupted by a coughing fit, which ended with him vomiting up a tiny bit of bile.

"The cavalry?" Doc finished, grimacing.

He gave her a thumbs up.

She slapped him on the shoulder. "Exercise, man. Honestly. You'll live longer."

Doc picked up her old plastic blaster and inspected it. "I'm not going to ask where these came from right now," she said, fixing Jake with a look, before tentatively slipping the console onto her back. "But after this is done, you owe me an explanation."

"I think I'll take my chances with Evil Santa," Jake replied, slipping on his glove accessory.

Michelle glanced around the group. "I'm having serious déjà vu, though I'm not quite sure why." As she flicked the switch that lit Jake's War Wizard up, she watched her brother flex his fingers.

Electrical static flew up the cord and drifted around his palm like a mini aurora borealis.

"Whoa, cool."

"Careful with that," Cisco said quickly. "It packs a punch."

"This old bit of plastic?"

"It's a bit more than that, as I think you already remember. You built it, after all."

"They're just old Halloween costumes, Cisco," Doc said, although he could tell by the waver in her voice that even she wasn't sure about that statement anymore. "Are we going to defeat the bloody monster out there by making him split his sides with laughter? Or are you hoping Jake here is going to snap his fingers and erase him from existence?"

Cisco turned to Natalie in the car. "We're going to go and help the people out there. Stay in the car and stay safe. We'll be back soon, OK?"

He didn't give her a chance to respond. Grabbing Jake by the shoulders, he led him away from the car to the next level down and the entrance back to the shopping centre. Doc and Michelle followed warily.

"Cisco–" Doc began.

He shook his head, spun Jake around until his War Wizard faced Doc, then flicked open the cartridge door and pointed inside. "You don't remember yet, but you will. Jake built these to cause maximum damage depending on whatever game you inserted into the slot."

She looked in. "*Punch 'Em Up*?"

"It was Jake's go-to game back in the day. And to be honest the only one that ever worked with the glove. But it does the trick."

Her eyebrow raised. "And what have I got?"

Cisco grinned. "Your go-to game was *Blastoid*. Michelle's was *Ice Castle Princess*. Mine was *Mega Boy II*."

"Show me."

Stepping far enough aside to ensure he did this safely, Cisco levelled his blaster at a sign for parking fines.

"Ready?"

"For what?"

He squeezed the trigger.

For a split second, nothing happened. He panicked. What if the consoles didn't work after all this time? What if the cartridges he'd carefully selected earlier were too old or dusty or just plain dead? What if the magic power source Jake had built into them had worn off?

Or, worst of all, what if he had been imagining their childhood heroics after all?

But just as he heard another roar of the angry Father Christmas in the distance, and the building shook again, he felt the familiar kick as the handle bit into his palm. And a neat 8-bit chime sounded at the same time as an electric wave shot out of the barrel of his blaster and melted the parking sign in a blast of blue and grey pixels.

"Mother*fucker*," Doc breathed, glancing between the sign and Cisco and then back to the sign. "It's real?"

Cisco regarded his friends, feeling a sense of warmth he hadn't felt in a long time. As the War Wizards had been pulled on, it seemed the years had slid off. As if time had suddenly gone full circle and he was a child again, strapping on the modified consoles and clutching the plugged-in blaster in his hand, ready to save the world.

"Let's go melt some shit," he said.

It felt good to be back. The gaming blaster in his hand, humming ever so slightly against his skin. The weight of the War Wizard heavy on the back of his winter jacket. It was difficult to remember they were about to properly face down a dark magic they hadn't seen in three decades.

And yet to Cisco it felt like no time at all had passed... except for the ache in his knees, the fact he was wheezing far more than he would have liked, and the way the straps holding the console to him bit into his clothes far more tightly than they had ever done as a child.

The mind is ready, but the body is middle-aged, he considered, as they ran back into the bright interior of the shopping centre, sliding across the polished floors, weapons raised and ready for action.

"What's the plan then?" Doc asked, jogging alongside him as they ran past *Planet Sport* and saw that it was mostly empty, except for a few frightened faces gathered in the back of the store, poking out behind the football boots. "I mean, you came prepared for this. You must have a plan. Because you totally understand what's going on and I don't even have the imagination to begin to pretend there is a reasonable explanation here."

Jake pulled up on the other side. "This is why you wanted to visit the suburbs on the way back, isn't it? You heard that ridiculous story about the snowman murder and you wanted to check it out because you knew something was happening. And that's why you brought the War Wizards?"

"I didn't know for sure…"

"It's the pirate, isn't it? He's still alive, isn't he?"

"What pirate?" Michelle called from behind.

"He's definitely dead," Cisco replied, ignoring her and gesturing to the roof that evil Santa was now trying to climb. "Or at least he was. But I think he might be waking up again?"

"The dead can't wake up!"

"You tell that to him."

"*What pirate*?" Doc insisted.

It was Jake who answered, with a sigh through gritted teeth.

"Deadman's Grin," he said. He gave Cisco an apologetic look. "There was no gas leak that Halloween, was there? It really all happened. We three don't remember, yet it all happened and that monstrosity outside is real, isn't it?"

"Yup."

They rounded the corner to the exit of the shopping centre and pulled up short, seeing the giant, ruddy-cheeked, inflatable face staring in. His eyes burned blood-red as he saw them and he threw his mittens against the windows, shattering the glass and sending shards exploding inwards.

Cisco pulled Doc back to safety under the porch of a confectionery store. The four of them looked at each other.

"A pirate brought that thing to life?" Doc asked. "This *Deadman's Grin*?"

"Deadman's Grin," Michelle echoed.

It wasn't a surefire sign they were remembering. But just the fact they uttered the words aloud, making them real, just as Jake had earlier, gave Cisco a sliver of hope that maybe they could survive this. That his friends would come back to him. The team would be back together.

"The Panic Stations," he said under his breath.

Now Doc's eyes crinkled in horrified recognition. "Now *that* I remember. Christ, was that the name you gave us? It was, wasn't it? No wonder I tried to block it out all these years."

"We were kids! We had to have a name, even if it was a bit shit." Cisco looked to Jake to back him up, but apparently his friend had already reached the limit of his memory for the moment. With a sigh, Cisco waved his blaster at the exit they'd been running towards. "It doesn't matter now anyway. Wherever we go from here, whatever we call ourselves, we need to finish off Evil Father Christmas first."

"We just going to fry him like you did that sign back there?"

"I guess."

Jake was staring at the electricity crackling across his fingertips as they twitched within the plastic glove. "Do you think that will work though? Just shooting or punching him in his boot or whatever? He's pretty huge. What if it doesn't affect him?"

"Got a better idea?"

As it turned out, Jake had. But before he could tell them what it was there was a scream from behind them and they scuttled to the edge of the balcony to look down at the ground floor.

There was a security guard there, among the scattered tables, chairs and drinks. His arms and legs were bleeding, pinned to the floor by light-up icicles, and he was groaning and squirming in agony. What looked like an angel was shoving a glitter-filled candy cane down his throat. Its eyes were also glowing a bright, sickly red.

"What the *hell?*" Michelle breathed.

"This is all escalating a lot more horrifically than I thought it might," Cisco replied, feeling queasy. He turned and sat with his back to the barrier, so he didn't have to watch the festive angel violating the man. "Deadman's Grin's magic must be growing stronger. Father Christmas must be a conduit or something, helping to possess other things? Maybe if we take him out...?"

Doc raised her blaster carefully and pointed it over the railing. "The dude down there can't wait for that. I'm going to shoot the angel."

"You can't shoot angels!" he hissed.

"Why not?"

"It's... it's Christmas?"

"You literally just said we should take out Santa."

"That's different! Angels are–"

He didn't get to finish. There was a desperate scream and they peered over the railing again to see it was already too late. The angel's grotesque job done, the guard convulsed once. Twice. His back arching against the floor, before a bloody line ripped its way across his white shirt. There was the sickening sound of skin tearing.

And a glittery festive penguin burst out of his chest.

It tossed one of the man's organs up in the air and swallowed it whole.

"Fucking *what?*" Doc cried.

She hadn't meant to be so loud. Yet as with all shopping centres everywhere, the Arndale was notoriously well designed to amplify the noise of toddler tantrums, family arguments, and public breakups as much as possible. Consequently, her words carried. Enough to draw the attention of the chestbursting penguin below. Its entrail-smeared beak tilted up towards the middle-aged gunslingers and it cried out for reinforcements – following which dozens of festive penguins streamed in from surrounding storefronts.

"Shoot them, shoot them!" Cisco said, trying to ignore the knowledge there must be other empty-chested shoppers dotted around having met the same fate. He stumbled backwards as the evil birds began to flap their little wings and fly slowly towards them.

"But penguins can't fly!" Jake insisted.

"*That's* what you have a problem with here?" Doc shot back.

Cisco barely had time to get his blaster up before the first of the creatures leapt over the barrier towards him, but the electricity wave he fired spiralled clear over their evil little heads. Luckily Doc didn't miss. She swept in, shooting fireballs into their midst and kicking their flaming winged corpses back down to the food court.

"This is nuts," she said, grabbing his hand and hauling him up. "We're leaving."

Yet as they ran for the exit – bursting into the night beneath the dangling legs of Father Christmas, shooting over their shoulders as he began to chase them – Cisco realised the glittery penguins weren't the only decorations standing in their way.

Over the tramlines, towards where Debenhams had been, they threw themselves into another section of the Christmas markets, only to be confronted with stall upon stall of festive shit stirring into life as Deadman's Grin's evil worked its magic.

Jake ran into a life-sized gingerbread man and only just managed to throw out a punch that split it in two, sending the torso flying into the tram power lines overhead where it was quickly toasted. Michelle, meanwhile, had accidentally pulled out her blaster cord and was spinning in circles trying to reattach it to the console as she ran, while kicking away the wind-up toy soldiers that were circling and bayonetting her legs.

Then a skinny little shape leapt straight out of a stall, landed on Doc's head, and with a loud shriek tried to gouge her eyes with a glittery pine-cone ornament.

"Whattheshi–"

Doc spun and tore at her face, trying to get the thing off. Cisco reached over, snatched the creature from his friend and jammed it headfirst between the safety bars of a heating grille at the next stall along.

The machine's hum instantly increased in pitch as the Elf on a Shelf's legs flailed wildly and then caught fire. The entire thing then exploded behind them.

"Creepy little shits," Doc muttered, as they continued to run.

The shaking underneath their feet increased as the furious Father Christmas thundered after them. They kept shooting, sending a variety of electricity waves, fireballs and icicles towards him, but it was becoming clear their 8-bit firepower alone wasn't going to bring him down. He might be weakening, the glow in his eyes flickering with each smoking hit, but there was still enough of him to continue to gain on them.

Exhausted, Cisco felt his body begin to weigh up the pros and cons of just lying down and becoming a host for all kinds of Christmas ornaments.

The giant roared as though he sensed victory.

So this is what happens after the credits roll, Cisco thought. *Once you've defeated the bad guys. Once you've saved the day. This is what you get for your trouble. You grow up to have to do it all over again but it's worse and you're too tired and maybe you figure death isn't as bad after all.*

It didn't seem fair. After somehow saving the town of Dark Peak from being overrun by improbable monsters and a pirate unleashing the underworld, this was the fate they'd won. A lifetime of being a joke, of running away, and returning to die in the same ridiculous manner they had only narrowly avoided in the first place.

"Jake!" he moaned. "This isn't working. He's too big and it's going to take too long to finish him off like this. We need something else to help bring him down. What was that idea of yours?"

His friend threw his gloved hand to the side, pointing.

"The wheel."

And there it was. Looming over Piccadilly Gardens, the Manchester Eye. A Ferris wheel nobody had really wanted in the city, but that had grown into a familiar comfort for locals over the years.

A comfort that just happened to be bigger than the giant chasing them.

"*That's* your brilliant plan?" Doc asked Jake, as the four of them ducked behind the pigeon-shit-encrusted statue of Queen Victoria.

"Admittedly, it's less of a plan and more of a hope."

"Hope is all we need," Cisco insisted, feeling like he might be sick again. He looked up fearfully at the statue in case she came to life to rebuke him. She was still, for now. "We need to finish this before it gets any worse."

"Whatever *this* is," Michelle said, looking at the scratches on her leg and wincing as she pulled out a tiny wooden bayonet.

Jake nodded and leaned on the stone plinth as he glanced around.

"Doc, Michelle, stay here and cover us," he said. "Wait for my signal. Cisco, you and I are going to make a run for it. We'll be the bait. Keep firing at Father Christmas, weaken him a bit more, and as soon as we've drawn him into the shadow of the wheel, I'll punch out the supports underneath."

"Right on top of the bastard," Cisco nodded. "Nice."

"I figure the sheer force of the impact should crush him enough to let us blow up whatever dark magic you say is controlling him?"

Despite feeling as though he might collapse at any moment, Cisco felt a tiny buzz of excitement inside him. Without even thinking, he stuck his fist into the centre of the group.

"Panic Stations!"

His friends looked at him with horror. He withdrew his hand slowly, feeling his cheeks colour.

"We'll need a new name," Doc said firmly.

"Fine, whatever."

"I'm serious, Cisco. I can't be doing with that shit. We're grown-ups and this is serious stuff." She sighed. "Now go and entice Evil Santa to his death please."

Cisco and Jake burst out from the side of the statue like a modern-day, far-less-cool Cassidy and Sundance. Cisco yelled and fired electric shots as they dodged the boots that came stomping down, repeatedly hitting the monster as they circled him, until he finally swung his face around and began to follow them.

"It's working," he cried to Jake. "Go!"

He ducked as the other festive nightmares came swarming out of the market stalls and fireballs from Doc started shooting past the pair of them, interspersed with the *thwack* of Michelle's icicles finding their targets. Clearing a path towards the wheel.

The stomping followed in their wake as they pulled into the shadow of the towering attraction. Jake leapt over the barrier to position himself by the supports. Cisco stood in the clearing beside it and turned around to face off against the big man himself.

"Oi, dipshit!" he yelled up, taking another shot and then waving his arms to get the giant's attention. "I've got a gift for you down here, you inflatable prick."

Father Christmas's evil, foul-smelling breath washed over Cisco as he leaned over, his eyes burning fiercely.

"*Dieeeeee!*" he roared.

"Now!" Jake shouted.

Cisco took one last shot, then turned and ran. The wheel above them groaned as Jake used his glove to punch the joists out from under it, before the metal screeched as it tore free and it began to tumble sideways. The pods dangled, then came loose and crashed down like gigantic hailstones. The Evil Father Christmas cried out in anger, but it was too late.

Cisco was thrown in the air as the wheel finally collapsed and the ground shattered behind him. He stumbled behind the graffitied concrete wall that cut the gardens in two, before peering out and watching the giant inflatable decoration slowly deflating beneath the twisted city attraction.

The being's eyes flashed momentarily, before Cisco took aim and unleashed a final volley of pixelated gunfire. It did the trick. With one last roar, the glow finally went dark, and the gas inside the giant ignited and exploded, sending shards of metal and colourful Christmas critters rocketing into the night.

Doc, Jake and Michelle hobbled over, just as the other creatures closing in around them collapsed like puppets whose strings had been cut – their conduit of dark magic extinguished, for now.

The friends sat back, exhausted, against the concrete.

"Is that really what we used to get up to when we were kids?" Michelle asked between gasps and the sounds of things breaking nearby. Her neat blonde locks now looked bedraggled and unkempt. "Is that why Jake and I ended up grounded after that Halloween, unable to hang out with you, even after they fixed up the school enough for us to go back for the final term?"

Cisco leaned back and closed his eyes. "Basically, yes. Although I don't remember it hurting quite this much."

A head found his shoulder. Doc's. Her hand patted his leg and gave it a gentle squeeze. "I'd say it's not the years, it's the mileage, but it's probably both. I know you came back to save us, Cisco. But don't you think these kinds of escapades are best left to the kids? We're too old and tired for this crap."

"I'd love to find a group of kids and pass on the baton," he said, any glimmer of relief evaporating along with his foggy breath into the chilly night. "I'd love to do that and then retire somewhere quiet and watch it unfold on social media as I sit by the fire and sip my hot chocolate and take naps until the sweet, sweet release of death. But it wouldn't exactly be fair, would it? We've given them enough shit to have to clean up in this world as it is. Besides, we've done this before. We sort of know what we're up against. And we've got a Jake."

"Huh?"

He feebly held up his blaster. "Jake built the weapons that helped us survive last time. These things were constructed using the same magical energy that had stopped the bastards before we'd even been born. Nobody else has that. It might not have worked as quickly as we needed on giant Father Christmas tonight, but we were definitely weakening him. They could have sent in the army tonight and it probably wouldn't have done any good. Can't imagine bullets work on evil, it'd be a bit like firing them into the darkness, when what you really need is light."

"You're welcome," Jake said, wincing as he touched a graze on his cheek. "Though I'm starting to regret ever hanging out with you guys."

"OK, so we have special magical weapons," Doc continued uneasily. "But I think we just established there is unbridled evil at work here and it's pretty annoyed. Also, it's a bit of an ask to have us fight something we can't properly remember. Even *you* said there were things that were still a little fuzzy. Stuff you missed."

"And?"

"I'm just saying, do we need help? Is there anyone who understands what this is? I think we could really use a wizened mentor right about now."

Cisco sat quietly, chewing his lip, weighing up the pros and cons of being honest with his friends about last night. Then he patted Doc's leg and rose to his feet, surveying the chaotic scene before them.

They'd have to believe him after tonight, wouldn't they?

"Cisco?" Doc persisted, letting him pull her up to stand beside him. Jake and Michelle stood too, wincing and stretching. "You've got that look on your face again. The one I hate. What aren't you telling us?"

As sirens began to blare in the distance, Cisco gestured for them to follow him as he staggered off back to the shopping centre car park.

"Well, there's this talking fox…" he began.

CHAPTER SIX

A Bun in the Coven

"I told you, I don't know how to explain it," Jake said again. He kept his volume quiet but forceful as Natalie paced around the kitchen. Every so often she'd glance at the knife rack, then go back to striding back and forth, circling the island in the centre of the room. Jake wasn't sure what was going through her mind, but it probably wasn't anything good. He hoped the kids and Cisco stayed watching TV in the other room.

"Are you saying it didn't happen, Jake? You can't possibly be trying that on me. I won't buy it. We didn't run for no reason. I heard the screaming and the shouting and the chaos around us. I felt the ground shaking and saw that bloody Father Christmas decoration after it had... I don't know, come loose? Blown from its mooring on the Town Hall and floated down the street crushing people? Shit, whatever *that* was, I've never seen you so scared. And the others too. I didn't imagine all that."

Jake sighed as carefully as he could. There was a fine line between claiming ignorance and accidentally getting your wife to attack you.

"I'm not saying you imagined anything. Something definitely happened, Nat. We all saw the news reports afterwards. Town was a mess."

She pushed back the strands of thick brown hair that had

broken loose from her ponytail during the argument and fixed him with a stare he'd come to love and dread in equal measure. "But you were involved, weren't you? That's why you left us in the car and went off with Cisco and Doc and Michelle. Why you took those toys of yours and came back all bloodied up. It was almost like you'd expected something to go wrong. You were prepared for it."

Jake laughed nervously.

A mistake.

"What's funny, exactly?"

"Oh, god no, I wasn't laughing at you... or that." His mouth began to dry up as he tried to find the words to clamber out of the grave he was digging for himself. "I wasn't prepared at all. It was Cisco. He brought the toys. Except they're not really toys, more science experiments from when we were kids and I have to be honest I was as surprised as anybody when I saw them in the car and discovered they still worked." Jake saw the look of patience wearing thin in Nat's tightening frown and continued quickly, "Anyway, it's a long story, but what happened in town was related to something we went through together as kids."

"And Cisco?"

Jake's eyes darted to the living room door. "What about him?"

"I know he's your friend, Jake, and he needs us, and he's lovely, he really is," Nat dropped her voice and leaned in, until their noses were almost touching. "But if this is anything to do with him, are we in danger if he stays here? If he put those toys or experiments or weapons or whatever they are in the car without telling you, can you really trust him?"

"I'd trust him with my life," Jake said, adding quietly, "Have done, in fact. Or so he keeps insisting."

"But it's not just your life now, is it, Jake? It's mine. More importantly, we have to think about the kids. And George."

Jake pulled her close, trying to offer some semblance of comfort and reassurance. He pressed her to his chest and stroked her hair as they hugged. She fell into it willingly.

"I just... worry, Jake."

"I know. And Cisco has been through a lot, that's definitely true. He's not been in a good place. But that event wasn't his doing and his being there actually helped to stop it. If we can trust anybody, I know it's him. I'm his friend, Nat. We went through a lot together once and I need to stand by him again now. It might be the only way to get through this."

"What is *this*, though?" she asked despairingly. "Is it over or is there more to come?"

Jake gave a little shake of his head, unable to answer the question. At least not truthfully. All he knew was that he trusted his friend. He might not remember all the reasons why just yet – although some of the memories were starting to come back, popping into his mind at awkward moments – but he had a feeling they were all going to need Cisco if they were to survive what was coming.

"We can trust him," he repeated, glancing to the door again, beyond which he could hear Cisco leading the children in a far-too-loud opera-style rendition of the CBeebies goodnight song. He pursed his lips and continued, "You'll be fine. We'll be fine. The kids will be fine. He'll make sure of it. From everything he's told me and what I'm beginning to remember, Cisco will know what to do."

"What the fuck do we do?" Cisco muttered, peering through the decorations in the window of Bay Tree Books as the snow began to fall around them. His frosty-white breath fogged the glass. He wiped it clean with the sleeve of his ski-jacket, until he could see back into the candle-lit room, just as the gathering of witches, wizards and a single stormtrooper made their way up the stairs. "We're too late, it's already started."

Doc, currently, was more interested in the fantastic window display than what lay beyond. What looked like a traditional nativity scene, except the three wise men had been replaced by *Minecraft* zombies, bringing gifts of iron ore, diamonds, and a pickaxe.

"The sweet baby Jesus would surely be pleased," she said, her bright red scarf unravelling as she bent down for a closer look as snowflakes settled on the glass. She blew them away.

"Are you even paying attention, Doc? We've got a job to get done that's now going to be made ten times harder thanks to the hordes of otherworldly creatures in there. What are we going to do?"

She laughed, each breath a chime of delight in his increasing unease, and gave him a gentle pinch on his cheek.

"A couple of days ago we faced down killer festive decorations and a Godzilla-sized Father Christmas. And from what you've told us about that Halloween when we were younger, we've been through hell before." She waved a gloved hand at the shop, to the big, yellow sign in the window, and pointed to the large, bold words. "It's just a local Dark Peak book reading of *The Dark Is Rising* put on by a nice old lady author. And they're just kids, Cisco. Children just like George, who got dressed up and came to listen to someone read a beloved story to them. They're here for fun, they're not about to attack us."

Cisco bristled as he buried his chin deep inside his jacket collar. "You can never know for sure with kids," he said, glancing into the window to see the last flash of a black cloak disappear up the stairs, leaving an empty room filled with small, stained, discarded mugs. "They can be little devils sometimes. Especially when they're swimming in hot chocolate or whatever sugary mess they've just been given in there. And I swear to god, Doc, they can sense fear." He shivered. "Besides, I didn't go through hell that Halloween. Hell literally went through me."

Doc shook her black curls softly. There was a little grey there, but it only served to make her look even cooler in his eyes. As though she was some kind of bad-ass warrior queen but one who had strands of tinsel woven into her hair.

"Every time you talk about those days, Cisco, I begin to wonder if my memory lapse isn't intentional. Because it sounds like it was pretty horrific."

He shrugged. In truth, it *had* been pretty awful at times. But as the years passed the horror had been pushed aside by the nostalgic longing for the adventure and excitement and his friends. He supposed he should be pleased that his return to Dark Peak had brought him tumbling back through time to face up against the same foe, while standing alongside the people he had thought lost. Yet he was a bag of mixed emotions right now, not helped by the fact George had slept most of the day after the Arndale fight and had been wide awake as soon as Cisco had tried to sleep last night, leading to a fitful night's rest on the couch, while his son bounced beside him watching a season's worth of some Australian show on Netflix about investigative school kids.

"Do you think the police will catch onto what we did in the city?" he asked, wondering what on earth George would do if he was hauled into jail on some kind of 'wielding dangerous games consoles' charge. "They're covering it all up right now, of course. All a terrible accident. A mini-earthquake right in the centre of town, bringing down the wheel and causing a stampede through the markets. Total bullshit, but we're still in the darkest timeline, aren't we? So much misinformation out there, people will buy anything."

"Jake said we got lucky with the CCTV going down all over the city. And there are no phone videos doing the round on social either. Total visual blackout, they said. Maybe an EMP?"

"All *his* work, I'm sure," Cisco said, thinking about the pirate. "Lucky for us in some ways, but it doesn't give us any proof that what happened was real."

She glanced at him. "You're afraid that people will simply move onto the next news story and forget, just like last time?"

"Damn right I am. You don't know what it's like to be the only one who remembers things a certain way, Doc. It's like losing a part of yourself. A part that was kind of important to being able to move on in life."

"But you got married, had George, got some job in dinosaurs or something."

"I work in archaeological museum exhibitions."

"Same-same."

"All I'm saying," he continued, rolling his eyes, "is that moving on and actually *moving on* are two different things. I moved on in life. But inside… I didn't. Do you actually feel like you thought you would when you grew up?"

That kept her quiet. After a moment's thought, she replied, "Not really, no. I don't feel much different to being younger. Just a bit more confident maybe. A bit more able to bullshit and pretend I know what I'm doing."

That's the trick to everything, Cisco decided. Being an adult was all about bullshit and spin and trying to convince everyone else that you knew what you're doing, when, really, everyone was in the same boat. Faffing about, trying to keep the world turning and often failing miserably.

He stamped his feet, unwilling to enter the bookshop now. He really didn't want to have this conversation in front of a room full of sugared-up children. They'd see right through his attempts to pretend he knew what he was doing.

"Maybe we should wait until after the reading to talk to the author?"

"To ask about the *fox*, you mean?"

The way Doc said the word "fox" said everything about how exactly she was taking this little escapade of theirs. She might have witnessed what they'd experienced in the city, but she still couldn't quite get on board with a talking fox. Even after he'd explained everything about the meeting in the attic, how Tabitha had warned him that Deadman's Grin was back, Doc was struggling to believe it.

She might be here this evening, but Cisco couldn't be sure if it was to support the cause or simply for his own protection, to make sure he didn't push his delusions too far in public.

"Tabitha said something was waking Deadman's Grin up again, bringing him back from the dead."

"But why?"

"I'm not sure. But I believe it's real. I saw him in town just before everything went down and I know he was behind it. If we can find Tabitha again we can learn more. And I think this woman knows where she might be, given that her mum and Tabitha used to hang out, and she wrote a whole book series inspired by her."

It was a stretch, but Cisco had nothing else to go on now. He'd returned to Jake's loft earlier and waited at the window for hours, staring out across the darknening world, then had braved the freezing winds in the garden to call out for the damn fox. Only the owls had answered him.

Yet he'd remembered the book he'd been holding when Tabitha had first appeared, written by a woman who'd once lived in Dark Peak. And although she had died long ago, her daughter, Elenora Thompson, still lived here. An author herself, she did regular book readings for the local children.

If they were going to find any clue to tracking down Tabitha, it was here, tonight.

Taking a deep breath, he linked his arm in Doc's.

She noted the panic in his eyes.

"Time to face your greatest fear, Cisco," she said with a wry smile. "Scary children and public speaking."

The door chime sang out as Doc marched him from the cold gloom of the high street into the shop. They stood for a moment inside, enjoying the stifling warmth of central heating and far too many candles to be safe in a bookshop. The scent of hot chocolate, slightly burnt marshmallows and shelves full of exciting paperbacks hung heavy in the air.

As so many things lately, it felt like childhood.

Then Doc nudged him in the ribs again and Cisco reluctantly moved towards the stairs, where he could now hear the riotous cackling being dramatically shushed in the reading room above.

"They're about to start reading," he hissed as the first step creaked under his weight. "We probably shouldn't–"

"Climb," Doc insisted.

"But it's Susan Cooper's magnum opus. Some things are too sacred to interrupt."

"I said climb!"

With a defeated sigh he continued up the stairs as they wound around the corner and led to a dimly lit room covered in an array of beautiful paintings – each a book cover, from *The Snail and the Whale* to *The Hunger Games*. More shelves lined the walls underneath the paintings, while in the centre of the room, spread among brightly coloured pillows and fleece blankets, around fifteen costumed children sat cross-legged as they stared at a grey-haired woman in a long robe with a copy of *The Dark Is Rising* resting open on her lap.

She looked up from the book and regarded them with narrow eyes magnified behind thinly framed green spectacles.

"Are you here for the reading?"

Cisco immediately felt the quizzical stares of all the young faces – and several accompanying parents – turn towards him. His cheeks began to burn, which was pathetic after everything he'd faced recently, especially given he was an actual parent himself.

Unfortunately, as he had discovered, having your own children didn't necessarily make you less socially awkward in front of others. Sometimes, it just made it worse. Because you knew what they were going to tell their parents about you.

Doc dug him in the ribs again.

"Oh, yes, no, sorry," he said, smiling rather too intensely at everyone. "We didn't want to interrupt you, Mrs Thompson, but we have a quick question. About a book."

The woman tilted her head.

"Aren't you the boy and girl who had something to do with the Halloween gas–"

"Yes, yes, we're *that* boy and girl. Well, we used to be anyway, before we got old. But don't worry, we're not about to start any gas leaks." One of the little boys sniggered to his friend and Cisco stammered on quicker. "And you don't need to worry about us destroying anything in here. Unless you count these lovely iced buns!"

He picked up one of the pastries that had been put aside for refreshments, waved it awkwardly, regretted everything he had just said, then half-heartedly shoved it in his mouth.

A piece of icing flaked off in his throat and he started to choke.

"Jesus wept," Doc muttered, as all the children began to giggle. "I literally can't take you anywhere, can I?"

She slapped him on the back – rather harder than was needed – then beckoned the author to the back of the room. Excusing herself from the children, Mrs Thompson got to her feet and smoothed down her skirt as she tiptoed through the fidgeting mass.

"Aren't they those monster hunters who blew up the school?" Cisco heard one of the parents quietly ask another as he continued struggling for breath.

"Monsters aren't real," a boy said, matter-of-factly.

"Yes, they are," said another.

"Are not," said a girl.

A little boy with ginger hair stood up. "There's an invisible man under my stairs."

"Liar, liar, pants on fire."

As the arguments grew in number, and a few wands and magical staffs were produced and pointed at each other, the author reached the back of the room and gave Cisco and Doc a look of disdain.

"We have a minute, at best," she said tightly.

Cisco reached into his bag and pulled out the book from Jake's loft, holding it up in front of her. She frowned, then grew sad as she saw the cover.

"That was my mother's book. She wrote it a long time ago and although I must admit it was one of my favourites, if you are here to get it signed I cannot help you. My mother passed away some years ago."

"We know and we're truly sorry about that. But we came here to see you tonight about something else. Specifically, we need to know more about your mother's inspiration for the talking cat."

Mrs Thompson's face grew suddenly youthful under the festive glow of the fairy lights that were dangling all around the room.

A childlike sparkle danced in her eyes and she regarded them both eagerly, as if only just understanding why they might be there.

"You mean Tabitha?"

"Yes."

"Is she back?" she asked hopefully.

Cisco tried hard to suppress the grin that wanted to tap dance across his face in that moment. Like everything else, Tabitha was real, and now even Doc knew it.

"Holy shit, you weren't kidding," she whispered.

He nodded at Mrs Thompson. "Tabitha visited me not so long ago and, well, I should have paid more attention. But now things are getting serious and I need to find her again before it gets worse for all of us. I've waited at the same window, at the same time of night, but she hasn't returned. I've called into the garden in the dead of night, at the foot of the hill she appeared from. And nothing."

The woman smiled. A lovely, grandmotherly smile full of kindness and wisdom.

"Oh, you won't find her that way. At least not without some help, if it happens to be around. It's best if you get her to find you."

"And how exactly do we do that?"

The children in the room were becoming louder now and some of the parents were having to step in to separate arguments over elves and wizards and, to a couple of them, who was the best at *Roblox*. Mrs Thompson had to lean in to be heard.

"Foxes are strange creatures," she intoned. "They go where they please and they do what they want. Which makes them perfect for slipping between worlds. Nobody questions where a fox has been, because nobody wants the trouble of knowing the answer. Humans have long known this about them, it's just that we've forgotten it over time." She took a step back, indicating the conversation was nearly at an end. "You haven't found her because Tabitha doesn't particularly enjoy spending time in our world – she never did – so you will need to encourage her back if you want to talk to her. Sometimes there will be those who can get her a message to her. But there is a more direct route."

"Which is?"

"Find the standing stone on Dunmow Hill. It is on the south side of the field with the big oak. There is a hole in the top. Most dismiss it as a gatepost or some such, but the hole is natural. And if you know your folklore, you will understand that a natural hole in stone is a thin place. A crossing between worlds. And at certain times of day, that hole becomes a looking glass through which the world beyond our own can be seen and reached. Leave Tabitha a note in the hole. If it is still there at midnight, it will reach her on the other side."

With that she nodded at them both and strode back through the increasingly impatient group of children, where she picked up her paperback copy of the book with the shadowy Rider on the cover, softly flicked through the pages to the bookmark, and began reading.

The room settled and went quiet. Cisco looked towards Doc half-expecting some kind of snarky remark, but there was none. She just motioned towards the stairs, indicating she wanted to leave.

Before he could reach the top step, however, there was a little tug at his sleeve. He looked down to see the ginger-haired boy staring up at him.

"The invisible man with red eyes really does live under my stairs," he repeated in a tiny voice, pushing his fake glasses back up his snub nose. "He appeared there the other day. He said to say hello to you and that he'll be seeing you again soon."

"I told you so," Cisco said to Doc as they left the shop a little later, having instructed the boy to lock the door under the stairs and given him a scrap of paper with their details on it to give to his parents. Not that either of them thought it would reach them. They knew enough about the school letters that their children always seemed to lose between being handed to them and home time. But they had at least tried.

"What's that?" Doc asked, shivering as she zipped up her coat.

Cisco gave her a grim smile as he shoved his hands in his pockets. "Kids are scary."

CHAPTER SEVEN

Messages on the Dark Hill

Doc sat wrapped in a camping fleece by the window in Jake's loft.

She was trying to keep her focus on the torchlight darting rather aimlessly across the hill outside, but it was difficult considering she was surrounded by her entire personal history. A history she had always felt a little trapped by and had once tried to get rid of. A bittersweet reminder of a father's love for both her and an era for which she had never really understood the attraction, even though she'd lived it.

Jake hadn't said a word as he'd led her in a couple of hours ago. Of course he hadn't, he was too scared about what she might do to him. But then again Cisco hadn't said anything either. In fact, he'd bowed his head almost respectfully, or possibly out of fear, as Jake had led them up to the loft and slid the bookcase aside to reveal the secret room.

Only Michelle had commented.

"What the *shit?*" she shouted, the shock in her words reverberating around the upstairs of the house. Jake's cheeks immediately coloured as he dived to shut the door to ensure no further expletives drifted down to the various children playing quietly in their rooms on the floor below.

"Keep it down, sis," he'd hissed. "Nat's already on my back about all this secrecy and plotting between us. I just about managed to convince her what happened in Manchester was more or less what the news stories said it was. If she discovers we're up here planning to sneak out in the middle of the night to leave messages on the hill for a talking fox in another world I think I'll be heading for divorce."

Michelle pulled a face at him, but she did drop her voice a little.

"I just can't believe you actually went and collected all this crap? After Dorothy specifically told you not to."

"This belonged to Doc's dad," Cisco had said, rather meekly. "It's not crap. Jake did something wonderful here."

"For you maybe. Because you never grew up."

"That's a bit harsh."

Michelle tilted her head. "Am I wrong?"

At the time, Doc had looked despairingly between the two as they sparred. These were the people she loved most in the world, in vastly different ways of course, and at different times of her life.

She almost appreciated Cisco jumping to the defence of her father's collection. Or she would have done had she not been so creeped out by seeing it all again after she'd intended to get shot of everything and move on with her life. On the other hand, she definitely appreciated Michelle sticking up for her, knowing how difficult it had been in the first place for Doc to even put it up for sale.

Cisco had gone quiet after that exchange. He'd sat down on the edge of the desk and stared out of the window to the hill, watching the sun begin to set, burning through the remnants of the curled-up leaves still clinging to the skeletal trees, unable to let go despite winter being upon them.

Those leaves reminded Doc of a long-ago memory. Something she couldn't quite place or put a finger on, which wasn't unusual. There was a whole chapter of her life that she was fuzzy about these days. But was it age, as she had always thought? Or was Cisco right? Was there an entire swath of her childhood that for some reason had been blocked out? Her memory wiped, like some droid in *Star Wars*?

It was a ridiculous thought. But then again Father Christmas had tried to kill them the other day, so, really, what did she know about what was possible anymore? The politics of recent years had certainly shown any outrageous notion was up for grabs. Why not killer mythical figures and toys and talking foxes?

"So, what's the plan?" she had asked, coming to stand beside her friend at the window.

Behind the wrinkles and his patchy beard, his face beneath those sweeps of black and grey hair was still as kind and handsome as she remembered growing up. Like a slightly unkempt Henry Golding. But the spark in his eyes was somewhat diminished, and he looked far too tired for all this. Beaten down by all the recent events in his life.

"The plan?" Cisco repeated, his head resting against the window frame now. He continued watching the sun finally disappear beyond the wood at the top of the hill.. "You mean the plan to get the supernatural fox to talk to us again and explain what the hell is going on? The same plan none of us can believe we're actually considering, because it's ridiculous? Because we're grown-ups and should be past this shit by now?"

"Aye, that's the one."

He cracked a smile at that. "Fine. We sneak out at eleven tonight, after the kids are in bed. Two of us, for safety. If only in case one of us falls and breaks a hip or something."

"To be fair, that could happen before you even leave the house."

He gave her a sideways glance. "Someone will need to stay with Natalie. The less she knows about any of this, the safer she will probably be. Jake said she's been wanting to watch that new costume drama on Netflix, so maybe that's a good excuse? Michelle, you can suggest watching the first couple of episodes and we'll probably get an hour to get up the hill and deliver the note while you watch it."

"Hell yeah, I'll take a torrid love affair between attractive people in nice outfits over slopping about in the mud," Michelle said, pleased.

Doc scowled at her to be quiet and continued, "And by deliver the note, Cisco, you mean scribble something on a bit of paper and shove it through a magical stone in a field."

"Yep."

"Do you know where the standing stone is?"

"We used to do cross-country runs on this hill and I vaguely remember seeing it, but that was before it became an estate." He had glanced at Jake. "But *he* knows."

Jake nodded. "Yeah, I know where it is. Walk the dog up there often enough, so shouldn't take me long to find it even in the dark."

Doc bristled as she saw where this was going. She was going to be shut out of the adventure already, wasn't she? Made to keep watch, just like when Cisco and Michelle had teamed up that one time at the incredibly haunted William House and–

An image formed in her mind.

Suddenly she could remember. Really *remember*. Vividly, a snapshot of that little trip when they were teenagers. An avalanche of emotions and feelings – the rising moon and gale force winds – and her stuck with Jake "keeping watch" as Cisco had told them. All so he could run off to explore the house with Jake's sister, who he had a crush on at the time.

It all hit her with a shudder. She had to lean back against the dormer wall, next to the window. Good grief. Where had all that come from?

"You OK?" Cisco asked, looking concerned. He stood, put his arm around her shoulder, just like he used to whenever the balance of power shifted between them and she had one of her rare moments of losing confidence. Or at least one of the rare moments she let the mask slip.

She shrugged him off. "Nothing, it's fine. I just remembered something, that's all. You were saying? I'm guessing if Jake is going because he knows where the stone is, then you have to go in case the fox turns up, right?"

"Her name's Tabitha," Cisco replied, "and yes. Jake and I have to go."

"Which leaves me to keep watch up here, while pretending we're all together reminiscing or something in case Natalie yells up the stairs to check in on us, right?" She looked around, unable to contain the shiver that took hold. "I mean, sure, the weirdness of having the entirety of my father's basement relocated to Jake's house and having to sit in the middle of it again waiting to lie to my sister-in-law probably beats running around a hill in the dark. But are you sure you two will be OK up there by yourselves? You won't disappear down a mineshaft by accident? Be eaten by some hillside nightmare come to life?"

Cisco looked hurt. Jake looked worried.

"There are mineshafts?"

"*That's* the thing you're worried about?" Doc replied, laughing. "Never stop being you, Jake. Yes, there are plenty of old holes up there, but they're probably all blocked up. Honestly, you've got bigger problems given our childhood nightmare is apparently back."

"We'll take the War Wizards, it'll be fine," Cisco said. He took his battered phone out of his pocket and checked the time, as the kids downstairs became louder in their games and a row started between two of them. "Come on, we have plenty of time to kill and I can hear George getting hangry. Let's go grab some food, put a movie on for them, and chill out for a bit."

He left without waiting for the others, seemingly lost in his thoughts. She could tell he was nervous. Cisco had always been nervous about this kind of stuff. And yet he never stopped to think twice, just got on with whatever crazy idea he figured needed to be got on with. There was a lovable aspect to that. A charm in his naivety and sense of duty, no matter what lay ahead.

Michelle hung back as Jake disappeared too.

"I'm so sorry," she said, gesturing to the shelves encircling them. Like the entertaining prison bars of a childhood she had thought she'd managed to escape. She put her fingers on Doc's shoulder, gave it a squeeze. "Had I known what the jerkwad was planning, buying all your dad's stuff and keeping it here… in a secret room no less… well, I would have stopped it. And perhaps punched him a little."

Doc shrugged, though not enough to displace her wife's hand. It was a light touch, but it meant everything. Always had.

She was still thinking on the memory as she wrapped the blanket more tightly around her shoulders and checked the *Thundercats* talking alarm clock on the shelf.

Still working, even after all this time. They made them solid back then.

11:45pm.

Cisco and Jake had been out there, making their way up the hill for about twenty minutes already. She had watched their twin torchlights amble up the garden, then slowly over the fence, at a speed not unlike two middle-aged men trying to climb over something in the dark with games consoles strapped to their back.

Then up the slope they had gone. Their lights moved around in circles for a good long while – Jake clearly trying to find his bearings – until they found what they were looking for.

At which point they had been relatively still, clearly focused on something.

She hoped it was the standing stone and not another monster.

It occurred to Doc that she hadn't really questioned the supernatural element of this evening's adventure. She'd spent her life moving away from those notions of fantasy that had swept away her father with his collectibles in the 1980s, following her mother's death when she was barely ten. They had saved Mr Forbes for sure. But for the most part Doc had not been too fussed. Even when they used to read the millions of comics he owned, played his consoles or watched the VHS videos of their favourite movies – always with the swearing dubbed over with random words by the English TV channels – she was only really in it to spend time with him.

Cisco had then compounded matters by being just as much

of a dork as her dad and she adored him enough to deal with
him always wanting to hang out, exploring the books and shows
and films and toys. And it hadn't been until he'd left Dark Peak
that she'd really been able to leave that aspect of her life behind,
far more content to enjoy the present with Michelle as they left
school, got jobs, and lived their lives together.

Yet, it seemed all those years of soaking in a universe of
science fiction and fantasy stories must have taken their toll on
her cynicism. Because leaving a note for an animal in the hole
of a mystical standing stone was a plot straight out of a kids'
picture book. One she was fairly sure her daughter Cecilia would
have raised an eyebrow at and commented in her whimsical,
chipmunk voice of hers, "That doesn't make much sense,
Mummy." And Doc would have smiled and kissed her daughter's
forehead and said, "No, of course it doesn't", and that would
have been the end of it.

Yet here she was, watching through a window as two childhood
friends ran around in the dark playing ghosts and goblins, and she
had accepted it.

Because she sort of believed again.

The afternoon and evening spent with the others had been
so much fun. Spent for the most part running around the house
with the children, playing hide and seek with Cecilia, George and
Emily, leading a merry chase from room to room, with George
especially completely failing to grasp the concept of hiding and
almost always wanting to be found.

The best part had been seeing Cisco join in. Scaring the
children, then pretending to run away from them, then throwing
his son about his shoulders and tickling him whenever the boy
had run up to him demanding he show his friends "the tickle
monster".

For a few hours Cisco had returned to who she remembered in
the childhood of that fuzzy haze of hers. The boy who had been
her best friend. Full of hope and optimism and excitement for
anything and everything. Almost glowing, like the Ready Brek

kid from that old advert. Certainly not the worn, deteriorating husk of a person that had come back to Dark Peak devoid of spirit, surprising her in the café the other day.

She wouldn't admit it to anyone, especially him, but she had missed their time together. Yes, people moved on. And she still had Michelle and Jake and this wonderful town where she lived. But after Cisco had left, things hadn't been the same. She had really missed them all hanging out.

And now they were back together again, doing things rational adults shouldn't be doing, while she was sitting in the midst of a childhood she had long forgotten.

"It's fine," she whispered to herself, trying not to look at the books and games and toy models around her. Each one a nostalgic gut punch. Her dad's entire life. The life that for so long had stopped him being the kind of father that she wanted.

Except, perhaps, in the end it had made him the kind of father she'd needed.

She smiled as some new memories found their way into her head.

For a second she forgave Jake his little secret. Forgave her father for wasting so much time on literally anything that wasn't her. And remembered what he had finally given her.

Life.

She was suddenly enveloped in a warmth that could only have been him. The love he had once poured into this collection, pouring back into her. The memory of their years together following the moment he had saved them all that Halloween, stepping into the fire of the school gym to rescue them. Those long, glorious years after that moment, where she won him back from all the toys and they made up for lost father-daughter time.

Sniffing, Doc shuffled under her blanket and blinked away the tears. Then looked back out of the window again, hoping to see the men returning.

But all she saw was darkness.

The torchlight was gone.

Cisco and Jake crouched in the mud behind the long grass, holding their breaths.

The moonlight streamed down across the slope of the hill, lighting up the canopy of trees to the north of the field they were in and filtering through the grass now dancing in the icy wind blowing across the valley that held Dark Peak.

"Should have brought a bigger coat," Jake muttered, flexing his weaponised glove and adjusting his footing. His wellies gave a soft squelch of a burp in the swampy ground beneath them.

Despite his tall, muscular, gym-inherited frame, right now he still looked like the boy Cisco had once fought monsters with. All anxious energy and nervous tick, trying to push those glasses that didn't exist back up his nose as they waited.

They had turned their lights off a minute ago. As soon as they had heard the trees.

Normally the wind blowing through the leaves wouldn't have alerted Cisco to anything other than the fact that they were up a hill in the middle of the night and it was getting windy. But there had been something in that rustle of leaves and branches. An underlying… something. Words. Language. He didn't know. But it felt like they were trying to whisper to him that change was afoot. That the veil between worlds was thinning and the moment was almost here.

So he'd immediately thrust the note he'd written earlier into the hole in the standing stone, grabbed Jake, and rushed them both into the crop of long grass near the blackberry bushes, where they might stand some chance of not being seen.

Seen by what, he wasn't sure. In fact, there was a lot going on that left him unsure about a great many things. But he felt it necessary to play it safe, just in case.

"Can you still see the stone?" Jake whispered, quieter this time, his words so soft they were almost stolen away on the breeze.

Cisco nodded slowly.

About a metre or so high, the stone stood near the edge of the field, bathed in silvery light. It was roughly cut, almost tear-shaped, and was likely mistaken by most as a gatepost worn down by time and the elements.

I guess it happens to us all, Cisco thought.

The hole at the top, all the way through the stone, seemed innocuous. Somewhere to attach the gate, people most likely thought. Hikers, ramblers, families taking the kids out for a run just to get them out of the house – this was a stone that a lot of people passed and nobody really saw.

Yet even as the pair of them had approached it, Cisco knew there was something odd about its nature. That hole hadn't been cut by human hands. As the author had said, it was entirely natural. Just big enough to get a hand through.

Or a note.

"It's still there, isn't it?" Jake said again, clearly not wanting to sit here in silence if he could help it. "The note. I can see the edge poking out."

"Uh-huh."

"What if the wind blows it out?"

"Then I'll go put it back in. Now shhhh!"

Cisco badly wanted to check his phone for the time, but he didn't want the light to give them away. It must be only a few minutes until midnight though? All they had to do was just sit here as quietly as they could, not give themselves away, and...

From out of nowhere, there was a small chink of light.

It came from the hole in the stone.

A golden glow, pouring through, as though someone had opened the door to a pub with a roaring fire behind it. Cisco and Jake both held their breaths, feeling a sliver of warmth trickle through the opening onto the hill, before there was a rustle and the note slid from view.

Something, or someone, made a curious noise.

Then the light disappeared again.

"Awesome," Cisco said, his heart racing and turning to Jake with a little grin of excitement. "Message delivered!"

Even in the moonlight, Jake looked a special kind of pale.

"Yeah... but to what?"

CHAPTER EIGHT

The Stone Giant

Every night after the note had been delivered, Jake and Cisco entered the loft to wait for Tabitha.

They usually left it until tea had been made and consumed by the hordes. Sometimes this was undertaken as a collective family meal when Jake was able to finish his work early (work he had been putting to one side a little since his friend's arrival). But other times the kids would eat first and the three adults afterwards.

Aside from the trauma of trying to feed two extra mouths every evening – with George entering that picky stage Jake definitely remembered all three of his daughters going through – he and Cisco were both slightly distracted by the whole note thing.

Consequently, they'd barely be paying attention, while constantly checking the windows to the garden, or to the front, hoping for a glimpse of large yellow eyes peering back at them from the darkness to confirm they had sent a message between worlds.

And thus mealtimes were beginning to become a big, tangled knot of frustration and excitement, just like he remembered when he lived at home with his parents and Michelle. When food was an obstacle to get through before he could rush back to his lab to pursue more scientific breakthroughs.

"Finish your mouthful before you leave the table," his policeman father would grumble after him, as he skipped down the stairs to his basement lair. Meanwhile his mother would be disappointed that once again they hadn't had the "good quality family time" she always hoped a meal around the table would bring.

Jake knew that Natalie was fast forming the same mindset. It wasn't just Cisco and George being here that was the problem. She loved them both dearly, especially George with his cute head tilts and contagious giggling. But whenever the adults sat together without the children to distract them, the conversation was stilted and quite clearly played for show. She must be wondering what the hell was going on.

Then again, so was Jake.

Father Christmas illuminations coming to life? A talking fox from their childhood warning about dark magic? A murderous pirate back from the dead to take his revenge?

He'd always found comfort in science. Spent most of his early years within those boundaries of proof and evidence and logic. Yet there was no comfort to be found here. There was evidence that *something* weird was happening, but no discernible scientific proof as to why and certainly no logic behind any of it.

Was his family in danger? If Tabitha had found them at this house, then surely Deadman's Grin could, too? Should he get Natalie and the girls out and take them somewhere? And should he go with them or stay here to help Cisco battle whatever lay ahead?

Because, like it or not – and he *really* didn't like it – Jake had a churning in his gut that this wasn't over. Not by a long shot. Their childhood wanted them back, by whatever means possible.

And yet every night he continued to dutifully sit in the loft without success. Taking turns with Cisco to sit by the window, peering into the night to spot any movement heading their way. Ideally in the shape of a small, conversational animal. But Jake kept the War Wizards nearby just in case it came in another form.

For good or for ill, nothing came their way.

By the fifth day they were just hanging around, not even

bothering to look out of the window, just exploring the collection. Reminiscing over lost moments.

"Remember these?" Cisco asked, waving still-wrapped comics of *Spider-Man and Zoids* at him. Jake nodded to be polite, not really sure if he remembered this stuff from way back when or from when he had bought everything and stacked the shelves here. Meanwhile, Cisco had started into a little monologue about what it meant to him, revealing quite clearly that his soul was still trapped in 1989.

It was both admirable and tragic.

Admirable because Jake couldn't hold onto the past if he tried. Bits and pieces came through occasionally, more so after the Christmas markets fiasco, but the rest was still foggy and uncertain. And he was almost jealous sometimes when he saw the joy in Cisco as a particular bubble of memory burst in his mind's eye and soaked him in nostalgia. There was definite merit in being able to hold onto that stuff sometimes.

On the other hand, Jake also saw the disconnect in Cisco's ability to function in the moment, holding him back from embracing the now. He was simply too distracted with what had been. For now, George hadn't noticed. Not quite. The little angel was quite content to run around and do his own thing. His dad was still present in body and that was all that mattered for the most part. But it wouldn't be long before he needed something more. Before he became aware. He was fast reaching that age where he was going to need more than occasional tickling and hide and seek. He was going to need to look into his dad's eyes and know that he was *present*, looking back.

"You should bring George up here," Jake suggested again, casually picking up a model starfighter – although which fictional fantasy it came from he wasn't really sure – and waving it pointedly in front of his friend. "He might like to play with some of this stuff with you."

"Yeah, I will," Cisco replied, flicking through his comic.

Jake bristled and tossed the starship at his friend.

"*Now* is a great time, don't you think?"

It hit the comic and landed in Cisco's lap. Cisco looked up to complain, but saw the look in Jake's eyes and had second thoughts. *Good*, Jake thought firmly. Perhaps it was time for a bit of tough love here. To wake him up from his stupor.

"Look, Cisco, I can wait up here a little bit longer in case Tabitha shows up. Why don't you take that ship and maybe this," he grabbed a black toy van with a red stripe, "and go play with your son before bedtime?"

"But these are collectibles."

"Collectible toys are still toys, and toys are made for playing with. You must know this, mate, hasn't George made you watch *Toy Story*, like, a thousand times? You'll be doing them a favour."

Cisco cradled the spaceship and van, looking uncomfortable with the thought. But Jake held his nerve and his gaze until his friend relented.

He got to his feet, looked at the toys again, then put one back and picked up another that looked, to Jake, totally the same.

"OK, but we need to keep the fictional universes consistent, Jake. You can't mix and match *Battlestar Galactica* and *The A-Team* because..." he paused and looked suddenly pleased, "...no, wait, yes, you can. OK, good call!"

With that, he swapped the spaceships again, then was through the door and hustling down the stairs. Jake heaved a huge sigh of relief and got up to shut the curtains, before restacking the comic books back onto their respective shelves. He glanced again at the other toys all lined up, unable to ascertain which shows most of them might have come from and not really minding. He'd never been able to fully indulge in all those stories as a kid. They seemed far too unlikely for his mind to embrace.

Any time Cisco and Doc had invited him to watch movies or read or play games together in her dad's basement, he'd politely sat with them. But his mind had always fixated on key issues in whatever plot was on show.

Why would such a dangerous, planet-destroying weapon

have a ridiculously easy way to destroy it built in? How did that archaeologist stay attached to the submarine when it dived and why didn't he drown? And who on earth thought it was a good idea to give that Goblin King a giant codpiece in a kids' movie?

Like it or not, Jake just hadn't been like his friends growing up. Perhaps he'd always had adult sensibilities, he wondered, finishing his tidying and getting ready to turn out the light. He pushed a finger to one of the consoles to nudge it back into hanging straight on the wall. Maybe his mind was just designed not to see the fantastical things that others could. Which made it easier for him not to remember what they'd all been through growing up.

He was about logic and reality and things making sense, and–

The knock at the window made him jump.

His heart began to thump out a message to his brain–

What

The

Hell

Is

That?

–it said, to which his brain had no response.

Suddenly he doubted everything he had been telling himself. Because no matter that he had been up here for several nights waiting for an otherworldly being, had he really expected anything to appear? Even after seeing the note disappear through the stone, he couldn't fathom something might actually climb up to this loft window to come and find them.

"Cisco," he hissed, hoping that his friend was somehow still lingering on the stairs and could hear him. "Cisco!"

Nothing.

The window rattled again.

Oh god. What should he do? Did he have time to run and get his friend? What if by doing that he missed whoever it was at the window?

Whatever not whoever, his brain finally said.

Semantics, he told his brain. *There's a creature from another world at my window. Pull your shit together and help me figure out what to do.*

He took a step towards the curtains he had only just closed.

Reached out a hand.

Then jumped back as the window rattled for a third time. Loudly, as though whoever was outside was getting impatient. And with enough strength for Jake to know it was unlikely to be a small, furry paw.

He should run. He really should. But he didn't want to let Cisco down.

"Screw it," he muttered, then stepped forward and ripped aside the curtains.

To reveal a face.

A giant face.

A giant *stone* face.

Jake's entire body shook as he was hit with a blast of déjà vu. Assaulted by feelings, images, and the distinct feeling of having seen this very face close up before, while being cradled in a stone hand.

He reached out, slowly, and unlocked the window.

A rough, grey finger of rock pushed it open gently.

"You have grown, young Jake," the face rumbled. "It seems you are not so young anymore. Is that why it took you so long to respond? I must say, you used to be a lot quicker to open the window whenever I knocked." His eyes, narrow crevices in the stone, seemed to blink. "May I come in?"

Jake's own eyes widened to the point he felt they might actually pop out of his head and smatter the face pressed close to the window frame with goop.

"I- I don't think... um, there might not be... much room?" he stammered.

The stone giant laughed softly, the noise like gravel sliding down a slope. "Still no more used to my jokes, though."

"What?"

"I cannot come into your tiny little house, Jake. We have been over this before."

"We have?"

They had. Jake knew it the moment he said the words. He couldn't remember the conversation, but rather the texture of it against the fabric of his past. As easily as he knew the touch of his children's foreheads after years of kissing them goodnight while they slept.

A sigh issued through a fissure in the rock. It smelled of earth and moss and ancient things.

"Things that once were have been forgotten, I see," the stone giant said, frowning. "Tabitha warned me that might be the case. She sent me because she knew you and I were once friends a lifetime ago. We used to walk together in the moonlight, cresting the hills around this town of yours, meeting the hidden people, conversing with my stone kinfolk in the north, dancing with elementals. You were never sure of what you saw, but you had fun. I remember that much."

Jake couldn't talk. It was as if a wall around him was being knocked down, showing glimpses of everything he had long held at bay. Illogical adventures he had shared with his friends. Human friends. Otherworldly friends.

And this stone giant. This…

"Boulder?" he said softly, the name feeling all too familiar on his lips. Tears began to creep into the corners of his eyes. He didn't bother to wipe them away. "Oh my god, Boulder?"

A wash of emotions cascaded over him, as if he had discovered a new part of himself that had been lying dormant. A piece of his soul that had somehow been overlooked all these years of growing up, taking on responsibilities, becoming an adult, a husband, a parent. A piece of who he had once been. A sliver of magic that he hadn't known had been missing from his life.

He suddenly understood a little of what Cisco had been trying to cling onto all this time.

"You remember my name," the being said, the fissures around its eyes deepening as it seemed to smile ever so briefly. Then he became solemn again. "That is a good start. But, for now, that's all it must be. I have returned with a warning."

The cold breeze wasn't the only reason for the shiver that slunk down the entire length of Jake's spine in that moment.

The giant face leaned in.

And told him everything.

CHAPTER NINE

It Begins

"You must prepare for battle as you once did. For the forces of evil are gathering at the gates and the powers of Deadman's Grin grow stronger. The fate of all our worlds rests on your shoulders." Jake paused and cleared his throat, looking a little bashful as though even he couldn't believe how melodramatic he'd sounded. "At least, that's what he told me."

Cisco watched as his friend paced around the dining room table, animatedly recounting his tale from last night for the benefit of Doc, who sat opposite, and Michelle's disembodied head from the video call on the tablet between them. He had heard the story already and although slightly annoyed he'd missed out on the actual conversation, he couldn't help the little tingle of excitement knowing the other side had been in touch.

Doc's face was a picture of weary disbelief. She had only just arrived after dropping Cecilia off at school and still looked pretty flustered after apparently fighting for twenty minutes to get her daughter to put on shoes.

"Right, so this stone giant of yours," she began, addressing Jake. "A stone giant you apparently used to hang out with. He came to tell you that we're all in deep shit?"

"Pretty much."

"And for some reason him and all these other talking rocks and foxes and supernatural beings with powers beyond comprehension are relying on *us* to save the world?"

"Yes, but he definitely said worlds. Plural. They're relying on us to save multiple worlds."

Doc blinked and gestured around the group. "*Us?*"

"No pressure," Michelle's face said despondently. She was calling from work, having slipped off to a spare meeting room in her office. "I thought I had a difficult day ahead here with another dull HR meeting and now suddenly I'm partly responsible for the continuing existence of other planets?"

"Not just other planets, I think. Other dimensions. Including the one Tabitha lives in."

Doc rubbed the back of her neck. "Speaking of which, Jake, this fox of ours. Where was she last night? If this is so important, why didn't Tabitha come herself to meet us instead of sending her proxy?"

"She was off on a quest."

"I can't believe we're even discussing this seriously. She's a fox, not fucking Gandalf."

"Look, I know, Doc. Believe me when I say I'm distinctly uncomfortable being the one to bring you this information. Flights of fancy regarding fantastical creatures from other worlds is Cisco's domain. He's the dreamer. I'm the scientist."

"My dad would have kittens if he knew you'd inherited his collection, Jake."

"I bloody well saved that collection! And feel free to kiss my arse."

"Oh, bite me."

Cisco sat back calmly, watching the two of them bicker as they had always done. Now *this* felt like a proper homecoming, seeing the pair trade insults over the trivialities of the madness they were involved with, neither happy with the other.

He glanced to the screen and saw Michelle was still being smart enough to stay out of the trouble that often brewed between her wife and her brother. Which left him as the only one who was prepared to say what needed to be said.

He cleared his throat.

"I didn't remember the stone giant either, you guys. Or, perhaps I did, but it was smudged a little in my brain. However, Tabitha is real. I believe Jake saw Boulder. And we all saw what happened in Manchester." He looked between his friends, from face to face to screen. "I didn't come back to Dark Peak just because of what was happening in my marriage. I came here because when I heard about the baby monitor murder, I figured what we went through was starting again. And it clearly is. Things are about to get messy."

Jake swallowed, his face growing sickly. "Boulder told me we needed to prepare. The tendrils of the shadow world – and he used those exact words – are infiltrating ours as we speak. He implied we're seeing glimpses of it around our own planet. The growing hatred, spreading like a virus."

"All because of a pirate we killed?" Doc said.

"That's the thing," Jake replied. "I don't think Deadman's Grin's body was ever properly destroyed. Dad said the government took it to a special laboratory nearby. I didn't realise then, but I guess even they didn't know for sure if what happened was a gas leak. Or maybe they were sure it wasn't. Otherwise, why keep the evidence?"

Cisco leaned back in his chair with a sigh, trying to contain a very big "I told you so" that was itching to get out. "And all this time I thought I was the only one."

"Sorry, mate."

"Whatever. It doesn't matter now. We just need to prepare for what's coming."

Doc glanced at the video screen and shared a look with Michelle. Cisco saw the flash of concern pass between them, though neither said a word. He felt guilty about that. As though perhaps his return had ruined the wonderful life they'd made together. He wouldn't have blamed them if they were thinking the same thing, even if the truth was that this bullshit would be happening regardless, with or without him here.

"And what exactly is coming?" Michelle asked her brother. "Did your big friendly giant tell you that, scuzzbucket?"

"Chaos," Jake said, giving the screen a finger. "As Deadman's Grin is brought back to life by whatever darkness is out there, his powers will get stronger. Which means there will be far more inexplicable monsters coming our way."

Then his phone vibrated across the table and he picked it up to have a look at whatever message he'd just received. His jaw hardened as he read it.

"And it's started already, hasn't it?" Cisco said, his heart racing.

"It has."

Doc crossed her arms on the table and lay her head down, burying her face. "I'm not going to get any work done today, am I?"

CHAPTER TEN

Swashbucklers

The three of them stood outside the gates to the Old Shire Primary School on the edge of town.

"I'm not sure this is a good idea," Jake said for the fifth time in as many minutes.

Cisco secretly agreed with him. Which is why he was relieved Doc had insisted upon a little discretion, making them carry their consoles tucked safely out of sight in backpacks.

They had parked in a quiet side street, under the shade of the leaning stone terraces and their snow-covered slate roofs, and hurried along the gritted paths to the school Jake had told them about.

Cisco couldn't help but think how much times had changed since the 80s. Once upon a time they'd thought nothing of rocking up to investigate strange occurrences with the weapons strapped to their backs, blasters already in the holsters, like young gunslinger wannabes. Nobody had really questioned it. While these days if you went out looking like that you'd be photographed and videoed and be a meme on the internet before you knew it.

Of course, Doc was a face about town now, a well-respected member of the community. Her little company, Green Goodness, was well known for helping those most in need. And although they all agreed that struggling families wouldn't give a crap if she was running around dressed like she was late to a Halloween party, they acknowledged that maybe, for now, they should keep their battle against the encroaching darkness as quiet as possible.

Cisco was fairly sure the others had already started bearing the brunt of the *Gasbuster* whispers that had resurfaced upon his return. He'd noticed it more and more, usually when dropping George off at the primary school he'd prearranged to place him at. He'd seen the other parents pointing and staring. It was only a matter of time before their kids started to bring it up with George during playtime.

But what could he do, other than explain to his son that Daddy was secretly having to save the world again in between school pickups?

"What did the message say, exactly?" Doc asked Jake, as she rang the buzzer.

"It was from Marilyn, the head. You know, Rose's sister who was in the year below us. She remembered the," he used air quotes, *"shenanigans* we used to get up to. And she said she had a bit of a problem we might be able to help with. Something of a paranormal nature in one of the classrooms this morning when they arrived."

"A paranormal nature. Brilliant. Did she give any more details than that?"

Jake didn't get to answer. The crackle of the intercom gave way to a shaky voice.

"Hello?"

"Hi!" Doc replied brightly, holding up a finger to make sure Cisco and Jake stayed quiet. "My name is Dorothy Forbes, and my acquaintances and I were sent a message asking us to come to the school to see Marilyn… Mrs Thomas, the headmistress? Apparently she needs our help with something of a specialised nature."

"*Paranormal*," Cisco mouthed.

Doc scowled and shushed him.

"Oh, thank god," the man's voice replied, clearly not needing any further information. He spoke in a hissed whisper, almost as though he was trying not to be heard by anyone at the other end. "You're the Panic Stations, right? Come in. Quickly. Please!"

Cisco grinned as the gate buzzed open. "Hey, we're famous!"

Doc held out an arm to prevent him from walking through.

"I hate that name, Cisco. I *hate* it. I'd forgotten how much, but it's all flooding back to me now. We're not doing that again, understand? I am barely hanging onto my sanity here as it is and I'm not going to compound this mess by running around referring to myself as a Panic Station. I'm a responsible adult with adult responsibilities."

"What should we call ourselves then?"

"Do we need to call ourselves anything? I'd very much like to just turn up, save the world, and fade back into normality. Why do we need something people will label us with for the next few decades?"

"Every team has a name, Doc, it's the rule of these things! *Ghostbusters, Monster Squad, Goonies…* they all had names. The good guys need a name for the viewers to get behind and chant in their heads."

"And yet this is real life and we have no viewers. Nobody is watching this shit. It's embarrassing."

"Doc, come on."

"Bloody hell, you just won't let it go, will you?" She eyeballed him. "Fine. I suppose you have a name all picked out? Come on then, spit it out."

Cisco opened his mouth and closed it again. Maybe he shouldn't say it. Maybe she was right. Their original name had been his suggestion and even now he could remember the bloody pirate laughing any time he said it.

And yet he couldn't resist.

"Swashbucklers," he blurted out gleefully.

Doc's mood visibly darkened. "Veto."

"It's perfect."

"It's really not."

"Come on, think about it! We're like those old-school heroes from the black and white TV serials, brought back for one last fight.

Ready to swoop in and save the day from the terrors of the high seas – which, in this case, is a very cranky undead pirate. It's perfect. We're modern-day swashbucklers!"

Swearing under her breath, Doc pushed her way through the gate and let it go without waiting for either of them to follow. Cisco just about got a hand to it, then dragged Jake after him as they made their way to the school office.

"Is that a yes?" he called after her.

The office was empty.

Or, at least, that's how it seemed at first.

The lights cast intermittent shadows across the paperwork spilling haphazardly over the desk. A coffee cup had tipped up and was now dripping onto the beige carpet. Files appeared to have flown from the open cabinet and were now all over the room. One hung from a row of festive paper chains that had been slung around the ceiling.

All three stared through the sliding glass window that had been decorated with painted snowflakes, took in the scene of what might have been a struggle, then unzipped their backpacks and strapped their War Wizards on.

"Hello?" Cisco whispered, poking his blaster through the opening, then following it warily with his head.

He jumped and smashed his ear into the glass when a voice under the desk hissed back, "Down here!"

Two eyes appeared in the darkness.

"It's in Room 2B," the office secretary said. The short, balding man glanced around as though half-expecting whatever it was to have perhaps escaped 2B and be sitting in the office waiting to eat him. "Mrs Thomas and the other teachers got the kids into the library and barricaded themselves in, while I waited for you here. They've told them it's just an impromptu story time. Most are buying it so far. But if that thing gets loose who knows what might happen?"

Jake leaned in, next to Cisco. "If it's that dangerous, why didn't you call the police?"

"We didn't want to spook the children." He paused. "And this didn't feel much like something the police could do anything about, to be honest. Mrs Thomas said she went to school with you all. Said you'd know what to do." The man whimpered as he saw Cisco's blaster. "You can get rid of it, can't you? That's what you do?"

"That depends. What is *it* exactly?"

But at that moment a falling sheet of paper drifted to the ground from a file at the back of the office. As it hit the carpet with a gentle rustle, the cowering man let out a small yelp and scuttled back into the relative safety of his desk, pausing only to reach up to hit the entry button.

The door to the main corridor opened.

"2B!" he hissed. "It's in 2B!"

Doc held the door open for Cisco. "After you, my dashing, old-school hero. It's time to buckle those swashes."

He pulled a face and strode into the school.

CHAPTER ELEVEN

The Stickle Brick King

"This doesn't feel like a very good plan," Jake whispered, although Doc wasn't sure if he was talking to himself or to them. "Using the War Wizards in the streets of Manchester was bad enough. Using them inside could be really dangerous. Should we rethink this? We don't even have insurance…"

"Bit late for that," Cisco replied. "But I think we've got this. Did I ever tell you about the care home ghost we had to fight? It was a tough one, but we managed not to burn down the building from what I remember."

Doc sighed inwardly as they trod the rough, ageless carpet familiar to most primary school kids. For some reason the care home ghost rang a bell in her head, but she didn't really want to get into all that now. Those memories were most likely lost for a reason. She began counting down the numbers on the doors they were passing. *5A, 4C, 4B…* they were heading in the right direction at least. Although whether or not that was a good thing remained to be seen. They had managed to avoid being caught for bringing down the Manchester wheel on the inflatable Father Christmas. Would their luck hold in the event they ended up destroying a classroom or two?

She tapped her finger on the vertical glass pane in the door of 3A. There was a picture there of a big, bearded man and a crown, but more importantly beyond that she saw a classroom in disarray. Chairs scattered in all directions. Desks upturned.

A shadow moving across the back wall.

"I think it moved from 2B," she said.

Cisco scooted along the corridor, the console hugging the back of his ski jacket, his blaster raised and ready to fire. He looked ridiculous. But, she considered, glancing down at the suit she'd forced herself to wear for the investor meeting she had later, probably no more than she did right now.

"This is 2B," he replied, looking in the next window along. "And the rooms are connected. So, yes, I think it went for a walkabout. Shall we split up? Jake, why don't you and your glove take this room? Doc and I will hit 3A with the blasters. We'll converge in a pincer movement."

"You've been playing way too much *Call of Duty*," Doc whispered, as the two men swapped places.

Something crashed in one of the rooms. Feeling a bead of cold sweat trickle down her neck, under her collar, she realised it was the one she was about to enter.

"Ready?" Cisco asked.

Doc nodded unsurely. With a deep breath, Cisco turned the handle and they burst into the room.

To find absolutely nothing.

There was no response from any improbable creature. No nightmare come to life jumped out at them. It was just a room full of jumbled chairs and desks and school books scattered around.

A jar with a garden in it sat on the windowsill, through which the rays of the low winter sun were pouring as they drifted off the snowcapped hills in the distance. Some handmade crowns, swords and shields lay on a cabinet nearby. There was a life-sized *Stickle Brick* model of what looked like King Henry VIII eating a chicken drumstick in the corner. Next to him was a shoebox diorama of a jungle. And–

Doc and Cisco froze as there was the slightest twang of little plastic spikes pinging against each other.

The yellow-bearded blocky face of the infamous king turned slowly towards them, his eyes bursting to life in a fierce and sickening red glow.

His mouth opened.

"Off with your heads!" he growled.

The attack was faster than either of them expected. Doc barely managed to get a fireball off – which fizzed wide and scorched a mural – before the fake chicken drumstick flew through the air and smacked Cisco in the face. Doc immediately saw the red indentations appear in his forehead, akin to all *Stickle Brick* injuries of her youth, and for a second didn't know whether to laugh or run.

Then the figure was on the move, waddling around the desks at the back of the room, his open mouth still roaring indiscriminate insults that would have been perfect for a bad medieval movie, but felt completely inappropriate for a primary school. He grabbed one of the tiny chairs and threw it at them. A metal leg grazed Doc's shoulder, as Cisco only just yanked her out of the way.

"Run!" he urged.

She followed quickly, looking for something to hide behind. Her weapon was forgotten for a moment as she dove through the classroom detritus to put as much distance as she could between herself and the mad king – who was now humming Greensleeves as aggressively as he could.

"Divorced," the king suddenly rasped at them.

Cisco fired over his shoulder in a panic. The electric wave hit the glass in the door, which exploded outwards into the corridor.

"Beheaded!" the king continued.

Doc glanced back to see plastic bricks reshape themselves at the end of the nightmare's hand, moving unnaturally in ripples up his arm until he appeared to be holding a broadsword. Her eyes widened.

"Oh, come *on*!?" she muttered, as he swung it her way. She tucked into a roll and went sliding through a bunch of homework, the sword whistling over her head.

"Died!" the king added, smashing through a desk next to her legs with the weapon. Despite its plasticity, it appeared to have some kind of magical properties that made it far more dangerous than it looked.

Because of course it did.

The desk split into two clean pieces as Doc slid away on her bum, pushing herself back with one hand, while the other raised her blaster.

She fired so many fireballs she lost count. Yet the *Stickle Bricks* rearranged themselves in an instant, expanding to form a doughnut-shaped hole through which the discharges passed harmlessly before turning the stationery cupboard in the corner into a bonfire.

The sprinklers erupted.

"Ciscooooooooooo!" she called, as the king grinned at her and brought the sword down again to bury itself in the floor between her legs. "Where the hell are you?"

Cisco appeared, leaping through the spray and smoke with wild, crazed eyes. His blaster was still clutched tightly in one hand, but they both knew his electric pulses would probably kill them all given the water now pooling across the floor. So he'd leapt for the king to engage in hand-to-*Stickle-Brick* combat.

It was the smartest, bravest, and quite possibly most foolish thing she'd ever seen him do.

The king saw him coming, however. He disassembled himself – avoiding the attack – then reassembled behind Cisco, grabbed his legs and threw him straight through the doorway to the next classroom.

"Divorced," the murderous school project rasped, continuing the little poem that most children in the country had been taught about the bastard king.

Doc pressed herself back against the arts and crafts drawers, feeling desperately around for another weapon. Something useful against… whatever this thing was.

"Beheaded," the creature breathed on her, putting his plastic beard against her face.

Then her fingers felt something she recognised. Something all kids remembered from primary school. Something that could actually help.

"Survived," she finished for the king. Then pulled out the triangular glue bottle, popped open the lid and squeezed as hard as she could.

The ooze spurted out all over the plastic menace. Enough to cause him to pause and wonder what the hell she'd just done, as he looked down at his sticky hands and discovered the mess dripping down his being.

Then he looked up and laughed. Literally raised his head to the ceiling and laughed and laughed and suddenly Doc realised that it wasn't *his* laugh. The noise was coming through him, but it was clearly coming from somewhere… someone… else.

It was a laugh she recognised from the very depths of her nightmares over the years. One she had clearly blocked out. But now knew exactly where it came from.

Deadman's Grin.

Anger wasn't the feeling she expected to be hit with. Panic, maybe. Terror of hearing his voice again. Fear of what was going to happen next – that she'd never see Michelle or Cecilia again.

But anger was what flooded through her in that moment. Anger that she had forgotten just what he had once put them through. Anger that she had let Cisco carry the burden of memory all this time.

Anger that the pirate was trying to kill them all again.

Her boot shot out. This time the king wasn't ready, still too busy enjoying her poor efforts to subdue him with glue. He partially collapsed, falling backwards. He reassembled himself almost immediately, but it wasn't as quick as it had been… the glue made sure of that.

It was enough to give Doc the space she needed to scramble to the side, back through the debris, sliding through the puddles in the carpet, until she was far enough away to know she was safe to do what she was about to do next.

She raised her gun and fired.

The king was slow to reassemble. He got most of the way out of the shot, but left sticky strands of the glue across the gaping hole he'd tried to make. Strands of glue that, despite the water spray around them, happened to react badly to the searing heat of her 8-bit blaster fire.

Within seconds the monstrosity was alight, the fire racing across his bricks, the little plastic prickles curling as they melted. The king's face roared with anguish and frustration as his body began to fold in on itself. He reached out the arm with the sword, but the weapon sagged harmlessly as its molecular structure collapsed in the heat.

Even as the sprinklers continued to flood the room, the monster burned fiercely, slowly fading away before her eyes.

Until, quickly enough, it was just a heap of burnt plastic on the floor, into which the king's face melted and had time for one last scream before his red eyes rolled backwards, disappeared and became slag.

Doc crawled to her feet, her soaked suit sticking to her skin in every conceivable place. Her boots squelched as she trod towards the plastic mess, before stepping over it and heading into the next classroom where she could hear a kerfuffle.

"Cisco?" she asked.

But he was motionless on the floor. The noise was instead coming from Jake, who was hanging from the ceiling suspended by paper chains wrapped around his wrists, while being slowly strangled by tinsel.

The toilet roll Christmas angel that was trying to kill him turned in surprise to see the visitor and exploded in a puff of shredded paper as Doc blew her away.

Jake immediately dropped to the floor as the last of the dark magic faded away with the monsters.

Doc offered her hand. He took it gratefully.

Then both of them surveyed the carnage, as Cisco began to groan nearby.

"You OK?" she asked Jake, as he continued clutching his neck.

"Got in a bit of a pickle for a minute there," he replied weakly.

"I hurt everywhere," Cisco complained from the floor.

Doc shivered in her sodden clothes, feeling the bruises from the fight begin to burn across her entire body. Clearly they were all too old for this. But at the very least she knew a little more now about what exactly *this* entailed. Because that pirate laugh had brought some of her past back to her, blowing away a few of the cobwebs of what had happened that Halloween. It had given her a sense of what the four friends had once fought and would have to fight once more.

If there was one bright spot to this absolute garbage fire of a day, it was that.

She believed again.

CHAPTER TWELVE

Date Night

Belief was a bitch, it turned out.

It was all very well having some of her memories back, Doc decided. But it turned out some things were best forgotten. Like the ability of inanimate objects to be possessed by evil and animating themselves into a killing frenzy. Or the fact that underlying all the horror was the knowledge that someone... or some*thing* was behind it all. Squirming fingers of darkness creeping into their world from a place beyond, through the devil pirate himself.

Or, perhaps, the fact this was the second time in their lives they'd had to deal with it.

That part was especially unfair.

Even after they had left the primary school, hobbling and holding each other up, trying to ignore the hundreds of little faces pressed to the window of the gym – and the horrified looks of the teachers behind them – Doc had tried to reconcile what this meant for her. For her life. For Michelle and Cecilia.

Unfortunately, the *Stickle Brick* king had changed everything. There would be no going back to a time before she remembered this was all real – a time when she saw the bad stuff in the world being solely man-made. Evil, yes, but fixable. Now it included some undisclosed menace and dark magic wreaking havoc from the underworld.

Worse still, the knowledge of what they faced meant Doc could no longer allow herself to be snarky about any of the crap that had happened since Cisco's return. She loved her friend, always had, and she'd missed him something fierce over the years. But there had been a part of her in the last week that wished he hadn't come back.

Now she had to fight that thinking. Because he wasn't the catalyst for turning her world upside down again, she had to remind herself. All this shit would have happened regardless. It would have rained hellfire upon them all and without Cisco they would have been totally unprepared for it.

In bringing himself back to face the humiliation that had once driven him away, Cisco had done a brave and honourable thing. Making sure his friends and everyone else weren't going to have to face it alone, without the benefit of hindsight.

She had to give him that.

Giving Cisco a begrudging look of adoration as they arrived back at Jake's car, she saw the pain etched on his bloodied face from being unceremoniously thrown through that door by King Henry VIII. She helped him in, giving his arm a little squeeze as she did so.

He looked up, through the mass of dark hair plastered to his head with sweat and sprinkler water. The graze down one cheek crinkled as he gave her a wincing grin.

"Good to be back, huh?"

"You bet."

He looked like he was going to say something else, but was cut off as an alarm in his pocket chimed repeatedly. Slowly, wearily, he slipped his hand in and tapped his phone off. Then rested his head back on the seat and closed his eyes.

"It's time," he said with a sigh.

Doc didn't need to know what the alarm was for to understand his reaction. Neither did Jake. They simultaneously checked their watches.

Three pm.

The school run.

If there were indeed thin places between worlds, portals from this Earth to another, then this was the parent equivalent. The moment where the day's freedom ended and the transition to chaos began.

For the briefest of moments, she looked back towards the primary school and envied the melted mass of plastic that had slipped back into the darkness from which it came.

"Are you absolutely sure you want to do this, Cisco?"

Michelle stood at her front door, dressed up far nicer than she'd been in months – perhaps even since before the pandemic. Dorothy was still inside, just putting on her shoes. And Cisco stood framed in the soft lamp light of her house, trying to shoo them both away.

"I'm serious," Michelle said again. "Cecilia is a bit of a handful at the moment. The full moon, the wind... you know how kids get. Are you sure you can cope with both her and George together? Why don't I just stay home and let you and Dorothy go out and catch up some more?"

"Not a fucking chance," Dorothy muttered as she slid past Cisco and linked arms with Michelle. "Do you know how long it's been since we've been out together, just the two of us? Cisco offered and we accept. In fact, we take his offer and we run the fuck away to the pub with it as quickly as possible. That's how this works. Don't question it now, I'm begging you. I've earned this date night."

It was two days after the incident at the school and, after what Dorothy had told her, Michelle was partly glad she'd missed out on the near-death experience and partly envious the others had gone to relive their teenage adventures without her. But she couldn't help wondering now if somewhere during the fight Cisco had banged his head and lost leave of his senses. He had barely managed to take care of himself lately, let alone George. Babysitting for other people seemed a stretch too far, surely?

As if sensing her doubt, or perhaps seeing it transparently

written across her face, Cisco tilted his head. It gave him the look of a dad embarking on an admonishment and to her surprise it helped settle her nerves a little.

"I'm not a complete loss to parenthood, Michelle. This is the least I can do for you two. Doc told me the last time you went to a restaurant and I'm not going to lie to you, even *I've* been out on a date in that time! Trust me, you need this. You deserve it. And I can survive for a couple of hours, no problem."

"Yes, you can," Dorothy confirmed. "You've got my number in case of emergencies, right?"

"Of course. Have you both got your consoles in case things go tits up and the tarka dhal gains sentience and tries to kill everyone at the curry house?"

Michelle laughed, only to realise he was being serious.

"Just for once," she said with a sigh, "I would like to have a regular conversation with you."

She turned on her heels and walked down the garden path, although not before hearing her wife dash back into the house.

"What?" Dorothy said innocently, as she popped the backpacks containing the War Wizards in the boot of the car and slid into the passenger seat.

Michelle scowled and started the engine.

They got lucky, as it happens. Not only was the Indian restaurant only half-full – lessening the anxiety Michelle had about dining inside since the Covid lockdowns had lifted – but she was delighted to find nothing remotely deadly try to kill them for the entire meal. Except for the vegetable jalfrezi, which was so hot they both felt like they were bleeding from their eyes.

Even then, it was fun to be out. Although maybe fun wasn't quite enough to describe it.

No, it was *freeing*.

Michelle and Dorothy were able to sit back in the booth, drink, eat, drink some more, and not have to worry about guiding someone else through a meal or feel guilty they were actually talking to each other as partners while Cecilia played a game on one of their phones.

They talked for ages in between bites. About everything and nothing. Kids, politics, work, kids some more, and especially the return of Cisco. Neither of them had seen his marriage lasting, but they'd both been disappointed to see their fears borne out. Although Michelle could see behind Dorothy's finely honed barbs about their friend's aptitude for relationships and knew she was secretly glad he'd returned.

They'd been close, those two. Always scheming, occasionally with Jake in tow. The three of them had been in the year below Michelle at school, and although she hadn't given them the time of day for much of their school lives, somewhere along the line she had joined their merry little band of trouble.

Somewhere in a car park, she thought suddenly. Had they gone bowling? Why was she suddenly picturing a splodge of blue ectoplasm smeared against a shitty carpet?

She shook away the thought. Whatever, she was sure it had happened around that particular Halloween. An event in her life that caused her, even now, to fidget in her seat. Uncomfortable about what had happened, even though she couldn't rightly remember much about it other than the stories of the gas leak. Plenty before it and plenty after it, just not those few lost weeks in the autumn of '89.

Why was that? Cisco had always insisted it had been real. He'd remembered the most out of all of them and obviously that was the reason he'd come back now. But even Jake and Dorothy were beginning to remember bits and pieces of what they'd gone through – as though reliving what they'd apparently done as kids enabled them to recapture the memories they'd lost.

What was wrong with Michelle that she still didn't remember as the others did? Had they held onto their childhoods tighter than she had? She definitely had fun back then, in those endless summers, playing out from dawn to dusk, enjoying those first burning crushes that chewed you up and spat you out, and the faintest fumbles of love in the shadows of the roller disco. But she'd never felt as strong a connection to that magical moment in time like they did. Childhood had just been a means to an end for her, a stepping-stone to the best bits that were to come.

Like the wonderful life she now shared with the beautiful woman opposite her, which she knew she wouldn't trade for anything long since gone.

Dorothy, whose eyes, like dark pools, were busy soaking up the view around them, a frown creeping across her flawless brow.

"Do you remember what this place used to be?" she asked.

She did it in such a casual way that Michelle initially didn't notice the importance of her tone beneath the words.

"Um, not really. We've been coming here for years, haven't we? Since way before Cecilia?"

Dorothy nodded but said nothing. Michelle suddenly panicked that this was some kind of test. Had she forgotten their anniversary or something? Was this where they'd first gone on a date? Shit, should she have bought a present?

She tried to think, staring first at the bar near the front where a customer had rushed in for his takeaway, then to the window beyond which spanned the entire façade of the restaurant.

And that's when it happened.

Something came back.

A moment in time that jarred in her memory. An image like a shadow emerging from the darkness. Not quite tangible or distinct enough to grab onto, but enough to know that there was something important on the edge of her vision where before there had been nothing.

Glass across the floor.

She could suddenly feel it under her feet even now. Slipping, splintering, as she strode through it.

"I can't quite remember," she said, a little frightened. All too quickly the image fragmented away. "It wasn't always a restaurant, was it?"

Screaming. Out in the street. People being chased.

"No, I don't think it was," Dorothy agreed, stabbing at the last onion bhaji on the hot plate with her fork. She was looking as anxious as Michelle was beginning to feel. "There's a reason we come here, though, isn't there? Somehow, I know that, but I can't remember why we started or why here? I just know it's important. This place is important to us."

Michelle nodded as another vision popped into her head.

A girl sprawled on her back.

It's Dorothy.

It was clear as day for a split second. Dorothy, as a teenager, lying in this very shop in an explosion of glass. And yet the image wasn't as terrifying as Michelle knew it should be now, because that feeling of anxiety wasn't to do with any darkness. It was anticipation. Of the kiss that was about to happen.

Our first kiss. It was here!

In the midst of…

There was no end to that thought. The memories slipped through her fingers and left her grasping at strange and wonderful feelings, that themselves dissipated without any tangible connections to hold them in place.

Then Michelle was back in the present, the only thing remaining being a little regret that she had so easily let those memories go in the first place. And perhaps a little more understanding about Cisco, feeling a pang of horror for what he must have experienced all this time.

Remembering brought both pain and pleasure, it seemed.

"He was right," she said quietly, unsure even now what had just happened to her. "Cisco, I mean. He was right about everything, wasn't he? We've forgotten a lot. Some of it has come back, but I think there's a lot we're still missing somehow. Like, it's trapped in… in a…"

"A fog?" Dorothy gave a thin smile. She felt it too. "Yeah, there's a lot I'd like to remember but can't. Some things are coming back, but a lot is still lost. Pieces of the jigsaw that have fallen out of my brain. I guess that's what happens when you grow up?"

She reached her hands across the table and Michelle did the same, meeting her in the middle. Their fingers intertwined beside remnants of papadam and they held tightly to each other.

"I love you, you know?"

"I know."

Dorothy did her best impression of Michelle. "*And I love you too, Dorothy.*"

Michelle smiled, the fuzziness of the wine and her feelings enveloping her in a warmth that even the meal hadn't matched. "And, *yes*, I love you too, Dorothy. Through all these chaotic years. Through the current nightmares. Through parenting and pandemics. Even if we can't quite remember how this started, for whatever reason, I'm glad I found you and you found me, and we got to grow up. Together."

Dorothy blushed, unable to say anything back. And that's how they remained for a moment, just holding hands and saying nothing. Until finally the bill needed to be paid and Dorothy drove them home, where they discovered to their total surprise that Cisco had indeed managed to survive looking after the kids – they were all asleep on the couch, sat in front of the TV as E.T. said goodbye to Elliott and took off across the sky.

CHAPTER THIRTEEN

Excuses

Cisco sat opposite George at the dinner table, attempting to discuss the school day. This was one of those parenting moments he'd always looked forward to enjoying. Just a regular chat between father and son, a time of bonding, laughing over funny incidents, and perhaps a chance to offer some sage advice – to which his son would listen intently and remember for all time.

In reality, it was almost always a police interrogation.

"So did you do anything interesting?"

A shrug.

"Come on, you must have done something."

"It was school."

"OK, smart alec. What did you have for lunch?"

"Can't remember."

"It was literally only three hours ago, George."

George frowned and gave another shrug.

"Was it pasta or rice or curry or something like that?"

"Nah."

"How about pizza?"

The boy picked at the food in front of him, pushing around the peas on his plate. He picked one up, licked it, then pulled a face.

Fuck me, Cisco thought wearily. He had half a mind to bring out the desk lamp and do this properly. *Nobody told me it was going to be easier to communicate with magical animals in other worlds than finding out what my kid did at school. Why don't they warn you about this stuff?*

He rested his elbow on the table, chin in his hand, trying his best to be "in the moment", as Jake had been while his own children had been eating without fuss not so long ago. Unfortunately, this particular moment sucked and had already dragged out for forty-five minutes. Everyone else had eaten and left. Jake was in the kitchen with Natalie loading the dishwasher and they were talking in low voices.

Meanwhile, George was dissecting his meal like a forensic food archaeologist. Inspecting every morsel, sometimes tasting it, mostly chucking it back on his plate.

Cisco's mind raced as he watched. Thinking back to the fight at the school again. Unable to stop picturing the glowing red eyes on the *Stickle Brick* king that felt like they'd been burnt into his retinas. Same as on the giant Evil Santa.

Those eyes were something he remembered all too well. The dark magic of Deadman's Grin, devilish puppeteer and all-round pain in Cisco's arse.

Jake walked back into the dining room and rubbed a cloth around the table, studiously avoiding the two people still sitting there, although he gave George's hair a little ruffle as he moved past.

"How's it going, kiddo?" Jake asked the boy.

"Great, thanks!" George sang, stuffing in a forkful of peas and beaming in an effort to impress the man. Cisco's shoulders sagged.

Giving into temptation, he finally reached into his pocket and pulled out his phone to quickly check Twitter.

"Did you update your notifications?" Jake said, balling up the cloth and setting it on the table in front of him as he took the chair next to George. "You said you were going to set some alerts or something. To keep an eye out for anything else we need to be aware of?"

Cisco shrugged. "I set up some keyword phrases for it to pick up. We got lucky with the school – if lucky is the right word – but we can't rely on a Mrs Thomas to remember us and get in touch when things get freaky. Social media works in real time. It's a proper wasteland sometimes, but for this it's perfect. We can be sure as soon as someone in Dark Peak sees something weird, they'll post about it."

Thankfully there wasn't anything of interest right now, so he put the phone down in front of him. Jake glanced quickly in the direction of the kitchen to make sure his wife was out of earshot, then leaned across the table.

"It's not going to be easy to get out to any future jobs whenever we want, you know? First the Christmas markets and then a couple of days ago we came home like drowned rats from the school. Nat's not happy."

"I bet. What did you tell her?"

"Nothing, yet. But it's getting tricky to fudge my explanations and at some point she's going to see through the bullshit. To be honest, I really don't like lying."

"Tell her the truth then?"

Jake's laugh was a little high-pitched. "The truth?"

"Yeah."

"Are you kidding me? *I'm* still struggling to believe all this and I'm part of it! No way will she believe what's going on, with ghostly pirates and possessed classroom projects. There's never any proof, other than how we look when we've had a battle and the destruction in the aftermath. CCTV always goes into static whenever the dark magic is used. Cameras don't work. All of which is convenient and yet gives us nothing to wave at the authorities to shout 'SEE?'. And even the school, who called *us* to save them, never reported what happened because they weren't even sure what it had been. Nobody wants to be that guy who claims they've seen what we've seen, because they know it's impossible to believe. If you weren't already part of this, would you?"

Cisco frowned at George, who was now picking off the breadcrumbs on his veggie dippers and attempting to lick them from his fingers one by one. "Probably not," he admitted. "But these things aren't going to go away. As your stone giant said, it's going to build from here. We need to find solid excuses to get out and take care of stuff. Like going to the pub or bowling or something."

"There hasn't been a bowling alley in Dark Peak in forever. Not since you were last here."

Cisco immediately pictured a row of scorched bowling lanes and a café door covered in exploded blue ectoplasm. He wondered if Jake remembered that too.

"Well," he said, "you're going to need to find something to say to Nat. Because Deadman's Grin is coming for us and it's only going to get worse. If we don't step up to fight back, people are going to get hurt."

His phone buzzed, vibrating the entire table.

All three of them stopped and looked at it.

"What's that?" George asked, using his fork to scratch his nose.

Cisco glanced at Jake, then reached out for the device.

He read the notification with dread, before throwing on his best unconcerned smile as Natalie breezed into the room, gave them all a slightly fixed grin, then went out through the door to the living room.

"Eat up your peas, son," Cisco replied as soon as she was gone, slipping the phone into his pocket. "Jake and Daddy have to go bowling."

Natalie didn't seem to believe the excuse. Cisco could see it in her eyes as he and Jake headed for the door.

"Seems a bit far to drive just for a game of bowling," she said, warily eyeing the pair of them. "But OK. Go relive your childhoods. Soak up all that nostalgia you keep banging on about. I'll look after the kids and get George to bed for you."

Cisco tried and failed to fend off the guilt. Was he being a complete arsehole here? A terrible friend? A worse father?

No, the world needs you, he told himself. *This is something you have to do. Nobody else can.*

"Thanks, Natalie," he said, then as he saw George wave from behind her legs, "Be good, George. I'll be back to sing all our goodnight songs, I promise."

Natalie narrowed her eyes ever so slightly, knowing he probably wouldn't be back in time and she'd have to put all the kids to bed by herself, then she shut the door.

"We need to get this done and then we need to find out how to kill the pirate again, properly this time," Jake said, as they walked quietly to the car. "Because middle-aged ghostbusters having to fight demons around school runs and bedtimes and wives who don't buy bullshit about bowling nights isn't going to be sustainable."

"Yep."

"So where are we going?"

Cisco strapped himself into the passenger seat and checked his phone.

"The Jousting Inn. On Summer Street, behind the library."

"Did you warn Doc and Michelle?"

"Yep. Michelle's working and Doc's trying to find a babysitter."

"Shit. Babysitters are like gold dust around here at the moment. As soon as the last lockdown lifted, they all got booked up for months. It's probably just us then?"

"I guess so. You got the War Wizards in the back?"

Jake held his friend's gaze. "Come on, mate. This isn't my first time."

Cisco grinned and gestured for him to drive.

CHAPTER FOURTEEN

Not As Easy As It Used To Be

The Jousting Inn was ablaze with Christmas lights. They blinked around the doors and windows, wound around a big, jolly tree next to the porch, and illuminated the plastic reindeer on the roof. Yet the place was empty when they arrived, with only the terrified owner, all greying mullet and grizzled beard, wrapped in his wife's dressing gown, there to meet them.

Old Bill stood in the doorway, chain smoking the fear away and shivering in the cold. As the pair arrived, he reluctantly stepped back into the bar.

"Are you the guys from the Twitter?"

"That's us," Cisco nodded solemnly. "From the Twitter. You said you had a weird problem? Like something moving when it shouldn't?"

"Aye. You said you might be able to help?"

"We'll try."

Old Bill pointed towards the pool room.

"Crazy puppet," he said.

The description turned out to be pretty accurate.

The Jousting Inn was so named because of the small suit of armour that had been displayed at the pub for as long as anybody could remember, its gauntlet glued to a wooden joust. Cisco vaguely remembered seeing it one afternoon Doc's dad had taken the pair to teach them to play pool. It had been distinctly less animated then.

Now it greeted him and Jake – against a rousing background of Slade's "Merry Christmas Everybody" playing on the jukebox – with a flurry of catapulted pool balls, which were, inexplicably, on fire.

Jake yelled out in shock as he was grazed by one and Cisco tripped over a bar stool as he pulled them both out of the way, collapsing into the cover of a table.

"I'm sure this used to be easier," Jake moaned, gingerly touching the charcoal stripe down the side of his face.

"It did."

"Then what happened?"

Cisco gripped his blaster tightly and popped his head up to see the knight pretending to gallop around the back of the room, making clip-clop noises. A powerful red glow seeped through its visor.

He crouched back down again as another ball flew his way.

"At some point we got old and slow and more susceptible to being hurt by demons from other dimensions. But, honestly Jake, these bastards were just as bad back then. It's a wonder we made it out of childhood."

"Reckon we'll make it out of adulthood?"

"Maybe. Ready?"

"No, but let's do it anyway."

The battle didn't last long. Cisco kept his distance, trying to draw the creature's attention by firing as much as he could while circling around the pool table one way, while Jake went the other. The electricity waves didn't do too much against the evil possessing the armour, other than scorch it as they bounced off. But the distraction was enough to allow Jake to sneak up and use his glove to punch the thing back to whatever hell it came from.

After it was over, having destroyed both the evil and much of the back room, they staggered out of the smoke, leaving the proprietor to gape after them with the cigarette hanging limply from his bottom lip.

The pair stepped out into the night-time drizzle.

"Pub?" Cisco suggested, as a joke.

Jake's laugh degenerated quickly as he began coughing out the smoky remains of the firefight. Then his phone buzzed with another notification.

"Night's not over yet," he said with a groan.

The next job had come from Michelle and Doc, who had managed to find a babysitter in the end – and it was actually her who alerted them to "gnomes and shit doing weird things" at the homewares store where the teenager had just finished work.

Apparently, she'd just locked up and left, claiming it was trouble beyond her paygrade. So Doc grabbed the keys off her, pulled Michelle away from her work, then hurried to meet Cisco and Jake outside the big stone building with the crappy blue and orange sign out the front. With a collective breath, the four then opened the place up and stepped into aisles of madness, full of not just gnomes, but all kinds of crazy-looking garden decorations and an entire department of plastic toys come to life. All bathed in a red glow. All baying for blood.

At first, Cisco wasn't sure how Doc was going to deal with this regurgitation of their childhood trauma. The fight in Manchester against Santa had been entirely reactive. The one at the school a tentative first step. But turning up tonight had been an informed choice, knowing full well what she might find. Was it a reluctant one or was she starting to believe again?

As soon as they came up against an attack of cheap, knock-off "Larry Blotter" dolls, and she kicked the boy lizard himself in the nuts, he knew he needn't have worried.

Side by side their 80s blasters blazed as they took on the masses, spraying pixelated fireballs and electricity as they moved from aisle to aisle.

Jake and Michelle had gone the other way, to garden furnishings. Cisco could hear their yells piercing the noise in the air – cries from Jake, swearing from Michelle, and occasionally the *thwack* and *crash* of a living ceramic nightmare being punched across the store and shattering across the tiled floors.

In the heat of battle, Cisco couldn't help but feel a little delighted. Even as a squadron of plastic drones dive-bombed into the pair and they had to duck into a treehouse, poking out of the tiny windows to pick off the attackers one by one, he felt something akin to contentment. It wasn't the fighting, he acknowledged, as some discount "Schlego" characters slipped down the chimney and scattered themselves across the floor beneath them like little landmines, with Doc launching into a wave of cursing as she accidentally kneeled on one. No, it was the camaraderie. Being back with his friends. And having a goal that he could actually accomplish to a degree of satisfaction.

Together, he and Doc finished cleaning up aisle five – pausing only to make the obligatory joke – then ran back through the store to where the battle was still raging through homewares. Jake was on the floor, bleeding from being stabbed in his arm by a sentient BBQ skewer. Michelle meanwhile was pinned to the wall by a life-sized winking sailor statue.

"Seriously…" she gasped, as the decorative monstrosity leered at her, "…who would ever buy anything like this?"

She collapsed forward as the sailor suddenly disintegrated. Doc holstered her weapon and enveloped her wife in a hug.

"Evil knows evil," she muttered, as the others quickly finished off Deadman's Grin's minions around them.

And so began the ritual of making excuses, finding babysitters, straight out lying about where they were going, and facing down evil to smack it back to hell. Night after night, day after day. Always on the quiet, always leaving behind chaos, and, somehow, always managing to avoid being seen on CCTV or recorded on anybody's phones, thanks to the evil energy disrupting the video feeds any time these events kicked off.

Sadly for Jake, there was nothing wrong with his wife's ability to spot trouble. Nat found the skewer injury a few nights after the fight in the homewares store, as he got out of the shower and they passed in the bathroom.

"What the hell, Jake! What'd you do to yourself?"

"What?" he said, before realising with horror his large plaster had come loose in the water and she'd glimpsed the angry red wound underneath. He laughed nervously. "Oh, *that?* That's nothing. I just bumped it on a… a door handle… or something."

He'd tried to quickly cover himself up with the towel again, but some sights cannot be unseen by anxious wives. Nat grabbed him firmly and investigated closer, before she saw another cut that quickly led her to discover more of his injuries. She followed them like a trail of destruction around his body and sympathy quickly subsided into fury.

"Mum?" Emily said, appearing at the bathroom door.

Nat shut it without missing a beat, turned around and folded her arms.

"Are you kidding me with this shit?" she whisper-screamed at him, knowing that their daughter was probably still listening outside. Her normally pale cheeks burned furiously with worry and anger. "Is this what's been going on behind my back? Is it, Jake? Holy hell, I've put up with so much since Cisco came to stay. The whole incident in town, the truth of which I know full well you aren't telling me. And then there are all the nights out. And all the secretive discussions you and Cisco and Doc and Michelle have been having when you thought I wasn't listening." Jake wrapped the towel a little tighter around himself, as though it might offer some protection from the tirade. "You promised me everything was OK, Jake. That the weird stuff wasn't going to keep happening and you were just taking Cisco out to look after him. I even bought your shifty excuses that you were 'just going to the pub again'. But that's not it, is it? What the hell have you been doing? Have you joined some kind of fight club for sad middle-aged dads? Is this your version of a mid-life crisis? Because, quite honestly, I'd rather you bought a fucking sports car or have an affair like regular people and be done with it!"

"I–"

She shut him up with a raised finger. "Don't even try it. I've tried to be the sympathetic wife. To be here for you as you tried to help your friend. I cleaned up our spare room for him and I put up with him hogging the main bathroom as he tweets god-knows-what into the universe from the toilet. I've put up with his moping about and I've even taken his son under my wing in order to make sure he has a chance to figure stuff out. I've literally added George to our own three children in my head. Remember our children, Jake? Because I'm not sure you do, given you've been going out getting the crap beaten out of you night after night with what looks like swords or some ninja shit."

She turned and left the bathroom with a muttered, "Fuck," leaving him clutching his towel, before Emily's head popped back into view.

"Oh, you are in so much trouble," the girl whispered in awe.

Jake nodded sadly, unable to argue otherwise.

"We're being overrun," Doc said to Cisco the next night, as they pressed themselves against the basement door of their favourite café. Scratches and moans filtered through the thick wood as it inched open again and skeletal fingers slipped through to grasp at them.

Cisco shoved his blaster in the gap and fired off a few fizzing rounds of electricity into the skull behind it. Shards of bones exploded against his face, but Doc saw it had done the trick. The undead fingers fell apart, clattering around their feet, and they were able to shove the door closed again.

"You think?" he gasped, sweat dripping down his face as he collapsed with his back to the barrier, looking remarkably heroic. He wiped his sleeve across his face, trying to blink away the exhaustion. "I don't know where that blocked up door in there used to lead to, but I'm guessing it ends in a place under Dark Peak where they buried a lot of bodies. Did you see how many skeletons had broken through? We're going to be here all night."

Doc shook her head, feeling her heart thumping in her chest as she tried to catch her breath. "I didn't just mean tonight. Every day now we're being overrun by the evil and ridiculous, and there's only so much we can handle by ourselves. Michelle and I have already gone through two babysitters and Cecilia called the last one 'mum' the other night, she sees us so little. I know Jake is getting some grief from Natalie, too. And when was the last time you saw George?"

"Earlier tonight, as it happens."

"Oh yeah? What'd you do?"

Cisco paused. "I was on my phone while I watched him play Roblox."

The banging and undead groans increased at their backs. Doc banged back harder. "Shut the fuck up, you turds." There was a brief, shocked silence. She continued, "I'm just saying that maybe we need some help, Cisco. Maybe it's time to call in the magical cavalry? I mean, a stone giant would be handy on most of these jobs. And I bet Tabitha has access to some pretty sweet otherworldly beings to help us."

"But she told us we needed to do this. It's our destiny or something."

"Screw destiny," Doc whined. "I want a hot bath and a night in. Come on, Cisco, all this saving the world business is exhausting. Let's ask the fox for some help? Please?"

Cisco's head began to bounce repeatedly off the door as it started banging again. "Tabitha said they've been watching over us all this time. Like, the garden watches us. Or something. I can't remember right now with all this going on. But I think the author said something like that too, didn't she? Maybe we can reach Tabitha that way?"

"The garden watches us? Like... the literal garden?"

"I think she meant the creatures. Like a bird or some other animal or maybe a pixie or a gnome or something. She said the shadows in the corner of your eye aren't always shadows."

"Are you telling me you think we should go and talk to the shadows in our gardens?"

"Well, I tried it before at Jake's and nothing happened. But maybe the garden was taking a break. If we all give it a go, maybe we'll get lucky?"

Doc shoved the soles of her boots as hard as she could into the concrete floor for purchase as the door began to give behind them. "Mate, that doesn't sound like something I can reasonably do and be able to live with the embarrassment. Isn't there anything else? What about sending another note through the standing stone on the hill behind Jake's house?"

"I don't know if we have time. Let's just try this and hope Tabitha wasn't blowing smoke up my arse?"

Doc grit her teeth. "Fuck it. OK. I'll talk to the garden."

The groaning and scratching and banging grew in intensity at their backs. The wood slammed into them harder. Inch by inch, they began to slide as the door was pushed open again.

Cisco lifted his blaster as skeletal arms snaked out and tried to choke him. "I'm all about respect for the dead," he wheezed, "but shall we just run in and waste them all?"

"Sold," Doc replied, clinking her plastic weapon against his.

The next morning, Doc woke early. Michelle was already checking her work emails, but Doc managed to persuade her back under the covers to enjoy a long, luxurious moment of simply lying there and holding each other.

Thirty seconds of it, anyway, before Cecilia called out wanting her breakfast.

Not long later, Doc was standing in the kitchen in her dressing gown, fuzzy-eyed as she let the steam from her cup of tea warm her face, staring through the double doors into the garden. Cecilia was in the other room watching TV, slowly increasing the volume as if her mums wouldn't notice if she did it incrementally. By the time *SpongeBob*'s theme tune blared out and was shaking the foundations of the house, Doc had already convinced herself to slip on her wellies and sneak out.

Thank god for double glazing, she thought, quietly closing off the noise and treading softly across the patio to the edge of the garden, across which there lay a light white winter frost. The sky was a pale blue, barely visible through the mist. But as Doc waited, the sun slowly poked over the old stone wall that bordered the side of the house, its rays filtering through the ivy that twisted and weaved through the rocky cracks.

She closed her eyes and let it soak into her skin. Enjoying the warmth on her cheeks, juxtaposed against the cold biting at her hands and feet. Listening to the birdsong in the trees. Not bothering to move, even as she heard the door open and shut behind her.

"Are you doing it?"

Doc opened an eye to find Michelle waiting expectantly next to her. "Doing what?"

"You know," Michelle said, dropping her eyes as though she couldn't really believe she was saying the words that followed, "talking to the garden. Asking for help. Seeing if someone can get Tabitha and an army of enchanted creatures to help us, like you told me last night we should."

"Oh, that. I haven't decided yet."

"Well, it's freezing out here, so can you decide quickly please?"

"Don't rush me. I had a tough night. I'm going to need to work up to it."

Michelle sighed, causing the garden to disappear momentarily behind the frozen mist of her impatience as her breath clouded the air. "Do you think those birds know anything?"

She didn't wait for Doc to reply. Lifting her chin, she called out, "Hey, birds. Can any of you talk? We need to get a message to a fox."

The birdsong continued, unabated.

"I don't think that's how you do it," Doc said, trying and failing to hide a smirk.

"Fine, genius." Michelle shoved her hands into her robe

pockets and stamped her fluffy slippers on the flagstones to warm herself. "Show me how you talk to magical woodland creatures then. I'm sure you're a bloody expert in it, as you are in so much else. A regular fairytale princess in your *She-Ra* dressing gown and Darth Vader wellies."

"This is exactly how I imagine a modern-day princess would dress, as it happens."

"Stop stalling, Dorothy. Talk to the birds! Call out at the shadows! Whatever it was you and Cisco decided last night, just get on with it. It's cold and I need to get back inside to get ready for work. I've already had to leave early twice lately to swashbuckle and I think it's a written warning if I don't turn up early today."

"Please don't call it that," Doc said with a grimace. "Swashbuckling was Cisco's idea. We didn't vote that in. He can call us what he wants, but for the love of all that's holy, let's not verb it."

"Fine. Whatever. I've had to leave early to fight killer Christmas decorations and homewares possessed by a dead pirate from some distant evil realm for reasons nobody can really tell us and what's more–"

Doc held up a hand. "Fine. Swashbuckle is fine. Did you come out here to torment me or does it just come naturally?"

Michelle laughed and kissed her on the cheek. "Get on with it now please. Call for help. Stranger things have happened recently than being answered by your garden."

With a deep breath, Doc nodded. The frost cracked beneath her feet as she stepped onto the grass, trying to attune herself to the world around her. They weren't quite on the edge of nature as Jake and Natalie were on their fancy estate. Doc and Michelle's modest stone terrace was a little more enclosed by the suburbs of Dark Peak. But the garden still had that feel to it, bordered on all sides by ancient mossy stone, wild hedges, and one beautifully gnarled tree that leaned overhead and creaked pleasantly in the wind whenever you listened hard enough.

"Um, hi," she began to the garden in general, immediately feeling silly. A glance over her shoulder showed Michelle wasn't laughing though. She gestured for her to continue. Doc nodded and tried to focus. She lifted her head to the birds in the old tree. "Can anybody up there hear me? We need to speak to Tabitha. *Tab-i-tha.*" A couple of the birds stopped and peered down at her. Doc's heart began to race and she moved closer, standing below them. Did they understand? Were they about to talk back? She called up again, more confidently this time. "We need your help. Things are getting out of control with Deadman's Grin and his magic. There are only four of us and we can't juggle this and everything else. Are any of you able to help us? With magic, or whatever?"

One of the birds fluttered down to a nearer branch. Tilted its head.

This is it, she thought.

The bird did a huge shit and flew away, cackling.

A series of swear words ran through Doc's head, as though giving her the chance to pull the handle for the very best mix of them for this particular moment.

However, before she could utter a sound, someone in the garden laughed.

Not Michelle.

It was a small voice, raspy and fractured, coming from beneath the cherry blossom tree, next to the stone wall.

"They do that a lot," Roger the Gnome said. His cracked plaster head tilted up to regard Doc and the grin that had been painted on far too many years ago curled up even more at the sight of the white goo dripping down her shoulder into her cup of tea. "I should have warned you sooner, but I wanted to see what would happen. I've been here a long time and sometimes you have to make your own entertainment to get through the day."

Doc's eyes widened. She looked to Michelle for help and found none. Michelle's mouth was hanging open in disbelief at the garden ornament they'd discovered hidden in the overgrowth of the garden when they'd moved into the house. A familiar-looking fellow that reminded Doc of the one her mum and dad had kept in their garden when she was young. Old, slightly crooked, with a faded face and a broken red hat that had been badly glued back together. Hence his name: Roger Red Hat.

Roger.

"It's you," she said weakly. "We used to know each other, didn't we? My god."

The visible memories were still weak in her mind, cloaked in that frustrating fog, but the soft scratch of his voice brought with it a whole host of feelings she remembered all too well now. Of scrambling about the dirt, fighting off hidden creatures, a desperate swing across a river, and Roger packed tightly in her backpack, whispering encouragement to keep her spirits up just as they threatened to break.

"God?" he joked cheerily, eyes flashing to life as he saw the recognition in hers. "No, just an honest gnome for what it's worth. One that's been with you many years, first as your friend, and then keeping watch over you and your family ever since." His legs and arms split from his body and he stretched upwards, yawning. "Oh, that feels good! I've been waiting to do that for a while. Now, Dorothy, Michelle, what's your problem? I'll admit I was only half paying attention when you came out, as usually you don't try to talk to the birds. You need Tabitha, is that right?"

Doc nodded slowly, still trying to process this. She'd seen so many incredible things lately, but finding an old friend in the garden and rediscovering those forgotten moments hit her hard.

"I... Yes, I mean yes, thanks Roger. We need to talk to Tabitha. Could you get a message to her?"

He didn't bother responding. Simply put his chubby fingers to his mouth and whistled, a long, trilling sound, high-pitched and melodious.

To their surprise, a tiny purple sprite flew out of a hole in the wall. Roger whispered something to her and she nodded, waggled her four wings at the pair of women in their dressing gowns, and flew off.

"Itsy?" Michelle said aloud.

"The very same!" Roger replied happily. "You probably remember her well, Michelle. And she you. You were always her favourite. Don't worry now, if anyone can track down Tabitha on her travels, it's her."

Doc came over and crouched down beside him, still unable to quite believe what was happening. The magic had been here all along. Her old friend, standing diligently in the soil, fading in the winds and rain, as he watched over them.

He raised a stubby arm and held out his hand. "Nice to finally get to talk to you again, Doc. I missed you."

She shook it gently.

"Me too," she found herself whispering.

CHAPTER FIFTEEN

Pressure

As much as Cisco loved being back home with his friends, reliving their youth as they played heroes and fought to stop the darkness from overtaking the town, even he had to admit he was getting exhausted by it all.

Once again he'd had no luck tracking down any enchanted friends in the garden, succeeding only in scaring Jake's neighbour as he yelled out each morning at the birds, the trees, and basically anything he saw that moved. And even though Doc and Michelle had said they'd managed to send a message for help, there had been no word from Tabitha yet.

The four were still on their own.

He was on the spare toilet one morning when George burst in. "Look at this I've just built in Minecraft," the boy said proudly, waving his tablet in front of him.

Cisco ushered him back out again quickly, making a note to ask Jake to fix the lock properly as soon as he could, before he continued to scroll through some Google results. "Sorry, George," he shouted after his crestfallen son. "I have to go and fight a rather angry plastic plant that's come alive at the garden centre and I'm trying to find out if it's meant to be poisonous. I promise to have a look tonight."

There had been no reply to that.

Cisco got no respite elsewhere, either. He might have been in the middle of some paid leave, but he still had an important museum exhibition display to write for, which meant slumping behind the laptop and researching various eras of British history, while trying to ignore all the notifications that were coming through until he had time to go take care of them.

Luckily the others had now accepted what was happening. They might not have liked it and maybe their memories of the past hadn't all returned yet, but they understood there was trouble and they had a way of fighting it. So even though Cisco was the only one who could take a break when he wanted to go fight whatever Deadman's Grin had conjured up next, one of the other three always made sure they took time off to help him.

More often than not it was Doc, being as she worked closer to Dark Peak than Jake or Michelle. And although Cisco relished the fun they had together – fighting everything from the undead rushing through that door in the café basement, to a possessed sleigh that was hunting late-night commuters walking home – it wasn't like it used to be.

Sure, they were still the same as they had always been. He hadn't really ever grown up. While Doc soon remembered how to laugh in the face of the ridiculous danger they faced on a daily basis.

But age and adulting was taking its toll. School runs became last-minute dashes, past the judgmental faces of parents who had been there to collect their children on time. Work slipped and clients chased them at inconvenient moments while battling the supernatural. "No, I can't send you that email again," Doc growled into her phone during one particularly brutal fight, as she battled a couple of gatepost lions that had come to life and attacked a postman, "you should have bloody archived it the first time."

Meanwhile the kids still needed to be looked after when not at school and bills needed to be paid and Cisco felt that he was quickly overstaying his welcome at Jake's house, no matter how nice Natalie continued to be to his face. So he took to checking the online real estate agents in the local area when he was in between battles. Not that he really had a chance to go and view any properties. Every day new and more bizarre occurrences took place, notifications from Twitter popped up on his phone, friends of friends contacted the group to tell them "something wasn't right" and ask "could they pop over?". And up he got, strapping on his trusty War Wizard to get to work.

Worryingly, the badness was spreading. Cisco had always figured the ability of Deadman's Grin to possess things was local to wherever his body was being kept. His evil magic bound by physical elements. Yet soon events began to spread around the country, reported at first as strange, isolated incidents, then as a wave of horror.

Cisco was in the middle of trying to figure out his tax return one lunchtime, when the TV in the background erupted in a Breaking News item showing the two leaders of the main political parties in the Houses of Parliament come to blows. Not just flinging the odd punch, but actually stripping down to their pasty white chests and trying to kill each other. The next morning, while discussing Greggs' new batch of vegan sausage rolls, a TV presenter got so enraged he started speaking in tongues and then vomited all over his co-host before the camera panned away to the stunned celebrity guest. And the night after that, the latest episode of *BBC Question Time* came live from the London Dungeon, with an audience to match.

But the worst thing?

Nobody seemed to care.

It had been a weird few years. Nothing made sense anymore. From the Brexit mess to the single term election of President Fuckface, logic was often seen being casually tossed out of the window. Then the pandemic happened, some countries handled it well and some didn't, and others decided to chuck science out of the window along with the logic. Politicians everywhere tapped into the rising evil ideologies thought long since discarded and discovered there was nobody left with any energy to hold them to account. And social media platforms continued encouraging everyone to fake and share posts for clicks and likes, while huge chunks of the media did the same.

Trying to hold fast to sanity, while the world burned like this, was exhausting.

Consequently, the wave of horror gripping Dark Peak – and now the country – became too much for anyone to keep up with. Ridiculous incidents that once might have been worthy of a whole evening of shocked journalists reporting from the scene, while more shocked journalists in the studio shook their heads, became mere bullet points in the evening news. The only people who seemed to care were the morning show commentators, who relished covering every angle of the crap they could.

"What do all these incidents mean?" asked Betsy Goodacre on *Good Morning England* (formerly *Good Morning Britain*, the name changed in advance of Scotland and Wales most likely voting to become independent).

"It's a left-wing conspiracy," replied the blogger from his parents' front room. "Funded by woke activists to try to stir up trouble for the government. They've been the real menace all along."

Betsy didn't question it, just nodded sagely, before they cut to a segment looking at the latest trends in right-wing fashions, complete with a catwalk of well-dressed angry young men in the studio.

Cisco turned off the TV at that point, lest he be tempted to throw it through Jake and Natalie's lovely French windows. Evil was running rampant throughout the country now. Everything Tabitha and Boulder had said was going to happen was happening. And despite Cisco and his friends working around the clock – and school runs and mealtimes and homework and the new football club Tintworth FC that George was now goalkeeper for – there was no sign that any of this was getting better.

They might be keeping Dark Peak from sinking into hell, but it wouldn't matter in the long run. Everything else around them was getting worse and everyone was either content to ignore it or had built in the normalisation of ridiculous, supernatural incidents into their everyday routines. Even the local police seemed happier cleaning up the mess left behind than trying to question why it was happening in the first place – quite possibly because they didn't want to face the truth of what they might learn. So they left the Swashbucklers alone to deal with it all. Which, of course, the friends did. Running themselves into the ground as they went.

"The definition of insanity is repeating the same thing over again and expecting different results," Cisco sighed to himself as George wandered by. His son gave his dad an odd look, as he might upon seeing a complete stranger sitting in the living room. Then he continued into the kitchen to find Emily. Cisco didn't blame him. They hadn't spent much time together recently.

He ran his hand through his ever-greying hair, before pulling it down over his face and pinching the bridge of his nose.

There was a reason they hadn't made the *Ghostbusters* parents in the films. It just wouldn't have worked. You couldn't properly parent and do your taxes and try to pay the bills *and* save the world at the same time. It wasn't possible. He was exhausted, physically and mentally. He'd already lost a marriage and now his son was drifting away too. Meanwhile his work was piling up in the background and there was still no end to the fighting in sight.

It was the same for the others, too.

Jake was treading on eggshells after Natalie discovered his skewer injury and had to skip the last couple of jobs, distracting himself with research into some interesting stones he'd picked up from a shadow creature they'd fought at Buxton Museum.

"They're runes!" he'd announced late one night, bringing them in to show Cisco, who had just arrived home from fighting a particularly rambunctious Christmas pudding that had gone on a rolling rampage through a house, setting several people alight. "Pretty cool, eh?"

Cisco had waved him away, then passed out fully clothed on the bed.

Elsewhere, Michelle had been summoned before her employment's Human Resources team to explain why she was constantly taking sick days. And Doc had already lost a client she'd forgotten to meet, because she'd been too tied up in the Redwood Pub wrestling diners from paintings that had come alive and were trying to suck everyone into their hellscapes.

This saving the world stuff was just too hard as an adult. As children they'd been able to do what they wanted. They had the energy to sneak out at night, fight the monsters, then creep back into bed and return to their childhoods of little responsibility. But Cisco hadn't been prepared by how different it was going to be now. That late nights had consequences. That food on the run gave you heartburn, and that fighting evil created a little ball of anxiety in your chest that never went away and because you were older you had to take it more seriously.

He'd come back to Dark Peak wondering if he could recapture some of that old magic. Even hoping that the monsters would return so he could fight them again.

Yet it turned out you couldn't ever go back to how it was. And now the nostalgia might actually kill him.

Pulling out his phone, he made a decision. George came back into the room at that moment and Cisco felt a flash of guilt for again not being present, but he ignored his son and kept texting Doc anyway.

They needed to change the plan and end this mess, before it ended them.

They had to take the fight to Deadman's Grin himself.

And as the ball of anxiety and dread continued to grow in his chest, Cisco figured it might be better to do it sooner rather than later. He told Doc the new plan. Then he dialled the doctors' surgery.

Shit is a lot easier when you're a kid, he thought, as he booked a check-up.

CHAPTER SIXTEEN

Health Check

"So you say you're having a little chest pain?"

Cisco sat on the dull brown chair next to the doctor's desk, trying not to stare at the distressing medical images in the faded posters hung on the wall opposite. If he had come in with anxiety, it sure as hell wasn't going to go away in here being told about all the other ways he might die.

"Uh, yeah. I mean, it's not really a pain, rather just a strange feeling right here," Cisco pointed to the centre of his chest and to his left arm. "And pins and needles down here. Also, my right knee is giving me crap, but that's another story. Basically, I've been doing a bit of exercise lately. Running around, ducking, being hit. Far more stuff than I'm used to if I'm honest, so this chest stuff is a bad sign, right? I did a Google search to check out the symptoms and it seemed bad."

The doctor's lips thinned as he bent and scribbled something on an important looking piece of paper. "Always with the Google."

"Excuse me?"

The doctor ignored him. "You said it started a couple of weeks ago. Was there anything you think could have triggered this feeling? And anything in particular that made you book the appointment today?"

Cisco wondered if he should be honest. If any place was a safe space, it should be a doctor's surgery. And yet would the slightly impatient man now tapping his pen appreciate hearing that Cisco was seeing and fighting improbable and terrifying things, shortly after returning to his childhood town, the place where he had once had literal creatures from hell materialise from him at the behest of a murderous pirate?

"Nothing I can think of," Cisco said. He played with some fluff on his knee, brushing it aside.

"Are you sure?"

"Yep."

The man nodded and wrote something else in his illegible scrawl. Cisco tilted his head a little, trying to see what it was, but couldn't make anything out.

"Do you think I need to have some kind of test to check my heart?" he asked. "Get on one of those machines and do a run while I'm all hooked up? That kind of thing? I mean, I have a son, I don't really want to drop dead if I can help it."

"You're not about to drop dead, Cisco."

Cisco let out a sigh. "Oh. That's good, thanks. What's the problem, do you think?"

"The problem," the doctor replied, looking up, unblinking, "is that you're over forty. By that time in your life, if it hasn't already, the human body has started to decline. It's worn. Regular stress has greater wear and tear on it. You basically need someone to check under the bonnet now and then."

"I... need a service?"

For the first time, the doctor attempted a smile. It fell far short of anything resembling good humour.

"Yes, just like a car. One that's been run into the ground a bit, if I'm quite honest, but not beyond keeping on the road. As long as you keep up with regular services on an old car you can keep them running for quite a while. Are you planning on staying in Dark Peak long?"

"Yes, I think so," Cisco found himself saying, which was a surprise. He hadn't really thought about it, beyond needing to come back to see his friends and check out the strange occurrences. To be here if the town needed him.

Perhaps he'd underestimated how much *he* needed the town?

"Great," the man said, standing and gesturing towards the door in no uncertain terms. "Then book in at reception, we'll do a check over and blood test. And in the meantime, try to dial back your involvement in any stressful situations, OK?"

Cisco thought immediately of the daily encounters with the supernatural he was having and the general feeling that it was all building to something even worse, on a scale that could mean their entire existence was in danger.

He smiled and nodded. "I'll try."

CHAPTER SEVENTEEN

The Woman in the Dream

The woman in the dream reappeared on a wet and windy Friday night, the week before Christmas.

Cisco wondered if exhaustion had brought her back into his addled mind. Earlier that evening, he and Doc had collapsed in her car after a particularly nasty battle, pulling off their half-charred winter gloves and tossing them on the backseat.

"This is no fun at all," Doc had groaned, wiping a sleeve across her sweaty, smoke-smeared forehead and throwing her head back. "Did this ever used to be fun? It doesn't seem like this could ever have been fun." Her fingers gripped the steering wheel, as though trying to hold onto some semblance of patience, while her brain did its best to come to terms with current events. "I'm still only getting bits and pieces of what we did coming through. Snapshots. Feelings mostly. Did we really used to enjoy doing this stuff? The fighting, the killing, the almost dying at the hands of some fucking weird shit somehow made real by some undead ghost pirate?"

"Well, *I* enjoyed it," he mumbled.

She laughed bitterly. "Of course you did."

He closed his eyes, still able to see the jagged outline of the electricity monster they'd just fought in the local arcade. It had been burnt into his retinas. And, on some parts of his body, his skin.

"However, no, it's not really like I remembered," he admitted.

"My body hurts everywhere. I think my shoulder might have gone. Going to have to get out the heat packs again tonight."

"That's what I figured. How did I let you drag me into this again?"

"Because that's what friends do. We fight evil and try to save the world together. Like all those old movies we used to watch. Like *Stranger Things*."

Her face lolled towards his dubiously. "Those kids had youth, energy, and David Harbour's dad bod. No offence, dude, all I've got is you."

They didn't talk anymore after that. Simply nodded to each other as she dropped him off at Jake's place, he got out and went to embrace unconsciousness, pausing only to creep into George's room to give him a kiss and tuck him back into his duvet.

Cisco barely undressed before falling into the spare bed.

Unfortunately, a good night's sleep isn't what he found there.

As he slipped from this world into another, it became clear that this place was altogether new. There was no chaos like in his recent dreams. No head-scrambles of anxiety over money and work and his son, interceded with terrifying monsters and a country in ruins.

Instead, he found himself standing on a calm, quiet beach. Pristine turquoise waves lapped at the golden shore. A gentle breeze swished through the weird-looking palm trees behind him. It was so real he could feel the sand giving way under his feet as he shifted and looked up to the swirling galaxy of stars rising above him, with twin moons to the west and a chain of sky islands drifting through the clouds all around them.

He felt awake, although he was keenly aware that his body no longer hurt and the anxiety in his chest was completely gone.

He was calm. Content. Peaceful even.

Maybe this was death? Maybe in the middle of the night, something in Jake's spare room had come alive at the whim of a ghost and killed him in his sleep. And now he was in heaven or whatever lay beyond the horizon of life on Earth?

It was an uncomfortably calming idea. Until he thought of leaving George behind and the anxiety immediately bubbled underneath the surface again.

Yep, still alive then.

He blinked as three shapes lifted from one of the islands just floating off the eastern horizon. They shimmered through the sky, before landing gracefully on the edge of a waterfall cascading into the night.

Their bodies long and lithe, their wings huge and slow.

They ducked their heads to drink.

Dragons?

Cisco didn't get further than that astonished thought. A bedraggled woman tumbled out of the thick forest nearby and ran across the sand towards him, a look of recognition and hope breaking across her beautiful, if dirty, face. Her large eyes widened even further from beyond strands of shaggy, strawberry blonde hair, half of which had been tied back with knotted leaves. Lips that had set in a grim downturn for far too long suddenly split to reveal a smile of relief and... something else.

She leapt on him with a fierce hug.

"You came back!" she breathed in his ear. She smelled of berries and the sea, wild and free, as though she was nature herself. Even as her hands left him, he stayed momentarily frozen, his cheeks surely growing red as he breathed in her delicious scent, unsure of the etiquette for this kind of situation.

He felt like a little boy again, confronted with vaguely remembered wonderful and dangerous feelings – stirrings inside him of a time and a memory he couldn't quite place.

Had they met before?

She looked him up and down with a rueful smile.

"My eyes have played many tricks on me over the years. You've often found your way here, although only ever in part, a spirit of sorts. Nothing tangible and real. But enough to let me see you grow into the man you've become. Time has taken us both by its hand and led us to adulthood, it seems. And yet in my head it's like no time at all since you were last here."

Was she speaking in poetry? It was like he'd stepped into an old-time movie.

"And where is here, exactly?" he asked. "I'm not just dreaming, am I?"

"Not entirely." She waved her sun-kissed arm up to draw his attention to the islands above them. "It has many names, but we have always known this place as Lyonesse. The land that was lost from Britain. Torn away from Earth by some ancient magic, to break up into this dreamworld."

Cisco looked around him again, not really sure what to feel or believe. Was this a dream or was it real? Returning to the woman, standing there at ease, looking every inch a survivor of whatever this place was, he suddenly felt very self-conscious about how he might be perceived. He'd gone to sleep in boxers and... oh, thank god, his subconscious had managed to slip on some pyjamas he remembered owning once.

Still, it wasn't exactly a heroic look. He tried to shift his stance to something more casual, to alleviate the fact he'd come dressed for a slumber party. Unfortunately, it served only to push his left foot a little too far into the sand, giving him a slight lean, which he tried to offset by putting his right hand on his hip, a bit like Superman.

"You are literally awkward in every dimension," a voice chided him from the past. It sounded like Doc.

In fact, now he thought about it, it had been her! She'd said those exact words to him down in the crudely carved cave prison under Dark Peak. The one they'd found that Halloween, beneath old William House.

Which was when he realised who he was talking to.

"Oh shit," he gasped. *"It's you."*

Then it all made sense. This was the woman from his dreams who had once been the girl in his dreams. The friend from another time he had tried so hard to save, along with her two brothers, after they had first tried to defeat Deadman's Grin and had been lost to time ever since. The person he had found himself returning to meet year after year since that fateful adventure. The woman who had been growing stronger in his thoughts over the last few months, as she tried to warn him of what was coming.

"Amelia William," she said, grinning slightly as she held out her hand. "Nice to meet you, again."

Their palms slid together beneath the spiralling galaxies and floating islands and improbable dragons.

Amelia William.

All the memories Cisco had held onto for so long had revolved around Deadman's Grin, as if there was a piece of the pirate stuck fast in his brain like a splinter. But despite holding onto more of his childhood than the others, it seemed the ravages of time had also stolen some things from him, too. First Tabitha, now Amelia – friends who had been so dear and important to him.

Why hadn't he remembered them until now?

"It's the magic's will," she said, as if reading his thoughts. "Tabitha said you might have lost those moments we all shared together. The times we friends spent on the cliffs not far from here, watching the oceans rise and fall. The chases across the sky as we sought that lost treasure. The campfires we seven huddled around many a night." Her smiled softened a little, a touch of regret hiding in the corner of her lips. "Memories, so they say, do not carry well from world to world. Sometimes they only return to a person when prodded into waking again."

"Oh, of course," he said, his heart sinking. He didn't feel very charitable about accepting *magic's will* when all was said and done. All these years he'd somehow been given cause to forget some of his most cherished friends, yet the pain and agony and fear he'd faced was still as fresh as the days they'd wrecked him. It didn't seem fair to hold onto the worst of times and have to let go of the best of times. How might his life have changed had that been different?

"So you remember me now, Cisco? How we knew each other when we were children, along with my brothers Peter and John?"

"I do. A little anyway." He scratched at his hair and found most of it was sticking up, as though he'd literally been dragged from his bed by the dream. "You were one of the children from William House who fought Deadman's Grin the first time. You saved everyone, right?"

She laughed, though it was a little cold. "We did, though they cared not for such facts. And that's how we eventually ended up back here. Only to find ourselves all these years later standing once again on the shores of this world, facing the same foe."

"Deadman's Grin?"

"Aye. And it is a twist of fate that it's because of him, you and I are able to properly talk now. The evil that pours through his being has infiltrated not only your world, but others like this one. Each twist of darkness is helping to dissolve the barriers a little more, upsetting the balance between dimensions. It is to our advantage we have found each other for real again, but I have to wonder if it is already too late to offer you my warning."

That bloody pirate, Cisco thought. Even in his dreams he couldn't get away from the bastard.

"If you're here to tell me he's back, you needn't bother. I know he's back. I don't understand how yet, because we put a fucking hole in his chest and he died. Then Jake and Michelle's dad gave him to the government to take away, and they ran some tests and then buried him, I guess. But I'm assuming something-something-magic, something-darkness, and now *boom* – we have ourselves a whole new undead pirate party?"

Amelia lifted her shoulders a little helplessly. "That is probably a better explanation than I could manage, if I'm being truthful. However, he is still just a man. A flinty, murderous man, who even in death stole me and my brothers away and ruined our lives. But there is more to his story than either of us knew at the time."

Cisco nodded, remembering the conversation in Jake's attic that had started this whole ridiculous adventure. "Tabitha told me as much."

"As she did me."

"You know Tabitha? Wait, of course you do. That bloody fox gets around, doesn't she?"

Amelia's laugh was long and loud. "You'd be surprised where she can go and what she gets up to when we're not looking! Yes, we have spent many long evenings by the fire together here, curled up, telling stories of our lives. Beings of her ilk have far more adventures than any of us blinkered humans would ever dare to imagine."

"Literally everyone has a better social life than me," he said with a smile. "So, Deadman's Grin is coming back. For what exactly?"

She shook her head and more hair fell loose from her knotted leaf hair-tie. "That's the problem − it isn't only him. The pirate is just the vessel of evil. Like a ship carrying the plague. There is something… darker… behind him. Beyond the Cobweb of worlds. A darkness that's working through him."

"Great. Tabitha failed to tell me *that* part." Then he sighed as he remembered. "Ah, no, wait. She asked me to go with her, didn't she? And I didn't. I couldn't just leave like that. It was all a bit much and I didn't want to leave George and…"

"You weren't ready, Cisco."

"Why not though? I came back home for that exact reason! I knew something was happening. It was literally why I forced myself to return to Dark Peak. And yet when Tabitha appeared and tried to help me understand what was happening, I didn't go. I was too afraid."

He closed his eyes against the dreamlike paradise around him, unwilling to let it alleviate his sudden guilt. Had he gone, could he have stopped Deadman's Grin sooner? Had he stuffed this entire thing up already?

Jesus, what a dickhead.

Amelia touched her fingers to his arm. "It's OK. It's not your fault."

"It kind of feels like it is though?"

"Like I said, you weren't ready. Even if you had gone, you might not have taken on board what Tabitha was going to tell you. It's fine."

Cisco put his hand on Amelia's for a moment. Felt her skin comfortingly warm beneath his. Then he took a breath and let her go, straightening as best he could despite the sand and the pyjamas he was still wearing.

"Well, I'm ready now," he said, defiant in the face of his apparent failings. "Tell me what we need to do. This evil, it's waking Deadman's Grin for what exactly?"

"To finish what it started. To make him unleash it properly into the world and bring down the Cobweb of worlds for good. Which is why Tabitha came to you. And why I have been trying to reach you too. Not only to warn you, but to ask you and your friends to do what we never could. To finish him before he wakes. Before he ruptures the barriers and brings the balance of the universes crashing down."

Cisco blew out his cheeks. This was nuts. All of it.

"Why us? You're here living in this other world and, hell, you look like you can handle a fight with a two hundred year-old pirate. Tabitha is basically made of magic. Can't you guys go and, I don't know, band together with some other ancient heroes. Maybe go wake King Arthur and his knights who are all sleeping under that mystical, mythical hill somewhere. Isn't he supposed to handle shit like this in the country's greatest time of need?"

"Tabitha couldn't wake them."

"Of course she couldn't," he laughed, but it faded quickly. "Wait, are you serious?"

Amelia shrugged. "I guess when you've been asleep for so long, it's difficult to be roused out of it."

"Oh, OK, fine," Cisco said, feeling that none of this was really fine at all. "But there must be other legendary heroes out there who you can call on? What the hell could you all want with me, Doc, Jake, and Michelle? What's so special about us?"

"Nothing at all."

He wasn't expecting that. His face dropped. "Oh. Really?"

"Truly. There is nothing special about any of you. No prophecies that foretold of your coming. No bloodlines of power. No special skills. No knowledge to help you defeat evil that others do not already possess."

"You're not selling me on this plan very well, if I'm honest."

Amelia gave him a wry smile. "And yet, you four came together and saved us before. You stood up to him and survived where others like me had not. Courage. That's why we need your help again, Cisco. You have courage." She mimed finger guns and her smile grew. "Plus, those amazing wizard blasters of yours."

With that she began to shimmer, along with the horizon of trees behind her. Like ripples in a lake, only they were getting stronger by the second. He spun around to see the rest of the place doing the same.

"Cisco, you need to go and find Tabitha. The author will know where she is right now. Tell her we've found what Deadman's Grin was searching for and have kept it safe. Then let her show you where to finish the pirate before he has a chance to wake. Nothing must distract you from that task. Nothing, OK?"

"But…" he began.

Too late.

He sat up in bed, sweat plastering the pillow to his face. The sheets clammy and sticking to him in all the wrong places. The image of Amelia still strong in his mind, although the doubt of what had just happened was already clawing its way back into his head.

It had just been a dream. Hadn't it?

He looked down to his feet and wiggled his toes.

Sand drifted off them onto the sheets.

CHAPTER EIGHTEEN

A House of Many Secrets

"Let me get this straight," Doc said, warming herself over her almond milk hot chocolate in Pepino Deli, which had been cleaned up significantly since the undead had poured through the cellar the other night. "What you're telling us is that you've seen *Star Wars* too many times and are now actively dreaming about Force Skyping some lost woman in another galaxy. After all the weird crap we've been put through for the *second* time in our lives, you're stepping things up and saying you can now dream yourself to other worlds?"

"There was sand in the bed, Doc," Cisco said, trying not to let it show he thought it sounded ridiculous too. He scowled at the looks of incredulity that Jake and Michelle were giving him. "*In* the bed."

George had stopped playing the game on Cisco's phone and was now staring at his dad with a deeply furrowed brow. Cisco had been convinced his son wasn't listening to the conversation, because he rarely did. Adults were usually boring and said boring things. He only tuned in when it suited him. Which apparently was now.

"How'd the sand get there?"

"Wouldn't we all like to know, kiddo."

"But it was *in* the bed? That's weird. Aunty Nat will probably be cross."

"That she was," Jake confirmed. "But I think perhaps Daddy just accidentally trod in some sand outside and brought it in with him before he went to sleep."

Cisco sighed. "It's winter, there's no sand on your estate, and I was asleep. Sand might get everywhere, as we all know, but it never usually creeps up on you when you're unconscious." He stirred the spoon around his hot chocolate, mixing in the festive cinnamon dust that had been artfully sprinkled on top in the shape of a snowman. "You know, this saving the world lark was a lot easier when you guys didn't question everything. It's all nonsense, we can agree on that. All of it. Nonsense. But that doesn't mean it's not fucking happening!"

He closed his eyes with immediate regret.

"Fucking?" George repeated, still very much paying attention. "Fucking! That's the f-word, isn't it, Dad?"

The two old ladies in their knitted beanies at the next table turned and glared. Cisco accepted the accusation of his terrible parenting with a nod, cued up another random *Minecraft* streaming video on YouTube, and slid the phone back in front of his son. "Please forget I said that, George."

George was already too distracted to answer.

"I'll bite," Doc said.

"Huh?"

"Who was the woman in the dream?"

The others were looking at him still, but now they seemed to be actually listening. "Do you all remember William House? There was a place under there, buried deep in the hill, far beneath the town. A place we found called the Underworld."

A flash of recognition crossed Doc's narrowing eyes. "A cavern containing doors to other worlds."

"Yep, doors opened by blood. Which, it turned out, I got to know in agonizing detail later on. But that's beside the point. You see, the William House kids were three children who went missing a whole century before we got involved with Deadman's Grin. They tried to stop him, only to end up being trapped in another world. One of the three particular worlds in that cavern. Amelia was the eldest."

"She's the woman in the dream? Who is now all grown up, despite being in another world, with, I assume, a whole different set of rules about how time works?"

Jake leaned over the table. "If I may interject, she grew up in the time between that Halloween and now... and assuming these other worlds even exist and it wasn't Cisco's imagination... that suggests time moves at the same speed in that world as ours. *But–*" he continued, holding a finger up to shush Cisco and allow himself time to finish, "if that's the case, how come she wasn't already a hundred years old when we met her as children, as you told us we did?"

"I've no idea how time works in different worlds, Jake," Cisco said, gritting his teeth impatiently. "I can barely remember what day it is in this one. For the entire pandemic I thought it was March 2020 and time has since lost all meaning. Anyway, we're getting off-topic."

"What exactly *is* the topic?" Michelle asked, a piece of pancake flopping about on her fork paused halfway to her mouth, the maple syrup dripping into a pool on the table.

"The topic is how to stop Deadman's Grin. Amelia said time was running out. That he was close to waking. That we had to deal with him soon or else risk a shi–" he looked at George, who was too busy watching Stampy Cat videos now to notice, "a *shed* load of pain and hurt and maybe even some biblical end of the world stuff too."

"And to stop him we need to find Tabitha? I mean, we knew that already. But we've had no word back from Roger or Itsy."

Cisco gestured to George to finish his pancakes, but the boy ignored him, still mesmerised by the screen. "Amelia said the author will know where to find her."

"Mrs Thompson?" Doc asked, reaching over to cut a piece of George's pancake up and popping it in the boy's mouth. He opened obediently and began to chew. "Well, that rings true because she did before, didn't she? But that whole leaving a note in the standing stone and then waiting for an answer took a while. Do we have that kind of time?"

"No, I don't think we do."

"So?"

He sighed. "Maybe Mrs Thompson knows a more immediate way. Something she couldn't talk about when we saw her. Like a magical horn or talking mirror or whatever it is you use to make a call between worlds."

"Like a supernatural WhatsApp."

"Sure."

"OK then. Let's go pay her a visit again. Thankfully she lives around here, just over Redgate Hill from Dark Peak. So you don't need to embarrass yourself in public again, we can just knock on her door and ask."

Cisco raised his eyebrows in surprise. "Now?"

"Might as well. If Deadman's Grin is nearly awake, time is of the essence. We should hustle."

"Oh, well yeah, we should. But what about George?" He looked at his son guiltily, although the boy was now too busy devouring his pancakes to pay attention to anything else. "It's Saturday morning and Natalie has already taken the girls out shopping to Manchester. You've taken Cecilia to her grandparents' place. I've got nowhere to drop him off."

"Bring him then. Where's the harm? It's just a little old lady's house."

The house wasn't just a house. It was a place. A feeling. A moment in time, though one that wasn't of any particular point in history, just none of them and all of them at once.

Doc couldn't explain it, this feeling, yet as soon as they drove down the lane into the village and turned into the walled garden, the sense of foreboding and excitement overwhelmed her. She stiffened in the passenger seat, allowing only her eyes to move.

Watching the moss-covered trees welcome them with limbs stretched wide. Seeing the family of squirrels jumping between branches, then scattering away into the old mill house along the side of the front garden, its four-storey tower renovated, but the rest left in ruins.

The stone house itself stood front and centre. Four big windows in the wall and two gable windows in the slate roof. And a presence that made you feel as if you were being watched from beyond those dark panes of glass and judged and quite possibly found wanting.

They crunched to a halt on the gravel in front of a tall, slightly dirty front door. Five faces peered out of the car windows in silence, each of them wondering what awaited them.

"If portals to other worlds really exist," Doc whispered, "I reckon this is a place to find them."

Her gaze rested on the door knocker. It was one of those realistic faces of a wizard or a tree elf or something else you might find in the more magical corners of a garden centre. Except she'd never seen one quite as detailed. Like everything here, within these garden walls, there was something a little different about it. An underlying sense of being.

They got out of the car, Cisco lifting George into his arms and letting him rest his head on his shoulder. He gave Doc a look as he spotted the realistic door knocker, clearly thinking the same thing.

What if the eyes opened? Would they run? Or choose to knock anyway?

Doc didn't want to seem like she cared about such things, so with a deep breath she reached out, pulled the heavy iron ring in the being's mouth and dropped it.

The clang echoed within the house and seemed to reverberate around them, through the outer wall, through the branches and leaves and soil beneath their feet. And for several seconds there was no response whatsoever, just George occasionally sniffing against his dad's coat and the nervous scuffling of feet on the driveway.

Then there was a noise behind the door and it swung open,

fully, with confidence, and without even a hint of the kind of terrifying creak that Doc had expected to hear.

Elenora Thompson stood framed in the doorway, bathed in the soft glow of her hallway desk lamp. Greying hair shining brightly in the light. Her eyes weathered, but her clear white skin remarkably ageless. Doc hadn't understood the last time they'd met just how like an Old One the woman had seemed, as though, just like this house, she was of no age and every age all at once.

She didn't smile, exactly. But she did nod as though she had been expecting them.

"You'd better come in," she said.

They followed her inside, past the towering grandfather clock with stars across its dial, past a series of old rickety stairs winding their way up to the first floor, and down a corridor between huge oil paintings that dazzled with images of sailing ships and distant shores and alien landscapes. Down, down, down that corridor they went until Doc realised that it carried further than the house on the outside seemed to be able to accommodate.

The others noticed it too. Cisco whispered to Jake over George's resting head, "How big *is* this place? It's like the TARDIS of houses!"

Doc held back a grin as she watched Jake nod, while his brain clearly took a few seconds to place the reference. Yes, she was still annoyed that of all the people to have taken her dad's prized collection of beautiful and useless memorabilia, it was the boy who had never appreciated any of it. Yet she loved him even more for what he'd done. He had saved it, as Cisco had said. Not that she'd ever tell Jake that.

"You'll find not everything in life is as it seems," Mrs Thompson replied, without missing a beat. She didn't look over her shoulder, merely carried on along the hallway, towards the broad oak door at the end. It stood ajar. Afternoon light poured through the crack and across the faded rug beneath their feet. Her soft voice, warm and with a lilt to it, continued, "People are never who they tell you they are. You have to pay attention to the character they show you. The news you are fed is always curated, specially selected, to fit just the right agenda. Adults and children lie to each other and themselves every second of the day." She paused at the door, hand resting on the brass handle. "And everything you have ever been told about the existence of magic and mythical creatures and pathways to other worlds... isn't necessarily the whole story."

With that she pushed the door open into the room and the group stepped into the light.

CHAPTER NINETEEN

Green Moss On Old Stone

Doc had never been in a room like this one before. Oh, sure, she'd seen them in TV shows and movies and read about them in books, but never actually thought she might get to stand in a place as special and sacred as this one.

It was a library. A museum. A veritable cavern of bookshelves full of stories and strange artefacts in glass cases and tapestries hung from the walls that shimmered in the sunlight and seemed to move of their own accord – but in a pleasing and not a probably-about-to-kill-you way.

Unreal. That was the word. An unreal room in the back of an unreal house that was a lot bigger on the inside than it looked on the outside. Where the pale rays of the wintry sun streamed through bay windows, glittering off the spines of the books and illuminating the gold steps on the library ladders dotted about. Where the fir trees at the back of the huge garden beyond swayed gently every now and then, seeming to crane their necks to look in and watch over them.

And there, to the right, a fire in the corner was crackling away, without any logs or coal or any fuel that Doc could see. The flames naked and alive and free.

Then her gaze was held by the thing in front of them, perched on the arm of a long blue sofa.

A beautiful black fox.

"Tabitha!"

That the word came from her own mouth was a surprise to them all, because she spoke it with an air of confirmation that suggested she'd never had any doubts about the creature's existence.

Tabitha inclined her head gently, although she shifted her large mischievous yellow eyes to Cisco as he smirked and sat on the couch opposite, a nice three-seater with plump cushions which each had a different symbol on them.

Runes, like Jake's stones, Doc thought. They had that Celtic look to them.

"I told you they'd rediscover their belief," the fox said to Cisco.

He nodded and gently put down George next to him. To the boy's credit, he had taken the sight of the talking animal in his stride and only had a partial frown as he stared at Tabitha now, before switching his attention to all the cool things on the shelves around them. The concept of magical animals hadn't been bashed out of him by life yet, Doc realised. Not for the first time, she silently thanked Julia Donaldson and Axel Scheffler for their service to humanity.

"Belief is a tricky thing," Cisco replied, slipping his arm around George as though preempting his son's attempts to wander off and play with things. "But, yeah, I think you'll find there are only so many times you can discover yourself fighting possessed children's toys and evil homewares before you begin to accept things aren't normal. Right, Doc?" The corner of his lips turned up as he glanced quickly at her. "Anyway, it's a relief to find you here, Tabitha. We've been trying to get hold of you. We even sent a message through Doc's gnome and Michelle's sprite to ask for help. Where've you been?"

"Gathering what forces I could. Not for the battles you've had, but the one yet to come. I am sorry I was not able to help you sooner though, old friend."

Cisco grimaced. "Old is right. There's only so much juggling of ghosts and goblins and children you can cope with when you're the wrong side of forty-five. We're exhausted."

Mrs Thompson smiled for the first time and sat down next to Tabitha, picking up the steaming cup of tea from the table in front of her and taking a sip.

"You don't know age like we do, Cisco," she said mysteriously, then turned to the others. "Now come, sit. We have lots to talk about and not much time."

Jake and Michelle tentatively crept over and took their places next to Cisco. Michelle gave George a little head rub as she passed. He grinned at her, seemingly unperturbed about whatever was going on and more than relaxed in the present company.

Tabitha beckoned Doc to sit beside her, which she did.

"It's nice to finally meet you," Doc said.

The fox's tail twitched with amusement. "And it is nice to see you again, Dorothy. You must surely know by now we have known each other since you were children. A time when such interactions between us weren't quite so difficult to believe and hold fast in your mind. We spent much time together back then, although admittedly a lot of it was with purpose as we fought the darkness."

Cisco spread his hands wide. "And that's why we're here."

"Yeah, Cisco had a dream," Jake said, leaning forward, elbows on his knees, fingers knitting together in a gesture of scientific anxiety. "I don't quite get the science behind it and I'm guessing there probably isn't much because, you know," he waved at Tabitha, "*magic*. Anyway, Cisco here told us he went to sleep and had a dream, but it turned out not to be a dream? And there was a woman in it who we used to be friends with once, but it turns out she's trapped in another world. And I guess the point of it all is that she says Deadman's Grin is on the cusp of waking up properly and there's some greater evil at work, which, not going to lie, has me a bit worried. Because the supernatural stuff we've had to deal with has been pretty wild. If that's what he can do while he's asleep, how much worse can it actually get? And what's more–"

Tabitha's whiskers twitched sympathetically. "Breathe, Jake."

Jake stopped immediately and nodded, taking a breath.

"Good boy." Tabitha turned her gaze to Cisco next. "Amelia paid you another visit then?"

"Yes, and this time we were actually able to talk. She was the one who told us to come here. As well as explaining all that other stuff."

Mrs Thompson took over the story now. "The William House children were famous in their own time, you know. Perhaps not as much as you four, after you blew up your school," she took a long sip of tea, a teasing eye regarding each of them in turn over the rim of the porcelain cup, "but their initial disappearance made the papers in these parts, after Deadman's Grin and his ghostly crew returned and stole them away, into the murky world beneath our town. And then they made the papers again when they reappeared a week later, having prevented him from getting access to what he wanted."

"So they were like us?" Jake asked, looking around at his friends. "What we did, that Halloween… they did it first?"

"One hundred years before you, to be exact. Unfortunately, what they did to stop the pirate was only temporary. As you found out to your cost when you were but teenagers and he returned once more to wreak havoc upon us."

"And as we are finding out now," Doc added.

The more she heard in this strange room, with these strange but kindly folk, the more the veil that had fallen over that part of her life began to grow transparent. She was steadily recalling glimpses of the past, filling in the blanks between all the other pieces of the puzzle that had recently fallen into place.

Skeletons with swords. A green witch. A giant boulder rolling down the Dark Peak high street. The entire town under siege by a variety of bizarre creatures.

Doc shivered at the thoughts. "But what *we* did wasn't permanent either, was it?" she continued. "We killed him. We shot Deadman's Grin square through the chest. But somehow he didn't die and he's been able to come back to give us all the shits. Right?"

"Always so eloquent, Dorothy," Tabitha noted with a nod. "And accurate with your analysis, too. Except for one minor detail. Deadman's Grin is not back. Not yet, at least."

"Good. Then, if you don't mind, can you tell us where the hell he is and how we dispose of him properly? Because I've got a business to run and a daughter to raise with Michelle and all this battling living nightmares has really put a dent in our lives."

Mrs Thompson laughed lightly and put her hand on Doc's shoulder. It was the gentlest touch and a heat, of sorts, flowed through the woman's fingers. Doc felt the tension she'd been carrying around with her for weeks begin to dissipate. She felt calm. At peace. Content.

"Patience, my girl. I understand more than you think how these strange events must be reshaping your lives even as you try to live them. I am one of those who have told the stories of such things over the years, as my mother did before me. There is such magic around us, across these lands, and so many stories beneath the surface of what you see." She leaned over and pointed out of the window, to the landscape beyond the trees at the back of her garden. "That's a stone circle on the hill behind my house, you know? Up on old Owl Tor. It's nothing to look at from here, but it's an entrance to the portals below Dark Peak, the ones you found as children. A magical entrance that can only be opened with the use of some runes, although they have likely been long lost by now. I had many adventures on that hill as a child, creating my own stories that would guide my life in different ways and not all of them in ways I would have liked." She sighed wistfully as she stared out, seeing something in her head that they could not. "Now, we must let Tabitha finish telling this story as she sees fit. It is not often she gets to come and spend this much time with us. A fox's business is always somewhere else, isn't that right, my friend?"

With her other hand she scratched Tabitha behind her ears. Doc wasn't sure if that was considered polite where Tabitha was from, but the fox seemed to enjoy it.

She shuffled her paws and raised her pointed nose straight and true.

"I have many friends across the vastness of the Cobweb and often I am only afforded a brief visit before I have to leave them behind to attend to other matters. It is a rare treat when I get to spend time with friends like now, even if it is to discuss such things as the impending destruction of everything we know and love."

Doc had been letting herself lean back into the delicious softness of the sofa. Yet whatever the old author had done, whatever magic her fingers had infused in her, suddenly drifted away as reality struck home.

"And we're back to the end times," she sighed. "OK, I've been patient, but let's cut to it now, shall we? I've been told a lot of different things lately and it would be good to finally have it from the fox's mouth. Is the fate of our entire world at risk?"

"Yes."

"And there are others out there which are also in danger?"

Tabitha blinked. "All worlds. Everywhere. The Cobweb of lands and the paths between them, all at risk of being consumed by evil. One that works through the pirate you know as Deadman's Grin, as many have found to their cost. He wasn't always so in life, but is very much in death a man of dark intentions and ambition, and it was to your credit that you stopped him getting his murderous hands on that which he sought the first time you met. But now we have come to know what lies behind him and indeed what set him upon his path. The antithesis of all that is good and pure and hopeful. The darkness that lies beneath and between our worlds. The void in between the real. The–"

"Christ, OK, we get the idea," Doc said, lifting her hand to stop the snowballing tension as best she could. Michelle's face was paling quickly on the opposite couch. Her normally piercing blue eyes wide and watery and terrified. "So how do we stop him, Tabitha?"

Sadly the fox didn't seem to have the answer. She scratched herself, then glanced at Mrs Thompson, who shrugged.

"We don't know yet if anything will work," she replied for them both.

Doc blinked, stood up and strode over to the giant bay window to stare into the greenery of the garden, as the afternoon sky darkened beneath clouds and the first sweep of evening drew in between the bushes and above the trees encircling the land. "Bloody hell," she muttered. "You know, this really is the least fun conversation I've had in a long time. And I had to argue with my daughter this morning over whether or not looking at the hand soap counted as washing your hands."

It was then she saw the eyes outside.

Peering out from the low bushes and from high in the trees and even from the darkness of the old stone well in the corner of the grassy enclosure.

Thousands of eyes.

Watching her.

Doc's mouth dropped open. Her body froze, rigid with fear, just like in one of those dreams where you couldn't move no matter how hard you tried, but yet you were still awake.

Sleep paralysis. That's what this was.

Except, she was awake.

"Help," she breathed.

It took all her energy to summon even that. Her throat was suddenly constricted, her lips dry and struggling to part with any words if they could help it.

Thankfully someone heard.

"Do not fear, Dorothy," Tabitha said calmly, interrupting the conversation going on behind her. Her ears must have pricked up. Could foxes hear as well as dogs? "We are among friends in this house. Both inside and out."

Doc felt that soothing warmth through her once more. She glanced over her shoulder to see Mrs Thompson catch her eye and smile. The author, who Doc was now fairly convinced was also a witch of some kind, was up to her tricks again. That was fine though. Doc decided to just lean into it and enjoy the magic as it calmed the rising anxiety inside her.

"Friends, eh? You sure have a lot of them out there."

She let her gaze drift across the garden, watching the eyes staring at her. Gold, green, yellow. All kinds of sizes. All kinds of shapes. But thankfully none she could see that were glowing red, not like all the possessed entities that they'd been fighting recently.

Hopefully that meant she could trust the fox.

"You *can* trust me."

Doc spun. "You heard that?"

Tabitha gave her a wry, toothy grin. "I didn't need to. Once you have lived as many lives as I have, you come to understand the way of people and what they must be thinking."

Doc frowned and peered out of the window again, but she couldn't see the eyes anymore. Only the rustling leaves blowing across the grass, while from the dark, angry clouds overhead, a thick snow began to fall. Flakes quickly gathered in drifts on the windowsill.

"Hey, where'd your friends go?"

"They will be watching over us on our journey," Tabitha replied. "They come and go when they please, but with you four returning to us I think word got out and they wanted to see for themselves that it was true."

Michelle started. "They wanted to see *us?* We're famous?"

"In a manner of speaking. The story of how you fought Deadman's Grin and his minions on All Hallows' Eve is one that has been told many times. Your story is known." The fox suddenly tilted and leaned back to nibble at her crotch. The group's faces pulled in awkward directions as they looked away, before Tabitha carried on as though nothing had happened. "However, don't expect to be treated like celebrities where we're going. You have aged quite substantially. I doubt anyone will–" She stopped as she saw their horrified faces. "What? I had an itch!"

Mrs Thompson chuckled under her breath. "She's still a fox, you know. One that talks and traverses realms across the Cobweb and has seen more lives than you or I care to admit. But a fox nonetheless."

"So what's next?" Doc asked a little impatiently, although she wasn't sure if she even wanted to hear an answer to that question. "Where do we go from here?"

"Goodbyes are what's next," Tabitha replied. She rubbed her head briefly against the author next to her. Mrs Thompson gave her a tender stroke and a tickle under the chin, then lightly kissed her forehead. With that, Tabitha left the couch and padded across to the door to the right of the fire. Doc half-expected her to jump up and try to paw the handle, but to her surprise the door simply unlocked and swung open. The fox paused in the middle of the frame and looked back. "Come on then, we have a journey ahead of us."

They stood up, confused. Cisco stared in panic at his sleepy son.

"You mean now?"

"When else?"

"But I'm not really prepared for this, Tabitha. I mean, the weapons are in the car, but I haven't brought any snacks or wipes or a change of clothes for George."

"Does he have somewhere safe to go?"

Cisco looked to Jake, who shrugged. "We'd have to go find the girls and they could be anywhere in Manchester by now."

The fox tilted her head. "Unfortunately, time is of the essence. George will have to come with us. But I will make sure he is looked after, I promise."

Cisco didn't look at all sure about that, but had no chance to argue the point. As Michelle ran back to the car to get the War Wizards and the gang strapped on the backpacks, he continued to hold George and kept shushing him back to sleep, ruffling the boy's hair as he did so.

"Right," Doc said, when they were ready to go. "Where to, Tabitha?"

Yet it was Mrs Thompson who answered in a low, sing-song voice. "Into the future. Into the past. Along the strands of the Cobweb.

Scurrying fast." She and Tabitha shared a knowing look, before she clarified for the benefit of the four bemused adults in the room, "To the bottom of the garden, in search of green moss on old stone. That's always the clue to where magic has touched our world. Where the thin places live, where you can cross from here to there. As I did long ago, just a little girl, who had just met her first friend."

"One last trip?" Tabitha purred hopefully, a touch of melancholy in her voice now. Doc saw something unspoken pass between them. And a glint of sadness… or possibly regret… in the author's eyes.

"Not this time, Tabitha. I'm too old for such things. Give my love to the Tree. May I see her again one day."

"You will. And I will be waiting."

With that Tabitha's tail swished behind her and she trotted off down another hall. The others followed, although as they passed the giant fireplace the flames roared a little higher and made a noise that sounded very much like "goodbye".

"I would have bet good money that if Tabitha was going to take us anywhere," Doc whispered to Cisco, "it would have been through this ridiculously big fireplace. Isn't that how these stories always work?"

He shrugged against George on his shoulder, looking as though he'd been thinking the same thing and was rather disappointed to be leaving by a conventional human door.

Doc turned and gave Mrs Thompson a wave, then hurried after her friends.

Clicking open the back door with her magic, Tabitha led them into the falling snow and the gradually whitening garden. The trees around them seemed to chatter louder as they made their way over the ancient flagstones in the grass, past the well, towards what sounded like rushing water a few metres ahead. Doc shivered as they passed the tree line, thick with yews, their trunks like twisted and stretched skeletons. Their roots sprawled like broken limbs across their path, their branches creaking overhead and drooping to touch them. Occasionally one would tug at their clothes, yet Doc couldn't help but feel it was a friendly gesture, as though reaching out to wish them luck. They were shielded from the snow in here, the canopy above affording them a little protection and warmth. Until finally they stopped before a small, gently flowing stream that ran past a crumbling stone building covered in thick green moss.

"Green moss on old stone," Doc repeated under her breath.

They were here.

"Tabitha," Cisco interrupted, stopping short of the others. His tired eyes were suddenly worried. His head twitched towards his son asleep on his shoulder. "Is this, you know, safe?"

"As safe as safe can be," the fox replied vaguely.

With that out of the way, the group stared at the obstacle before them. Only a metre across, the stream didn't seem to be any different to any other stream Doc had ever seen. Crossing their path, it seemed to act as a natural divide between the edge of the property and the trees beyond.

But there was something strange about what Doc could see on the other side.

Nothing.

Nothing normal, anyway. She seemed to be able to sense there were trees ahead, but wasn't able to look directly at them, as though the vision wasn't real or kept shifting just out of her direct line of sight.

Cisco could feel it too. He leaned in close and whispered over his sleeping son, "I think everything is about to change."

She nodded. "Then let's get it done. The world needs saving, right?"

She turned to Tabitha.

"Want me to pick you up?"

The fox's tail flashed dangerously.

"I'd like to see you try," she said, and jumped across.

Only... they didn't see her land. Tabitha simply disappeared in a shimmer.

"And away we go," Cisco said to himself, before he, too, leapt over the stream with George and disappeared. Followed swiftly by Jake, then Michelle.

Doc took a breath. Looked around one last time, in case it actually *was* the last time.

Then she jumped.

CHAPTER TWENTY

The Enchanted World

Cisco held his son tightly against his shoulder as he landed on the other side.

The other side of what, though?

All at once nothing had changed and yet everything was different. They could no longer see hills of grass and sheep beyond the scatter of trunks in the author's garden. In that single jump, nature had swallowed them whole, dropping them into a dense, ancient forest, surrounded on all sides by eerie shadows among the crooked limbs of all manner of magnificent, twisting, climbing trees. There was a rich, pungent scent lingering in the air too. An otherworldly haze that told of decay and rebirth, and perhaps even time itself. Such a familiar scent kicked up by their boots as they trod softly through the woodland loam, that Cisco was forced to pause for a moment and close his eyes, breathing it in and letting it fill his lungs so completely it might as well have been the first breath he'd taken in decades.

And perhaps it had been. Here at least.

A soft breeze caressed his face, welcoming him back. It caught the dense foliage around them and suddenly everything shifted and swayed. The forest was answering in kind, the wood creaking and the leaves rustling, a secret conversation that grew in excitement as the interlopers appeared, following the fox.

"Wisha, wisha, wisha," George murmured, his little breath hot on Cisco's neck.

Cisco looked at the others and saw Jake and Michelle staring around with a similar level of awe, before Doc appeared, her tall figure shimmering into existence on the bank of the stream.

When she looked around, it was with a calm understanding. She smiled at Cisco and listened to the words George kept repeating as he dozed against his dad.

"Enchanting," she said.

Cisco nodded, clutching George even more tightly. He kissed his son's little cheek.

You know, don't you? You're asleep and you still feel what's happening here.

Children were inherently connected to magic. He'd always thought it and seen it suggested elsewhere. They had an innocence about them which allowed their eyes and hearts to see and understand it, without really knowing how or why. Just accepting it as it was.

It was only when you got older you lost that connection. Severed, through age and responsibility and stress and exhaustion.

"Tabitha, where are we?" he asked.

"You already know," the fox replied with a lazy grin, as she sauntered along a well-trod footpath. The others followed. "You haven't been here in person for many years now, but it sounds like you paid it a visit not so long ago with little George."

"No, but seriously. Where have you brought us?'

Cisco felt the hairs on the back of his neck rise as they walked deeper into the forest. Into their past. Slipping around tree stumps and through the hollows of fallen trunks, skirting around the mossy boulders strewn through the landscape like a giant's half-finished game of marbles – the shadows between which held eyes that blinked as they passed, while every now and then a long nose would poke out and sniff at them.

His eyes seemed to be acclimatising to the surroundings as one might acclimatise to the dark. Except it wasn't dark. The opposite, in fact. He was seeing things more clearly, the colours becoming more vibrant, and here and there things started appearing in the undergrowth and in the branches above them.

Flickers of lights.

Lanterns.

Doors in trunks, bolt holes in the moss-covered ground.

And movement.

Tabitha took a long time to answer him, as if she was waiting for the reality around them to do it for her. Michelle gave little gasps as a pair of small lights, like glow worms, buzzed in the air in front of her, then giggled and flew off. Jake flinched as a tall stick-like figure emerged from within a tree trunk and loped across their path, barely giving them a glance as it parted the bushes and went on its way. Even Doc seemed at a loss for words now, staring at the wisps of light and shadow dancing through the tree canopies above them, watching the unfolding magic without a hint of the usual cynicism that had formed her façade for as long as he'd known her.

"Tabitha," Cisco insisted. "Say it."

The child in him saw it all and believed. But the adult in him needed to hear the words.

And the fox understood.

In a small clearing, she leapt up onto a fallen tree and sat for a moment, curling her tail around her hind legs. Her eyes, like pools of sunshine in the shadows, regarded them kindly as everyone gathered around her.

"You know this place by many names and in many stories. Tír na nÓg, Annwn, the Otherworld, the Underworld. And, yes, even the fabled, beloved *Enchanted Wood* finds its truth in this wonderful land. It is one and all of them at once. A world of magic and secrets that overlies the one you know. You can still feel its existence in your countryside, if you are quiet and respectful. You might even catch a glimpse of its magic in the twilight, in the corner of your eyes, maybe a blur of the Woodwose behind the bushes or a Wild Elf watching you from the trees when they think you're not looking. But while our two worlds used to be a lot closer, now our existence is revealed only to a chosen few. To people who can bring it back into your world in the only form you humans would be able to accept." She paused and tilted her head. "Through stories."

Michelle looked confused. Jake looked troubled. But Cisco saw his own excitement mirrored in Doc's eyes as they glanced at each other. Excitement and a level of confirmation that everything he had felt in his bones, everything he couldn't ever have hoped to articulate – just *knew* – was real.

Tabitha smiled and loped off again. Winding through the branches of the fallen tree, leaping across to another log, and then back to the path. Enjoying herself.

"There have been others, you know. Other people in your world who have travelled these paths into other realms, meeting other beings, expanding the horizons humans often limit themselves to through their inability to imagine. We meet them by intention and by accident, but we always know if they are ready when we find them. Usually, the stories are already buried in them and we just unlock the door. Sometimes they use what they find through their adventures with us to feed their storytelling later in life, when the memories are foggy and half-remembered. They think they're conjuring these preternatural occurrences from thin air, when really they're remembering snippets of lives they actually lived."

Cisco felt a sense of his son growing heavy in his arms, but the clockwork cogs in his mind were too busy whirring to notice properly. Tabitha led them further into the wood, past clearings with colourful gatherings and figures leaping over bonfires, where shimmering beings were playing otherworldly music. Onwards, through tunnels cut into rocks whose insides were gleaming with stones of all colours. And, rather disconcertedly, underneath a tree whose branches were full of swinging cages containing the bones of what might well have been Orcs.

Thank goodness George was asleep.

"Are you saying that you've been to us many times before, visiting *writers*?" Cisco asked.

"They weren't always writers when we met them," Tabitha replied with a peculiar noise that sounded very much like a laugh, "but they certainly were afterwards. How could they not be? They saw new and wondrous worlds and came to understand the magic of the Cobweb that connected all realms. It seeped into their blood and bones, but when they returned they found they had nobody to talk to about it. Nobody would believe these far-fetched tales, unless they were actually spun as far-fetched tales. And so it began. Enid, Susan, Clive – although I knew him as Jack – they are the more recent names you know, whose stories you have woven into the fabric of your society. Yet these folk weren't the only souls we met as we went about our business. This is a journey I have been at a very long time. So you can imagine where those myths and legends and tales you read about in your history books might have come from."

"Christ," Doc whispered. "How old *are* you?"

The fox glanced over her shoulder as she leapt from cap to cap across a series of red and white dotted mushrooms at the side of the path. "Older than you'd care to imagine and too old to care to tell you. Now, please, be careful as we skirt the edge of the swamp we're about to come across. The Grindylow are resting right now, but children are their very favourite delicacy and they are drawn to their specific sounds. Cisco, hold George tight and try not to wake him or we risk having to break into a bit of a run."

They emerged from the trees at the edge of a body of water. Or at least it seemed to be water, beneath the wafts of lilies and straggles of long grass. On the island in the centre were a few pale green figures reclining on rocks and hillocks. One of them lazily looked over, scratching itself with a long, furry, multi-jointed finger. *Like a spider's leg*, Cisco thought, before he watched in horror as the creature yawned, revealing several rows of gleaming yellow teeth.

"Swamp-gremlins," Michelle whispered, moving to the right edge of the path, as far away as possible from the water. Cisco watched Doc take her hand and calmly squeeze it, before she added, "I have to be honest, Tabitha, this isn't feeling very enchanted at all right now. I thought this was supposed to be some kind of magical wonderland?"

"And I thought you said it was safe," Cisco added, wrapping his arms around George even tighter than he had been.

Tabitha didn't bother slowing down as she answered. "Magic can be good and bad and safe and dangerous. Enchantment is the same. You might have come to misunderstand the word as solely meaning wonder and goodness and fun. But, if so, you have missed the clues along the way. My home can instil in your heart the most gloriously beautiful feeling... or it can invoke despair and horror at the very real possibility of being torn limb from limb or being trapped in servitude by a Fae King or dragged to your death by Jenny Greenteeth. So as much as we are an enchanted world, we can also be a world of dangers. Now, hurry if you please, the Grindylow are starting to pay attention."

They were, too. It wasn't just the one head turning their way, it was most of them. One was even starting to wiggle its way down the slope like a crocodile in a cloak of shells, hissing as it slithered into the water and began swimming towards them.

"Go faster," Jake urged. Cisco felt a shove in his back as they hurried on.

The deeper into the forest they moved, the darker it got. It seemed to be approaching night, if they had such a time of day here. Yet, bizarrely, it was still remarkably easy to see where they were going thanks to the trails of lamp lights, bonfires, fairy lights and even the odd Will o' the Wisp that glowed brightly in all kinds of colours.

Doc dropped back alongside Cisco now, her face aglow in the firelight from a permanently burning bush lining the side of the path. They both eyed a row of cheery gnome-like characters who were busy roasting what Cisco initially thought were marshmallows, before he saw in horror the small, bound, winged figures struggling to get away.

"Do you believe all this?" Doc said, pulling a face as she plucked one of the twigs off a gnome before it could go fully into the fire. She ignored the annoyed shout in a strange language and carefully undid the spider's thread holding a partially singed faerie to the bark. "This land, all of it, it's everything we used to read about as kids. Everything we saw in comics and lived through books. Everything even my dad used to dream about. This otherworld exists. We're really here. I'm really saving this faerie! I'm not making it up, right?"

The faerie looked up at her gratefully as she freed it. For a second, Doc gazed down in wonder, a smile touching the sides of her lips. Then the faerie brushed its wings down, leapt up and bit Doc's fingers.

"Fuuuuu–"

She cried out and waved it away. It flew off with a tiny cackle. If that wasn't bad enough, the group of gnomes behind them broke about laughing too. Another admonishment followed and Cisco didn't need to understand the language to get the gist of it this time.

George stirred on his shoulder at the cacophony of noises. He patted him on the back softly, his palm moving in circles, as he'd always done to get him back to sleep.

"That looks like it might feel pretty real," he said quietly, wincing at Doc's bleeding finger. She squeezed it, as though trying to get any poison out, then sucked it with a growing frown knotting her brow.

"I thought I was saving it!"

He kept a close hold of his son as he watched the dancing light fly into the forest gloom. "What even was it? A faerie? I didn't know faeries bit." He paused and considered that comment. "I didn't even know faeries existed."

"Yeah, I'm getting the feeling that there's a lot of things neither of us know." Doc curled her injured finger into a tight fist. "But still. Biting faeries, enchanted trees and other worlds. This is all the stuff that dreams are made of, right? So, you know, thank you. I'm sorry for not believing you all this time."

"There's nothing to apologise for, Doc."

"I know. It's just… I spent years resenting being laughed at after what happened. That you got to escape and left us three to pick up the pieces of our lives. I guess I let it cloud my memories of all that stuff we used to get up to. Our friendship. Those early mornings you'd ride your bike over to mine to play video games in the basement. All those times my dad caught us and thought we were getting up to mischief." Her dark eyes lit up at that thought and they both grinned. "Do you remember that time we played *Alien* on Dad's old Spectrum and you jumped out of your beanbag with fright and my dad came running in and yelled at you, thinking that we were getting it on?"

Something crept into his recollection just then to spoil the moment. He remembered a piece of paper, a report, with crude pumpkins scribbled around the margins, sitting on his desk in his bedroom.

The good humour faded.

"That was the morning of the Halloween report," he said with a shiver. "The one I did on Deadman's Grin. Remember? That was the bloody start of the whole adventure back then. That was the last day everything was normal, before it all changed."

They carried on in silence for a few minutes. The only noise came when they passed three beautiful women dressed in layers of greens and browns, their hair like twisting, sweeping vines, who blended in so well with the surroundings Cisco almost walked right into them. Their collective laugh as they watched him stumble away, mumbling his apologies to their half-hidden faces, was like a summer wind through the trees.

"The Wood Witches," Tabitha said quietly. She tilted her little snout in a bow towards them and three white smiles appeared from the shadows, before they became part of the forest again. "As you know, they are those who can harness nature and have been its guardian."

"As *I* know?"

"Oh, of course," the fox said vaguely. "Never mind. They are a story of a completely different time for you, dear boy."

"More friends from the past?"

"The past? Not exactly."

More riddles. Cisco was getting a little tired of them and was about to ask another question when they arrived in a clearing.

The clearing, it turned out.

Everyone stopped and craned their necks as they looked up.

And up.

And up some more.

The tree before them was the size of a skyscraper. Its wood thick and gnarled and ancient as it rose from a hill of roots into the sky, beyond the canopy of the other trees. So high that Cisco couldn't actually see where it finished. Yet he could see a variety of creatures and figures and glimmers of light rushing up and down it. Mingling in groups at the bottom. Hanging from ropes that led into the boughs above.

Then there were the doors.

All the way up the trunks, and some in the branches, too – doors of all different sizes and irregular shapes and decorations were carved into the wood. Most wide open, allowing the visitors a glimpse through. Yet what they saw beyond were not rooms.

They did not lead inside the tree.

They led to other worlds.

"The Tree of Paths," Tabitha said softly with an air of reverence, gazing at the sight before them adoringly. Her ears twitched as she listened to the wave of noise flow down through the branches and crash over them. The sounds of a thousand or more different realms, mixed in with the comings and goings of the forest folk here. "You may know it differently, of course. It has been written about before. But that is the name I prefer. A place of possibilities."

Cisco stared in astonishment. Through one green door he caught a glimpse of a sunlit hill, beyond which the flags of a castle could just about be seen fluttering in the wind. Through another red, triangular entrance, he saw red skies and flashes of lightning illuminating a terrifying looking mountain. There was a patchwork quilt of countryside in another.

"And so our journey continues and the battle begins anew,"

Tabitha sighed, sweeping her tail from side to side and turning to her friends. For that's who they were and always had been, since their very first meeting. Even though Cisco couldn't remember it visually in his mind, he could feel it now. The shock and the excitement and the joy at discovering Tabitha as a child and having his eyes opened to the wider universe, the Cobweb, as the fox had so eloquently put it. She continued, "We must go up the tree now. To the place where Deadman's Grin can be found."

Cisco absently rubbed George's back, but found his son was already awake. Staring up into the worlds among the branches. "Pretty cool, huh?" he said quietly. George nodded, unable to speak.

Michelle's mouth gaped open as well as a tall, beautiful elf strode past and gave the woman a knowing smile. One that bordered on indecent. Doc narrowed her eyes and slipped her fingers into Michelle's, pulling her close.

"What makes you think we can do this?" she asked, watching the elf smirk and lope up the tree like a graceful, gravity-defying deer. The figure disappeared inside a door beyond which they could all see giant serpents swimming through a sky-bound sea. "Especially given that last time we killed the pirate he didn't stay all that dead? We've got the same weapons we had before, only they're much older and more likely to break. Hell, *we're* all older and more likely to break. You've got a vast universe's worth of beings to choose from here, Tabitha. Elves, nasty little biting faeries, carnivorous gnomes, freaking swamp-gremlins… and I don't doubt a whole host of other terrifying beings. Why the hell did you decide that us four, ordinary, slightly unfit, middle-aged human nobodies could take on this momentous challenge again and get it right this time?"

Tabitha stepped out of the way as a troop of pixies wandered past, playing instruments. The music was tinny, but beautiful.

"The first time you *disposed* of the pirate," she replied, "he was whole and it was in your world. You did actually end his time there physically, but his soul was trapped in a purgatory of sorts. It is there the dark magic has been working on him, patching him up, and coaxing him back to life to do its bidding once more. All the more powerful for it."

"Great," Michelle muttered, squeezing Doc's hand.

"And yet, the fact that his spirit and body remain separate right now means he is more vulnerable than he ever was or ever will be. To answer your questions, Dorothy, we are doing this because we no longer have a choice. We are doing this *now* because it gives us a chance to end him for good. And I have already told you why we chose you four. Because you saved us once and we believe you can save us again."

Doc, though, was unwilling to let it drop. Cisco knew she could sense something Tabitha wasn't telling them. "Courage isn't enough. What is it about us that you need?"

"I do mean it when I say we need you for your courage. That your actions in the past have made you symbols of strength beyond the world you know. But, yes, there is another reason you are the only ones who can stop Deadman's Grin." Tabitha stared at them all for the longest time, then finally relented with a long, troubled sigh. "It's because you're human. You have the capacity for violence, even when it goes against your nature. Right now you're the only beings standing between the pirate and the spread of destruction through all the realms of the Cobweb. Desperate times like these require desperate and violent measures, beyond the means and morals of magical folk."

"OK," Doc said with a nod. "Only we can kill the bastard while he's sleeping. That I can accept. So what do we do?"

"We need to find the doorway in the tree and quickly. Time moves in tricky ways here. Sometimes forwards, sometimes backwards, sometimes to the side. We can't risk waiting for too much longer and having him break through, back into your world. You must go to him now."

Tabitha turned and led them up over the twisting roots, towards the gigantic trunk before them. She gave a little bark once up the tree and a small platform came spinning down through the mist, onto which everyone boarded.

"Now this feels oddly familiar," Cisco whispered to nobody in particular as they began to lift up through the branches. He could only try to hold on tight, one hand gripping the woven barrier of twigs and the other grasping his son against his chest. He'd never been fond of heights. Not even magical ones.

"The Cobweb stretches across time and space and dimensions," Tabitha explained as they bumped their way up the tree. "The Tree of Paths is a nexus, if you will. The centre of the web. It contains the signposts and paths between the realms. Beings of all kinds are free to come and go as they please."

"And they all know about it?" Cisco asked.

"They do."

"So where are our signposts? The ones from Earth?"

Tabitha bowed her head, clearly having been waiting for this question.

"We are still *on* Earth."

"Wait. What?" Michelle frowned and gestured around them. "This isn't one of the other realms on the Cobweb? But it's so *different*."

The four turned towards the fox. Even George looked down at her. Tabitha took a patient breath and nodded. "Our enchanted world is still very much a part of Earth. As I said before, we are but a layer of what you already know, the world beneath, or above, or betwixt. The Otherworld of your myths and legends. The place where travellers sometimes wander and are never seen again. Where knights are led by beautiful Faerie Queens or tricked into following mischievous changelings. A place children may stumble into by accident and have the greatest adventures." She gave a toothy smile. "Have you heard of Beltane? Calan Mai? May Day? All celebrations throughout your land that commemorate special times when our worlds drift closer to one another in place. Where doorways can once again be found in mountains and woods and rivers that open for a short time to places such as this. Yes, once we were together, your world and mine. We were a whole. But then civilisations grew and society became more complex and humans, as you know, are territorial and violent and greedy creatures. There came a point where they grew to desire other worlds for their very own. Where they wanted to monopolise control of the magic and enchantment. Many didn't, of course. There are always the good and the brave, standing alone to hold back the tides of such horrors. But in the end the tide was too much. So we beings held a council here and all made a unanimous decision to hide this part of the world from you."

Cisco felt his insides contract, feeling the ancestral shame of what had passed and the sorrow of what was lost. All this magic could have been theirs. The wonder. The ability to move not just beyond the fixed horizon of their own world, but other worlds and times. What a place that could have been, had humans just not been so... human.

"This is why we can't have nice things," Doc sighed, her face a mirror of what Cisco felt. Although there was something else there. Something a little more raw. Anger. "You shut us out to protect everyone else? Hid the signposts from human eyes so we couldn't find this world again?"

"Almost entirely."

"Almost?"

"They left the paths open," Cisco replied, finally understanding. "And some of you continued to return to our plane of existence to meet a few of us from time to time? The writers. Us. Amelia and her siblings too, I'm guessing. Always children?"

"Children can be trusted," Tabitha said simply. "I'm sorry if our actions seem harsh. But you have to understand that we had to save the greater good. Not every adult human is like you four. There is always rotten fruit hidden away in the bushel. And, in the end, it worked in our favour. We may have our own little bad apples here, but nothing we can't handle. The Queen of Enchantment long ago disbanded our armies and we have lived in comfort and security in our diversity, free from the eyes of greed and fear of the other. Except..."

"Except now you need us humans to do what you no longer can. Because, despite some of our best efforts, we've got nowhere near being able to secure such peace for ourselves. We've been raised in a violent world. Losing ourselves piece by piece."

"And yet, your loss might just be our gain."

Cisco grimaced. "At least our inhumanity is good for something I guess."

"So, you can go literally anywhere from here?" Jake asked, seemingly having forgotten their dangerous predicament and in typical fashion retreating into his obsession with the details of the scientific impossibilities before him. Fascinated, he reached out and before anyone could stop him poked his hand through a doorway into a rainstorm beyond. When he pulled it out, water dripped from his fingers. He held it up for the others to see, his entire face lighting up with childlike glee. "So cool!"

Tabitha shook her little head. "Be careful, that's the realm of the Goblin City and they don't take kindly to hands, or other appendages, poking their way into their world. And, yes, the tree can lead you to any land you can imagine. Not to mention thousands you couldn't even dare to dream about." She paused. "Except two. Long ago, it was decreed that two of the doorways had to be closed here for all our sakes. Burned shut with a magic that cannot be undone. Those worlds are now only accessible via... *other*... means. But now isn't the time to talk about them. We are almost here."

The lift brought them to a thick, wide bough, a natural pavement of sorts, that stretched out into the mists. It stopped without word from Tabitha, who leapt off and walked along as though she had done this a thousand times before.

Cisco figured that, perhaps, she had.

He clutched George tightly and followed with great care. As they had ascended the tree he had become increasingly worried about the height, even though it was mostly hidden thanks to the surrounding mist. Yet there was still a cold panic in his heart at the thought of the drop beyond the path beneath their feet – a cold panic that grew as the branch changed from healthy brown to rotten grey the further they walked. The soft wood giving way to the crackle of dead bark with each step.

After a few seconds they came upon a doorway in the branch itself. A trapdoor.

"Here we must part," Tabitha said. "This doorway hasn't been open for some time and because of where it leads it won't stay open long, certainly not enough for us to hesitate. You must go forward now. Be careful though, because this is a strange land, but one in which you will know where to go. Find the pirate's spirit. Destroy him, no matter what happens. He is already nearly powerful enough to wake and when he does all hell will break loose. Quite literally." A flick of Tabitha's tail and the door slowly, reluctantly, swung open and crashed against the bark. "Now, go, quickly!"

Michelle and Doc barely took a breath before they pulled out their blasters. Then, glancing at the men, they held each other's hands, their eyes lighting up with grim excitement, before stepping forwards and down, disappearing into the portal.

Jake turned to Cisco and gestured to George. "You're not bringing him along, are you?"

Cisco couldn't answer. He was suddenly rooted to the branch, frozen in absolute terror.

"Go, Jake," Tabitha urged. And with a twitch of her ears, she nodded urgently towards the portal.

Jake took one last wary look at his friend, then jumped in after his sister and Doc.

Cisco, though, suddenly understood something awful.

He couldn't do this.

All this time he'd carried George through this strange and dangerous land, towards a battle he had to face, all on the promise that Tabitha would look after the boy. But what did that mean exactly? He'd been so preoccupied with rediscovering the magic of his childhood, he hadn't considered finding out how the fox would keep his son safe – especially in this world that seemed just as deadly as beautiful and enchanting.

"I told you I'd protect him," Tabitha said gently. "I can keep him here, perhaps take him to see some friends of mine in the tree. Does he like toffee?"

"I don't know..." Cisco replied quietly, squeezing George as he stared at the hole his friends had just jumped into.

He couldn't do this. He couldn't leave his son here.

"You can't take him with you, Cisco."

Shit. This isn't happening. What are you doing, you absolute bellend? This is what you came here for!

He began to sweat. His fingers dug into his son's back and he felt George return the emotion.

"Don't leave me," his son whispered.

Everything inside Cisco told him this was his destiny. He had returned to Dark Peak sure in his bones that he was going to be needed. And yet now he was standing on the precipice of his fate, to the place he knew he had to go, he suddenly understood the limits of his desire to relive his youth.

His son was more important. He couldn't leave him here, not in this strange place with biting faeries and god knows what else. Not even in the care of Tabitha.

"What if he falls?" he said to the fox. "What if one of those swamp-gremlins get him? What if he disappears into another bloody realm while you're not looking? Sometimes he wanders off..."

"*Cisco*, you have to go or everyone suffers. You have to go *now!*"

But it was too late.

The door squealed as the enchantment pulled it closed again. Leaving the magical fox, the boy, and his dipshit father out on a limb.

"Ah, crap," George said.

CHAPTER TWENTY-ONE

Cowards and Courage

The journey back down the tree was not a pleasant one.

Occasionally a figure or a moving plant or something equally bizarre would pass them by as they descended, or would call out from a nearby branch, or just wave. But Tabitha wasn't talking or listening to anyone right now. The fox sat perfectly perched on the basket rim, unfazed by the jolts and the swaying, simply staring off into the mist as if trying to see something.

Cisco wondered if that something was his courage, which he had clearly misplaced in order to have let his friends face Deadman's Grin all by themselves. But every time he shivered at the thought of what he'd done, he felt the tiny fingers of his son clasped tightly in his hand, and he gave them a squeeze and knew he couldn't have done anything else.

Just the thought of leaving George alone on that branch, high above this world, was enough to explode shards of terror in his stomach. What if he had fallen? He didn't know Tabitha as Cisco did, maybe he would have resisted, tried to follow Cisco into the in between place. What then? He would have been putting him right in harm's way.

You've already done that by bringing him here, genius. In fact, you already did that the minute you returned to Dark Peak, thinking that perhaps all the madness was starting again. Which it was.

George gave him another squeeze. "Are you OK?"

"I'm fine, George, thanks. Just a little concerned about Aunty Dorothy, Michelle and Jake, that's all."

"Where did they go? Into the tree?"

"Not quite…" Cisco looked up to see if Tabitha was listening. She wasn't. Or at least she was doing a damn good impression of not giving a shit. "They've gone on a special journey. Remember that old cartoon show I made you watch once, with the boy and the magic torch and the slippery slide under his bed?"

"Yeah?"

"Well, it's a bit like that. They've gone down the slippery slide into a new world."

George thought about this for a moment. "Are they ever coming back?"

"Oh goodness, yes."

I hope.

The rest of the journey to the forest floor was undertaken in silence. George kept looking and pointing and gasping at various things, as though he hadn't seen most of them on the way up. Cisco kept hoping Tabitha would offer him some consolation, a way to redeem himself, a titbit of information that could allow him to get George home and catch up with the others before they had to fight Deadman's Grin.

But the fox said nothing more. Not until they were down, out of the basket, and flitting quickly along a new trail.

"Do not dwell, Cisco," she said, not unkindly, though he sensed her words were a thin layer of ice hiding depths of disappointment. "What's done cannot be un,' as the Stone Folk often say. Let us get you and George home safely. I will take you the shortest way I know from here."

The path grew thin as it slipped into a darker, more tense part of the wood. No lamplights here. No glowing magical beings or bonfires or even the bright sparks of the woodland creatures. Just mossy rocks, roots, and crooked trees.

Tabitha suddenly stopped at a patch of bluebells. Leapt off the path and made her way to a cave of twisted roots beneath one such tree, in the middle of which was a dark burrow.

"Down there," she said. "That's the way home."

Cisco hesitated. "That's a rabbit hole."

"Have you ever seen rabbits that size?"

It was a fair point. And even if Cisco found the idea of crawling down there fairly frightening, George held no such fear. His eyes lit up and he slipped from Cisco's grasp, diving headlong into the burrow. "Coooooooool!" he shouted, before all that was left were echoes.

Ah, shit. With only an apologetic glance goodbye to Tabitha, Cisco took off his backpack and scrabbled into the hole as quickly as he could until he saw the dirty white soles of his son's trainers shuffling ahead of him. Falling to his belly – and pulling the pack behind him – he began to crawl after George, putting aside any concern that this might be a trap and focusing on just getting to the other side. *If* there was another side. Because what if this was a mine? Would there be shafts? Was he about to hear George scream as the floor fell out from under him and he tumbled like Alice into the endless darkness?

"George, wait up."

He crawled faster as the shoes ahead of him suddenly disappeared. Pushing himself through the hole, he tried to ignore the damp soil and bugs wriggling beneath his fingers as he dug in and dragged himself along. Something fell into his hair, crawled along his scalp. He kept going.

"George! Where are you?"

Suddenly there was light. A soft, pale glow only a few feet away. Where it had appeared from, he had no idea. But as he pushed himself ahead, he felt the tunnel widen. Until he was able to scramble out on his hands and knees.

Where he found George standing on the edge of a small wood on a hill as the midwinter dawn began to break over Dark Peak.

"Where the hell have you been!"

Natalie flung open the front door the second they reached the driveway, still in yesterday's clothes, her red eyes wild and angry. Her daughters' sleepy faces were pressed against their windows upstairs. Cisco and George were ushered quickly into the house, Natalie tutting over their dishevelled and muddy state, all the while her brow creasing in a heady mix of fear and anger as she realised they were alone.

"Enough," she said. "Enough of all this. You said you were going for a coffee yesterday. A coffee! That was nearly twenty-four hours ago!" She slammed the door behind them, got them to take off their shoes, then pushed them into the dining room and slammed that door too. "I'm sick and tired of your secrecy and nonsense. It stops now. But not before you tell me where the bloody hell you two have been all night and what you've done with my husband!"

Cisco glanced at his son, whose head hung low thinking he was the one in trouble. "Go and get changed, George," he said. "Then find one of the girls to play with for a bit. Me and your Aunty Natalie need to have a talk."

George scuttled off meekly and they listened to his little footsteps up the stairs and across the landing, before finally Cisco dumped his backpack and took a seat at the dining table. The surface was scattered with bits of material, ribbons, a pair of scissors and whole bundles of sticks and knotted branches, which he stared at in confusion for a few seconds. Until he realised what she'd been doing.

"The Christmas scarecrows," he whispered, grimacing as he inspected a white pillowcase Natalie had clearly been planning on using for the head. Its face was only half-decorated so far, with black eyes and scribbles of long hair that not only stunk of permanent marker, but gave the impression of something that had just crawled out of a well. "I'd forgotten all about these guys. Why the hell is our town so obsessed with terrifying the shit out of everyone to celebrate the good baby Jesus?"

He wasn't sure where the weird tradition had come from. All he'd known growing up here was that every year, the week before

Christmas, along with decorations in their windows and lights in the gardens, people would also tie horrifying festive figures to their houses, fences and gates. The Christmas scarecrows could be anything really, there never seemed to be a particular theme. Some were snowmen or gingerbread men. Others were celebrities or famous characters from films or just bad puns. There was no real consistency, other than of making small children cry and giving everyone nightmares.

Natalie didn't care so much about that right now though.

"Where's Jake, Cisco?" she persisted, snapping her fingers to get his attention, torn between anger and fear. "And Doc and Michelle, too? Jake's mum called me to say they didn't come home to pick up Cecilia last night. Where are they all and why are *you back* here without them?" As Cisco gestured for her to take a seat, she crossed her arms as if daring him to try and make her. "No, I'm not sitting. I've been sitting all night waiting for you all. I'm done sitting, Cisco. Tell me everything. *Everything.*"

Cisco clasped his grimy hands tightly in front of him. Half in prayer for himself. Half for his friends.

"They are safe for the moment," he said slowly and carefully, making sure he did this right. Or at least as right as one can when lighting a barrel of TNT underneath someone's entire worldview. He gestured to the seat again. "But you're really going to want to sit down, because this is a garbage fire of a story."

Natalie stared at him for a moment longer, then took the seat in the most furious way he had ever seen anyone take a seat before.

He discreetly slid the scissors on the table out of her reach, then told her everything.

The conversation went about as well as Cisco thought it might, in that it was full of disbelief and tears and anger and a whole lot of creative swearing of which the writers of *Veep* would have been proud.

We should probably take Natalie with us next time we fight Deadman's

Grin, he considered, as she spat accusations across the table at him, spittle flecking the polished oak top. *There's a special level of anger that worried parents and partners possess that only a fool would risk facing.*

Unfortunately, Cisco had turned out to be that fool. He'd let Jake, Doc and Michelle go to the in-between world to face the pirate alone, running away like the coward that he was.

Not a coward, a father, he tried to argue.

He sighed. As if that technicality mattered right now.

Natalie picked up an apple from the fruit bowl and bounced it off his head. "Did you just *sigh* at me? You sludge back into my beautiful house after apparently sleeping in the wild all night with your poor son, then dare to sit here and tell me fairy stories about where the father of my children is? Are you out of your shitting mind?" She got up and began to pace. "It was so good to see you when you came back to town. I couldn't have been more pleased to have you stay here, Cisco. To see Jake so happy again. He missed you so much. You were one of his few decent friends and I always liked you. You seemed decent. Honest. So what the *fuck* is this bullshit you're spinning right now? I know something went down in Manchester that night at the markets, but possessed ornaments? Talking foxes? Enchanted lands? A giant tree and a motherfucking pirate that's bringing shit to life to kill everyone and wants to destroy the world?"

"It's true... all of it."

Another apple hit him in the head.

"I swear to Christ Almighty, if you start pulling *Star Wars* trailer quotes out of your arse right now I will shove this entire bowl of fruit up it so far you'll be crying orange juice. Jake might never have understood the pop culture references you and Doc fling back and forth at each other, but I was *raised* on that shit. Comicon, Comicana, the Comic Art Convention, I saw them all with my dad, when I wasn't mucking about on the BBC Micro and the Amiga and the NES and devouring *Empire* magazine and *Starburst* and whatever else was out. I've lived and breathed everything you have, dipshit." Einstein the dog jumped up and put his paws on her lap, trying to see what all the fuss was about. She rubbed his ears. "And this one here? He's named after our favourite fictional scientist's dog. I just let Jake think we'd named him after the actual scientist, because he wouldn't have understood. And, no, don't you dare think this makes me just like you! We are not kindred spirits. I don't go around pretending that I'm still a child, playing pew-pew with old consoles and pretending my cosplaying is real. I grew up, Cisco. And now you need to do the same. For the last damn time, no more fantasy stories. Where the hell is my husband?"

Cisco felt all the emotions he'd been trying to keep under control bubble under his skin. But he let her finish and when he was sure she was done, he calmly reached into his backpack, pulled the blaster out, and fired at the Christmas tree in the corner.

It was, on reflection, overkill. But as Natalie gasped in horror and Einstein yelped and scampered out of the room with his tail between his legs, Cisco knew he'd made his point.

The pixelated wave of electricity hit the tinsel, baubles and pine, and in a momentary swoosh of heat it was engulfed in flames. The festive reds and silvers and greens quickly melted and dripped onto the wood floorboards.

Natalie's jaw dropped. She looked between the tree to the blaster in his hand and back again.

"Th- that's just an old light blaster. An accessory. How the hell did you do that?" Then: "Is *that* what's been hanging in our loft all this time? I thought they were just toys. I will kill him!"

Cisco put the blaster back in his pack and held up his hands in a gesture of surrender. "Jake built these when we were younger and I'm beginning to think he kept them just in case we needed them again. Which we do."

"Oh, Jesus," she mumbled.

"All those stories you've likely heard around town about what we did that Halloween here in Dark Peak? They're all real. Yes, we did accidentally blow up the school a bit. But it wasn't a gas leak. The town really was attacked by a dead pirate and a whole bunch of monsters and we really helped stop it. With these magical weapons."

Natalie's face had paled. She collapsed in her seat and put her head in her hands, vigorously massaging her eyes with her palms as though trying to rub away the visions Cisco was currently making her see.

"Where is he, Cisco?" she asked. "Where is my husband and where are my sisters-in-law?"

He held her gaze. "Everything I told you about where we've been is true, Natalie. They have gone to another world to fight the pirate and I should have gone with them, but I had George and I couldn't, and for that I'm sorry. After all this time I spent trying to convince them this was all real, and told them what they needed to do, they stepped up. And I'm embarrassed to say I hesitated until it was too late. I'm sorry. I really am. George... he's all I've got. I know I struggle with being a dad a lot of the time, I know you don't think I've grown up all these years, but it was too hard to let him go. I had to keep him safe." He chewed the inside of his lip for a moment, uncomfortable with what he needed to say next. "I know what I can do to make a difference now though. I know how to help them."

Her hands lowered. Her eyes blinked red and teary behind them. "How?"

"The body of the pirate is still here, on Earth. If I can destroy that while he's still under, he'll have nothing to return to inhabit. It should finish him off. They might not have to fight him after all."

He'd been thinking about that on the journey back. Whether it was possible, whether it would work, he didn't know for sure. It made sense though. Deadman's Grin surely wouldn't be able to return if his body was incinerated, like the government should have done when they'd picked it up in the embers of the school gym years ago.

Tabitha might not have seen any merit in the act, but it was the only thing Cisco could think of now to help his friends.

"There's just one thing…" he said slowly.

"You need me to look after George."

His cheeks coloured at the simplicity of her reaction. The acceptance of his predictability. The fact he was taking advantage of her again, and she was about to let him. Really, he didn't blame her for hating him. He hated himself.

"Yes, please, Natalie. He loves you. Probably more than me at this point and that's fair enough. But the fact is I can't take him with me and I can't trust anyone else with him."

She nodded and looked up as he walked towards the door.

"Just help them, Cisco, or I'll do worse to you than you've just done to our tree."

He looked at the slowly collapsing green, red and gold glittery mess. Then, as the charred angel that had topped the tree finally plopped to the floor, into the Christmas puddle, he swallowed, grabbed his backpack, and left the house.

Off to find the body of the man who had haunted him all these years.

To find him and kill him again.

CHAPTER TWENTY-TWO

Three Go On An Adventure (To Purgatory)

"I'm going to fucking kill him."

Michelle dutifully listened as Dorothy continued to vent, leading the way through the strange, multi-coloured undergrowth, using her blaster as a blunt machete to carve a path of sorts. Or at least Michelle *pretended* she was listening. In truth, she was only half paying attention to her wife in front and the swishing of Jake's footsteps through the grass as he brought up the rear. Most of her focus was really on the creeping sense of familiarity at where they had found themselves.

Because she'd come to realise she had been here before.

In her head.

Through a book.

A branch flung back towards her and she only just ducked out of the way in time. An apology drifted back, but Dorothy was clearly still fixated on what Cisco had just done. Leaving them to step through the branch into a whole new world, while he had...

Well, what *had* he done exactly? Had Cisco stepped through and gone somewhere different to them? Had he instead turned and run away with George? Or was this all an elaborate trap by Tabitha, whose existence she still wasn't entirely sure was legit?

The problem with the last one was Michelle knew this was all too real. Because here they were, pushing through impossible, yet really quite beautiful undergrowth, in this strange other world within another world, while giant butterflies and long-legged birds and even some tiny mice – all of which had cartoon-like faces – flew and ran and swung through this exotic jungle.

All things considered, Tabitha seemed pretty normal.

"Maybe there was a problem with the portal?" Jake suggested as helpfully as he could, although his voice was straining under the weight of such positivity in words he didn't really mean. "Perhaps it has a limit to how many people can come through? Or he's come through but landed somewhere else?"

"Then why did *we* all land together?" Dorothy replied sharply. "We three land in the same spot, next to the creepy caterpillar with the books and the pipe, and Cisco lands somewhere different? Nope, not buying it. He chickened out. We came through for him, but he didn't come through for us."

Michelle knew Dorothy's rage at Cisco had been simmering beneath the surface over the years. Any time his name came up she was always ready to rag on him, while clearly being unable to acknowledge she simply missed him.

Cisco had his faults for sure. And he had dragged them into something Michelle wasn't comfortable with *at all*. But he was still a sweetheart. A flawed man-child, but one who only ever had the best of intentions for those he loved.

"He had George with him," Michelle said again in his defence. She ran a weary hand through her hair, pushing it out of her face. She had ties somewhere, but couldn't be bothered to stop and locate them right now. "He couldn't have brought his son here. Not where we're going."

Dorothy harrumphed, spooking a cloud of fireflies or maybe faeries or something entirely new. She waved them away as they buzzed her face, their glow lighting up the dark, and there was a dangerous look in her eyes as she glanced back.

"We have a daughter too, don't forget. We still came through."

"A daughter who we left with my parents, where she's safe."

"And Cisco could have left George with Natalie. Not brought him on this ridiculous trip into god knows where. At the very least he could have asked that author Mrs Thompson to take him home, while Tabitha took us to the tree."

Michelle couldn't help the laugh that escaped her. "As if you'd leave Cecilia with a complete stranger! I still remember you being unable to let her go on her first day in Reception, even though we'd already had the meet and greet with the teacher and met the other parents and children. It was all tears and tantrums that day... and that was just you."

Dorothy mumbled something under her breath and kept moving. "Whatever. He came back to Dark Peak and rebooted this whole bloody shit-show we'd spent years forgetting. It's only fair he should be here to help us finish it."

Jake caught up with Michelle and they both shared a look that didn't need words. They might not have been the best of friends growing up – what brother and sister ever were? – but they communicated on their own frequency when they needed. And right now both of them were thinking the same thing.

Just agree with her and let's get on with it.

They soon reached a half-collapsed wall that ran as far as they could see in either direction. Jake paused, his hand resting on top of it. "I wish he was here too, but he isn't and we have to assume he's not going to be joining us. I think we just need to get on with this mission as best we can?"

Michelle nodded and urged her wife to do the same. Dorothy grumbled something else, pushed past them both, and climbed over the wall.

Only to get to the other side and scan her surroundings with mouth agape.

"Get the fuck out of here," she breathed in disbelief.

Michelle and Jake scrambled over the wall after her to find everything suddenly changed. Like they'd passed through some invisible boundary.

Gone was the forest of bizarre trees and undergrowth, and familiarly creepy bugs, all of which niggled at the back of Michelle's mind like a dream she couldn't quite remember upon waking.

Instead, hills stretched out on all sides. A sea of green, rolling beneath perfectly puffy clouds drifting across an otherwise blue sky, while over the grass a variety of wildlife roamed – although these were no creatures Michelle had ever seen before – half-human horse people, a beaver in an apron, and even a horned boy with the legs of a deer who was playing some pipes as he bounced past.

"Isn't that…" Jake began in earnest, watching the boy swinging an umbrella on his arm.

Dorothy gripped her blaster tightly as though trying to maintain some contact with reality. "Uh-huh."

"But doesn't that mean…"

"Yes, yes it does, Jake. And I'm glad something we made you watch as kids has finally sunk into your pop culture subconscious. This is exactly the same as the cartoon of the classic book. Except we appear to be in it."

There was a loud roar of a lion in the distance and all three heads swivelled to the right where they could now see a castle in the distance, flags fluttering atop its battlements.

Michelle's hand hovered over her holster again. She moved closer to her wife. But Dorothy's face had lit up in an expression of joy and wonder that she hadn't seen in years and her fingers relaxed.

"I think we're in some kind of malleable landscape," Dorothy whispered, taking Michelle's hand and squeezing it excitedly. "The way it just transitioned like that when we crossed the border. Did you recognise where we were before? I figured you would, because I've heard you reading that story with Cecilia this week."

Michelle's eyes lit up. That was it. *Wonderland!*

"And this place?" Dorothy continued. "I watched the cartoon with her on TV the other day. It's still fresh in my mind."

"Which proves what exactly?" Jake asked.

"Well, does it make sense to you we just happened to travel into two places we both have recent memories of?"

"Does anything make sense at the moment?"

"No, true. But I think it's likely that whatever this place is, it's reacting to our presence. To us. Maybe it's adjusting to the minds of whoever is travelling through it. Tabitha mentioned Deadman's Grin was in a kind of purgatory. Perhaps it's one of his own making – not a hellscape, but his own personal prison?"

Jake pulled a face as he looked around. "This doesn't feel much like a prison though."

"Depends on your perspective, I guess? To many this place seems pretty damn cool. But it's also a bit of a trap, a place that's easy to lose yourself in, never to return to real life."

"We should keep moving then," Michelle said quickly, not wanting to get trapped anywhere if she could help it. The thought of not being able to see Cecilia again made her nauseous.

"Yes, we should," Dorothy said, unable to help the corner of her lips twisting up ever so slightly into a smug grin. "And if I've learned anything from playing video games all these years, it's that what you're seeking is always to be found in the most logical place."

"Which is?"

But she was already trotting off along the hillside, scattering the centaurs and unicorns and witches, as she made her way to the fairytale castle in the distance.

To Doc's disappointment, they never made it to the castle.

Not *that* castle, anyway.

Because with each boundary she led them across, the world around them changed and the castle shifted into some new, weirdly familiar end goal.

Halfway across the perfectly green hills, they made their way over another collapsed stone wall and suddenly it was all bright colours and ninja tortoises throwing fireballs, and the castle ahead had become blocky and pixelated with a single flag flying above it.

Crossing the next wall the light went out and it became night.

Just like that. The sun was now the moon, the flights of birds in the sky were now speckles of stars. And before them the castle had grown dark and foreboding, towering above them into the dark, bat-filled skies as lightning crackled behind it.

Then Jake cried out as zombies, skeletons and werewolves began crawling from the land, loping towards them, and the three were forced to shoot and punch their way through the masses in order to reach the next wall, before leaping over to suddenly find themselves riding horses in a painting.

Not just any painting though. It was as if all the amazing fantasy book covers Doc had ever drooled over at the Trafford Centre Waterstones (a standard side quest she allowed herself any time she took Cecilia to the cinema there) had been amalgamated into one giant matte painting of which Ralph McQuarrie himself would have been proud. The skies above swirled in romanticised reds and pinks and oranges, the jagged mountains burst high on the right side of the pass they rode on, and to the left there was a sheer drop to a raging river.

Yet it was what lay ahead that had Doc's attention.

The fantasy castle to end all fantasy castles.

Despite never having ridden a horse, she managed to get it to stop with a swift, smooth tug of her reins, drawing up at the crest of the mountain path, before staring across the magnificent vista towards it. The others did the same, Michelle looking slightly queasy as she leaned over the improbable drop to one side.

"I don't get what's going on," she moaned. "Why does everything keep shifting here? Why are we on the horses from one of your book covers, Dorothy? Where did we even *get* the horses? We didn't have them in that last place with the vampire castle and that naked beardy man throwing daggers."

Doc couldn't offer much in the way of an explanation. In the past hour – if time was indeed ticking along at a normal rate – they had passed through several different places she recognised. Even if that last one had been a bit of a mash-up of childhood memories.

"The places here are shaping themselves around us, I guess. Stories from books, video game settings, and now we're in a fantasy novel. All scenes pulled from us as we passed through the world."

"I still don't get how this is purgatory though?" Jake said, frowning, as a distant steampunk-esque airship appeared from behind a cloud. There was a glint of sunlight from its prow as it began altering its course towards them. "I've never been religious, but I thought purgatory was meant to be a bad place? It hasn't all been bad."

Doc nodded thoughtfully. "Perhaps purgatory is all about what our subconscious makes of it? It adjusts to fit whoever is here and whatever's in their hearts and minds?"

"Which in our case was a load of nostalgic stuff pulled straight from that collection in your loft," Michelle said. "The book I've been reading Cecilia, the cartoon Doc watched with her, and I know you've been playing video games up there with Cisco recently."

She pulled her horse away from the cliff edge as she spoke. It whinnied softly beneath her, but did as it was told. Doc smiled to herself.

"What?"

"Nothing. You just look good up there."

"Oh." Michelle's cheeks coloured a little. It had been a while since Doc had been able to make them do that. The sight created a familiar little campfire in her insides and set it alight.

"If you two are quite finished," Jake interrupted, hand shielding his eyes as he looked skywards to the encroaching airship. "I'm pretty sure someone thinks we look good up here too. And this being a fantasy cover I'm guessing there's a chance whoever is on that airship is likely to be an antagonist of some sort. So maybe we should crack on and reach that castle?"

"Right you are, my liege," Doc replied. She gave Michelle a wink, then gestured for her to ride alongside her as they began the downward slope on what she hoped was the last leg of this bizarre journey.

CHAPTER TWENTY-THREE

The Princess is in Another Castle

"Cool backpack," the man on the train said.

Cisco gave a smile that was more of a grimace and gripped his bag a little tighter. Why had this wide, bearded bear of a man sat next to him? It was typical, that's what it was. The carriage was pretty much empty post-commuter time and yet this guy had chosen to park his sizeable behind right next to him.

What was worse, he had deliberately decided to ignore the earbuds Cisco was wearing. OK, so he wasn't *actually* listening to anything. He'd put them in as a polite deterrent. But maybe this guy knew that. Or maybe he just didn't give two shits about personal space and was intent on having a damn conversation anyway.

"Lots of weird shit happening, right? Figures you'd bring your own proton pack or whatever the hell you've got in there."

Cisco pulled out the earbud, feeling the colour drain from his cheeks.

"I'm sorry, what?" he asked, despite having heard quite clearly what the man had said.

"I said, lots of weird shit happening in the world right now, yeah? You see Piccadilly Gardens after all those fucked up loonies ran riot around it... place was a right state. Made me wonder if what people were saying about Santa really coming to life was real, you know?" The man jabbed a hairy finger at the backpack. Cisco saw the zip hadn't quite come down enough at the side, revealing the games console and electronic wizardry within. "That's some kind of ghostbusting shit, right?"

"Costume," Cisco replied, quickly trying to wrench down the zip.

"It's not real? It looks real, man."

"Sorry, it's not."

"Cosplay?"

"Something like that."

"Why you carrying it around with you then?"

Cisco thought quickly. "Got a party in town. I'm going as Venkman."

"Huh," the man mused as the train pulled into Broadbottom. The doors opened and the pair of them watched as a tall figure in a trench coat got on. The doors closed and the train moved off again. For a minute Cisco got to enjoy the silence and the hope that the man beside him might shut up for the rest of the journey. Until he added gruffly, "I reckon you'd be more of an Egon to me. Or a Stantz."

Cisco stared intently out of the window. In the reflection, he saw trench coat man move into their part of the carriage. *Christ, not another one.*

"Yeah. Sorry mate, but no way you're cool enough to be a Venkman. Don't get me wrong, the others were OK and everything, but he was…"

The man's voice trailed off as the new arrival pulled up next to them and his long, grimy coat swished around his legs. It only took a second for the smell that accompanied him to register, before Cisco saw there were no feet sticking out underneath. He was floating.

Both he and the bear man looked up into the face of a rotting corpse.

"Hiya fellas!" the corpse said, before crumbling fingers reached down and pulled open its coat to flash them.

What they saw inside was far, far worse than anything *Crimewatch* had prepared Cisco for over the years. As the bear man reached out to push the nightmare away, he only succeeded in losing his arm into the sticky interior, with a squelch they would both remember for the rest of their lives.

The man began screaming, writhing in his seat, trying to pull himself free.

Cisco stood up and unholstered his blaster. "Tell Deadman's Grin I'm coming for him," he said and fired a single blast of electricity into the terrifying apparition. Thankfully the bear man took the brunt of the explosion of ectoplasmic gunk, before he fell back clutching his arm and staring up in shock.

"What the fucking hell kind of cosplay is *that?*"

"The shut-up-and-leave-me-alone kind," Cisco replied, slipping the blaster back under his jacket, grabbing his bag, and stepping over the man to find a quieter carriage.

Nobody sat next to him for the rest of the journey.

Whether they'd seen what had happened, saw the lack of fucks in his moody gaze, or perhaps the splurges of blue death down the side of his shoulder, he managed to avoid getting roped into another unwanted conversation all the way to Piccadilly, then the slow countryside connection out to Grindleford Gorge.

The quiet suited him fine. It left him alone with his maelstrom of thoughts. About how he'd let down George. How he'd let down his friends and himself.

And how he could now fix it all.

Arriving at the tiny station, he strode out past the black and white timber office and café, taking the bridge over the railway line into the swath of twisted, ancient woodland covering the gorge.

This wasn't how things were supposed to have gone, he thought for the millionth time as he leapt up over a broken stile and broke through the thin sheet of ice into a puddle of mud on the other side. Growing up was supposed to make things better. He had fulfilled his hero fantasies as a kid, so why hadn't he gone on to do greater things as an adult? How had he gone from saving his town – arguably the world – only to end up a shit friend, a terrible father, and clearly a rubbish partner in life, trudging alone through a wood in the middle of the Peak District?

"Life doesn't make sense," he muttered to himself, as he took off his gloves for a moment to check the map on his phone, zooming into his location to see which of the two paths ahead he needed to take. He nodded to the young professional couple striding in the opposite direction in their fancy new hiking gear, clearly enjoying a romantic day out. Then he pushed on grimly, trying hard not to be jealous of those not spending their day hunting down an old government facility to kill an undead pirate.

The destination hadn't been hard to track down in the end. He'd asked enough questions of Jake lately to get a rough idea of where it was. And a quick not-at-all awkward call to Jake's and Michelle's dad filled in the rest.

"They took it by helicopter," the retired policeman had said down the phone after Cisco had explained himself, saying it was imperative he knew for Jake's sake. The old man's voice had been a little puzzled, but he spilled the information willingly, as though enjoying the chance to be useful again. "We all knew where. There was this abandoned gunpowder storage building in a forest beyond Hope Valley. A place where only hikers and squirrels go to play with the faeries. They said it was a storage facility, but we all knew the stories. How it was really a laboratory, doing secret experiments, all buried underground. A bit like the warehouse with all the crates at the end of that movie... oh, you know... that one with the palaeontologist."

Cisco only barely prevented himself from correcting the old man, before he thanked him and hung up.

Now he was here, trudging through a cold, wintery landscape, on his way to England's very own Area 51. And it was as British a locale as he could imagine. Nothing but mud and the occasional lost sheep, trails of wood ants, and a robin which landed on his path a little further along and didn't move, only watched him as he crested the top of a small rise and made his way further into the dangerous and foreboding sea of trees.

His breath grew heavier as he strode through the knotty twists of the bare ancient birches and oaks. The frosty clouds of his gasps were now accompanied by the cracking of twigs and pine cones, and the rustling of leaf litter beneath his boots.

It was another world in here. A fairytale of sorts. Woods and forests always were, even the Earth-bound kind. He'd always felt that in the deepest part of his being as a child. There was something primal about them, a reminder from a life long since gone, passed down in genes or DNA or whatever the hell else made up people.

Jake would know the science behind it. Something about the hereditary nature of memories and experiences. That the reason people feared spiders was probably because at some point in the past someone had been attacked by one and the terror had solidified into a genetic memory for the rest of their descendants to suffer.

Whatever it was, he thought, as he tried to simultaneously slow his pace into the unknown and hurry as fast as he could across the slippery tree roots curling across his path like Cthulhu's mossy tentacles, there was definitely some truth to it.

These places were alive. They were living entities, filled with shadows and monsters and faeries and goodness and light and darkness and death. They were history. They were longing. They were love and hate and fear and hope.

And, right now, they were watching him.

He couldn't be sure, of course. But as he put his hand down on the bark of a fallen trunk to climb over it, he saw faces. Not the kind he'd seen in Tabitha's world. There were no distinct creatures here. Rather subtle hints of something even more ancient and primal staring at him. From the cracks in the rocks. From the dark holes in the trees. A twitch of eyes hidden in the leaves.

It was like walking into a very beautiful British nightmare. Like an episode of *Detectorists* written by Guillermo del Toro.

The forest continued following him as he trod the meagre path nature had tried its best to reclaim over the years. Watching his every move. Listening to his breath as it came in short, middle-aged bursts while he hauled his aging frame further into the gloom. The tension mounting, he flinched as something crawled through the mulch ahead, then again at the sudden flutter of wings overhead.

The pale afternoon sun was poking through in places, sticking fingers into the dark around him. But the glimmers of light weren't enough to lift the dread he felt. He was in this good and proper now, and the doubt of his ability to survive it was ebbing away with his energy as the time passed. He paused only for a few minutes to eat a chocolate bar he'd brought with him, then pushed on as best he could. The undergrowth grew thicker. The land rising and dipping like waves on the edge of a storm, with boulders cast across it like men adrift.

Then he saw it.

Unnaturally straight lines in the gloom. A hint of man, overwhelmed by nature.

A small, crumbling building, with a red-brick arch at the front and steps leading down to a bricked-up doorway framed by damp stone dripping in green moss.

Of course it's bricked up, he thought, pulling out his blaster. Not even the government would abandon a scientific facility containing a creepy supernatural evil being in it without some kind of minimal precautions to stop people wandering in.

Looking around him to make sure he was alone, he fired repeatedly at the bricks, cringing at the 8-bit echoes erupting through the silence of the gorge, but thrilling at the Tetris-like way the lines of blocks crumbled away with each shot. Until finally the smoke and dust cleared, and he saw what it had been hiding.

An old, locked red door.

It was unremarkable at first glance. Yet to Cisco it spoke of a great many things.

Of being a doorway to nowhere. Or possibly everywhere.

A Pandora's Box of potential horrors from the past he had to climb inside.

Stepping over the rubble and shooting off the lock with his blaster, he reached out for the handle.

CHAPTER TWENTY-FOUR

Heartbeats in a House

"Are you sure we announce ourselves like this?" Doc asked, still picking thorns out of her legs from the field of roses they'd just had to wade through. She waved towards Michelle's hand as it hesitated over the large door knocker. The knocking bit was held in the mouth of an uncomfortably realistic face, just like the one at the house of Mrs Thompson, except this one made Doc feel distinctly uneasy. As though it was actually suffering the indignity of being a door knocker.

"You said we needed to get inside. What else do you suggest?"

Doc scowled as she accidentally stabbed her finger. "Something quieter. Where we don't hand ourselves to evil on a silver platter."

Michelle looked up to the castle towering above them. Although it wasn't really a castle now. It had changed again on the journey down from the pass. No longer the stuff of fantasies, it had morphed into a dark and foreboding tower that stretched far higher into the sky than any of them could see from the ground. One with many windows and plenty of shadows from which to watch visitors and likely plan their demise.

"I would think he already knows we're here, don't you?"

Jake nodded his agreement, trying to stifle a yawn with his giant glove. "Michelle's right. Let's just knock and be done with it. I want to send Deadman's Grin back to wherever you go when you're dead but you get killed again, then I can get home to my girls."

Doc rolled her eyes and wagged the plastic barrel of the blaster between them, as she pushed through to the door. "Fine, we'll do this the quick and easy way. But don't come crying to me when it all goes tits up."

She pulled the heavy handle and let it drop...

...the crash echoed through the forest, as Cisco's leg burst through the door.

It hadn't flown open like in the movies. Even after being unlocked it was stuck fast to the frame, so he'd had to give it a kick. Except, the rotting wood gave way too easily, which not only jarred his bad knee, but left him hanging half in and half out of the underground facility, before he lost his balance completely and sprawled onto the wet, sticky floor inside.

Not for the first time recently, he wondered why he'd been so eager to return to this adventure business. Would it have hurt to just grow up gracefully? Had he been a better husband and father, he could quite easily have been sat watching *The Repair Shop* right now, enjoying a quiet afternoon with a cup of tea and his wife, while George made festive paper chains to hang around the house for Christmas.

Sighing heavily, he pushed himself up, wiped his muddy hands on his jeans as best he could, and slipped on the head torch he'd brought just in case.

The room around him was unlike anything he'd expected to see. It was just like any normal office reception, with a curved desk against the far wall, a small lamp and telephone to one side, and a chunky monitor to the other. The only difference was the fact there were no windows because this was underground. Not to mention the pervading sense of death, which he now felt inside him like some kind of electrical current and made him wonder if that's what had led to the abandonment of the place. It was a feeling not at all helped by the multiple animal corpses in various states of decay strewn across the snazzy 80s carpeted floor. Creatures that had once sought shelter after the humans had left, yet hadn't managed to escape again once they realised what was lurking here.

"Bloody nostalgia," Cisco muttered, hopping between the skeletal bodies as he headed for the only door he could see, shot off another lock, and moved further into the facility.

Beyond was a corridor. Old wall panels were falling away in places. The ceiling was torn, tree roots were snaking their way through, and there was a constant drip-drip-drip of water like a ticking clock.

His eyes narrowed as they followed his torchlight, first to the left, then to the right. Which way to go? All he could think of was that the government must have stored Deadman's Grin as far away from the entrance as possible. It was a body, after all, not some ancient or supernatural artefact that could be boxed up neatly and put on a shelf. Bodies deteriorated in all kinds of messy and remarkably smelly ways. Plus, he was an evil entity. He'd have to be buried somewhere deep and secure, because surely there would have been health and safety standards that meant they couldn't subject the majority of their staff to that kind of horror. It would kill morale, for one thing.

He went left, treading carefully as he ducked under collapsing ceiling tiles and pushed through spider webs. Then he discovered the stairwell and took it down.

If upstairs had been the front-desk of the facility, then the next level was mainly offices and staff cubbies. Each filled with computer equipment he hadn't seen the likes of in years, like giant keyboards, floppy drives and dot-matrix printers.

Cisco inspected everything carefully with his torchlight, although he was unwilling to let the beam linger for too long in one spot in case something in the dark caught him by surprise. His mind was starting to play tricks on him. Twice he thought he heard someone creeping around behind and twice it turned out to be the hurried thumping of blood in his ears. And there was now a low, almost imperceptible hum accompanying his path through the remains of the facility, that he couldn't determine for sure was real.

Not until he found the central chamber.

The pulse in the air here hit him as strong as the stench of decay. A tangible force beneath the hum that shook him from the inside, through his bones, setting his teeth on edge. He stumbled onto a balcony of some kind, gasping as he yanked his snood up from his neck until it covered his nose and mouth.

"Holy death," he muttered, fingers clutching the rusting metal railing as he shone the light slowly around the level he was on and then... slowly... warily... down the gaping emptiness before him.

It was like a giant, circular lift shaft. Except there was no lift. Only motes of dust caught in the unnatural light as they fell towards the eerie red glow far below.

Towards the source of the hum.

The facility he'd seen above was just the top of this governmental ants' nest. Whether they'd occupied a natural underground cave in the gorge or carved out an apartment block's worth of dirt and rock in order to build this place, he had no idea. It would have been one hell of an undertaking either way. But here it was, he thought, as he leaned over and stared down. A big-ass hole in the middle of the forest and the only way down was the rickety staircase he found himself on.

He followed it around the chamber, down to the next level.

There were doors in the wall here now, each accompanied by a single, dusty window. The doors were locked, but peering through the glass he could make out that each was a small square laboratory with an object held in the centre by racks or hanging from the ceiling. Strangely, most of these objects were doors themselves, although the more windows he looked in as he descended, the more variety he saw, just like in Tabitha's Tree of Paths.

Old oak doors. Twisted iron gates. The odd tree trunk with a natural hole in the bark. A giant rock with a person-sized split in the middle. And above each of the external doors to the rooms were a multitude of faded plastic signs, denoting a range of mythical places, most he didn't recognise, but some he did – one in particular, beyond which he could see a plain stone archway through the glass.

Lyonesse.

Cisco stopped, frowning.

Didn't he know that name?

He tried the handle, wanting to get a closer look, but again it was locked. He debated shooting out the handle, but the thought of making any kind of noise down here creeped him out for some reason. As though it might draw attention to himself.

There was a presence here now. He had no idea how he knew. But he knew.

Eyes on the prize, Cisco. Or you won't get to leave this place alive.

On he went. Keeping his footsteps as soft as he could on the metal grates beneath him, treading down the steps to each descending level. No longer looking into the lab windows now – far more concerned with the glow slowly casting all around him in sickly red light that indicated not everything in this place was dead.

There was life down here, of a sort, and Cisco knew exactly what that meant.

He raised his blaster and kept moving…

…up, into the heart of the tower they went, winding their way up the stone staircase Jake had found behind a painting.

Doc was still concerned about just how easy it had been to get into the castle.

It should have been fortified, guarded by creatures of the night who were itching to pour boiling oil down the murder hole onto the interlopers as they came through the door.

But, no. The door had swung open on the second knock. And as the echoes of their announcement of arrival were still reverberating around the huge hall, they were greeted by nothing more dangerous than the crackling of a roaring fire and the rustling of a festive paper chain dangling over the gothic mantelpiece.

"This is all probably a trap, you understand?" she'd said.

Jake pointed out a strange tapestry of a tropical island and a sailing ship. It was all moving. Yet as he traced his finger around it thoughtfully, the tapestry swung a little to the side and revealed a staircase behind it. Heading up.

"We have no choice now though," he replied. "Shall we?"

Doc grunted and poked her blaster into the gap, ready to unload a few fire bolts in case anything leapt towards them. It didn't.

"People think the bad stuff is always found by going down," she said, leading them behind the tapestry and staring at the climb ahead of them. "It's such a cliché. The really bad shit is always at the top."

"Is that a yes to going up?"

"I guess so."

Up the stairs they went. Taking each well-worn step carefully. Eyes wide and wary as they scoped the path ahead of them, lit only by flickering torches hung from the curved stone wall. All three of them were on edge, despite the fact they hadn't been attacked at any point since arriving in this world. Which to Doc made the tension even worse, because she knew they were being invited into Deadman's Grin's very own personal purgatory here and danger was surely only moments away.

Surely?

But nothing happened. Not to them anyway. Meanwhile, each time they reached a new floor, they watched the stone rooms beyond the stairwell shimmer and shift, revealing curious scenes from the distant past. As though the building they were climbing was built of memories from someone's life.

Empty banquet tables and unlit fireplaces.

Cobwebs strewn across a damp, spray-soaked cave.

A spooky cabin, with darkened windows around the walls through which Doc could swear she saw trees swaying menacingly outside, despite the fact they must have been about five or six storeys high.

Yet despite the illogical changing scenery, each floor seemed devoid of life. The silence felt heavy, broken only by the scuff of their shoes and Doc's laboured breathing, until Jake grabbed her sleeve two floors further up, and nodded towards the end of the room they'd come across.

"What the hell are they?" he whispered.

Doc's knuckles tightened around the grip of her blaster. She hadn't noticed them on any of the other floors, but as her eyes adjusted to the gloom she could see shadowy tendrils writhing their way from the floor to the ceiling right at the very end.

They were thick and squirming, like some kind of tentacles from your worst nightmare, rising up and disappearing into the stone.

Whatever they were, they didn't seem to notice the intruders. But Doc wasn't in the mood to be taking any chances. She curled a finger and beckoned for Jake and Michelle to follow her up to the next floor as quietly as they could – only to find the tendrils were here too. Closer this time. As though the tower was beginning to narrow the higher they climbed.

"It looks like they're feeding on something," Michelle said with horror, as they peered down the deck of what seemed to be the representation of an eighteenth-century sailing vessel through which the tentacles of darkness rose. Her face pinched in disgust, watching ripples move down the tendrils. "Or something is feeding off them?"

"It's the latter," Jake replied.

"How can you be sure?"

"All this time, Deadman's Grin has been growing stronger, his evil spreading far beyond Dark Peak, all around the world now. Something has been helping him push beyond the bounds of his current predicament."

Doc stared at the forest of shadows, grimacing. "The void is feeding him its darkness. Just like Tabitha said. It's helping him to break free."

"Should we attack these things then? Cut him off at the source?"

She didn't have an immediate answer for that. Once again she wished Cisco was here. Not just so she could box his ears for leaving them to this quest alone, but because he would have somehow known what to do. He'd pull some random pop culture reference out of his arse and explain just how to fight these supernatural twisty things.

But he wasn't here when he was needed. Worse… despite her initial seething anger at him for deserting her in this moment of importance, she was increasingly worried about what might have happened to him.

"I don't know if what we're packing would do any damage to those," she admitted, feeling her energy ebb as she contemplated everything. She tried to straighten, for her own sake as well as the others who were now looking to her for leadership. Worry and anger seemed to be her default at the state of the world at the moment and it was exhausting. But she would not let it win today. Evil needed taking care of and she might as well be the one to get it done.

The tendrils pulsing suddenly grew in ferocity, as though sensing the danger she presented. A wave of darkness came crashing down on the deck of the ship and spilled over them all and Doc had to put the back of her hand to her mouth to try to stop herself being sick.

"Go, go!" she spluttered. "It knows we're here."

The stench followed them as they hurried as best they could up the tower. All three of them were relatively fit, yet each was flagging now and Doc panicked, wondering if they'd make it to the top at all.

And, if they did, would they get a chance to kill Deadman's Grin or simply collapse to the floor and die?

Panting, her fingers clutching the curved walls for support, Doc finally reached a landing and saw no more steps.

"Here," she gasped, the blaster raised but wavering in her hand.

How high had they climbed? She'd stopped counting at ten floors. The burn in her lungs and legs suggested it was maybe triple that and for a ridiculous moment all she could do was laugh as a movie scene replayed itself in her mind. They'd turned into the Ghostbusters after all. Middle-aged and struggling to climb stairs to fight the bad guy.

Cisco would have appreciated that. Even if there was no way he'd have made it past the third floor.

"If the bastard kills us, I'm not even going to be bothered," Jake wheezed, leaning back against the wall. "Let the darkness win. I'm tired."

"That's the spirit," Michelle replied, having collapsed to her knees on the top step.

There they rested for a few seconds, trying to right themselves, before the evil wave followed them up the stairs and pushed them into action.

Standing wearily, they moved towards the tall door that surely signalled the end of their adventure, one way or another.

Doc adjusted the grip on the blaster and reached out with her other hand to the door.

"Everyone ready?" she asked.

"No," Jake and Michelle replied together.

She yanked on the iron ring handle anyway.

Whatever she was expecting to see beyond the door, she didn't really know. But she *did* know that it wasn't the battlements at Conwy Castle in North Wales.

A distinctly more evil red dragon than normal adorned the flag fluttering above them as Doc, Michelle and Jake stared incredulously out over the old houses in the town, towards the harbour where the wind was whipping up a swell and throwing about the old sailing ships anchored there.

It was all at once familiar and strange. Doc and Michelle had been here only last year, having taken Cecilia on a weekend trip. They'd spent most of the day wandering the castle, but it had been all ruins and tourists back then.

Now?

Now it was real.

Or as real as it might seem given the sky above them was an ocean of blood red, filled with swirling, bruised purple storm clouds and cawing ravens.

They stood on the tallest tower of four, while around them the castle was not only intact, but bustling with people in eighteenth-century dress. Not far below the grass sloped away from the stone foundations towards crooked houses and smoking chimneys. Horses and carts trotted and weaved through the cobbled streets. Somewhere someone was singing drunkenly and merrily, "Leave her, Johnny, leave her!"

Doc wanted to say something to the others, perhaps to make sure they were still there and she wasn't the only one seeing this stuff. But she didn't.

Because ahead of them, in the centre of the tower, stood a man with lanky black hair and ghostly pale skin. His face cut and bleeding. His hands manacled to the stone floor.

His body, clothed in a ratty shirt and torn trousers, convulsed as smoke rose from the floor and poured into him.

Doc's lips mouthed the words, as Jake breathed life into them beside her.

"It's him."

CHAPTER TWENTY-FIVE

We... Are... Going... To... Die!

Cisco finally reached the bottom of the facility about seven levels down. The repetitive, echoing clank of metal under his boots immediately quietened, replaced by the soft scrunches of his heels against a concrete floor.

He swung his torch around, feeling the cold and damp bite deeper against his clammy skin. He wiped a sleeve across his eyes and gripped his fingers tighter around the handle of his blaster, as if fearing it might slip and roll away at an inopportune moment.

Five tunnels spread out from the central chamber and from each there was a faint, eerie glow seeping towards him. Enough light to see by. Enough light to put the fear of god into him that there was clearly still life down here, waiting for him.

It was strongest in one tunnel in particular, where the red light was pulsing fiercely as though feeding something at the other end.

That way.

Steeling his jaw as best he could, he lifted both his torchlight and the blaster, trying to keep his nerve as he crept into the tunnel. The hum grew stronger with each step, like a video game sign designed to alert the player to the upcoming boss fight. Or the rising crescendo of a piece of music at the end of a movie, geeing the audience into squirming to the edges of their seats in anticipation of what was about to happen.

Except, it's just you. There's no movie. This isn't a video game. It's just you, a gasping, forty-something dad trying to recapture the magic of saving the world like you did when you were a kid.

Put like that, it was ridiculous. And yet here he was, peering into the shadows, unable to stop hearing the mental *beep beep beep* of a motion tracker in his head as he followed the hum, sweeping the torch and blaster from wall to wall.

For the moment, all he saw were surgical trolleys filled with dusty, decaying folders, their paper intestines spilling out across the tunnel floor. Pausing at one he opened it a crack to see lots of barely legible notes scrawled around black and white photos of...

Cisco flinched as though he'd seen a ghost. Which, of course, he had. Because the object of the photos had been a corpse he recognised, even with the giant hole in his chest and without the tricorne hat that had terrified him as a child.

They'd been studying the pirate. Investigating his corpse after bullshitting an entire town into believing he was part of a collective hallucination and didn't really exist.

The righteous anger Cisco felt at this finally being confirmed didn't materialise as he thought it would. He'd always known, after all. He'd spent years raging against the injustice of being the only one to understand they'd been conned as kids. To finally arrive in this moment, having the reality of it laid bare before him, was almost an anti-climax.

All he felt now was a creeping sense of bile rising up his throat. Because this was it.

This was the place where he would face and kill the bastard.

Again.

A few more steps and he began to make out a doorway at the end of the tunnel, beyond which lay a room. The evil red light drifted down the corridor, beckoning him closer. The hum began to vibrate through his teeth.

He stepped into the lab.

It was a large room and clinical with it. He assumed the walls were white, but it was difficult to tell in the glow that pulsed through the tubes that were hung across the ceiling like intestines. A bench ran around the perimeter, filled with the dead faces of ancient computer monitors and one cracked SodaStream machine in the corner, buried beneath old fast-food wrappers and what looked like a half-eaten cheeseburger still remarkably preserved.

Yet as Cisco took in the sight before him, it was difficult to concentrate on anything but the glass coffin in the middle of the room that all the tubes fed into.

A coffin that contained the body of a man he hadn't seen in over thirty years – though one he met in his nightmares constantly. A gaunt, haunting figure that had fascinated him as a child and terrified him as an adult, stalking him through the decades even as Cisco knew he should have grown out of that fear. Because that's what adults did. They stopped believing in ghosts and monsters and long-dead pirates and men who came back to life to kill you.

Especially this man, who he had once put a hole in.

A man who now looked remarkably, terrifyingly intact.

The darkness has healed him, he thought in a panic. *Get it done, quickly!*

Cisco moved closer, eyes fixed on his lanky-haired nemesis, taking slow, deliberate steps across the floor, kicking aside folders and crumpling old reports, as he processed what he was about to do. The grip of the blaster felt slippery in his sweaty hands. His fingers flexed and his knuckles went white as he held it even tighter and raised it towards the glass, drawing it up the body in the coffin until the barrel was level with the man's head.

This was it. This was his moment. His chance to finally end it all and save everyone. Just one squeeze of the trigger and he could absolve himself of thirty-two years of nightmares and prevent an eternity's worth to come.

And yet he hesitated. His finger hovering, unwilling to commit.

Because if he did... it would be over.

Deadman's Grin had been the one to bring him back to Dark Peak in the first place. The pirate was the tie that bound Cisco to his friends, both now and in the past. *He* was their greatest adventure.

If Cisco pulled the trigger now and severed that tie, what then? Without holding onto that nightmarish nostalgia, would his memories of childhood – the bad *and* the good – finally leave him? Would they drift away, as they had from the others, like so many bright balloons released by a child distracted by something better?

Maybe it was for the best. To grow up like his friends had. To enjoy what adulthood and middle age and parenting had to offer, without all that longing for what had once been. But he couldn't help the surge of anxiety in knowing that those memories had kept him going all this time. They had been the key to his survival.

Without them, who would he be?

The blaster wavered in his hand. He used his other to try and steady it, holding his aim, but still unwilling to fire. And it was as he wondered if he could do it, if he could *really* do it, that the decision was taken away from him.

A noise crashed through his mind, like someone had tuned radio waves to the static in between stations of clarity. He clutched his face with one hand as he fell into a computer tower and tried to stay upright. The pain flooded him momentarily, until suddenly the dial was turned and there was quiet again. Broken only by a distant voice.

You need to save her.

He blinked his eyes open and spun around, half-expecting to see someone standing behind him. But there was nobody. He was alone, except for the corpse-who-didn't-look-quite-dead-enough in the glass coffin. The voice came again.

You failed her last time, Cisco. Now's your chance to save her.

Somehow, he understood what that meant.

Amelia.

And then it all clicked into place. The gateway he had passed on his way down, *Lyonesse. That* was the world Amelia had told him about in the dream, wasn't it? The world she and her brothers were trapped in. Trapped, despite his best efforts as a kid to save them.

Free her.

Yes. Yes!

He could free Amelia and her brothers and put everything right again. This was his chance to do what he hadn't been able to back then. A chance to rectify the mistake he knew now was another reason he hadn't been able to let his childhood go. Because he'd left them there, hadn't he? Abandoned and forgotten the siblings who had first put their lives on the line to save everyone from Deadman's Grin, just like he and his friends were doing now. What kind of hero would have done that?

He stared at the pirate's body. Then he turned and saw the lever on the wall beside the door behind him. One linked to the red tubes pouring their light around the room and into the coffin.

Turn it on. Release the magic into the facility and open the gateways. Free her.

The logical part of his mind tried to do the calculations. It was fuzzy, but the more he thought about it the more he felt he could do it.

All he needed to do was turn on the power here and it would open the gateways. He didn't know how he knew that, he just understood that's what would happen. Perhaps the government had been using Deadman's Grin to power the other portals? He didn't care for their reasoning right now. All he knew was that he could do this.

Turn the power on to open the gateways and as soon as they were open he could kill Deadman's Grin. It wouldn't take long. Seconds, probably. He could save the world *and* Amelia at the same time. Releasing the William House children – adults now – from their lifelong prison.

Alternatively, if he killed Deadman's Grin before opening the gateways? The power would be gone. He might not be able to open them ever again. So, really, this was the only way. A chance to absolve himself of all that hidden guilt he'd clearly been carrying all this time. A moment to finally do the right thing.

Do it, said the voice.

So he did.

* * *

The three friends stood on top of the castle, regarding the manacled pirate before them.

It's him, Doc thought again.

How she knew for certain, how she recognised his face, she didn't really know. She hadn't even seen him close up when they were children and since then the bliss of whatever had clouded her memory had kept his gruesome, thin figure from her thoughts.

Yet it was him and a deluge of emotions of what he had put them through – completely altering the trajectory of their childhood – came rushing through her now.

Chief among them was the cold, silent fear she realised had never really gone away. It had always been there, lurking patiently as she attempted to live a normal life, waiting for the day it would reclaim her.

Her knees wobbled and almost gave way, but Michelle had seen her go and quickly put a hand on the small of her back. It was enough to give Doc the strength to shake her head and brush her off, even as reality seemed to drop away from the tower, leaving them suspended in the heavens with this monster for company.

The monster who chose that moment to lift his head.

"How the skin ages," he rasped, the voice of a man who had been left to the elements for far too long. His fingers reached up to gently touch his dry, blistered lips, as he stared them up and down as though inspecting his next meal. "And yet, the eyes do not. For I see three pairs I recognise. Three faces that once watched me die. I have been waiting for you for so long, and now you are here… I am glad of it."

"You won't be once you understand we're here to watch you die again," Doc said.

Her shaky finger found the trigger of her blaster. Could she really do this? Kill someone? It seemed different to what they had done as kids. Wrong. Very *badly* wrong. Which was ridiculous, because they *had* done this as children and shouldn't children be more innocent about, you know, murdering people?

A smile crept over his lips like a spider emerging from a hole in the ground. Suddenly Doc understood that he knew. He *knew*. He had already seen she wasn't going to pull the trigger. That taking a life was now too complex and fraught with repercussions for her, as it should be for any sane adult.

Fuck, she thought, glancing to the side and seeing Michelle and Jake clearly having very similar thoughts about how this was going down. *We're going to die here and he's going to get free and oh god Cecilia!*

Without another word, Deadman's Grin lifted his arms in a gesture of welcome until the manacles grew taut. Then, to Doc's horror, there was a single final pulse of smoke into his form and the chains that had held him down for however long he'd been trapped in this place burst open.

He kept his gaze on them as he rubbed his wrists.

"I'm so sorry to disappoint you, Dorothy, but I do not plan on dying again. Unlike the last time we met, when you and your friends managed to prevent me from finishing the mission I had been tasked with, this time you have arrived too late." He stepped from the deathly tendrils of smoke, leaving them to writhe in his absence, and adjusted his tattered shirt as though it might make a difference to his grotesque appearance. "You do not catch me at my best, I must admit. You'll find that spending so many years in your own personal hell, in this castle where my suffering truly began, takes a toll on any fine fellow." He wagged a bony finger at her. "Unable to rest, unable to finally, mercifully, embrace the endless sleep of death, left in agony for however many years. No, you would not like it. It is remarkably unpleasant, even for those of us who have already been forced to suffer so much in this godforsaken life."

Doc could see the instability in his bloodshot eyes now, as though he was a glass teetering on the edge of a table, on the brink of tumbling and shattering. She and the others edged away as best they could, but it only took a couple of steps before Doc felt the cold stone parapet at her back, preventing their escape.

The pirate's smile widened, revealing blackened teeth and festering gums.

"I have felt you all, you know?" he whispered. She could smell the stink of his breath as the wind carried his words. There was a crackle of lightning above and the air grew thick with the threat of an imminent storm. "It has been so long, but the darkness in my soul allowed me to reach out into your world and taste your fear again. It is nothing like how it used to be when you were children, of course. There is nothing like the fear of children. But when you are in my position you will take anything… and your distress and terror was still a drink as sweet as any rain in the heat of a Spanish gaol. A moment of coolness and clarity. And hope."

Doc's gun was still raised, the console throbbing against her shoulder blades. She knew Michelle was aiming at the pirate, too and could see Jake flexing his glove in the corner of her eye, yet none of them had done a damn thing yet.

Screw it, she thought, and tried to pull the trigger.

To her surprise, nothing happened.

It was the longest nothing in her life. As though time had simply stopped and everything around her had frozen – along with her finger – leaving only her thoughts to fill the empty void.

Deadman's Grin raised a gentle hand and put it on hers. To her horror, she found herself lowering her weapon.

"Your minds are no match for me," he said gently, gesturing to the smoke behind him. "I am so much more than I once was. The darkness of the void fills my every sinew and fibre, so I can once again take up its quest. To recover the sword that will help it break the Cobweb and in doing so finally free me from its clutches." His finger traced a line from the back of her hand and up her arm. His fingernail scratched lightly against her cheek. She still couldn't move. "You have lost, children. Our time is at an end."

"*Children*?" she snapped back, relieved her tongue was still her own at least. "We're in our fucking forties! No matter how much shit you've thrown at us over the last few weeks, and no matter how bloody tired we are from life, we still managed to deal with all your nightmares *and* do the school runs on time." She tried to force her hand back up but it wouldn't move. Instead, her fingers relaxed and the blaster clattered to the floor. It served only to make her more furious. "You're talking to three people that had to parent through a global pandemic. That witnessed moderately sane countries completely lose their shit and elect total fucking buffoons. Three people of a generation that has to live with the fact we've done fuck all about the planet-killing society we inherited and can't get our act together to make it all better for the generations that follow us... while still finding time to binge-watch Netflix. That's us. We lose every damn day and we're still here, motherfucker."

His smile faded. A small victory, but one Doc would gladly take if this was to be her last moment alive.

She waited for him to reply. To zap her into a million bloody pieces. To conjure up some nightmarish beast and have it eat her.

He did none of those things.

Instead, he stepped back and nodded.

Suddenly the stone parapet at their backs grew soft and gave way. They fell backwards into it, only for it to harden again around them.

Michelle screamed, her face only just poking out of the top of the thick, rough blocks. Beside her, Jake had begun to hyperventilate. Doc panicked too, feeling the hard stone pressing against her chest, restricting her breathing to short, sharp gasps. Her fingers grasped air, looking for some kind of purchase, but found nothing of use.

Deadman's Grin leaned over them, his foul breath raining down spittle. "Your words are spirited, but in the end meaningless. I will not kill you. Not today. For you are a number short and I know enough about your stories to know that killing you will only serve to make him more powerful. For what pushes a man to his limits more than vengeance?"

"Ci- Cisco," Jake gasped.

"Yes, that bilge rat you call Cisco. He is still on Earth, isn't he?" The pirate closed his eyes and took a breath, as though he was smelling something delicious and couldn't wait to taste it. "Yes, *yessss*, I can sense him even now, creeping closer to freeing me. And he has no idea of the pain that awaits him."

With that, the pirate stepped back. Doc tried to angle her head to follow him, her lungs burning now, terrified that she didn't have long left. Through watering eyes, she watched him stride back to the smoke, take a breath, then step into its embrace one last time.

"Dorothy," Michelle breathed urgently. Her hand was reaching for Doc's, flapping helplessly against the rock that bound them. "H- Help!"

But Doc couldn't do anything other than watch Deadman's Grin through the tears forming in her eyes. The last thing she saw was his face crease in ecstasy as the darkness finished doing whatever it was doing, before he threw his arms up in the air and cried out.

And faded from existence.

That should have been the end of it for them. They had been left to die in this cursed world, trapped in the walls of this castle like some medieval Philadelphia Experiment gone wrong.

But it wasn't the end.

Immediately after the pirate vanished, the wind swirled to a gale around them. The flag ripped free of its pole and tore itself to shreds. The clouds darkened further and the blood-red sky started actually bleeding, while the battlements began to shake. Doc felt the rumble through her bones as the stone vibrated against her, crushing her lungs even further.

We... are... going... to... die, she thought.

There was a whip-crack and something beneath her gave way. She opened her mouth to scream, feeling thick globules of the blood rain splash against her lips, tasting the bitterness and death as it ran across her tongue and down her throat.

The wall crumbled. There was a collective gasp. And the three of them fell through the castle, as the world that had made up Deadman's Grin's purgatory collapsed upon itself. They tumbled into nothingness.

CHAPTER TWENTY-SIX

A Dark Force Awakens

Cisco pulled down the lever and it all went to hell.

The voice in his head was gone in an instant. The static it had appeared from was gone, too. Suddenly he was tuned back into his own unique radio station and the frequency was blaring out his usual song: *what the actual fuck have you done!?*

The room burst into life. The emergency beacons in the ceiling began to scream, while bubbles flooded through the tubes connected to the pirate as the red goo fizzed and churned. Monitors around the room suddenly began scrolling reams of pixelated text, before one by one the huge black screens exploded.

Deadman's Grin opened his eyes and twisted his head to face Cisco.

"Hello, old friend."

Cisco tried to get off a shot, but his hand was slow to move. By the time his finger found the plastic trigger of his blaster the coffin was bursting open like a grenade and he was thrown across the room. The projectiles tore at his hair and splintered his jacket as he spun, before he clattered into the wall, bounced off a bench and collapsed behind a bank of computers.

The alarm continued to blare somewhere in the back of his consciousness. He opened an eye and only saw red. Was it the alarm or blood? He could feel hot, sticky liquid dripping down his forehead and gingerly touched a hand to his hair to pull out a shard of glass.

"It is quite something to slip between worlds," the pirate said, his voice coarse, the words like bones being dragged across a mortuary floor. "You cannot help but feel the emptiness in the divide, either side of the strand of Cobweb you tread. The endless, infinite void that beckons you to slip and fall and fill its hungry maw." He laughed, a sound as bitter and cold as the winter wind blowing across the earth high above them. "After that, you begin to understand the fragility of our place in the grander scheme. If there is a god, they are no match for the void. I should know. I have seen more than most mortal men ever dared to dream."

There was a crunch.

A footstep on glass.

Moving towards him.

"You sent your friends after me, didn't you, little rat? Somehow you found the entrance to the world before death where you knew I'd be and you let them come after me." The pirate's tone twisted upon itself, growing even crueller if that was possible. "Yet you didn't come yourself. Why is that? Did you grow up to learn life was not what you thought, that the bravery of youth fell away long ago and you have aged into a coward? Did you return to face your demons... to face *me*... to try and prove that you were still special, only to cower at the last minute and let your friends do it for you? Come, admit it, there is no shame to be found here now. Only your inevitable death."

Cisco squeezed his fingers to find his blaster was still in his hand. It had never felt more like a child's toy than it did right now. Plastic and useless in the face of the threat before him.

If he had always wanted to feel like a kid again, it was now his wish came true. He was helpless, unsure of what to do, terrified of this monster and full of regret he had got himself in over his head and was probably about to die.

He tried to gauge his surroundings, looking for a way out.

A place to run away again.

His mind raced, thinking about Doc, Jake and Michelle. His friends had clearly reached Deadman's Grin in the other world. The bastard had seen them. But he had still awoken here, now, back on Earth. What did that mean?

The ache of the scenarios racing through his head threatened to overwhelm him. It would be his fault if they were dead. He had come back to town intending to lead them down this path. They wouldn't have done it without him.

He scrabbled on his stomach through the glass and dot matrix paper that was spooling haphazardly from the printer on the bench as the computers went haywire. The ball of guilt in his throat was stuck fast, the tears already streaming down his cheeks. The ache in his chest fierce now. Was he about to have a heart attack? *Shit, not now. Please not now.*

Yet the adrenaline quickly kicked in and with it came focus and now a small amount of rage.

He was going to end this motherfucker if it killed him.

"Are you listening to me, Cisco?" Deadman's Grin called, his voice louder now. Cutting through the cacophony of the facility like a sword through flesh. The wailing alarm actually seemed to shrink in the presence of his words, as though understanding who held the power here. "Your time is done. There is no need to hide. I will kill you either way. But wouldn't you rather come and meet your fate like a man?"

Cisco was listening, but only to the approaching footsteps. It wasn't the stride of death he might have expected. The old pirate might have returned with greater powers than before, but the tentative sound of his movement laid him bare at that moment. He was back, but he was wary.

Cisco's knees cracked as he pulled himself up behind the desk. He'd taken so much for granted as a child, but chief among the benefits he felt was the freedom to move his body without it making noises. So as he thrust the blaster over and started firing wildly, he knew Deadman's Grin had already heard him and had moved out of the way of the burst of pixels that shot from the barrel. The wave of electricity harmlessly charred calendars and notes pinned to the back wall, as the pirate threw his hands up and spread them wide.

To Cisco's horror, a mass of cables suddenly wrenched from their ties on the walls and in a shower of sparks began squirming across the benches and floors like snakes.

He scrambled back through the door to the corridor. A heavy monitor flew out after him, narrowly missing his head and smashing down on the concrete in his path. He rolled to the side as another followed and he held his blaster up again, firing into the doorway.

It didn't help. Possessed equipment continued to pour out of the chamber of horrors, to the sound of the pirate's booming laughter.

A floppy disc drive scooted into the corridor after him, gnashing the five-and-a-quarter-inch wide set of teeth it had grown. Cisco gasped as he kicked it away, only for its tail plug to lash at his ankle, striking him hard, pins down, on his shin bone.

A burst of white-hot agony shot up his leg.

He grit his teeth and shot the thing to pieces, still stumbling up the corridor, until he realised there was no way out. Nothing that could get him out of this mess. No handy button that seemed like it might activate a barricade and shut off the room and the pirate from the world, if only he could reach it. No bag of explosives he might be able to lob in there and dive to safety at just the last moment.

It was just him and his War Wizard against the impending apocalypse.

Limping and firing his weapon over his shoulder like some aged action movie star, he knew he wouldn't get too far. More objects started coming to life around him. He neared the central shaft and saw the stairs he knew he wasn't going to reach.

There was a substantial fire now behind him. It began to spread beyond the door as the silhouette of Deadman's Grin appeared in its midst and walked slowly towards him. Cisco realised the damage didn't really matter, because it wasn't like the government was going to make him pay for anything.

In a matter of days there would be no government.

Ghosts were walking the Earth again and this one had powers beyond comprehension.

"Cisco," Deadman's Grin hissed. A dozen steam pipes burst free of their brackets and squirmed into the corridor, the metal groaning as they bent at unnatural angles and wrapped around his ankles. Cisco slammed into the floor and was flipped onto his back, only to find his wrists quickly bound up, too. The pipes pulled him into a star shape, directly underneath the central shaft. The tendons in his arms and legs strained and threatened to snap completely.

Then all became quiet.

The tall figure leaned over him, face cloaked in shadow beneath the tricorne hat he had obviously recovered from somewhere and placed at a jaunty angle on his head. Only the whites of his dead eyes could be seen.

"Was it worth it, Cisco? What you did to me back then, was it worth it? You bought yourself only the smallest reprieve, enough to grow old and waste your life." The pirate sneered. "Look at you now, even more helpless and harmless than before. You would have done well to let me have my way the first time. Now you are a father there is so much more of you to hurt."

Cisco went cold. He was unable to help the look of sickening despair that escaped onto his face.

George.

"You wouldn't," he breathed.

Deadman's Grin's smile grew wider. "That's the problem with becoming a father, my boy. It leaves you wounded and vulnerable and open to all sorts of nasty terrors. It is a gash in your soul, a hole in the fabric of your being that keeps you up at night from the moment they are born to the day one of you dies." His boot kicked out and caught Cisco in the kidneys. The pain was immense, too much even to let him utter anything more than a gasp. Then the boot struck again, stamping on his hand, and he screamed.

The agony was intense, burning through his fingers. It ran up his wrist, into his arm. He grit his teeth against it as the pirate laughed and stepped back, drawing a knife from his belt. One he must have picked up in the lab that was now on fire, because *surely* the scientists hadn't left the strange undead corpse in their lab armed with his own knife?

"You should take comfort from the fact that I'm going to gut you first," the pirate said. "But rest assured your boy will follow soon enough. As will the rest of the world."

Cisco heard the words through the pain and fog spinning around his head, but he could do nothing about it. He had no more energy to fight. All he could do was moan softly as his old nemesis bent down and stretched out with the knife.

BOOM.

Deadman's Grin lifted up his head, the tendons in his neck straining as he looked to see what was happening. Cisco could only watch through the stinging tears in his eyes, confused, until he saw the red light flowing up the sides of the cylindrical chamber, before all the doors burst open and a menagerie of monsters poured out of them.

The power had taken its time to work through the old system. But once it had, it lit up the entire chamber and opened all the doorways he had passed on the way down. Except, there were a hell of a lot more than he remembered and he hadn't expected there to be so many terrifying nightmares ready to pour through them as soon as they'd been unlocked.

White spirits flew out, joined by dark, evil creatures he knew instinctively were a fabric of these lands and were eager to roam them freely again. A horned beast with goat legs loped up the staircase. It was followed swiftly by what looked like goblins.

And then…

Oh god.

The giant snout of a dragon pushed through a door only three floors above them, before the wall burst open to reveal a thick, scaly body and leathery wings. Digging its talons into the stone, it quickly crawled onto the wall and looked around, as though confused by its surroundings.

Cisco tried to wrestle free of the pipes that still pinned him down, as bricks and mortar crashed around him.

Deadman's Grin looked back to his struggle and slipped his knife into the sheath at his hip. "I think this will be more fun," he said, then put his fingers to his lips and whistled.

The dragon's eyes snapped towards him. It circled the shaft once more, then snaked down towards the pirate, before letting him sling himself up onto its back. With a hissed incantation in the creature's ears, its wings unfolded and the pair lifted into the air, pausing only for Deadman's Grin to tip a finger to his hat at Cisco.

Then they swung around, letting the dragon's tail cut through more of the wall, before they burst straight up, through the roof above them, into the night.

As the rubble fell towards him, Cisco knew it was all over.

He'd let his friends down and now he'd got himself killed. Worse still, he hadn't saved the world – rather it looked like *he'd* been the one to end it.

And that's when he saw the glimmer on the stairs to his right, as a blonde woman and two fierce looking men leapt the last few metres and landed in a crouch next to him. He caught a scent of strawberries as the woman leaned over him, brushing his face with her hair and sparking a memory of something he could have sworn was a dream.

Then she stretched out a hand to the wall and said, "*Protego.*"

Immediately something shifted. The pipes around his limbs grew rigid and snapped off. And the wall of rock quickly formed a giant hand and became a shield over their heads.

Just as the facility collapsed.

"I've got you," she whispered in Cisco's ear, as it all went dark.

CHAPTER TWENTY-SEVEN

The Wood Witch's Cabin

The woman's voice was soft and warm in the darkness beneath the earth. It spoke to Cisco of adventure and love and all the worlds you ever saw in sunset clouds or dreamed lay beyond the horizon. It told him he was safe, despite the darkness threatening to suffocate him. It eased the pain burning its way up his arm as he clutched it tightly to his chest.

It was a voice from a long-ago dream.

But also, somehow, it was of now and maybe even the future.

Or, at least, *a* future.

How did he know that? He had no idea. Perhaps he was just delirious, lying as he was here in the dark, after witnessing an ancient evil fly out of a secret government facility on the back of a dragon, while other creatures of myth and legend and horrible campfire tales were now running amok through the forest above them.

No, not above them. Around them now. Because as Cisco flitted in and out of consciousness, he discovered he had moved and was now travelling. Being dragged by his upper body, first through some kind of tunnel that smelled damp and earthen, before feeling a fresh smack of winter's night on his face as they broke through to the surface.

"His trousers are coming down," someone said. A gruff voice, but well spoken. Like an English actor from an old black and white movie.

Cisco was barely awake, yet he could feel his jeans were indeed sliding down his bum with each crunch of his legs against the soil and leaf litter. In his head he pulled the trousers back up again, but in reality he knew he hadn't.

"Dignity is a privilege he doesn't need to worry about," replied another voice that seemed out of place in this time. "The bugger's lucky not to be dead."

"Aye, true, but still it might be better on the eye if we hitched them up. I have no wish to see more than I already have done."

"He has undergarments on. What's your problem?"

"Will you two *shut up!*" the woman cut in. Her voice was a little breathless against the night's breeze as they stumbled through the forest. "Please, Peter, John, stop your bickering. I refuse to let you ruin this moment with your continuous back and forth."

"You've waited for a moment to see him with his trousers askew?"

There was a laugh, then a sharp slap. No more was said after that, until a few seconds later Cisco felt the jeans find his ankles.

"On second thoughts," the woman relented, "yes, please hitch his trousers back up. They are all the way down now."

Cisco blinked his eyes open briefly as a rough pair of hands grabbed the belt of his jeans and hoisted them up. He heard a grunt – his own – but couldn't do anything other than that. All he could do was let himself be carried, watching as the constellations of Orion and Isis made an appearance between the drifting snow clouds above the trees, while his boots bumped and jolted over roots and fallen branches. His last thought before he passed out again was that they were still in the forest. What forest? He couldn't remember. The events that had led him to this moment were suddenly a little murky and fuzzy, as though his brain felt it best he shouldn't remember just yet to give the rest of him a break. A kind gesture, he decided, as he slipped into unconsciousness again.

He woke properly to the dark interior of the world's most haunted cabin. A scene straight out of every horror movie ever made.

Rotting wooden beams crawling with bugs, spiders skittering across webs over the walls, faded paintings with creepy figures in them fallen and smashed on the floor, and shadows in every corner. If he hadn't been so tired, he would have been terrified.

Lying on his back, he felt something soft behind him. A coat, perhaps? It wasn't enough to cushion his spine from what he felt were some pretty unforgiving timber floorboards.

He groaned loudly, shifting as best he could to find a better position and feeling every sinew of his being admonish him angrily.

"Welcome back," the voice said from the rocking chair in the corner.

Had he been slightly more conscious, he might well have dropped dead of fright there and then. Thankfully his wits were still a little numb and he soon remembered their journey to the cabin and who the voice might belong to.

"Amelia?"

His long-lost friend leaned forward, her smile matching the moonlight drifting through the skeletal frame in the glassless window. She looked tired and exhausted. Her clothes dirty and ragged, and her eyes cloaked in shadow – although Cisco thought he saw a glimpse of a twinkle in them now, like the stars he had seen earlier.

"Where am I?" he asked. "What happened?"

In an instant everything changed. A flash of light caused him to squeeze his eyes tightly shut and swear under his breath, before he opened them to an entirely different scene.

The same cabin, as far as he could tell.

But now he was lying on a couch, a thick quilted blanket sewn with strange symbols tucked up to his chin, and he could see the room around him properly. It was warmly lit, with fairy lights draped around the window and across the mantel of the fireplace, while within it he could see the flames of a roaring wood fire just visible through the smoky glass of the cast iron burner.

Amelia was still in the rocking chair, leaning forward and watching him. The light in the room seemed drawn towards her, dancing across her skin, giving her a kind of fairytale glow. She was finely dressed now, wearing a beautifully simple green gown, while a pointed hat with a pleasantly crooked top was slung on the corner of her chair.

"You had a fall," she replied kindly, although to what question he wasn't sure. His eyes wandered the room, noticing that the abandoned cabin – terrifyingly dilapidated a moment ago – was now full of life and warmth and joy. Most certainly not abandoned any longer. A place of refuge and peace.

Home?

It felt like home. Although how could that be? He had not been here before.

The feeling was all at once familiar and strange. A memory that wasn't really a memory. A flipped coin still spinning through the air, yet to land on any side – with both outcomes still possible.

Where the hell am I?

"I had a fall?"

Amelia nodded, her face brightening to see him talking again. Her eyes greener than emeralds, matching her dress. Her hair golden yet flecked with strawberry. She looked both familiar from the dream in which he'd last seen her and all at once more vibrant and excitingly real.

"You fell, but you're safe now," she said and he realised that's exactly how he felt. Safe. Not alone and empty as he had been for so long. He was home and he was warm and loved. What was this place? It was both the broken cabin he had been brought to and yet it wasn't. Which one was real?

A child's scream of excitement broke his concentration. It erupted from the doorway to what looked like a kitchen beyond. A pot was bubbling on the stove. And through wafts of sweet-smelling soup pouring from it to infuse the air in the room, a boy ran towards him, his arms outstretched.

"Daddy! You're awake!"

"George? What are you doing h–"

"–ere?"

Cisco readied to embrace his son, just as the vision vanished. His empty arms fell back to the coat. His breath fogged the freezing air in front of his face, lit by the low moonlight streaming in through the broken window.

Amelia was now standing before it, rubbing a graze along her arm and peering out as if watching for something.

"They're still out there," she said.

Cisco rubbed his face to try and wake himself up and slowly got to his feet.

"Who?"

He drew up beside his strange and beautiful saviour. Still dazed, he couldn't help but let his weary gaze flicker in her direction, even as she continued to peer out into the night.

"Knuckers. Ogres. Lantern Men. Nightmares from every folktale and legend you've ever heard and plenty more I'm sure you haven't. Though I've never seen so many of them in one place before." Her face darkened with worry. "There were always one or two that flit between the different worlds and sometimes wandered into ours. And we used to see a few whenever we ventured into the Valley of Mirrors – just their reflections, of course, but it was enough to be able to go away and ask the cauldron about them." She held her hand up, knowing full well he had no idea what she was talking about. "I know you don't remember, so I will explain another day. Either way, this is something different. Something I do not like at all. The pirate's dark magic opened the gateways and released all the nightmares back into this world. They will be more difficult to kill now they are here properly and I can only pray Peter and John will be careful."

"Your brothers," Cisco said, remembering now.

"Yes, my bickering brothers who helped carry you here. They

have gone off already to begin the hunt, to try to stem the tide of darkness as the creatures flood these lands once more."

She grabbed him suddenly and pulled him into her to the side of the window. Their bodies pressed together. A finger held to his lips.

Heavy steps were crunching through the leaves outside.

Coming closer.

The cold was already deep in Cisco's bones, yet he still felt a shiver of dread creep from his boots to his legs and up his spine as whatever it was approached the cabin.

Amelia pulled him even closer, if that was possible. He could feel the soft rise and fall of her breath now, and...

...her heartbeat against his.

They were dancing in this new vision. Slowly, in the middle of the cabin, bare feet padding across the boards bathed in the warmth of the evening light. The fire was out, yet the summery glow that streamed in through the open window, filtered by the lush green trees surrounding their home, was heat enough. That and the closeness of their bodies, pressed together in a way that felt both long overdue and as fleeting as a wish for something that hadn't yet happened.

His son's soft snoring drifted from another room, while there seemed to be music outside, though not any he had ever heard before. Birds chirping, crickets buzzing, the breeze rustling leaves... all in a rhythmic way that was all at once entirely natural and like something out of an old-fashioned animated movie. As if nature was serenading them.

Amelia looked up at him with a lazy smile.

"You've got that faraway look in your eyes. Where are you?"

"I- I'm not sure," he replied honestly.

Her smile grew and she rested her head on his shoulder, her hair tickling his neck. "Well, don't stay away from me for too long, Cisco. I've waited long enough for you to come back into my life.

Living here alone in this wood, learning my role, watching over what I was meant to and hearing from Tabitha about my part in the world. But you're here now. And I'd like to keep you with me, if that's OK?"

He gave her a squeeze, knowing that's both what he was meant to do and what he wanted to do. For the first time in his life, he understood he was in the right place. His brain wasn't trying to retrace its steps into his past. He wasn't thinking about what had come before. He was finally living in the moment.

What moment? He wasn't sure.

Perhaps the past. Perhaps the future. Perhaps an entirely different time altogether.

Maybe he was just trapped in the facility and this was some kind of seconds-before-death vision conjured up by his mind to show him what life might have been like, if only he had made a different decision along the way.

Or maybe it was real.

Either way, the moment was good.

After a minute more of dancing, Amelia lifted her hand to the window and gestured, and the music outside slowed and stopped.

"You know, George is asleep..." she began, a glint in her eye.

"*...so don't say a word or we're both going to be eaten,*" she finished back in the abandoned cabin.

Cisco blinked, out of balance in both himself and quite possibly time. Yet he felt the threat nearby and continued to listen, as still as possible in the bitter cold, even as snow began to fall through the cracks in the roof and drift in through the broken pane of glass beside them. Listening and waiting, as the heavy, deliberate footsteps circled the cabin, as though they couldn't come too much closer, before they quickly moved off into the trees again.

All became quiet.

Amelia let go of Cisco and stood back. For a second or two they just looked at each other, while the rain of snowflakes fell around them and little eddies of white blew into the darker corners of this strange place.

"How are you feeling?" she asked.

Cisco blinked, first at her, then at the window, beyond which the snow was beginning to fall faster and in bigger clumps, slowly blanketing the clearing outside.

"I still might need a little explanation of what the hell is going on," he said, rubbing his eyes as though it might help him see all this a little clearer. "For a start, this isn't a dream, is it? You're actually here?"

She moved away and he was immediately colder for the empty space she left. Yet she seemed entranced by the cabin as though seeing it for the first time. Her fingers reached out and touched the timber beams above their heads, then around the doorframe, then tapped a nail against a familiar-looking rusty cauldron hanging above the blackened fireplace.

"I'm not sure where *here* is, exactly," she replied, "although I always wanted to live in a little cabin in the woods like this one. My brothers said it was the witch in me trying to get out, which might be true, I guess. There was a story, when we were kids, about the Wood Witch who lived in such a place and looked after the forest and the animals and guided lost souls. She was so in tune with nature, she was even allowed to harness it. I always had a fancy for that life. Spending my days roaming the trees and brooks and hills. Then perhaps leaving the fire on late in the evening, to let my husband follow the smoke on his way back from whatever he was doing out in the world." She sighed as she swept her hand over the mantelpiece and twirled around lightly to face Cisco again, her face at once pensive and hopeful. "Do you remember we used to talk about that, as children? I suppose you don't. Maybe that was just a memory I had to hold onto in order to survive out there. Although I'd like to think I could see myself here."

"Yeah, I think I can see you here, too," he said, the visions he'd just witnessed still strong in his mind. He wondered what they meant.

She collapsed in the old chair again, full of relief and exhaustion. "To answer your question, Cisco, I was always real. Whatever you did with that pirate back there, it opened the gateway Peter, John and I have been staring at for so long in our world. That's what allowed me back here tonight, in person."

"Just in time, too. You saved me back there, thank you."

"As you once tried to save me, I remember."

She looked sad at that and for some reason it stuck like a splinter in the back of his mind, as though it should be something he needed to remember.

Something important.

"It was all Deadman's Grin, you know," she said. "He was the reason why we ended up in that world, even after we'd escaped back to Earth. We knew he had been tasked long ago with retrieving an item from it. An artefact that could help the void destroy the Cobweb for good."

"What kind of artefact?"

"It was a sword. One forged across multiple worlds, with the power to break the strands that connected them all. A weapon of such power it destroyed the very place where I've now spent most of my life. A place that used to be part of this world, before it was ripped away into its own dimension." She sighed with no small amount of regret. "Yet even after we stopped Deadman's Grin returning to Dark Peak, we knew he wouldn't rest. We decided to return to that world and make sure he could never find it. And in doing so we trapped ourselves."

Cisco frowned. "I remember reading about what happened to you when you came back to town. How nobody believed you. How they treated you. I'm so sorry."

"Oh, no matter. It made our decision to return to that world easier. And we eventually found what he was searching for, which made it worthwhile."

"The magical sword that could break the universe?" Cisco felt something akin to hope, a burst of warmth in the cold. "I don't suppose it's the kind of thing we could use to kill Deadman's Grin?

To finish him for good and stop this madness before it brings about the apocalypse?"

She stared at him thoughtfully, before giving a brief nod.

"I have been wondering the same myself. Although it's the sword the pirate wants and if we use it against him, we risk it falling into his hands. I'm not sure Tabitha would approve."

They both yelped in horror as a shadow leapt through the window and landed next to them.

"I wouldn't approve of what?" the black fox said, panting as though she'd run a long way to get there. Her shoulders dipped and she sat on the floor with obvious relief. "I must say, I'm glad to see you both alive. When I saw the cavalcade of terrors moving through the forest, and saw the beast carrying that pirate fly overhead, I knew there was a chance I would find you both together. But in what state, I wasn't sure." Her wide eyes blinked as she looked around. "Thankfully you found a place to hide that carries a magic few can overcome. It is lucky the cabin appeared to you in your time of need, for many have sought it over the years and most have lost themselves to the trees in their search. The Wood Witch was never one to want to be found."

"The Wood Witch?" Amelia repeated, staring around her with renewed awe. "She was real? This was hers?"

Tabitha peeled back her lips in some semblance of a knowing grin. "There have been more than one in the role over time. But yes, this was theirs. And although we are lacking one at present," the fox glanced at Cisco with a strange look in her eyes, "I hold out hope that may yet change."

He frowned at that and opened his mouth to get Tabitha to explain, but she had already twisted away to lick at her back leg, which he could now see had a nasty gash across it.

"Oh, my poor little one," Amelia cooed, scooting over and wrapping the fox up in a gentle hug. "What happened?"

"I got between a Bloody Bones and his pond," Tabitha said, wriggling out of her embrace and trying to stand tall. "It's fine, the old thing barely nipped me. But the Dead Folk that grabbed at me when I got too close to the water caused some bruising that will ache tomorrow." Her tail swished impatiently. "It matters not though. Right now we need to get you back to the others and quickly."

"The others?" Cisco said, suddenly remembering what Deadman's Grin had said about his friends and feeling a spark of hope again. "You mean, they're still alive?"

"Alive and pissed *all* the way off," Tabitha replied.

CHAPTER TWENTY-EIGHT

A Midnight Bridge

The three of them moved quickly through the night, sweeping from tree to tree, occasionally pausing to listen to the distant howl or screech of something unnatural.

Each and every time Cisco said a silent prayer, hoping whatever it was hadn't found someone to eat. He wasn't religious at all, so he figured he'd just offer up the thoughts to whoever was listening. And, out here, in the countryside, the dark of night overhead and the blanket of snow shrouding the hills, it was very easy to feel that something was indeed paying attention to them.

That his friends were alive was a revelation that gave him hope they still had a chance. Deadman's Grin might have been released into the world, along with hordes of beasts that had crawled out of all the portals the laboratory had gained access to over the years. But knowing Doc, Jake and Michelle hadn't been lost was everything.

He still wasn't entirely sure how they'd survived the pirate. Tabitha had been vague on the details, but apparently the Tree of Paths had alerted her to an occurrence in that world and the fox had sent in some acquaintances to retrieve the other Swashbucklers and take them home again.

Which is where she was leading Cisco and Amelia now. To regroup, equip their weapons, and go face the ghostly son-of-a-bitch who'd almost killed them all.

Under the gaze of the silent, snowy hills, the troop wound their way down the trail into the nearest village – although Tabitha made sure to lead them on a path that skirted the softly lit streets, before appearing in a large white field beside a playground.

"There are gateways all over this country of ours," she said casually, as if preempting Cisco's question of exactly how they were going to find their way home at this time of night. "Remember how we found our way to the Tree of Paths at the bottom of Elenora Thompson's garden? Well, the gateways don't just jump between worlds. Some of them can carry you across this land, too."

"Shortcuts," Amelia said.

Tabitha nodded. "This one is on a Midnight Bridge, just beyond the Stone Guardians."

"The stone what?"

Cisco had barely got the words out, before he jumped and gripped Amelia's hand tightly. One of the huge rocky mounds dotted around the field had lifted its head sleepily as they passed and blinked open a giant eye.

"Protectors of the gate and cousins of your friend Boulder," Tabitha explained.

She trotted past the giant head, while Amelia raised a hand and waved. The Guardian yawned and a small scatter of pebbles fell out of the corner of its mouth, before it shook the snow off itself and settled back down to sleep.

They reached the bridge soon after that. A beautiful stone curve over a gushing river, only wide enough for Cisco and Amelia to walk single file, while Tabitha trotted along the mossy stone wall at the side. Halfway along, she paused and looked up at the sky where the snow had stopped falling and the stars twinkled once more beyond the drifting clouds.

"Ready?" she asked them.

Cisco looked at Amelia, who didn't seem to mind what was going on. He got the impression this was a relatively normal night for her.

"For what?" he asked.

Tabitha gave him another toothy grin, before a burst of what could only be described as stardust cut across the centre of the bridge. A split in the air appeared and revealed a doorway leading somewhere completely different.

"Midnight," Tabitha repeated and crossed through.

"Of course," Cisco said, following after.

He knew instantly where he was when he reached the other side of the bridge. Moor's Clough. It was a popular trail just on the edge of town, with its own bridge across the Dark Peak Brook. And although that bridge was mostly a modern construction of wood and wire fencing, Cisco figured that there must have been a stone predecessor at some point in the past. That's how this magic worked. *Green moss on old stone,* Mrs Thompson had said.

It being late, they had no trouble finding their way home without bumping into too many people. Just the odd bunch of friends out for a festive drink and a man walking his dogs. Certainly, nobody who cared too much about a couple following a black fox.

Past the crooked cottages of Old Dark Peak they went, with their Christmas decorations beaming festive goodness out into the streets to banish the shadows. Then they crunched across the snow-covered footpaths to the main part of town, striding past Norfolk Square, down the alleyways beyond the church, then up the hill to Jake's estate.

It took forty-five minutes all told, Cisco occasionally glancing down at Tabitha, Tabitha softly rumbling to herself beneath her whiskers. And Amelia clutching Cisco's hand as she stared at the shop windows and the tall, proud tree near the memorial, and the occasional car that whizzed past.

"How things have changed," she replied softly, as though either on the verge of tears or confused about what she saw or maybe both. "From where I was trapped, I've been able to see you grow and see the world grow around you. We could catch glimpses of life unfolding here without us. But to see it for real, to know that I'm back here, finally, and everything I know is gone? It's a lot."

There wasn't much he could say to that. She had disappeared

from the world over a hundred and thirty years ago. Everybody she had known was dead, except for her brothers who, after pulling Cisco's jeans up during their escape from the lab, had disappeared to hunt the roaming beasts across the Peak District.

He gently warmed Amelia's cold fingers between his and drew her tightly to his side. It wasn't much, but it was something. A moment of quiet companionship, before they reached Jake's road and headed for the house where all the lights downstairs were blazing through the curtains, behind which shadows could be heard arguing loudly.

"You fucking left us!"

The trebuchet combination of the bowl and spoon fired the milky cereal across the table as Doc slammed her fists down and accidentally caught the midnight snack she'd been eating. Everyone in the room flinched and straightened. Jake looked to his wife whose weary face was a furious red, but thankfully Natalie opted to stay quiet for now. Michelle silently wiped the dripping milk from her cheek and leaned over to put her arm around Doc's shoulders, possibly to comfort her, probably to prevent another messy outburst.

Cisco stayed on the far side of the table, out of range of the physical attack, but perfectly placed to receive the verbal grilling he knew he deserved. He shuffled on the spot, unwilling to look down at his feet, stubbornly defiant in his misery and guilt. Although he did risk a glance over to where Amelia had wisely taken a neutral position, next to the sideboard where Tabitha had squished her furry behind between Jake's perfect family photographs.

"I said I was sorry," Cisco said again, summoning up all his levels of humility to take this one on the chin. He couldn't blame Doc at all. He couldn't blame any of his friends. He'd absolutely screwed this up. Almost killed them. Possibly everyone else on the planet, too.

"I don't think sorry covers this," Michelle replied. Cisco's heart sank as he saw the look of disappointment in her eyes. Worse still, Jake wore the same expression.

According to Tabitha they'd had a hell of a time in the purgatory world. Trapped and left to die by Deadman's Grin, they'd then fallen into an abyss they all thought they were going to tumble through for eternity. Only being saved when Tabitha sent the Gabble Ratchets, hounds of the sky hunt, to squeeze their way into the deteriorating construct and drag them out again.

After that, they'd been forced to take a shortcut back to Dark Peak. Although this had been another one of those muddy tree root tunnels and despite having had showers, he could still see bits of leaf litter in their hair.

They were alive, though, and for that he was unbelievably relieved and grateful. If only they could forgive him for leaving them.

The television in the background continued to flash as the twenty-four-hour news stations replayed incidents and sightings across the country. Amelia's face, glancing towards it occasionally, was a ghostly white in its glow. Even Tabitha's sheer black fur seemed to have paled in the face of so much terror – all recorded and replayed on repeat.

Blurry CCTV vision of cars being attacked on the M6. A mobile video of a dark streak across the moon followed by a blaze of fire. Mythological creatures roaming the hills across the Peaks.

And that was just in the UK. Because images coming in from around the world showed that after a few years of very human horror, championed by clowns and dickheads, tonight was the night that the darkness had decided to join in.

It was utter chaos.

Doc pushed her hands across her face, groaning deeply.

"You shouldn't have come back," she said, her voice exhausted in its anger. "Ever since the day of that bloody Halloween report, you've been leading us into trouble and you just can't snap out of it. I've missed you all these years, Cisco, but you really shouldn't have come back. You've just been unable to grow up. To move beyond whatever you thought we went through back then." She raised a finger as she fixed him with a glare now. "And even though what we went through *did* happen and clearly has been happening again lately, maybe we could have dealt with it? Or maybe he wouldn't have woken up properly?"

Cisco tried to maintain his calm. "He was already waking up, Doc, that's the point. I had to try and stop him."

"Yet you didn't, did you? You let us go off to do it and nearly get ourselves lost in space. And now he's fucking escaped and also released a whole bunch of new nightmares into the world at the same time?"

"Old nightmares, actually," Tabitha noted from the back of the room, giving her ear a scratch. "Those creatures have been around for almost as long as me, slipping between the worlds. They've been seen here before, woven into your campfire stories and books. It's just that now they're here properly. Untethered to their own dimensions. Roaming free."

Jake left the relative safety of Natalie's side to draw back a chair at the head of the table and sit down near his sister. Now the three of them faced Cisco, like some kind of inquisition.

"Doc's right, mate. Whatever happened at the facility has stirred up a whole bunch of trouble. It's like a plug holding back evil has been yanked and now it's spilling out, so much worse than before."

The way Jake looked at him in that moment almost broke him. It was the way his mums always regarded him when they suspected he'd done something wrong. It spoke so much of how his friends had all grown up. Not just in age, but actually taking control of their lives and accepting the responsibilities that came along for the ride.

He had tried to do that, hadn't he? Or had he been too caught up in the past to get it right?

In the background, Amelia glanced over then moved deliberately to the table to join them. For someone so slight, she had a strength and presence to her that had everyone shutting up and paying attention. Even Doc kept her lips tightly pressed together for the moment as Amelia pushed her hair from her face and fixed each one of them with a look.

"I remember you all, do you know that? There's a chance you don't remember me still, other than what Cisco might have told you. But we knew each other as children, when you put your lives on the line to save me and my brothers. And even though that didn't work out, I never stopped being grateful for it." She turned to Cisco. "Or believing you'd return for us, even if we told you not to do such a thing."

He reddened under her gaze.

She knows I did it.

It didn't take a massive leap of intelligence to understand that the only way the gateways at the facility could have powered up again was if someone had physically turned them on. Someone alive. Now, one by one, his friends saw it too.

Yes, he *had* gone to kill Deadman's Grin. But he'd let himself be tempted by the opportunity to try to rectify a past mistake. To fix the past, of a sort. To save Amelia as he had once failed to do.

And it was going to cost them all.

"You let him out, didn't you?" Jake said, pushing his face into his hands.

Cisco blushed furiously under the heat of their collective shock and disappointment. Yet despite every instinct telling him to lie his way out of this, he nodded and quietly pulled up a chair. "I went to kill him. Honestly, I went to kill him. But when I saw the gateways, I thought I could get Amelia and her brothers out first. There was a voice in my head telling me I could do it. Switch everything on, power the gateways up, and then kill him."

"It was his voice you heard," Tabitha said unhelpfully as she leapt onto the table next to Amelia. "You two are connected and have been ever since you finished him off when you were a child. That's what happens when you kill another living being. He stays with you, like a ghost in your flesh and blood machine. This is partly why you have never forgotten him, like the others did. This is also how he was able to reach into your head and tug at the strings of your emotions."

"Jesus, Tabitha. That feels like a big thing I could have done with knowing! And you were going to tell me this *when* exactly?"

The fox bowed her little head, accepting some of the blame. "I didn't think I'd need to. If you had just gone into the portal with the others, as you were destined to do, confronted him in his very own purgatory where he was weakened, it would have been less messy. The real world, unfortunately, is far more conducive to evil. His dark magic held more power through his physical form and he was able to control your thoughts, to bind you to his will and make it feel like your own."

Doc rubbed the balls of her palms into her eyes as though it might squeeze out the madness.

"You were played, dude. Admittedly by a two hundred year-old dead pirate, but still. What the hell do we do now?"

The fox shook her head with no more answers to give. Instead, she glanced over to the television, where the latest breaking story was being covered by a rather miserable and cold looking reporter standing out in the snow. A story that involved sightings of a dragon flying out of the hills and heading towards Dark Peak, while a strange mist began to grow across the land.

Cisco put his face down on the table.

Deadman's Grin was coming for them.

CHAPTER TWENTY-NINE

The Mist

Cisco stood at the edge of the wintry garden, huddled in his fleece, watching Einstein become a little black and white blur against the snowy ground and the thick grey of the mist that had appeared.

Looking for a place to do his business, the dog's tail was low as he sniffed around. Cisco didn't know much about dogs, but he understood that wasn't a good sign. He wondered if Einstein could also feel the oppressive presence all around them. The sense of foreboding, as if they were all just waiting for something bad to happen.

Or someone bad to find them.

"Did you see the news this morning?" Doc asked, her boots crunching against the frozen steps from the back door behind him. She pulled up alongside and he saw she was wrapped up in her ski jacket, festive gloves cupped around a steaming mug of hot chocolate.

She took a sip, waiting for him to respond.

"I caught a few articles on Twitter," he replied carefully, back to watching Einstein who had wisely decided not to venture to the end of the garden and had circled back towards them for safety. The Christmas lights Jake had put up along the fence that led to the hill could barely be seen now. Their faded flashes seemed weak and on the point of giving up. "The mist is everywhere. Everyone around the country woke up to it and nobody can explain why."

"Except us, though. Right? Because it's the pirate and whatever magic he had while dead has got worse now he's back. And even Tabitha doesn't know what to do." She sighed. "Speaking of whom, is Fantastic Mrs Fox still here?"

"I'm still here," a soft rumble said from behind them. Tabitha's tail swished below her as she sat on the edge of the mosaic garden table, watching the pair of them. "I'm assuming you were trying to be funny, Dorothy? You always were the one with the driest sense of humour."

Cisco watched Doc's cheeks grow hot, despite the cold. She quickly mumbled an apology and took another sip of her drink, hiding her face in the steam. He stifled a grin, momentarily taken back to the good old days when the unlikely group had first hung out together and life had been about jokes, even in the face of evil and death and otherworldly beings.

How had the children survived that and not worried so much about it, yet the grown-ups were a hot mess of anxiety and stress?

The momentary cheerfulness passed quickly. Cisco stamped his feet to warm himself. It was beginning to snow again and he saw Einstein stop and look to the sky.

"What are we going to do, Tabitha?" he asked. "Do we still have a chance to stop him?"

The fox's eyes narrowed in disdain as she watched the dog twist his head this way and that, trying to lick the icy flakes from his nose.

"Maybe," she replied with a sniff. "This isn't like last time. Deadman's Grin was a ghost when you were children. He passed through the boundaries between worlds and had no need to acclimatise. After he came back, you took him down and his body was put in stasis. He's been there for decades now and while the spirit is always willing, the human body is fragile and slow. He is awake, but he will need time to regain his strength before he faces us himself."

Cisco thought to how the pirate had set the laboratory alight, brought the place crashing down around him with ease. He'd hate to see the pirate even stronger than that.

"How long do you think we have?"

The tail twitched again. "I'm not sure. A couple of days, maybe."

"You want us to grab the War Wizards, don't you?" Doc asked, a hint of resignation in her voice. "Get the old swashbuckling team back in business one last time, ready for the third act battle? The climax where we win or lose?"

Tabitha thought quietly for a moment. Too quietly, Cisco decided, shivering again as the snow grew heavier, the thick flakes drifting between them. Likely she was working out new ways to send them into danger.

To his surprise though, she only said, "Do nothing just yet. I need to go back to my world. I will try to rouse our old friends to join us once more in this fight."

"Except this time we kill the bastard properly, agreed?"

"Agreed." With a nod at them both, the fox then leapt from the table and trotted through the snow up the garden, pausing only to give Einstein a look of bemusement as the dog began to circle.

"So what do *we* do while she's gone?" Cisco whispered, watching the black shape disappear into the mist.

"You heard her, Cisco, we just stay put. Maybe we just get to be parents again for a day or so. The Christmas nativity is on at the school tonight. God knows how, with reported sightings of bloody dragons and whatnot, but I guess nobody really knows what to believe any more. They're just trying to keep life going as usual. So let's go. Let's be parents and offer some semblance of normality for the kids. It doesn't make sense given everything, but we all lived through reality starting to come undone in ridiculous ways in 2016 and everything that happened in the years after that, so we're used to it by now. Sticking our chins out and getting on with pretending to live our lives, while the world goes nuts."

"The nativity's tonight? Shit. Of course."

There was no "of course" about it, he'd forgotten all about the school play. No wonder Natalie had packed George off with a bag of spare clothes before school this morning, including a tunic and a cardboard shepherd's crook. In his exhaustion, his mind on the various news notifications pinging up on his phone and his impending fight with evil, Cisco had barely seen it.

He really was the worst.

"Think we can trust her?" Doc asked, still staring into the mist. "Tabitha, I mean?"

Cisco chewed his lip. "The same fox we once knew as children, who lives in another world that overlaps ours, who hangs out with faeries and goblins and all kinds of magical creatures, who once asked for our help to defeat an otherworldly evil, almost got us killed, and is now asking for our help to do it again?"

Doc's smile was genuine this time. Without saying another word, she softly pinched Cisco's cheek and headed back into the warmth. But not before gesturing to Einstein.

"Time to clean shit up, Cisco."

He sighed and crunched across the garden to where the dog was stood still next to a steaming hole in the snow. As Cisco pulled one of Jake's plant-based poo bags from his back pocket and crouched down to clean it up, he noticed Einstein had his tail up, eyes fixed at some unseen thing in the mist.

"What's up, boy?" he whispered. "Is something out there?"

And although the dog couldn't answer him verbally, Cisco had a creeping feeling the answer was a resounding *yes*. They hurried back inside, pausing only to toss the bag into the black bin, before slamming the door shut behind them.

Unfortunately, the impending sense of doom followed him. But as they all got ready for the big event, Cisco couldn't decide what worried him the most.

The approaching end of the world?

Or the idea of sitting through another school nativity?

The atmosphere in Jake's car was the worst kind of awkward.

Cisco had asked to take Nat's car with Amelia, which left Jake in the SUV with his wife riding shotgun, Doc and Michelle in the back seat, and Emily tagging along in between them, eyes closed and listening to her music. Her sisters were at their friends' houses, far too cool to attend nativity plays now.

Nobody had said anything since they'd left the house. Which had only been five minutes ago but had felt like a decade.

It was like the world's worst double date, with his daughter as chaperone.

Nat still wasn't talking to him and Jake knew that was a bad sign, even though he'd simply had to bring the War Wizards along, shoved in the boot of the car, just in case.

Dark Peak was quiet as he drove up the high street. A little too quiet. He decided the mist must have something to do with that, because at this time of day it was usually chaos, as parents dashed between the seven different primary schools for after school clubs or just to go shopping.

But there was very little traffic now, few headlights punching through the shroud across the town. It was as if everyone had decided to head home after the school run and lock up tight, closing the curtains to whatever their instinct had told them was coming and hoping to let it pass them by.

"Did you get Amelia's ticket, Doc?" he asked, trying to lift the gloom that had set inside the car, as miserable as outside. He caught the barest nod in the rearview mirror.

"I still don't remember who she is," Michelle remarked, staring out of the window. "She has a familiar face, but I can't place it from anywhere in particular. Was she really someone we met when we were younger?"

"She was," Jake replied, fingers gripping the wheel as though he was trying to ground himself, even as he let the fanatical notion loose from his lips. It wasn't scientific what he was admitting, but he remembered enough to know that everything Cisco had told them in the past – and had told them recently – was true. All of it.

"Then why don't I remember?"

"We all suffered some kind of memory loss that Halloween, Michelle. Blocking out the ridiculousness of what we experienced. Especially as the town came to grips with what happened, it was the only way most people could get past it and move on with their lives."

Doc tapped her fingers on the back of Jake's seat. "Then how come Cisco always remembered more than we did?"

"Maybe like Tabitha said, his connection to Deadman's Grin has something to do with it," Jake mused. "But maybe also Cisco remembered because he needed it to be true? He lived for stuff like that. He so badly wanted to be living in a fantasy that as soon as it actually happened he held onto it, even when the adventure was over and the rest of us moved on. For him it was everything. While for us it was easier to believe we *hadn't* fought an ancient evil trying to wreak havoc, along with creatures from television and films coming to life to kill us... it was all just a gas leak."

"What the hell did I marry into?" Natalie muttered under her breath.

Jake looked into the rearview mirror to meet the separate, but similar frowns of Doc and Michelle as they struggled to find a response. Between them, Emily caught his eye and gave him a grin. Then all of them went back to staring out of the windows as they took a right at the deserted traffic lights in the centre of town and climbed the hill to the school.

Only then did Jake realise what the strange thing was that had been nagging at his brain this entire trip.

Despite the mist, he'd been able to see the shopfronts as they'd travelled from street to street.

And for some reason, all the Christmas scarecrows were gone.

Cisco turned off the engine to Natalie's car and sat for a moment.

They had parked in the school playground, right behind Jake's bigger car. But as the others got out of the vehicle and headed up the brightly coloured walkway to the hall, following the twinkling Christmas lights, Amelia waved them to go on ahead. There was a dip in Cisco's stomach, partly through excitement, partly fear. He was glad they might have a chance to talk, although he wasn't sure what to expect. Perhaps he could offer an excuse or apology or *something* to make things right again. Or perhaps they could just sit quietly, as he vaguely remembered them doing once, sat on a cliff top, looking out across an improbable world in another universe.

He glanced to the side to find her continuing to stare at the inside of the car with a crease in her otherwise perfect brow. Studying it as though it was the most magical thing she could imagine, while puzzled as to how it all worked.

"Times have certainly changed," she whispered eventually, then gave him a grin.

She was wrapped up in one of Natalie's old coats, a thick brown piece whose buttons she'd left undone. Yet she showed no signs of being affected by the freezing cold weather that had descended upon the town.

He understood she was tough like that though. Tough like nature. He wondered what she must have suffered over the years, trapped in that other realm with her brothers, never to return to their family. Having to grow up away from everything they had ever known, in a world they had to learn to understand even as it tried to kill them.

They'd only spent a short time together as children, him and her. Cisco wished he could remember it properly and wished it could have been longer.

And yet he also wished he could have saved her back then and got her back to her own time. As he'd promised.

"Are you all right, Cisco?" Amelia asked gently. Her frown was gone now. She had seen in him whatever she'd been looking for and a gentle smile broke her lips. "You look tired."

"I feel it too," he said, resting his head back on the seat. His sigh misted and faded in the cold air, like his spirit leaving his body. "I'm sorry for what I did. For making a selfish choice, even though you told me not to let anything stop me from finishing him. I know he tricked me, but there was a part of me that honestly thought I could have it all. To rescue you and save the world, too. I could hear the plan in my mind, plain as I'm sitting here with you now."

She shrugged, as though it was nothing. It was a kind gesture, because they both knew it wasn't nothing at all, it was possibly a world-ending something.

"He is very persuasive, Cisco. Yet rest assured I didn't need rescuing as such. We had made a home in Lyonesse and of course it wasn't quite as I'd expected but we had made our peace with where the course of life's river had taken us. I missed you though. All these years I missed you and your friends. It sounds strange considering we were children from different times, thrown together for a short while in this other place, but I just knew that perhaps if we could be together somehow..."

Her voice trailed, unable to finish the thought. Yet he understood. He'd felt the same about her since they'd met, even if he hadn't remembered the reason behind that feeling he'd had all his life.

Then a car pulled up next to them and a loud family spilled out, wrecking the moment forever.

Amelia sat up straight, cleared her throat. "Now, I believe we have a play to attend? I haven't been to one in over a hundred years, so I must admit I'm a little excited! Come, let us go in and cheer on your boy and celebrate the festivities, shall we?"

She turned to get out of the car, then paused. Cisco took a second to realise she had no idea how to open the door. He grinned and pointed to the handle. "Just pull that."

"This is all going to take some getting used to," she noted, then leaned back over to kiss him on the cheek. "Thank you, Cisco."

Suddenly warm in his chest, he followed her out of the car, and arm in arm they went into the school, unaware of the hundreds of pairs of eyes staring at them through the falling snow.

CHAPTER THIRTY

Nativity

Doc didn't want to sit anywhere near the front of the audience. In her four-nativity experience that was the nervous projectile vomiting range and she'd already been hit twice in the last couple of years. First by Cecilia and then some poor boy playing a sheep.

She'd said all this walking in. Yet Michelle always wanted to be as close to their daughter as possible, to get good pictures without people's heads in the way. "They can't possibly throw up *every* year," she said, as they pushed through the double doors into the stuffy and slightly stinky school gym, only to find that they could.

Mrs Barnstance gave them a weary smile, crouching on her hands and knees just inside the entrance, scrubbing with paper towels.

"If you had a vomiting angel on your nativity bingo card," she laughed somewhat hysterically, "you may now mark it off."

Michelle, Doc, Jake, Natalie and Emily all smiled, then immediately headed for a group of seats on the far side of the hall, away from the smell and out of range of any more surprises. They sat down together while Doc stripped off her coat and put it on the two shabby plastic seats next to her, for Cisco and Amelia.

"I knew you'd forgive him," Michelle whispered.

Doc grasped her wife's knee and gave it a playful pinch, before the two linked arms. "It's Christmas," she said. "Who knows if we have many more left?"

Let evil do its thing out there if it must, she thought. Tonight there was nothing to be done other than enjoy the simplicities of nervous children singing Christmas songs to the slight whiff of sick.

Cisco and Amelia quickly slid into the seats next to them. He gave Doc a nod. She smiled and punched his shoulder.

"Hey!"

"That's for everything."

"I said I was sorry?"

She grinned and whispered. "I know. Merry Christmas, dickhead."

His cheeks reddened and he scratched at his beard, casually shuffling his backside further into the seat, before hissing out of the corner of his mouth. "Same to you, fuckface."

A moment of them, just as it used to be.

She had missed this so much. The boy and girl they had been. Their friendship, which should have lasted forever, but stumbled and fell in adolescence. She should have made more of an effort to keep in touch with him. He should have been less distant. It should have been better between them.

Regret was a heartbreaking thing, it turned out. Pity there was often so much of it to be found in growing up.

Before too long the hall was full. All the rows of seats were taken. Harried parents with red, sweaty faces – huffing because of whatever nonsense their other children had pulled before leaving the house – were beginning to line the walls now. Dads trying to lean and act casual while holding everyone's coats, as though they couldn't care less about missing out on cramming themselves into the tiny seats. Mums pulling all kinds of snacks out of their bags for the younger siblings.

Then the lights dimmed and Jake grinned excitedly down the line at his friends from where he sat with Natalie and Emily. Next to him, Michelle squeezed Doc's hand. And Doc's knee nudged Cisco (whose own knee was nudging Amelia's, she noticed).

It felt good, just for a moment, to be back together again without a creature in sight.

Yet as the children trooped into the hall and took their places on the stage of boxes – Cecilia and George dressed up as shepherds among them – and tiny frightened eyes scanned the audience for comfort, Doc realised she could see many more eyes than there were children.

Because in the windows at the back of the room, through the steamed glass and mist and falling snow beyond, she could see others appearing.

Eyes that were all kinds of wrong.

Glowing red.

And as the tiny voices on stage broke out into song, the wrong eyes outside blinked in unison and attacked.

Winter howled through the shattering windows, sending a blizzard of snow and glass into the crowd. It was followed by a mass of twig-like fingers and branches for arms, scrabbling and tearing their way into the hall.

Jake knew instantly what the hideous creatures were, even before they pressed their soulless faces into view. He should have expected this particular nightmare after noticing the town looking emptier on the journey here.

He looked to his sister. Michelle's face had gone as white as he'd ever seen it.

"The Christmas Scarecrows!" they said in unison.

Children were spilling off the stage into the audience, as the parents who weren't panicking did their best to scoop them up and try to escape. Yet as Jake turned, he saw more odd-shaped heads lunging through the snow against the windows on the other side of the hall.

They were surrounded.

"Get the kids," he urged Michelle, kicking aside the chairs in front. Her and Nat immediately ran through, yet it was his daughter Emily who bravely dove into the crowd and managed to grab Cecilia. She would have grabbed George too, but the boy was too fast and quickly squirmed away on his belly under the legs and chairs, thankfully heading straight for them anyway. Cisco scooped him up and balanced him on his hip like a pro.

"Tabitha was wrong," he shouted. "Deadman's Grin must be here already. He's brought those bloody abominations to life with him, too. Did you bring the War Wizards, Jake?"

Jake couldn't answer though, because there was a climax of screaming. A scarecrow dressed like a giant elf was now scrambling through the glass, severing a wooden limb in the process, before vaulting across the stage.

Distressingly, it was heading straight for him.

Unlike his daughter, Jake panicked. He did manage to shove Nat and Emily away from the monster, but in an effort to avoid it himself he tripped over someone's fallen scarf and tumbled into the chairs.

The creature leapt through the air and landed on him. Twigs scratched his face, teeth snapped and blew foul-smelling breath over him, and its hand-drawn mouth rasped a single word into his face.

"Runes!"

Jake's stomach doubled in on itself. He felt his dinner pushing its way up his throat, only to be pushed back down again as one set of stick fingers constricted around his neck, and the other set started what can only be described as *fondling* him.

Oh no, no, no, what is happening, please no, don't go in my pocket!

Then as the fingers skipped on past his nuts, he understood what was happening. It wasn't trying to turn him on. It was looking for something. Something he'd picked up a week ago and put into his coat pocket for safekeeping, only to forget about it altogether.

The runes. The sharp little stones with weird engravings he'd rescued from his battle with the demons at Buxton Museum.

Two figures suddenly appeared overhead, as Cisco and Doc lurched forward and between them tried to drag the scarecrow elf off him. It continued calling out, "Runes! Runes!" stopping only when Doc picked up a chair and smacked its stuffed head clean across the room, scattering a group of huddled families.

"Into the kitchen!" she ordered everyone around her. Without waiting, she began pushing all the mums, dads, teachers and children she could reach towards the steel door beyond the storage area, before dragging along Jake after her. He only had time to turn and see Cisco following close behind, with George wailing softly in his arms now, before realising Natalie, Emily, Michelle and Cecilia weren't following.

Split by the advance phalanx of scarecrows, they were heading in the other direction, towards the classrooms, with Amelia and a whole bunch of other families in tow.

"Nat!" Jake cried, before he was bundled into the kitchen and the door was slammed shut behind them.

"Everybody down, stay away from the windows, find somewhere to hide!"

Doc flipped the kitchen light off, relieved to find most of the other parents she knew were listening without question. In the dark, she could just about see their faces were torn between confusion and terror, not sure what they'd just witnessed. Yet at least willing to accept someone stepping up. Even if it was her.

Others weren't quite as compliant.

"Who put you in charge?" one of the year-five dads snapped. He stood there with his slicked-back hair, posing in front of the snow-buffeted window in a suit that probably cost more than most of the people in here made in half a year. His gold watch glinted in the low light. "I don't know what any of that was, but I'd like to speak to someone in an actual position of responsibility, not some bloody lesb—"

He stopped talking as Cisco gently put his son down and punched the man in the mouth. It was a solid crunch that reverberated around the benches and echoed off the hanging cooking utensils. It didn't put the bastard down, but it did shut him up.

"Take a seat," Cisco said firmly.

Fingers to his jaw in shock, the dad stared around as if perhaps expecting a lawyer to appear from nowhere and leap to his defence, but none came. Everyone else began to crouch lower behind the steel benches, cramming their kids into the spaces between the pots and pans in the cupboards. Reluctantly, the man sat down with his mortally embarrassed wife and crying child. He took care to push aside the girl's tear-stained, snotty little face from his suit first, which was lucky because then she vomited all over the floor.

Doc reached into her back pocket to pull out the wipes she always carried and handed the entire pack to the man. He took them without a word and began to awkwardly clean up.

Cisco crouched down next to her. "You always come prepared?"

She patted her various pockets, pointing at the different bulges in turn. "Eco-friendly wet wipes. Compostable dog poo bags from the last time I took Einstein for a walk. Muesli bars to prevent hungry meltdowns. I'm always prepared." She touched his arm. "And thanks, Cisco. For *that*."

He gave a dismissive wave as though it was nothing.

"You always were prepared. Remember that lighter you used to carry? How we used it to create a torch with a human femur wrapped in pirate shirts that one time? Man, saving the world was a lot cooler when we were kids. You don't happen to have anything on you that can help us now, do you?"

"No," she said, her eyes fixing on Jake. "But maybe he does. Jake, that thing back there was talking to you. Groping you too, which was a gross image I'll never get out of my head, but it said something, didn't it? It sounded like *runes...*"

The sheepish grimace he gave them both told her all she needed to know about their predicament. He reached into his coat pocket and pulled out nine white ceramic runes, each with a strange symbol carved into it in what looked like blood.

"We picked these up from one job fighting the demons at that museum. I wondered why they might be after them, so I did a bit of research."

"And?"

"Well, they're runes. But I didn't get much. They were found by a priest during an excavation at the hill fort on Mouselaw Castle. You know, the one with the antenna on the hill, just north of Dark Peak? I'm afraid nobody knows what they were for though, some ritual probably."

Doc closed her eyes. "I think I know what they were for."

Mrs Thompson, the author, had told them as much during their visit to her house, when she'd pointed out of the window, across the garden and beyond the trees.

That's a stone circle on the hill behind my house, you know? Up on old Owl Tor. It's nothing to look at from here, but it's an entrance to the portals below Dark Peak, the ones you found as children. A magical entrance that can only be opened with the use of some runes...

"Deadman's Grin sent them for these little stones," she muttered, banging her head against the steel countertop. "He wants to get back to the caves under Dark Peak, but after the collapse of William House and with him being a physical man again, he couldn't possibly go the way we went as kids. He's brought those bloody scarecrows to life to fetch these runes for him to take him another way. Shit, Jake, why didn't you tell us?"

"I forgot I had them! I put them in my coat to take back to the museum, but I think I got sidetracked with one of the girls having a drama over something."

Doc chewed her lip. How the hell were they going to get out of this? They were all trapped in here without so much as a blaster between them, just a bunch of terrified families, harried teachers, and a few kitchen utensils.

Could you whisk a scarecrow to death? Probably not.

"The War Wizards," Cisco asked Jake again. "Please tell me you brought them?'

"I did."

"Great!"

"They're in the car."

"Bloody hell."

"Yeah, sorry, but I couldn't exactly bring them in, could I?"

Cisco popped his head above the counter to stare out the window and saw shadows moving in the falling snow. "I don't think we've got long," he said, knowing it was only a matter of time before they were hunted down in here. "We'll have to make use of what we've got."

"Are you serious?" she asked, unable to help the laugh that escaped. Perhaps Cisco was seriously considering breaking out a spatula or saucepan.

"Just hear me out, Doc. Deadman's Grin seems to only be able to bring to life manmade things, right? I think he can control people, to an extent. He tricked me, after all. But the stuff he's manipulated to use against us – that night in Manchester, the decorations, the giant Santa, now these abominable scarecrows – it's all been unnatural."

"So?"

"*So* we should fight back with things he can't control. Natural weapons. There have been loads of stories where they have certain trees that ward off demons and monsters and things. Hazel trees, birch trees, even holly, I think. Maybe if we can find something like that, we can fight our way out or barricade the doors until we can figure out how to get down to the car and get the weapons."

"And where the hell are we going to get a bloody hazel tree from? Who the hell even knows what a hazel tree looks like? Do either of you?"

Cisco pulled a face and immediately waved his phone at her. "Nobody needs to actually *know* things, Doc. That's what Google's for."

She scowled as he began to type, only for George to tug at his arm.

"I'm bored, can I have that to play–"

"Are you kidding me?"

George's sulky look suggested that he hadn't been. Cisco took a long breath, then pulled him tightly into the chest of his jacket and kissed his hair. "Sorry, George. Dad just needs to look for something, OK?"

"Fine."

There was suddenly more smashing glass from the hall and a rush of scratching across the wooden floor. The army of scarecrows was now properly in. As everyone held their breaths and pulled their children closer to them – or shut the cupboard doors they were hiding in – it was Jake who decided to act.

"I'll go find us something," he said and scuttled off on his hands and knees heading for the pantry.

For a minute, it all went quiet. Nobody else dared to move. Then the scratching outside the door grew louder and a face appeared at the window.

The fake plastic snowman mask looked in, coal eyes glowing a horrible red as if they had just been plucked from a fire.

His breath fogged the window.

And the handle began to turn.

Clever boy, the voice in Doc's brain remarked.

Suddenly Jake reappeared, running across the room, leaping over the benches and slamming his body into the door. He reached into the crook of his arm and into the glass jar he held there, before his fingers reappeared sticky and brown. He began to smear the horrifying looking mess across the door. The gathered parents looked at him as though he'd lost his mind.

"Jake… what the hell are you doing?" Doc hissed at him.

He held up the jar proudly. "Vego chocolate spread!"

"What!?"

The door began to bulge open. Jake shoved himself more tightly against it.

"It's got hazelnuts in it. From the tree, right?"

Cisco put his head in his hands and groaned.

"That's not the same thing, mate. That's not the same thing at all!"

And it wasn't.

Two scarecrows shoved the door open, despite Jake – and what now looked like his dirty protest – being behind it. They bounced in and he fell away, throwing the jar of spread in desperation. It dented the snowman's head, enough for him and the gingerbread-dressed scarecrow beside him to bare their teeth at the chocolate-covered man sprawled before them.

Jake screamed as they fell on him. The gingerbread man then bit into his arm and Jake's scream became a howl of pain.

Doc grabbed a frying pan and cracked it again and again over the head of Jake's attacker until it let him go. She then tilted the pan on its side and split the scarecrow's broomstick spine in two. The thing collapsed, eyes suddenly cold and colourless.

Yet before she could pull Jake out of harm's way, Cisco pushed past and bundled into the snowman that was about to attack her.

The pair spun away towards the back wall, smashing into the sink. Cisco tried to get purchase, tearing off the creature's costume until it was just a bundle of knotted sticks tied beneath a fiercely round head. He grabbed the thing's right arm and shoved it into the waste disposal, before flicking it on. Yet even as the nightmare howled its rage, a supernatural echo of Jake a moment ago, it still kept slashing.

Cisco slipped backwards and lost hold of the other arm, and the branch fingers quickly stabbed down into his shoulder.

He screamed.

"No!" George yelled.

They'd forgotten about him in the attack. Doc had hoped he would stay put, hiding like everyone else. But he must have had his dad's genes for getting himself into trouble.

He ran over and began pummelling the scarecrow's spindly legs. "Let him go, let him go!"

The snowman's glowing eyes spun down. Cisco tried to lean down to push his son out of the way, but the sticks twisted in his flesh and he groaned through gritted teeth.

"Run," he whimpered desperately.

George didn't listen.

He kept banging against the creature, then tugging at his dad as though he might be able to pull him to safety.

The snowman grinned, its teeth sharp and salivating.

Then its head exploded.

And as the rain of splinters subsided, and Cisco wrapped up George into his one good arm, four figures stepped from the doorway.

Clutching her daughter with one hand, Michelle lowered the blaster in her other, its barrel still emanating 8-bit smoke.

"We thought you might need some help," she said, as Cecilia stared in shock at what had just happened, while Natalie and Emily stood by her side.

"Oh, Michelle, Cecilia, thank god," Doc whispered, wrapping them in a hug, as Natalie dove on Jake, stared in shock at the teeth marks in his jacket, then punched him in his good arm.

"What the hell?" he moaned, before his mouth disappeared beneath a brief, angry kiss.

"That's for making me worry," Natalie said, finally letting him go and dropping the heavy bag she was carrying. "Now, I brought your deadly weapons. Go out there and show me why I married you."

As the Swashbucklers suited up into their consoles, Emily stood in the centre of the group, hands on her hips as she surveyed the scene, from her chocolate-covered dad to the branches sticking out of the garbage disposal in the sink and Cisco's bleeding shoulder.

"And you parents worry about *us*?"

Doc caught the girl's eye.

"Growing up can be complicated, sweetheart," she said as she slipped on her War Wizard and shoved it against a cabinet to turn the thing on. The blaster hummed comfortingly in her hand. "Now stay here please. We have to go and save the world again."

The air was full of 8-bit chimes and fizzes and swirly noises as the friends fought their way out of the kitchen.

Cisco's arm hurt like hell. Yet it wasn't his blaster arm and with Doc's help he'd been able to clip his pack on and was taking out his pain and anger on every supernatural festive nightmare he came across.

They could have left. Run out of the school and made a break for it, hoping to draw the scarecrows with them as they sought the runes. But they had brought the pain here and they figured they needed to stay and fight it.

So they held tight in the hall, standing in the centre, as the scarecrows surrounded them and surged forward, limbs flailing as they ran into a stream of electric waves, fireballs, icicles, and the fury of Jake's glove.

Yet even as their numbers began to dwindle and Cisco thought for a moment they might yet escape this, there was another noise. A thumping he felt in his chest more than heard. Something big and heavy in the air outside.

A gigantic shadow appeared in the mist and snow, dropping straight onto the reception flower garden, squashing the children's carefully maintained plants.

"It's him!" Cisco shouted to Doc. She was close by his side, but the constant barrage of computer game violence erupting from their light blasters was deafening. He nudged her in the ribs as they finished the last of the scarecrows off. "Doc, he's here!"

The wall suddenly split in two, bricks and plaster and children's drawings of reindeer spilling down across the nativity stage as a dragon's head burst through and roared at them.

Cisco felt George tug again at his leg and say something, but he didn't hear it. This was the moment it had all been leading to. He had to stay focused on the figure on the dragon's back as the wintery wind and swirls of snow blew in and whipped across the hall.

"It's over," Deadman's Grin called, his voice muffled only slightly by the gush of weather assailing them. He sounded pleased, which wasn't a good sign. Cisco took aim and fired, but missed. The dragon dropped his head and glared at him. Teeth bared, there was a rumble and a fiery glow beyond them, growing deep in his throat.

The light inside got brighter.

The heat became intense.

It opened its jaws to incinerate them all.

Only for a giant rock-like fist to explode through the wall and clasp its fingers around the dragon's neck. The fire that had been about to snuff out the group was swallowed again as the beast's head was pinned to the floor.

Deadman's Grin didn't have time to react before his ride was wrenched from beneath him, the dragon's body taking the rest of the hall wall away as it was yanked out and flung off into the snowstorm.

Boulder the stone giant leaned down to wave at them. Then to Cisco's relief, Amelia appeared next to his rocky leg, with Tabitha bounding along beside her.

"I brought help," the woman said, before her look turned to absolute horror as Cisco collapsed to his knees in front of her.

Ah shit, he thought weakly. *This isn't it, is it?*

He suddenly felt far too hollow and spent. What was that old line about being bread and butter and all thinned out? He couldn't remember it off-hand, his brain was fuzzy and his eyes swimming a little, but he knew it captured what was happening to him now. The blood was warm and sticky as it continued to trickle out of his shoulder, down his arm and chest, soaking his clothes. He grimaced as Amelia ran over, reaching down to slip her arm around him.

"You'll be OK," she insisted, though he wasn't sure she believed it herself. Her fingers were soft and warm on his skin. "Tabitha can find someone to help you."

But Cisco shook his head. There would be time to fix him up later. He was probably going to be OK, just a bit of blood lost, maybe some more scars and some splinters to pull out of him.

The main thing on his mind now was whether it was all over.

The dragon was gone. The scarecrows seemed to have either been destroyed or had run off.

It was quiet and peaceful, and nobody was trying to kill anybody else.

Had they just saved the day again?

Not quite.

He realised with a sudden horror that his leg no longer had a tiny arm around it. There was no body huddled against him for warmth or protection. Cisco twisted around shakily, but there was no sign of the little boy he loved more than anything in the world.

The hall was rubble and snow and charred sticks and Christmas costumes and blood and even some more vomit.

But his son was gone.

Out in the cold winter's night, there was a distant laugh.

CHAPTER THIRTY-ONE

The Stone Circle

Cisco stumbled into the blizzard outside the school.

His head was dizzy and he didn't know what he was doing. All he understood was that he must follow that noise. The laugh of a pirate who finally had what he wanted within reach. A sound colder than the fear now gripping Cisco's insides, squeezing the life out of him with icy fingers.

Deadman's Grin was on the cusp of revenge.

Staggering over the rubble of the smashed wall, feeling the crunch of broken glass turn to the crunch of snow, Cisco walked without really seeing. Out of the broken school building. Past the stone giant. Past Tabitha.

To find himself in the midst of the most unlikely gathering imaginable.

A crowd of faces stared at him through the falling flakes and the mist that still clung to the land like evil incarnate. Eyes of all shapes, sizes and hues, belonging to a host of beings that were all at once familiar and forgotten, as if he'd tumbled into some high school reunion and couldn't quite place anyone but just knew they had once been a part of his life.

Faeries darted around in the cold, their glowing trails skimming the gathering snow drifts as though they might be scouting for danger. Bearded gnomes frowned seriously as they retrieved their tiny pickaxes from the broken bodies of the scarecrows they'd stopped from making it inside. Beyond them a host of beautiful, ageless tree people warily tilted their heads, letting their willow hair cascade around their shoulders as they regarded the bleeding and broken parent in their midst, silently communicating with each other as if sizing him up for what lay ahead.

"He took my son," Cisco said weakly, looking around, hoping they would understand him. Hoping that one of them would step forward and comfort him and tell him it was all going to be OK. That they were going to save George and stop the man who had stolen him away.

Yet while he knew they were here to help, had helped already, they were also far too still for his liking.

They seemed to be waiting for something.

Or someone.

He realised with horror it was him.

Tabitha brushed up against his legs suddenly, a warm companion in the empty chill. The nimble black fox leapt onto the stone giant's hand and was lifted before Cisco.

"One of the scarecrows snatched him away," she said solemnly. Cisco waited for the explanation that they had rectified the matter and George was waiting over there with the pixies or the leaf maidens. He felt like collapsing when it didn't come. "I'm afraid, Cisco, that Deadman's Grin has him now."

"Where?" Cisco asked, his voice barely a whisper. But he already knew, didn't he? His head bowed momentarily, his strength wavering. "Owl Tor. The stone circle."

Tabitha inclined her little head. "I do not believe he will harm your son, Cisco. Not yet. Not while you still have the runes he came for. He needs them to open the gateway into the dark beneath these hills. To access the portal he has been trying to get into for two hundred years. We do not know what he seeks. Only that if he succeeds, it will bring an end to everything we know."

"What he seeks?" Cisco repeated, then turned to Amelia. "You told me you'd found it, didn't you? I... I forgot to tell Tabitha.

I'm sorry. But you found what Deadman's Grin is after, in your world?"

Amelia stepped forward. There was a reluctance to her movement that indicated a wariness about what she was about to do. How Tabitha might react. Yet she reached to her side anyway, grabbing hold of something nobody could see, before it materialised in her hands as she held it up for them all to view.

It was a sword. But that was like saying a rose was just a plant.

The grip beneath her fingers was gold and inlaid with all kinds of gemstones that glowed brightly as she tightened her grasp and turned the blade over to catch the light. And what a blade it was, glistening pure white and as thin as a razor, its length seeming to ebb and flow before their eyes as she moved it around, entranced, as though still in awe of its power.

"The Breaker of Lyonesse," Tabitha said in a reverent and hushed voice. Then she looked up to Amelia with narrowing eyes. "You brought it here?"

Amelia nodded as though having expected the accusation.

"We found it, Peter, John and I. After all these years of searching, we found it. And though we argued over leaving it be, we did not believe you sent us to find it only for it to remain in that world. We knew he would be back for it one day. We felt it safer for it to remain with us, especially once the gateway was opened again."

Tabitha seemed to consider her explanation. Her eyes flashed furiously between fear and understanding and back again.

"We cannot let him even touch it. If he does…"

"I know. I won't let that happen."

The fox's bushy tail swung back and forth. "I do not approve."

Amelia smiled a little at that. "I know."

Finally, Tabitha sighed, finding some level of acceptance. The tail stopped moving and curled beneath her again.

"You did as I asked and I can expect no more of you than that," she said. "And now we are here, we must continue the story to its end regardless."

Amelia nodded, then slipped the sword back to her hip. As she did so, it disappeared again.

"That sword," Doc said. "Can we use it against Deadman's Grin?"

Tabitha shifted on the stone giant's hand. "It is entirely possible it may help. But only one of us may wield it with any chance of killing him and destroying the dark magic that brought him back to life." She turned to Cisco. "I'm afraid, my friend, that we need your help again. You have been chosen for this moment, because you were the one with the greatest connection to him. You *must* stop him."

Cisco found an arm scooping him upright as Doc drew alongside and held him tightly. "He can't possibly hold that thing, look at him!"

"I will keep it until he needs it," Amelia said. "I will stay with him until the end."

She and Cisco shared a look. He gave her a weak nod.

"I need to get George back," he said.

Doc gave him a squeeze, as Jake and Michelle appeared on the other side of him. "And that's exactly what we're going to do. Together."

"I still have the runes," Jake said. "They should give us some leverage. Buy us time to negotiate and get George out of harm's way?"

"Before we fry the devil," Michelle added, raising her blaster.

Cisco swung his head limply from side to side. In his mind's eye, just for a moment, he saw his friends beside him once again, as they had been all those years ago. For what, he couldn't quite remember. But there was Doc with her crooked grin and fierce passion. Jake pushing his glasses up his nose, terrified, but determined to stick with them. Michelle glowing with attitude. And around them, all those they had met and shared adventures with. Friends from the other world who had relied on the children back then, just as they were relying on the adults now.

Was he dreaming, seeing them all again like this?

Or were these the last moments of a dying man?

He couldn't be sure of either. Only that as he felt everyone around him once more, he could feel a warmth flood through him. It was enough to make up for the cold that was now creeping into his soul, just as his blood was seeping into the snow around his boots.

He hoped it was enough to get him to his son.

"I just need George back," he said, trying to speak to Tabitha, but perhaps also addressing those other supernatural beings around him. "I'll do what I can with the sword and the pirate, but I'm not anybody's chosen one."

Maybe he had been when he'd been younger, but who was he kidding? There was no way to recapture the past. He wasn't the same person, even if he had tried so desperately to hold onto his childhood. Time and age had betrayed him. He was old. He might not be able to save himself, let alone anyone else. All he cared about now was George.

But then Tabitha lifted her head, eyes sparkling and her voice loud and clear. It cut through the harsh howl of the wind rising against them and the snowfall trying to muffle their spirits.

"You might not be the chosen one, Cisco. But you are in the right place, at the right time, with the right weapon. And we will do what we can to help. We have been watching over you all these years. Wherever you touched upon nature, we were there. We were always with you, even if you didn't know it. And we will fight with you again now."

The faces around him nodded, including a familiar group of crooked-hat-wearing women who had gathered instinctively around Amelia. She hadn't noticed though. Her gaze was reserved for Cisco, giving him a smile that reminded him she had been with him all this time too, in a way.

A beautiful, dark-haired faerie with blue wings buzzed past his ear, so fast he couldn't quite catch her words. But she didn't bite him at least and the melodious sound gave him heart. The mud-red beard of the nearest gnome twitched and twisted into some semblance of a grin of pride, displaying a row of silver teeth. Even Boulder the stone giant rumbled his approval.

Cisco tried to straighten. He looked over his shoulder to where Natalie stood on the edge of the chaos, remaining with Emily and Cecilia clutched closely to her. Natalie didn't nod. But there was an acceptance in her eyes that told Cisco she had come to believe, even if she didn't exactly like what it was she was being asked to believe.

"Quickly," he said to his friends.

They knew what he meant.

Jake, Doc and Michelle left him swaying there to say their goodbyes. Jake gave Emily and Natalie a fierce hug, no words needing to be said.

"We'll be back soon, kiddo," Doc said to Cecilia as they, too, embraced tightly. "Stay with Aunty Natalie now, OK? We have to go and rescue George."

"I know," the little girl said.

"We love you so much," Michelle added, clutching the pair of them.

Behind her, the other families were peering out now, so many shocked faces staring at the mythical army gathering in the snow outside.

Wiping her eyes, Doc returned to Cisco, then gestured to the incredulous faces of the other parents. "This is the second school we've destroyed now," she whispered. "I think we might be cultivating quite a reputation for it."

Cisco nodded at that, then looked over to Tabitha who was waiting.

"Let's finish this," he said, and began trudging off into the snow.

After his son, into the fight, trailing blood with every step.

The battle through Dark Peak was intense.

Cisco kept shooting his blaster into the maelstrom of 8-bit weapon fire, watching wave upon wave of his electric bolts fly through the air, joining the fireballs and icicles, decimating the evil surrounding them on all sides. Setting alight, electrifying, or impaling whatever slithered or crawled or loped towards them, while Jake continued to batter anything else that made it through.

Meanwhile Tabitha and the army of nature streamed out around them, doing their best to protect the humans in their midst. Buying them the space they needed to chase Deadman's Grin on foot through the centre of town, towards Owl Tor.

As waves of freshly baked gingerbread men scampered like gremlins across the snow from the bakery, the stone giant's fists slammed through their number, splattering biscuits and icing across the stone terraces. The good witches were flying overhead on crooked branches, reciting incantations and casting spells on flocks of possessed Christmas tree angels who were falling from the heavens with murderous intent. Their wings shrivelled up and they tumbled screaming from the skies to fall with soft thumps in the snow.

Cisco and his friends kept to the middle of the streets where the snow was lightest, huddled together for safety, avoiding the sides where the thick drifts were blowing up against the shop windows. Inside these – and the windows of the stone terraces around them – he caught glimpses of people he knew engaged in their own battles, tangled in snake-like tinsel, being strangled by wreaths, or thrown across the room from the force of explosive Christmas crackers.

His shoulder was numb now. He figured that was probably best. At least the pain had gone with it. Yet his body was growing colder by the second, the blood still leaving him. And he could feel the thick magic of Deadman's Grin suffocating them through the mist and snow that shrouded the town in a deathly white.

So he kept his legs moving, ignoring the ice sticking to his jeans in clumps, making sure his boots took step after step, always forward, after his son.

They can't be far ahead, he thought. He hoped it was true.

Tabitha leapt through the drifts beside him, snarling and biting any who came near, tearing into the legs of slendermen and ripping out the throats of a pack of goblins. Leading by example, even as she directed her army against the incessant threats. Because it wasn't just the possessed Christmas nightmares they had to deal with now. The beasts of myth and legend who had escaped the gateways in the facility had heeded the call of evil and been drawn to Dark Peak, too.

A gnome was picked up and tossed into the night by a skull-headed beast. A good witch fell not far ahead, her crumpled form swallowed by the thick snow, while the evil gargoyle who had killed her swiftly darted after her sisters, pushing through a flock of faeries who quickly found their sharp little teeth had no effect on the rocky monster.

And as a white-furred, devil-horned Krampus-like monstrosity bounded down the street, it was closely followed by a river of baubles pouring out of the local homeware store to drive themselves under Boulder's feet.

The road shuddered as their huge companion tumbled backwards with an earth-shattering crunch. Krampus leapt on him and instantly began to chop at his limbs with a fiery pitchfork. Jake and Michelle went to his aid, but Boulder waved them away even as he was swamped by more nightmarish creatures.

Cisco watched it all through bleary eyes.

They were losing, weren't they?

He almost gave up in that moment. Felt the cold begin to claim him and wondered if it wouldn't be best just to lie down and let whatever beast came along finish him off for good.

Yet once again Amelia was there to pick him up. She wasn't using the sword, perhaps not to draw attention to the fact they had it, so all she could do was stay with him, lifting him back to his feet whenever he fell. Helping him to raise his blaster hand and fire to clear the path ahead.

"Keep going." Her breath was warm in his ear. "George needs you. We all need you."

No, you don't, he thought.

But he kept going anyway.

Out of the centre of town, they began up North Road. Past the pubs where fights were in full flow – although whether they were being attacked or it was just a regular Friday evening, Cisco couldn't tell. Under the low bridge they went, then up the hill, spraying their colourful and deadly retro-fire at their enemies. Ducking as creatures Cisco couldn't even explain threw themselves at him from the snow or dived at him from the air. Letting his friends shield him where they could and barely protecting himself when they couldn't.

The road grew steeper, lined with trees whose many and twisted branches were thick with white, like winter coral. The snow had drifted deeper up here. Cisco's legs were frozen and he struggled to move. Yet somehow he kept on. Up. Up. Up the road. Senses overwhelmed from the firefight around him, the stink of the weapons fire, the crackle of the shooting, all punctuated by unearthly cries, screeches and screams.

"Across the field, follow that path, we're nearly there," Doc urged through the chaos. Together they pulled themselves over the wooden fence and struggled across the field, following the slight dip in the blanket of snow that took them underneath a solitary crooked tree. There they caught their breath for a moment as the tree did its best to swat at the enemies overhead and protect the friends beneath, before they shuffled on again.

After the field they found the cemetery. Cisco's eyes wanted to shut for good now. He could quite happily have curled up in this spot he'd always loved, overlooking the town, out to Shire Hill and the fringes of the Peak District. It was the perfect place to rest for all eternity – or at least whatever was left of it once Deadman's Grin destroyed the Cobweb.

But still Cisco kept moving. Towards Owl Tor. More through habit now than intent. One step at a time along with his friends, leaving footprints, blood, bodies, and a great deal of destruction in their wake.

Then they were there.

A little past Hodge's Sanctuary Farm they began the final ascent. A stone wall ran the height of the Tor and they huddled up against it, using the barrier for cover and leverage as they climbed towards the stone circle – a monument that had stood for millennia, forgotten or ignored by all but those who knew its magic.

Cisco didn't know how close they were when he heard it. All he knew was that he was on the verge of passing out when the tiny, familiar voice split through the snow and wind and fighting.

George's voice.

Talking to Deadman's Grin about...

Fortnite?

Cisco would have laughed had he the energy. Had his lips not been blistered and frozen solid in a permanent grimace. Had his throat not burned with a fury of exhaustion and despair.

"...and then I- I got a battle pass, which meant I c-c- could get my favourite skin..."

"I said *shut up*!"

"...but it wasn't the r- right one, because I wanted the back bling and the starship glider..."

"Are you not afraid of me, boy?"

"...and D- Dad said he'd give me the V-bucks but he forgot. He's always forgetting s- stuff..."

There was a loud sigh as the friends quietly crested the hill in the blizzard and slowed their advance. Sharp jagged outlines could be seen not far ahead. The circle of half-buried stones. And in the centre, two figures. The tall one had removed his hat and was wiping a sleeve across his forehead.

"I will kill your father for this. I will gut him and make you watch as he breathes his last breath, I swear it."

Cisco noticed that George didn't seem particularly bothered by the threat. He didn't know whether to be proud or upset, as he let himself slide behind the stones with his friends.

Doc gestured down the slope and leaned into his ear. "There are more of his freakshow creatures coming up behind us. We don't have much time. What do you want to do?"

Cisco shook his head. What he really wanted to do was let his friends go. To face Deadman's Grin alone. They had all done enough. Every one of them, even those not from this world, who remained familiar but forgotten reflections of a life he had once lived.

Perhaps Deadman's Grin would give George up if Cisco offered himself in his place?

Yet even now Cisco could see the shadowy shapes massing on the hill below them. Fanning out. Surrounding the survivors. There was no escape to be seen for any of them.

Not unless he killed the pirate.

Or... took him away from here?

A plan formed in his mind and he reached out a shivering hand to Jake.

"The runes," he mouthed, flexing his numb, bloodied fingers. "Quickly."

"You're not going to go by yourself," Doc hissed, knowing what he was planning. She grabbed him by the collar. "Let us spread out. Maybe we can catch him in a crossfire?"

"She's right," Amelia said, crouched on the other side of him.

She looked down to her hip, but Cisco shook his head.

"Not yet."

In truth he knew he wouldn't be able to lift the sword at all, let alone use it before the pirate could end him. He couldn't take the risk. There was a better way out of this for the rest of them and he would take it, even if it killed him.

Jake dropped the runes into his hand and Cisco clamped his fingers around them. He smiled at his friends. At Amelia.

"Stay here," he ordered as firmly as he could.

"But–"

"I have to do this alone, remember." He looked to the fox, beaten and shivering, but still with them. "Tabitha, make sure?"

It was the first time he could remember seeing the animal taken aback. Surprised, almost.

Slowly, her little yellow eyes blinked.

"Good luck, Cisco."

Sticking his fists into the snow, Cisco pushed himself slowly, shakily, back to his feet.

But as he undid his pack, dropping the smoking War Wizard and blaster into the snow for the last time, he found he wasn't alone.

Stepping into the stone circle beside him was Amelia.

"Never alone," she whispered. "Not then. Not now."

Deadman's Grin saw them then.

Despite the heavy mist and the swirling snow, the delight on his gaunt, skeletal face was plain to see.

"And so, we come to the end," he called, his words loud enough to carry across the hill. Perhaps even across the blanketed countryside, over the snow and carnage, and through the December winds that blew with a force that suggested they knew what tonight meant, and were both celebrating and mourning what was to happen.

Deadman's Grin spoke as though he knew the others were there. Perhaps wanting them to witness the moment he finally got his revenge.

Cisco didn't care. He was too tired. Far too tired for all this. He held out his hands and let the stones in his palm draw the man's gaze.

"I have your runes. Give me back my son."

George saw his dad then. Still dressed like a shepherd, his eyes widened beneath his little tea-towel headdress, even as he shivered in the bitter cold. Deadman's Grin pulled the boy close to his leg before he could move. The pirate's attention flicked to Amelia.

"And if I did, what then? You live out your days as the happy family you always wanted to be?" He laughed, a sound colder than the frigid air battering them atop the hill. "You cost me much the last time we fought. You and your friends and your fancy pistols." He thumped a fist against his chest. "You put a hole in me here. Not enough to kill, however. Oh no. Just enough for you and your people to force me to endure a timeless agony in the other world, trapped upon that blasted castle top. Punished by one world for my sins and by another for my failure."

To Cisco's surprise, the man's fingers released George.

He nudged him in the back.

"I have no need of you now, boy. Go to your father while you still can. Say your goodbyes."

The little shepherd looked up at the pirate and blinked in confusion, then at Cisco. For a horrible second, Cisco wasn't sure his son would actually come back to him.

Until slowly, but with increasing speed, George stumbled away from the man who had taken him, then broke into a run through the snow and collapsed into Cisco's arms.

Cisco realised, right then, everything he had done wrong as a father and everything he had done right. Life hadn't been perfect. He'd stuffed up more than most, made mistakes, had more regrets than any of his friends. Yet as he wrapped his arms around George, pulling the shivering, freezing boy into the warmth of his blood-soaked coat and burying his face into the boy's neck, he felt the love there. Somehow, despite everything, there was still love between them.

"I've got you," he whispered into George's hair, ruffling it with his fist of runes. "It's all going to be OK."

But it wasn't.

There was a scream and as he opened his eyes again and stared through the tears, he saw that Deadman's Grin had stretched out an arm and beckoned Cisco's weapon out of its snowy grave. The console flew through the air over his head. The grip of the blaster found the man's palm.

His fingers closed around the trigger as he pointed it at the boy.

"No!" Doc screamed, standing from the cover of the stones, her own gun up. Michelle and Jake were only a split second behind her. But Cisco knew they would all be too late.

Not Amelia though.

Without a word, she threw herself forward, into the line of fire, whipping the materialising sword out before her, swinging it around in an arc, ready to spear the pirate to the stone behind. Cisco cried out. Somewhere else, Tabitha did too.

Yet none of it mattered.

The trigger had already been pulled.

A wave of electricity shot from the barrel of Cisco's blaster and splintered the air, sweeping across Amelia's back in a burst of charred clothes and smoke. Her eyes squeezed shut in pain, before she collapsed into the snow before them.

Cisco didn't know if she was dead. His mind didn't have time to rouse him enough to figure that one out. All he could do was scream silently as he stared from her beautiful face to the sword that had slipped from her grasp.

The pirate's features flickered in puzzlement as he regarded the object that had clattered into his boots. Then, slowly, the smile crept back to his lips and grew wider as he lowered the blaster, crouched down and picked up the sword with the other hand.

"You brought it to me?" he said in disbelief, a chuckle beginning deep in his throat and then erupting from his jaws as he leaned back and yelled it to the night. "You actually brought it to me! The Breaker of Lyonesse. Soon to be the Breaker of Cobwebs. The key to my freedom. The sword I have tried to claim all this time… you fools actually delivered it right to my feet!"

Still dazed and clutching George in one arm, Cisco reached out to Amelia with the other. She was cold to the touch and unmoving, her cheek laying softly against the snow, the flakes continuing to fall across her hair. He could only stare at her, as he heard the last acts of battle continue around him.

Doc charged from cover, taking advantage of the pirate's distraction. Yet he was too fast now. Without even looking, he raised the blaster again and found his target. Cisco looked up just in time to see her take a blast to the edge of her hip that sent her spinning sideways through the air. Jake leapt up to drag her behind a stone only to take a hit in his glove, which exploded in a fiery blaze as he fell back trying to shove it into the snow to put it out. Michelle then dragged her wife to safety, as the barrel of her blaster erupted in covering fire.

Cisco looked from his friends to the pirate who was still gazing greedily at the sword.

Still distracted.

Pulling his son around until he was shielded, Cisco grabbed the boy's shoulders and kissed his forehead.

"I have to go now, George."

Their eyes met for only a split second, not long enough by far for what Cisco wanted to convey in that silent way that parents and their children have, but enough to say he was sorry. To say thank you. To say all the other things that fathers could never tell their sons and their sons were too embarrassed to tell their fathers. To acknowledge the regrets and all the good intentions that had fallen by the wayside. And for them both to understand that despite the fighting and misunderstandings and stress and laughs and tears and tantrums, there was and always had been love.

It didn't make amends for what had come before.

But it would hopefully make amends for what came next.

Cisco turned and ran. Legs like stone and his entire body either numb or in agony, he charged the laughing pirate, staying in the line of fire of his own blaster to keep protecting George. And even as Deadman's Grin realised what was happening, and tried to take aim, Cisco slammed into the bastard's midriff and threw him back towards the far side of the circle.

Together they hit one of the standing stones.

Cisco's fingers tightened around the runes.

And they vanished.

CHAPTER THIRTY-TWO

An End of Everything

Whatever power Deadman's Grin had used to conjure his army of shadows quickly dissipated and blew away in the snowstorm as soon as he vanished.

The dark mythical figures he had drawn to aid him, the ones surrounding the stone circle, on the verge of falling upon the group and tearing them apart, now halted. Slowly, as if waking from a dream, they began to turn and one by one staggered off into the night to find their own mischief.

A single word drifted across the blizzard and blood.

"Daddy?"

Jake crawled through the snow and wrapped George into his jacket, holding the poor boy tightly to him, unable to respond as he knew he should.

He couldn't explain what they'd just witnessed. All he knew was that as Cisco had tackled the pirate and pushed him *into* the standing stone, they'd just disappeared. And if that wasn't terrifying enough, through the asteroid field of snowflakes that swirled around the stone circle, he could now see strange new markings on the rock that had swallowed his best friend.

A carving of two figures locked in battle.

The tall and thin Deadman's Grin.

A beaten and terrified looking Cisco.

Jake pulled the boy's head away from the horrible sight, rose to his feet and moved them to where Michelle had propped Doc up against one of the stones. He almost called out a warning, lest she disappear into the rock next, but he remembered that none of them had the runes now.

Cisco had taken them with him as he dragged the pirate to god only knows where. Which meant they couldn't possibly hope to try and get him back.

He was gone.

As Jake reached the others, he found Tabitha had left Amelia to inspect Doc's wound. She grimaced as the fox sniffed at it. Beside her, Michelle looked on worriedly, pausing only to glance up at Jake and George, tears in her eyes.

Finally, Tabitha sat back on her haunches. Tired. Relieved. Upset.

"I am thankful to say you will be OK, Dorothy. We have friends who can heal such injuries and maladies. Poor Amelia has fared worse, yet she might live too if we can get some help and quickly." She threw her little head back and yowled into the night. The noise was swiftly smothered by the blizzard, yet to Jake's relief a call was not long in answering. The smacking together of rocks. And soon the rumble of Boulder's footsteps approached. Tabitha stood. "I suggest we move off this hill, out of the cold. There will be no more fighting for us now. I believe the imminent danger has passed and there is nothing more to be done here."

It was then Jake caught the subtle flash of the fox's eyes towards the stone where Cisco had disappeared.

The sag of her shoulders was something he felt in his very soul.

As George sobbed into his jacket, whimpering for his father, Jake pulled him tighter and squeezed him as gently and as fiercely as he could.

"Don't worry, kid, we'll figure this out," he said, trying to sound hopeful and failing miserably.

* * *

It was Christmas Eve.

Doc sat in Jake's front room, in front of the roaring fire, next to the new and hastily decorated tree, bought for the kids' benefit. She continued to hum "Silent Night" even though she knew George had fallen into a fitful sleep in her lap long ago.

Beside her Michelle was drifting in and out of consciousness, Cecilia tucked in her arms as they watched the festive edition of the girl's favourite baking show. On the big armchair across from them, Jake and Natalie were huddled together. Emily, Anne and Lea were lying on the floor watching TV, listening to music and playing on their phones.

Nobody spoke.

Nobody needed to, because it was as perfect a Christmas scene as anybody could hope to experience, except for the one gaping void in the room.

Cisco had been gone for two days now. Despite her injuries still giving her grief, Doc had insisted on going back up to Owl Tor the next morning to make sure he hadn't somehow come back. After having his magical battle with the pirate, maybe he had been thrown back by the hillside victorious, only to face the threat of hypothermia.

She wanted to make sure she was there for him, as he had been there for all of them in the end. So she had set off through the town, past the groups of people trying to clean up the mess of the battle, still unsure of what exactly had happened, while whispering to each other of "another gas leak".

Doc let it slide, refusing to put things straight. *Let them enjoy the bliss of ignorance*, she figured. It had served her well all these years, after all.

Yet as she reached the stone circle, crunching across the perfect white snow beneath the clear blue skies, she found there was nothing there. Just the half-buried stones and the carving in the rock she couldn't bear to look at.

Now she didn't know what to do. Tabitha had brought one of her healers, a leaf maiden, into their house to make the best of the wounds she and Jake carried. Then after they had been suitably patched up, the fox had bid them a temporary farewell and with the help of the stone giant had carried Amelia back to their land. The woman was alive, but only barely, and unwilling to wake. Tabitha promised them she would help her. She also promised to get word to her brothers, who were still out there catching monsters, trying to tidy up what Cisco had done.

Doc couldn't concentrate on that now though. Amelia had Tabitha and the land of enchantment. Her own focus was needed here. With Michelle and their daughter. With Jake and his family. And with George.

The poor boy had suffered so much. It was almost a blessing that the authorities had too many incidents to deal with across the country, allowing Jake and Natalie to quietly take in George for the moment, until they could track down his mother. Making sure he had his found family around him as Christmas approached, trying to find some normality in the horror for the sake of the children.

Unfortunately, as the baking show finished and Doc went to grab the remote control to flick it onto the next episode, she realised that normality had once again taken leave of its senses.

Her hand was disappearing.

Eyes wide with terror, she lifted her arm up in front of her face and stared through where her fingers could only partially be seen, directly into the eyes of Jake, who had sat bolt upright in his chair to look at her after seeing he no longer had feet.

Everyone in the room was slowly vanishing.

Being wiped from existence.

"Oh hell," Doc muttered, as she felt the rest of her begin to thin. "What's he done now?"

Cisco and Deadman's Grin tumbled down, through stone and soil, darkness and dust. Roots scratched at their faces and tugged at their limbs, as they fell and fell and fell into the unknown, both a part of the earth and transient visitors passing through.

Finally they slipped out of the hill, fell through the air of an enormous cavern, and landed on the wooden deck of an ancient sailing ship that inexplicably happened to be sitting beneath the Peak District on an underground river.

Cisco didn't have time to try to understand what was happening or where they were. Only that he must get up. He had to ignore the pain wracking his body and the throbbing in his knee, somehow pull himself up again and finish this.

He reached out for the rigging that spilled across the timber boards. The runes clattered from his fingers and across the deck as he grabbed a rope and pulled himself to a sitting position.

Deadman's Grin was faster.

It helped he wasn't injured. Not bleeding across the wood like Cisco was. He hadn't had to fight his way across Dark Peak, beaten and bloodied by evil forces. He was full of life and ready to kill again. The sword clutched tightly in his right hand, the other finally dropping Cisco's blaster and War Wizard and kicking them away.

"You found my ship!" he laughed, grabbing Cisco by the scruff of his shredded jacket and pulling him up until they were eye to bloodshot eye. "The Cutlass and Shark. I haven't been aboard this fine vessel since I sailed in to find the gateways to the other worlds. Do you remember them? I'm sure you do."

He sneered and ripped open Cisco's shirt, tracing the point of the sword down the scars Cisco still carried. The ones the pirate himself had made.

"Does it still hurt, boy?" he taunted.

Cisco tried to offer some kind of resistance. A kick to the nuts. A wry, knowing grin that showed he wasn't scared.

"Fuck off," was all he managed, before Deadman's Grin threw him over the side.

He hit the water like a dead weight. The world closed in around him and he awaited the end, until boots stomped down beside him and he was hauled out again, coughing and spluttering into the chilly, damp air.

"You don't get to die that easily," Deadman's Grin muttered, his boots scattering pebbles as he dragged Cisco onto the small beach that lay at the edge of the water. "You'll see me finish what I started before you go, of that you have my word."

Cisco was pulled along as the pirate climbed up onto a carved path and walked by the side of the river, until it branched off into a wide tunnel filled with carvings and inscriptions covering every inch of the walls that stretched up into the dark.

They were broken only by tall, arched doorways. More gateways to other worlds, Cisco knew. Each framed with pictorial inscriptions that showed so many weird, beautiful, unnatural images he figured he must be hallucinating.

The pain, however, was all too real.

"Here," Deadman's Grin said, finally. They had stopped before a doorway across which images of floating islands seemed to ripple against the stone. Cisco recognised it. Lyonesse. The world where he had met Amelia in his dreams. The one she had been trapped in with her brothers. The pirate traced his fingers across its surface, then looked at the sword. "This is where I would have gone, until you brought what I needed to me. You've saved us all time, thank you."

With that he carried on up the path, the cold and darkness embracing them both, as the pirate looked around him and finally settled his gaze on a split in the rock that looked nothing like a door, but rather a divide between doors. A tear in the Earth itself.

Shit, Cisco thought, the panic really beginning to set in. *That's it. The void.*

The pirate touched the jagged edges of rock briefly, then turned to Cisco and dug a grimy finger straight into the wound in his shoulder. Cisco screamed as he felt the man's nails scraping underneath his skin, ripping it back until more blood spilled out, down his shoulder and across the floor before the tear.

The magic here had been waiting for such a sacrifice. A beam of dark light exploded from the crimson pools of Cisco's lifeforce and illuminated the rocky split, which began to widen before their eyes. Deadman's Grin gasped in wonder, dropping his victim to the side as if discarding a plaything.

"Yes, that's it. Awake with the blood. Awake and come take your sword. Destroy your blasted Cobweb. Then free me as you promised!"

Cisco slumped on the ground as his knee finally capitulated in the face of supernatural punishment and middle age. He was unable to do much but watch in horror as something within the rock began to move.

This is it. We're all dead. We're all fucking dead and it's all my fault. My friends. My son. I've killed everyone, everywhere. The void will take us all.

He shifted on the floor, feeling hot, wet patches beneath his fingers. His blood was still dripping across the stone and he could see it was filling small grooves carved into the path. Secret pathways that now burst into life with the same dark light, carrying threads of it twisting and turning throughout the tunnel.

It reached the other doors and one by one began to open them.

Weak and despairing, and on the edge of passing out for good, Cisco blinked through his tears to see other worlds blaze into existence around him.

But not just other universes or dimensions, he realised.

Other times, too.

His breath caught in his throat as he noticed one past in particular. Just the sight of it ignited an explosion of nostalgic longing that burned through his insides, filling him up with unmitigated excitement and agonising loss until he couldn't think straight.

No, that's impossible, he repeated over and over in his head. *That can't be real. That cannot be real.*

And yet it was.

An image through a doorway of a place he'd often dreamed about, but hadn't seen in decades.

The moment where this whole ridiculous journey had started.

Unfortunately, with this vision came a very clear understanding of what must come next. Of the terrible choice that was now laid out in front of him. A choice that was really no choice at all, because he would lose either way.

Either they were all going to die at the hands of the pirate. Or they were all going to die at his hands.

He was going to have to kill them all to try and save them.

He'd have to give up George.

Fuck, no, please no.

His head dropped and he spat a glob of blood out onto the path, gritting his teeth against the decision he'd already made in his head. The only one that made sense, even though it was going to end him. Because time was running out and there was only one way forward that had any hope.

A way forward... by going back.

George. I'm so sorry.

The tears streamed down Cisco's cheeks as he began, unseen, to slowly crawl across to the doorway on the other side of the tunnel. He hated himself for moving at all. Hated knowing he was going to be the one to make this happen. Yet still he dug his fingers in and dragged himself across the rock, smearing a bloody trail that spoke of one last desperate act. The act of a madman. Or perhaps only of a father clinging to a sliver of hope.

Or maybe both.

"George," he sobbed quietly, his words thin and spent. Delirious. Despairing. "I promise, son. I'll get you back. I'll fix it, somehow. I promise."

There was no sense in what he was saying. His brain was already whirring, trying to figure out what it all meant, piecing together what he'd have to do to fulfil that promise, but there was nothing.

Still he crawled towards his end. His beginning. Unable to stop thinking about the irony of what he was doing, imagining Doc's incredulous laughter if she were here to see it.

I've got no choice, he told her. *I'm so sorry.*

Inch by inch he moved, across the damp rock, feeling the dregs of his life still seeping out of him. Knowing he didn't have long left. Just enough time for this moment of agony at understanding what lay ahead and his part in it.

His fingers reached the step to the doorway. Beyond he saw a familiar sight and a familiar face.

For a second he paused, thinking it was George before him. Yet when he blinked, he saw the truth of it again.

It wasn't his son in there.

It was him.

Only then did Deadman's Grin turn around. Even as the pirate knelt before his dark mistress, he must have sensed something wasn't right. He hesitated. Pulled the sword just a little out of reach of the clawed hand that was stretching out of the void to claim it and end them all.

Too late came the shout of "no!" that spilled from his lips as he saw what was about to happen. An act he was finally powerless to stop.

Cisco closed his eyes.

I will find you again, son. I promise.

With that, he pulled himself up with bloodied hands and fell through the door.

And reality began to rewind.

EPILOGUE

A wind chime.

That's what it sounded like. A twinkling wind chime in the recess of his mind, as he woke face down in his bed with his bedside table rattling beside him.

Cisco raised his head, blurry-eyed, confused by the sound because it was somehow familiar, yet definitely not his usual phone alarm. In fact, it wasn't a phone at all. It was his old DeLorean-shaped radio alarm clock, chiming to get him awake, before switching on the local radio station which was part way through *You're History* by Shakespeare's Sister.

His face hit the pillow again momentarily. Was he concussed? It was a distinct possibility. The last thing he remembered was dragging himself, bleeding and dying through an underground portal, as a pirate screamed in the background.

The thought seemed like a good one, but it quickly brought a frown to his face.

He'd beaten the bastard, hadn't he? He could still picture the look of abject rage and fear twisting the man's gaunt, thin face as he'd been prevented from passing a sword into an evil-looking black hole. That must have been a good sign.

And yet there was something troubling him beneath the apparent victory. A sense of loss he couldn't quite place. George. It was about George. And yet that didn't make sense, because his son was still with the others, safe now that the pirate had been stopped. So why did Cisco feel a hollowness inside him that didn't make sense? Hadn't he just saved everyone by doing whatever he'd just done? By pulling himself through the gateway that led here?

Except... where *was* here, exactly?

Blinking his eyes open again, all he could really focus on were the horrific fluorescent zig-zag patterns on the pillow and duvet wrapped around him. Before slowly his sight began to adjust and the detail of his destination became apparent.

He was in his old room.

In his old house.

In his old life.

The boxy black and white television sat on his desk, beneath the *Indiana Jones and the Temple of Doom* poster. The Airfix models of the X-Wing and Viper that Doc's father had given him for a birthday present sat on the shelves on the other side of the room, next to the door. Across the floor were scattered some Zoids, mixed in among mismatching ski socks and a few VHS tapes. And his NES console was sitting on the floor, with various game cartridges sat on top.

The same games console he definitely remembered donating to a charity shop... twenty-five years ago.

Oh shit. What did I do?

He leapt out of bed with shock, gaping at everything around him, before being even more shocked that he'd managed to leap out of bed in the first place – rather than roll out grumpily as he normally did when George woke him up early to watch cartoons.

Looking down at himself he saw no bloated stomach beneath the bedtime Batman t-shirt he wore; Michael Keaton's chin was fairly straight and smooth against the teenage chest beneath it. Which also explained why he suddenly didn't feel so tired. He was in his old – young – body, awake and ready to bounce around the room at finding himself back in the place and time he had longed to return to for so long.

And even though a fog was beginning to settle in his head,

as though his memories were succumbing to the light that fades any dream upon waking, he couldn't help the mix of horror and excitement swirling inside him.

Here was everything he treasured, the memories he had so badly tried to cling onto. It was all here. *He* was here.

And yet.

His stomach collapsed in on itself and he had to put a hand to his desk to stay upright.

If he was here, George wasn't anymore.

George was gone.

His son didn't exist.

And the others...

A voice shouted through the door, muffled and familiar.

"You're running late if you want to get over to Doc's house before school," Bernadette, his mother, said, rapping three times on the wood, before adding, "And don't forget your Halloween report."

Fuck, fuck, fuck!

Cisco spun in a panicked circle, breathing in short, shallow gasps, not knowing what the hell to do. And yet inevitably the spinning slowed and the breathing settled again, as the fog continued to drop between the child he had become and the adult who had just dragged himself back in time. His panic at what he'd done began to subside. The agony of the loss he'd brought upon himself now fading quickly. The memories of George slipping through his fingers.

He thought of his friends and hoped they were alright, although he couldn't quite remember why he was concerned about them. He thought of a brave woman whose green eyes he could picture as she fell before him, and of a sleek black fox who could talk.

And he thought of his beautiful son. His son. Whose name he could no longer remember, though he had definitely made a promise to him, hadn't he?

He could feel the boy's shoulders in his fingers still, see the light in his eyes as they looked at each other across the snow... yet even that touch was beginning to soften and fade.

Had that been real?

He wasn't sure now.

It was all increasingly fuzzy.

Until, finally, it was all just a fleeting sense of déjà vu and he was left with only the words of his mother chiding him through the door into getting dressed and reminding him of the talk he had to give today.

The Halloween report.

The thing that started it all.

His teenage eyes widened at the enormity of what lay ahead, as some deep part of him that wasn't quite lost yet – the part of us that holds onto those dreams we've had, because sometimes they are not always dreams – understood that this was the moment where his story began. There was a splinter in the back of his mind now, something important. And he knew he must do better this time around if he was to fulfil a promise and save everyone he had ever loved.

Because somewhere out there, they were all counting on him.

"Oh, boy," he muttered, and rushed to get ready for school.

ACKNOWLEDGEMENTS

Swashbucklers is a strange mix of who – and where – I am and have been, both as a child and as a 'grown up' (which, by the way, is a milestone I still don't feel I've reached). It wasn't intentional when I set out to write it, but in the end I think the book speaks perfectly to how I see the oddity of growing up.

Clearly a lot is owed to my 80's childhood. The stories we grew up on back then really got under your skin and had the power to change you in ways you couldn't put words to, you could only feel. I wanted to capture that magic if I could. And although I haven't clung to that sweet, sweet nostalgia as dangerously as Cisco had, I certainly understand the pull of it. The yearning for cherished memories and adventures. The draw of the freedom and possibilities you had. The lure of an escape from a modern life that isn't quite what you planned (it never is), back into the comfort of fantastical other worlds.

So, a huge thanks to all those writers and creators who made that part of my childhood so damn enjoyable. I could list all the books, movies, TV shows, comics, and games that influenced this story, but then my acknowledgements would be bigger than the book – and I promised Rob Greene I wouldn't do that again. However, if you've read this far, you already know what the inspirations were. If it appears I was trying to channel all that ridiculous 80's fun in here, you're absolutely right. I steal from the best.

My friends at the Transpatial Tavern, including Rob, Brenda,

Patty, "Cats" Sarah Jean, Ginger, Halla, Char, Dave, Gabriela, Caroline, and Reese – plus other chums Kate, Gemma and Anna – thank you all for keeping me going this past year with your love and jokes (and bean gnomes).

Special thanks to Noelle and Chris for (respectively) the midnight writing sprints and unflinching support on edits, and the unflinching hair/feedback I needed to properly nail the ending.

Huge appreciation for all the amazing book people who take the time to read, rate and review stories like mine. With a special shout-out to Nils who I knew was looking forward to this 80's adventure for ages.

Sara Megibow, literary agent rock star, you continue to be the very best champion and cheerleader of my stories, thank you.

Eleanor Teasdale, your editorial feedback is always wonderful and a joy to work with. In fact, thanks to the whole publishing team at Angry Robot – including Gemma, Sam, and Caroline – who continue to be brilliant. (And I still can't get over how great the cover is, thank you Karen Smith!)

Finally, to Elliott and Noah, who continually teach me what it means to be a dad. Even though I'm not nearly the best around, I will keep trying to be better for you both. And Fiona, to whom I owe so much and always will, thank you.

As for you, thanks for reading this funny little mash-up of a story, set in this enchanted landscape I love so much. I hope you enjoyed it.

ABOUT THE AUTHOR

Dan Hanks is a writer, editor, and vastly overqualified archaeologist who has lived everywhere from London to Hertfordshire to Manchester to Sydney, which explains the panic in his eyes anytime someone asks "where are you from?". Thankfully he is now settled in the rolling green hills of the Peak District with his human family and fluffy sidekicks Indy and Maverick, where he writes books, screenplays and comics.

Liked what you read?
Fancy some more Dan Hanks?
Good news! Check out
Captain Moxley and the Embers of the
Empire

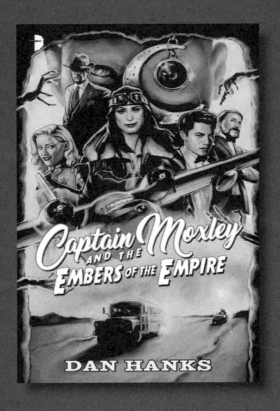

Read the first few chapters here

CHAPTER ONE
Lady Liberty

New York, 1952

Shards of moonlight cut through broken windows, bathing the hidden warehouse beneath the Statue of Liberty in an eerie glow.

Rows of wooden boxes marked 'Authorised Personnel Only' filled the shadowy interior. Crates in their hundreds, stacked from the cold, tiled floor to the ceiling. All neatly arranged. All quietly waiting for their turn to be shipped off-site to destinations as yet unknown.

All except the crate that suddenly exploded in splinters of pine.

A man burst through it headfirst and fell to the floor in a bloody heap, his once immaculate grey suit in tatters.

His fedora rolled to a stop in front of him.

"I already told you—" he muttered, blindly searching the floor for something. His hat? A gun? Whatever it was, he didn't find it in time.

A dusty brown boot connected with his stomach. He doubled over again, coughing and wheezing like the last gasp of a Spitfire running out of fuel. He had to spit the final few words out, along with several gobs of blood.

"– I don't know where she is."

The figure standing over him paused for the briefest of seconds. Head tilted, as though contemplating the merciful option.

Then Captain Samantha Moxley stepped into the light and kicked the man in the face.

I don't believe him.

He began to crawl his way back across the chipped black and white tiles, leaving a bloody smear in his wake.

Why would I?

She began to follow slowly, keeping a deliberate distance between them. Enough to make him expect another attack. Enough not to be caught by a trick up his sleeve.

I know what lies he's been trained to tell me. How to manoeuvre the conversation around until I'm not sure what's up and what's down. How to make me doubt what I know to be true. He and his friends are masters of spin and bullshit, twisting perceptions to suit their agenda.

Reaching a stack of crates, the man pulled himself until he was sat up. He looked tired and beaten. She knew how that felt.

I know, because I used to be just like him.

He coughed and more blood splattered his shirt. Yet a surprising sound issued forth from his broken mouth now. Filling the cavernous warehouse with an exhalation of pain and laughter. Had she broken him already? Cracked his facade?

Well, that hadn't taken long at all.

He smiled through shattered teeth, knowing his guise of innocence wasn't going to delay the inevitable any longer.

Sam put a boot on his shin bone and crouched down, taking care to dig her heel in just enough to make him realise she could break him further.

Her fingers reached out for his tie and straightened it. Then she slipped the knot right up to his windpipe and leaned in close.

"Last chance, Agent. Tell me where she is and I might just let you live."

He gave a whispered laugh.

"It no longer matters. You'll never reach your sister in time. The Nine are not to be refused, you know that. I guess you should have done what we wanted when you had the chance?"

Sam nodded and let the cheap, charcoal tie fall to his chest.

"So should you," she said.

She reached into her pocket for the silver disk she always carried in case of emergencies. An experimental piece of weaponry that she'd been given when she used to work alongside people like this. About the size of a dollar coin. Small and unthreatening.

Unless you knew what it did.

The man's eyes widened as he saw it. His lips started protesting weakly. But she didn't hear him now. Her boot held down his chest and she bent down to slam the gadget onto his exposed neck. There was a sharp THWACK as the hooks on the back fixed tightly to his skin.

She pressed the button in the centre.

5...

He grasped for the disk, but she punched him in the face. Hard enough to buy her time to rifle through his suit pockets.

4...

Her fingers found a folded piece of paper. She pulled it out quickly and glanced at what it said, as he groggily struggled beneath her.

3...

Yep, this was it. Exactly what she had come here to find.

2...

"Best of luck," she said. "I believe you'll need it."

1...

She lifted her boot. Just as a shimmer of purply black light silhouetted the man. And pulled him screaming into another dimension.

The heavy metal door to the warehouse slammed shut as Sam strode into the cool October night beneath Lady Liberty herself. The young pilot who had been waiting for her – no more than eighteen or so, with grease smudged across his white, freckled cheeks – was doing his best to appear casual as he leaned on the railing and stared out at the city lights beyond. He dropped his barely smoked cigarette, scuffed it underfoot in a scatter of autumn leaves, and raced over.

"What's with all that screaming in there?" Charlie asked. "Sounded like a fella. You okay, Miss?"

His boyish face, half-hidden beneath an oversized cap, showed genuine concern as he handed back her brown pilot's jacket and battered Smith and Wesson Victory. Sam holstered the revolver and slipped into the jacket, trying to hide her wry amusement as she discreetly pocketed the flyer she'd just retrieved.

"I'm fine, thank you Charlie," she said. "And, don't worry, there won't be any more screaming from that gentleman for a while. I've just packed him off on a small trip. We all set?"

"Uh, yeah. Good to go whenever you are." His gaze wandered across the bloody smears on her ripped shirt and his head tilted. "You can tell me to get lost, because this *might* not be any of my business… but you know the war's over, right?"

"If only that were so," she sighed. The concept of there being peace in our time wasn't one that had borne much fruit in her life. She'd left the battlefields of Europe only to find herself in a war of a different kind. And now this? Wasn't this America? What happened to that quintessential American dream of finding a quiet part of the world to call her own, free from being knee-deep in other people's shit?

She started walking towards their transportation – a Grumman UF-2G seaplane, bobbing gently on the choppy waves of the bay as it clung to its mooring on one of the long timber docks.

Ex-coastguard and apparently ex-military, given its faded star and stripes insignia on the fuselage. It had been 'liberated' for the night by Charlie from where it was usually locked up in his dad's Bronx marina. Not the sleekest or fastest bird in the sky, but Sam couldn't help but fall in love a little bit with its homely, no-nonsense design. A great way to get about New York City if you had some cash to part with and were in a hurry. Which tonight it turned out she was.

Charlie jogged to keep up. "Hey, whatever Miss Moxley. I didn't mean nothing by it. It's like I always say, the customer's got reasons and nobody needs to know 'bout them but them. By my reckoning you've still got a few dollars left to burn tonight. You wanna take in a Broadway show? Or how about a flick? My sister said that new all-singing, all-dancing one with that fella Gene

Kelly is pretty gangbusters. Although, she'd probably go watch him do anything, she's that mad in love with him." He looked up at her earnestly. "Seriously, I can take you any place you like. So where do you wanna go?"

Sam glanced to where the sprawl of city lights in Lower Manhattan twinkled and danced in the distance.

"Back, kid. By my reckoning, about ten thousand years."

His face was the picture of confusion, but she didn't have time to elaborate further. Because at that moment a shadowy break cut through the illuminations reflected in the bay.

A boat. Full of armed figures. Heading straight for them.

"And it seems I'm not the only one," she added, grabbing Charlie's arm. "Come on, best foot forward!"

They heard the yelling over the hum of the boat's engine before the gunfire started. Then a hail of bullets pinged off the granite walls and the ground around them. And even though she knew the men were too late and too far behind to be precise – no matter how many times in the past she'd tried to instil in them a sense of instinct – there was every chance their angry, scattergun approach could still take one or both of them down. A bullet in the shoulder. In the leg. A lucky ricochet.

That would end her rescue attempt real quick.

"Go! Go!" she yelled above the din, and thrust the young pilot towards the seaplane. She quickly untied the mooring and jumped in after him, slamming the door behind her.

"Who the hell are those guys?"

Charlie flinched as bullets started pinging off the metal shell and he attempted to strap himself into the pilot's seat. For a second, Sam considered letting him. But he was fumbling his belt, she could hear the shortness of breath in his words and despite the terror that had suddenly started to roil in the pit of her stomach, she knew there was no way he was going to get them out of this.

She grabbed his shoulder and yanked him out of his seat before he could buckle up.

"They're old friends," she said, ignoring his yelp of protest and collapsing into his place. She felt the thrum beneath her fingers, reaching deep into her bones as she started the engine.

Her hands fumbled over the controls, almost as awkward as Charlie had been, all sweaty and trembling. Was this the first time since the war? Since the crash that had put her on this path? She suddenly felt like she was once again in the ATA pool of trainee pilots in Hamble Airfield, back on the green, green grass of England. Just a rookie recruit, all fresh-eyed and eager to do her part for the war effort... before being confronted with the flying bus that was the twin-seater Magister and wondering if she was about to get herself killed.

More bullets bounced across the cockpit.

Life was a ridiculous circle, she decided.

"You're a pilot?" Charlie cried as she pushed them away from the dock.

"I am."

"But... but you're a woman!"

She gave him a death stare.

"I just mean, on the way over you were all fidgety and nervous and stuff, Miss Moxley. I thought you'd hired me by mistake, seeing as you seemed more scared of flying than anybody I ever knew. Figured the jacket was just for show, maybe the latest fashion on 5th Avenue or whatever?"

A glance out of the window and she saw the group of men gaining fast. Six or seven of them, all in suits. More bursts of light flashed from the muzzles of their guns.

Only a matter of time before they hit something useful.

"Miss?"

Her fingers gripped the throttle and lurched them forward.

"It's *Captain* Moxley, Charlie," she snapped, swallowing her fear as best she could. "And I don't mind flying, it's the crashing that upsets me." She fixed him with a look. "Now strap the hell in. We're leaving."

The small cargo ship bobbed uneasily as it made its way through the bay. The grandeur of New York City to its right. The Statue of Liberty lit up with gunfire to its left.

Standing quietly on the deck, a shadowy figure watched events unfold.

Agent Taylor's fedora dipped ever so slightly in resignation, as the seaplane they were trying to apprehend finally bounced off the waters and clung desperately to the sky. Away from the bullets. Into the safety of the night.

She's made this far harder than it needs to be, he thought with some irritation. *As usual.*

He raised his hand and beckoned the two hulking, fiercely unnatural figures nearby.

They stomped forward, each with a pair of guns in their clawed hands, while enormous leathery wings unfolded in readiness like bats preparing for their evening meal. As they reached him, their misted chrome and glass helmets inclined his way, revealing the spiderwebs of hoses connected to tanks at their backs – a potent mix of gases that kept them alive in this realm's atmosphere.

Looking up at them, he hesitated for a moment, wondering if using these… specialist tools… might be overkill, but his concern didn't last long.

Overkill was the only thing that had ever worked with Samantha Moxley.

"We can't allow the Captain to beat us to the prize tonight," he said loudly, once again feeling a deep sense of regret about setting foot on that beach in Normandy all those years ago. He pointed to the speeding light in the night sky. "Bring her down."

CHAPTER TWO
Sky Fight

Sam's fingers gripped the cold, shuddering metal of the yoke as they pulled away from the water – and the gunfire.

The plane bucked and fought, but she'd danced with worse partners in her life. That Spanish prince in Nantes for one, during a particularly traumatic undercover mission the year after the war ended.

And, of course, more recently there had been Taylor.

Is he down there now, orchestrating events from a safe distance?

As usual.

She watched the fine water spray streak across the cockpit window as they pushed through the skies above the bay. The idea that he was behind this made her shiver, but not as much as the terrifying thought of what his men would do to her sister if she didn't beat them to her. If there was one thing about Agent Jack Taylor that could be relied upon, it was that he always kept himself out of harm's way. Yet he had no qualms about instructing others to get their hands bloody – he had ordered her to enough times over the last few years, that was for damn sure.

A crack, like localised lightning, sounded just outside the window. A familiar noise, muffled by the engines, but loud enough to make both occupants jump and Sam's heart sink.

A bullet.

It shouldn't have been possible. They were too high, too far from the men they'd left behind. Yet it was what it was.

Sam immediately tensed in her seat, her eyes scanning the dark night outside, watching for whatever she could feel approaching. But it was Charlie who saw it first. The tight angles of his jawline immediately slackened as he stared out of his window in horror.

"Oh God."

She twisted around, but couldn't see past him. "What?"

"That's... that's not possible!"

Another gunshot, another crack against the plane. Then a whistling sound as air rushed out through a brand new hole in the fuselage behind them. Sam wrestled with the aircraft as it shuddered violently.

"Be more specific please," she urged.

The young pilot's gaze slowly returned to the neon-lit cityscape before them. His face was as bone white as the moon rising above Lower Manhattan.

"I think we're in trouble, Miss Moxley."

Her knuckles tightened on the yoke as she glanced sideways.

"I told you, it's *Cap*–"

Then she saw the giant-winged figure behind him, careering through the sky towards the plane.

"Holy Christ," she gasped, yanking back hard on the stick, as whatever it was – a man? A dragon? – raised his guns and fired again.

The bullets screamed past as the plane groaned and fought against her reckless flying.

To her relief, it did what it was told. Just enough to get them out of trouble in that instant. Yet the flash of wings that suddenly shot past on the other side of the plane told her that she probably wasn't going to be able to keep this up. Not if there were two of those things out there.

She spun the plane left and right, as the creatures weaved around her, wings beating and folding, skimming the currents with ease. Cats toying with a cornered mouse.

Whatever they were, and whatever nightmare Agent Taylor might have recruited them from, didn't matter right now. The immediate problem was they were able to manoeuvre far more skilfully than this heavy bird. Even with her at the controls – and she'd been known to make broken Spitfires dance.

The Nine had truly outdone themselves this time. She'd been party to some of their tricks in the past, of course. The horrors that roamed the corridors beneath the city streets where they'd worked in secret over the years. The dimension disk that had sent that stooge at Liberty Island into godknowswhere. (Whether it actually was another dimension, she still wasn't sure. Some of her old colleagues had thought it might be. Regardless, wherever it sent people, they arrived back on Earth in a completely different location, and were almost always catatonic.)

But armed dragon...men? Well, they certainly weren't the strangest shit she'd witnessed in her time. Not by far. But right now they were enough to cause a small level of concern.

She turned to the boy shrinking into his jacket beside her. His fingers whitening from clutching his seat, trying to hold onto some kind of sanity. Part of her wanted to do the same. But she'd seen and done enough to be able to roll with the ridiculous now.

The dragonmen circled again, before one pulled away and fired. This time she felt rather than heard it. A shudder as bullets ripped into them again, somewhere at the back.

Somewhere important.

She pulled back on the stick but nothing happened. The city buildings directly ahead stayed at exactly the same height they had been in her eyeline. Growing closer with every second.

"Son of a bitch," she muttered.

For a moment she threw the stick back and forth, as though her sheer force of will would somehow fix whatever had been done to the elevators. But they didn't respond. The plane stayed level, unwilling to move up or down. Heading straight towards the Manhattan skyline.

Charlie twisted his head towards her. "You're going to climb above those buildings, right?"

"We lost the elevators, I'm afraid. Can't go up or down."

"Go around then!"

Sam opened her mouth, then closed it again. She licked her dry, cracked lips – tasting blood from the earlier fight. And considered the thought that just popped into her head.

Oh, what the hell. I need to get to the museum anyway.

"Don't worry, Charlie. I'm going to get you out of this mess, I promise." She shoved the throttle forward and the plane leapt towards the urban labyrinth.

"We can't fly into the city," he yelled. "Are you crazy?"

"Possibly," she admitted. "Hold onto your hat."

The Grumman UF-2G skimmed the tip of Battery Park and shot between the tall buildings.

The dragonmen dropped back momentarily. She didn't think it was owing to fear. Whatever these creatures were, it was unlikely they would be scared off by the neon lights of New York City, but she'd long ago found that the surprise of doing something unexpected had always caused others to hesitate. Buying you enough time to figure out how to get out of almost any ridiculous situation.

And this was one of the most ridiculous she'd faced in a while.

Over City Hall they flew. Then up Broadway. Tall stone buildings streaked past on either side. Flashes of incredulous faces pressed up against windows, watching the strange chase pass by.

Too soon came the thump of wings against her window, as one of the beasts pulled up and spun away again. *Shit.* They hadn't been put off for long. And she still had no idea how to get out of this alive.

"I can't believe you're doing this," Charlie muttered beside her. Then, as more gunfire erupted from behind them, driving up the side towards the cockpit, added, "I can't believe *they're* doing this. What even are they? And what the hell did you do to piss them off?"

Sam shook her head as she suddenly tilted them a full ninety degrees to avoid a large American flag fluttering proudly outside the NYU campus.

"Long and painful story," she said, levelling them out again as the boy fell back into his seat with a gasp. "You'll be unhappy to discover there's a whole world of horrors out there that most people don't know about. And these appear to be some of the creatures who deal with them. Dangerous creatures for a dangerous job." She glanced over. "I know because I used to work with them."

"It sure looks like you left on bad terms, ma'am."

She let out a laugh; loud but humourless. "Don't ever do a deal with the government, Charlie. You'll be paying for it for years."

THWUNK.

Her eyes widened and she glanced over her shoulder.

That was heavier than a bullet impact.

She flinched as the rear door buckled, before a chunk of it came off completely and flew away into the night. A clawed hand swept in through the hole and pulled at the metal, fighting the air pressure to wrench it open inch by inch.

They were coming for her.

"Take over!" she yelled, leaping up and stumbling over the seat as she pushed the kid towards the stick, while keeping her eyes on the door at the back as it was finally torn off its hinges, allowing one of the dragonmen to squeeze himself in.

"Wha– what the hell am I supposed to do?" Charlie yelled in her wake.

"Keeping us alive would be great," she called back.

Framed in the doorway against the moonlit night, the dragonman's bulky figure seemed almost human. If you looked past the faceless helmet and the fact he was trying to fold his wings in behind him.

Sam leapt forward, meeting the creature with strength and fury. Still stuck in the doorway, buffeted by the winds outside, his gun barely had time to lift towards her. She kicked it flying out of his hand, then swept what she figured was his foot with hers. Off-balance, she grabbed his helmet and rammed his head against the doorframe with a sickening crash.

Noxious gases began to seep out of the glass, searing her eyes and throat. But the beast himself didn't go down. Claws slashed across her shoulder and shoved her away.

"It's ov-er, Cap-tain," his low, inhuman voice rasped in staccato fashion. It was, she realised, surprisingly loud against the screaming rush of wind filling the plane. An inbuilt speaker system, perhaps? Just another one of The Nine's little party tricks, designed to intimidate and terrify. As if the bloody claws and dragon wings weren't enough. He gestured towards the cockpit. "Land the pl-ane now or–"

She took a swing. Hard, into the face mask again, cracking it further. Her knuckles exploded in agony, but it jolted him back for a moment.

Not today, you winged shit.

He slugged her back across the jaw and she fell against the opposite wall hard. Breath lost for a second, she couldn't move as he approached.

She snarled with what energy she had left. At him? At herself? She didn't know. Her sister would have found it amusing, if she was here.

Behind the dragonman, buildings whipped past in flashes of grey and neon. Until finally they disappeared as his lumbering figure filled her vision.

A great big target.

Her foot shot out and caught him in the groin. There was a satisfyingly pained exhalation through the speaker as he doubled over, before she followed up to the back of his knee and dropped him half to the floor.

All those years of working for them. Working with them. And they still don't understand who I am.

She leapt up and grabbed his reptile-like shoulders. Kneed him in the stomach then followed up with an elbow.

There was a loud fizzing as the speaker gave up the ghost.

More gases poured out. He tried to stand, but only succeeded in staggering back towards the door, coughing and wheezing.

She stalked towards him, balling her fist.

These lackeys they'd sent to do their dirty work probably didn't even have a clue. She had seen things… done things… that would make most men vomit into their precious fedoras.

CRACK. A punch to his throat. Not hard enough to crush his windpipe – if he even had one – but a nice little distraction.

It's over when I say it's over.

She reached for the tubes connecting his failing helmet to his tanks and yanked them out. Each came free in an eruption of whatever hellish gases he needed to stay alive.

"Give Taylor my regards," she said, and kicked him out of the plane door.

She watched him fall for a second or two. Just enough to make sure he didn't somehow survive and chase after them. Then, wiping a gloved hand across her lip and glaring at the crimson streak that came with it, she pushed herself back towards the cockpit.

Only to look up in horror as the young pilot cried out.

"Captaaaaaain!"

Beyond him, through the windshield, the other dragonman had appeared. Wings spread outward. Flying backwards before the plane.

Raising his gun towards the boy.

The windshield burst open in an explosion of bullets and wind. Sam could only throw her arm up against the deadly debris as she leapt forward. Catching a glimpse of the holes ripping through the back of the young pilot's seat.

He shuddered within it.

"No!" she screamed with fury as she raced forward, feeling the plane tilt beneath her feet.

This wasn't fair. This wasn't the boy's fight.

"Can't… control…" he groaned as she reached him. But not fast enough to prevent him collapsing against the yoke and pulling it hard left.

Their entire world of existence shifted to its side and dipped dangerously towards the ground. The boy fell against the cracked side window, his breath coming in ragged gasps. She couldn't hear it beneath the roar of the wind through the plane, but rather felt it under her fingers as one hand fought to keep them airborne and the other sought to see how badly he'd been hit.

"Hold on, Charlie," she yelled above the din, digging her knees into the back of the seat to stop her falling onto him. "Stay with me, kid. Don't let g–"

The glass that held his weight cracked and shattered outwards.

And with a look of silent horror he fell through.

She clutched the seat as his shadow disappeared from view beneath the plane. Towards the line of police cars she could see snaking after them through the traffic below. His scream already lost beneath the steady roar of wind and the whine of the plane as it began to dip.

My fault.

She blinked, feeling her stomach churn. But it wasn't the dangerous descent. It was the thought that once again she was taking the burden of blame when it lay with others.

Wrestling the yoke, she slipped onto the torn fabric of the seat and brought the aircraft level again as it continued blasting through the streets, towards Midtown. Then she looked up, fixed her glare on the dragonman flying backwards in front of the plane.

A trick of the light, maybe. But she could almost see a devious smile flit through his otherwise intact and misty helmet.

And it made her angry as hell.

She reached for the handle of the harpoon gun she'd seen wedged down the side of the seat. The kid had told her he'd gone fishing with it in the Hudson once, pulled out half a shark. Didn't matter if it was true or not. She believed him.

No, not my fault at all.

The New York night raged through the shattered windscreen as she lifted the loaded weapon over the dashboard – and fired.

Yours.

The bolt burst through the dragonman's back and hit the gas tanks. His helmet lit up first, a beautiful ball of flame encased in glass – before the rest of him erupted in a giant orange explosion that blossomed out and out and out. Until he was just a flailing shadow of melting arms, legs and wings.

Without a thought, Sam jammed the gun under the seat. Wedging it firmly within the metal bars.

Just in time.

The rope went taught as the impaled body fell from the sky. It was a pretty unorthodox way to bring them both down to earth. Her old wingman Jenkins would have scoffed in that affable manner of his, had he survived the war to witness this – but he would definitely have approved.

"Darned good idea, Sam," he would have said, "but let's hope he had a heavy last meal, eh?"

The rope strained against the frame of the shattered cockpit window. It groaned with the force of the corpse's weight outside. But the gun beneath the seat held tight.

The plane began to tilt down, bringing more of the city street into view.

And there it was ahead.

Central Park.

"Thank fuck," Sam gasped, as she held fast to the stick, unwilling to let them drop too fast if she could help it. The streets were full beneath them, but the park held enough green soft landing space to make surviving this night without killing anyone else a possibility at least. In fact, she could just about see the glint of moonlight on one of the lakes through the trees as they dipped further towards the ground. There was a shiver of memory. She held it at bay at they descended sharply, bursting from between the buildings, and she made one last course correction towards the water.

"At least it's not the English Channel this time, I guess," she said. Then closed her eyes and braced.

There was the barest sound of a crack below as the dragonman's body hit the ground, before the rope finally snapped – and the plane flipped over and splashed down into the lake on its roof.

This time she was ready. As much as you can ever be for a ridiculously close call with death, but ready nonetheless. She went limp with the impact, then sprang into life as the dark, chill swirled around her. Through the shattered window she went, ignoring the glass biting and scraping at her skin. Pushing away from the cold metal frame and up, up, up... until she exploded from the surface and gasped in a lungful of the oil and fume-tainted air.

A few weary strokes were all that was needed to reach the bank. But even then her sodden clothes grew heavier by the second – and she briefly wondered if it might be easier just to let go, slip beneath the water, and let the world move on without her.

It would have been a relief, certainly. And perhaps part of her felt she deserved it.

But then she thought of Jess and it was enough to keep her going. She could not leave her sister to the mercy of government. Not to Agent Taylor and his sneering sidekick Smith and their insidious monsters.

Fingers found dirt and she pulled herself through weeds and moss, until she was on real land. Then she fell back onto her elbows and watched the still-burning dragonman scrape past her, as the plane sunk into the lake and dragged him after it.

"The pleasure was all mine," she called over, as his charred wings disappeared beneath the water with a hiss of steam.

Reaching into her jacket, she drew out the leaflet she had pocketed earlier, pulled the hair away from where it had plastered itself to her face, and read the wet, blotted words again.

THE NEW YORK METROPOLITAN MUSEUM OF ART INVITES YOU TO THE VIP UNVEILING OF THIS CENTURY'S MOST IMPORTANT DISCOVERY...

Sam looked to her right. Beyond the lake, at the edge of the park, was the shadowy outline of a large, imposing building through the trees – the windows lit and figures gathered within. She could almost have cried with relief, had her lungs not been full of water and near-death.

"I owe you one, Charlie," she said, getting to her feet.

Feeling like a swamp creature from one of those monster movies her dad kept trying to take her to at the local picture house, Sam wearily climbed the steps of the New York Metropolitan Museum of Art. Bedraggled and unkempt, she left behind sodden, muddy footprints, along with a trail of moss and only-the-devil-knew-what from the lake.

A man in a tilted grey hat gaped and dropped his pipe. Two women in blue polka dot dresses, arms linked, rushed on past, as if whatever had happened to Sam might be catching. Their black heels clicked furiously, like a typing pool under deadline, as they headed for the safety of the subway.

More stares as she burst through the revolving door of the museum into a sweeping lobby full of the city's brightest up and comers, all dressed in dinner suits and ball gowns. Heads turned, following the trail of water she dripped through their midst as she searched for the exhibition hall. Pushing through their finery, until she caught a glimpse, in the reflection of a silver platter, of a tall attendant in a black suit and tie, guarding a set of double doors.

The man's thin moustache twitched as Sam approached, pushing roughly through a small gathering of old, white men who were leering over a waitress.

"Can I help you, miss?" The attendant asked, stepping in front of her.

She slapped the wet invitation to his chest and strode past him, through the double doors and into the exhibition hall.

Where she found her sister in the clutches of an ancient evil.

Check out more great reads on our
website
www.angryrobotbooks.com
@angryrobotbooks

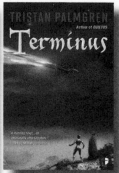
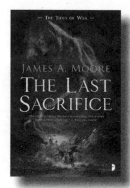
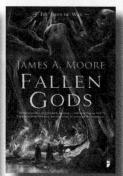

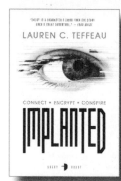

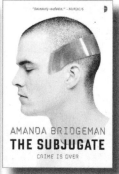